BETTY BLUNT was educated at Cheltenham Ladies College and studied Architecture at Liverpool University.

During the war she married an American, who joined the Royal Air Force and fought as a fighter pilot in the Battle of Britain.

When he returned to civilian life they made their home in America where she started her literary career, but in due course phased herself out of writing to bring up her two sons.

After the untimely death of her husband, she took up her pen again.

Now she has remarried and lives in the Isle of Man, and has since written two novels 'Treacherous Moon' followed by 'Deep Ran the River'. She has begun another novel with an American background.

Her children's book 'My Minimonks from the Himalayas', the first of a series, was published in the spring of 1983.

Treacherous Moon

Betty Blunt

DORSET PUBLISHING COMPANY,
MILBORNE PORT, SHERBORNE,
DORSET DT9 5HJ

First published in 1984 by
Dorset Publishing Company,
Milborne Port, Sherborne,
Dorset DT9 5HJ

Printed in Great Britain by
Wincanton Litho,
Old National School, North Street,
Wincanton, Somerset.

Binding by
Butler and Tanner Limited,
Frome, Somerset.

This book was designed and
produced by Rodney Legg.

Original cover artwork by D.G. Swinton.

International Standard Book Number [ISBN] 0 902129 57 0

Dedicated to my dear husband, Dudley,
in appreciation of his unfailing help
and patient hours of listening.

Winter in Sefton Park

I went for a walk in the Park
In the dusk of a winter's evening –
It was just before dark.
I shall ever remember the splendour there,
For I was a child and, 'till this moment,
Of such true beauty unaware.
Under the mellow gas lights,
Each branch a glistening sword.
My footsteps silent in the snow,
It was a wonderland of magic,
A sparkling place I did not know.

The gleaming carpet crisp beneath my feet,
Pristine, a world of pure perfection.
The moon a shining orb of light,
Then to my wondering eyes a joyful sight –
A lone red robin perched upon a tree.
His alert brown eyes, quite unafraid,
Quizzically gazing down at me;
But not a move as if he knew
The bewitching picture that he drew.
Forever on my heart engraved
A memory that will never fade.

B.B.

Prologue

ROSIE WANDERED slowly down the country lane with her black labrador, George, plodding along beside her, matching his pace to hers. She patted him affectionately on his grizzled old head. What a friend he is, she thought, never demanding, always loyal and anxious to please. He understands me: we're as comfortable together as a pair of old shoes.

Her slight figure of medium height was an arresting one and, despite the passing years, the beauty of her youth still shone through, enhanced now by an inner serenity. Beneath the surface, however, was a determination and unswerving resolve of purpose which, combined with her exceptional talent, had made her into one of the leading artists of the day.

It was early Spring and the trees wore their light clothing of green. The banks and hedgerows were fresh with clusters of primroses and violets. The countryside lay quiet, except for the cheerful twitter of the birds. Above her a skylark soared, its clear, liquid song a musical outpouring of joyful sound.

As they rounded the familiar bend in the lane, George quickened his pace a little, scenting the closeness of home. Rosie always looked forward to this moment, when she caught the first glimpse of her cottage through the trees, nestling serenely in the wooded countryside.

She opened the garden gate with its old familiar creak and remembered the very first time she had done this so many years ago, when she was a mere slip of a girl, and the pleasurable sensation, which she had experienced then, had increased a hundred-fold.

She loved every stick and stone of the place, for here she had experienced the most sublime happiness. It had sheltered her during the turbulent years of war, when she had suffered so many trials and heartbreaks – now it was a haven, which had brought her peace.

The old-fashioned garden was full of spring flowers and the early daffodils and narcissi, nodding in the gentle breeze, seemed to welcome her as she walked down the path. George stood panting, pleased to be home again, wagging his tail with a sharp rap-rap against the old oak door. She pushed it open and went in.

She looked appreciatively around the spacious room, with its pretty diamond-paned windows. A blaze of logs burnt in the large beamed fireplace, with her comfortable, sprawling easy chairs on either side of it. Close by, a bookcase, stretching from floor to ceiling, was filled with a miscellany of books on a variety of subjects. She was an avaricious reader, always anxious to keep abreast of modern trends in an ever-changing world. The brilliant white walls of the room were a perfect foil for her paintings, all water-colours, with one exception, a striking portrait in oils of a young R.A.F. officer, conspicuously apart from the others. Rosie had never painted a more brilliant study, but only she was aware of this, for it was the living image of the man she had so fleetingly known and loved. They had shared a wonderful dream together and he had left behind sweet memories, which lingered for the rest of her life.

She walked through to the kitchen and put on the kettle for her afternoon tea. Bronwen had been in that morning and left a tray set for her – everything was spick and span as usual. How fortunate she was to have this 'gem', dear Bron, who through the years had become such an important part of her life. They had grown old together.

George followed her in and noisily lapped up his water, splashing a great deal of it around the perimeter of the bowl; then, with dripping jowls, he returned with her to his usual place by the fire. From here she could see her favourite view – the simple back garden with its gnarled old apple trees and the magic of the Snowdonia range in the distance.

She settled down comfortably and sipped her tea. George leant slightly towards her, his flank touching her leg. The warm contact was reassuring to them both.

She glanced at her afternoon post and saw that there was a letter from the Managing Director of her London gallery, who over the years had become a close friend. He was asking if she had ever considered writing an autobiography. Knowing her interesting background, he felt that it could be a best seller.

She sat back in her chair, contemplating the form that such a book might take. She was encouraged by her vivid memories, as she tiptoed through the milestones of her life. Yes, there was undoubtedly plenty of good material for an absorbing story.

Leaning forward she stoked up the fire then, snuggling down in her easy chair, she closed her eyes and let the whole panorama of her life unfold before her.

1

ROSIE WAS born in Liverpool in the days of its prosperity and grandeur after the First World War. It was a delightful old city with beautifully laid out parks and elegant Georgian terraces.

Great fortunes were made from commerce and the thriving ship-building industry. Liverpool's vast dockland, stretching for seven miles along the banks of the River Mersey, was the hub of this great activity.

Merchant ships plied their flourishing trade across the oceans of the world, taking Lancashire textiles out and bringing back sugar and spices from the West Indies, tobacco and raw cotton from the southern states of America, and timber from Canada. These were among the important cargoes handled by this great port.

It was unique in having its own private exchange for the disposal of the massive cotton imports, destined for the thriving textile industry of Lancashire, then at its height.

The great luxury passenger liners, sailing to and from America, were a spectacular sight in the Mersey – such famous giants as the *Mauretania* and *Aquitania,* which maintained a prosperous communication with the New World.

Side by side with this prosperity and wealth was tragic privation, stemming from extreme poverty. The dockers' daily sustenance was often merely a hunk of bread, spread with treacle, and near-starvation was the order of the day.

Thin, ragged, barefooted children were to be seen running about the streets. These urchins were a common sight in dockland, standing beside the passenger boat trains with thin outstretched arms, begging for pennies – it was truly a heart-rending sight. Sometimes they were rewarded with coppers thrown to them by the more caring and compassionate travellers, but usually they were regarded as dirty little beggars and best not encouraged.

Despite this contrast of extremes, Liverpool possessed a charisma of its own – a great city of character – a giant of the North, dominating the estuary of the River Mersey.

* * * * *

Rosie was an only child and much adored by her parents. They lived in a large Victorian house within the boundaries of Sefton Park, overlooking an enchanting lake, surrounded by grassy banks and trees. In spring, these banks were covered by a great profusion of daffodils and the glens were thick with rhododendrons and azaleas.

To Rosie the park seemed like a fairyland and, when the bright sunshine shimmered on the water, this imaginative little girl believed it was the silvery wings of countless fairies dancing on the surface.

At night, she would look out of her bedroom window and see the lake, still and brilliant in the moon light – her fairies were now asleep!

Every afternoon she went out for a walk in the park with her nanny. She particularly liked going down to the lake to feed the ducks, though she was fearful of the swans, if they joined the party; they would hiss threateningly at her if she failed to throw the bread in their direction and she was always ready to beat a hasty retreat!

Her second choice was invariably the stepping stones which to her were most exciting. They were set above the lake with shallow water trickling between them, cascading like a miniature waterfall into the lake below. She would jump from stone to stone, taking care not to slip as there would be a stern reprimand if she splashed her gleaming white boots.

She was a pretty child, very chubby with golden hair and large blue eyes; she had a peaches and cream complexion with an enchanting bridge of freckles across her little snub nose. It was no wonder her parents were proud of her. She was always immaculately turned out, which she resented bitterly. Why couldn't she be plain and ordinary like other little girls? She was secretly rebellious of being such a showpiece and especially in the winter months when she was dressed in a white fur coat with matching hat and muff, all of which she particularly disliked.

She longed to discard this finery and throw it into the lake. Sometimes she imagined the hated clothes floating away and becoming wet and bedraggled like her old moggie, Snowy, after a soaking in the rain – she pictured them slowly sinking to the slimy bottom – good riddance!

One day she was openly defiant, determined to get her own way.

"No, Nanny, no, I won't wear these horrid clothes. They make me look silly," she said stamping her foot. "Other little girls don't wear them, so why should I?"

"Other little girls are not so lucky as you are, they don't have such lovely things," Nanny answered priggishly. "Now put your arm into this sleeve at once."

But Rosie held her arm rigid by her side and would not relax it and, when Nanny tried to force it into the sleeve, Rosie threw a tantrum: "I won't put the beastly coat on," she said, sobbing loudly. "Everybody stares at me."

"They only stare at you because you look so lovely," Nanny said proudly, for she enjoyed taking out her beautifully-dressed charge .

By this time Rosie had been forced into her coat and her hat pulled down over her pretty curls, but Rosie, determined to strike a last blow for freedom, tore the hat from her head and stamped on it, screaming lustily: "I hate you, hate you, hate you, Nanny."

It was only a minute before her mother appeared. "Whatever is happening, Nanny? I've never heard such a noise," she said reprovingly.

"I'm sorry, Madam, but Miss Rosie is being very naughty and is refusing to wear her winter clothes."

"What nonsense! Now stop all this screaming, Rosie, and do as you are told. I'm ashamed of you – you're behaving just like a baby," she said sternly. "Of course you must wear your fur coat and hat; it's very cold outside – now let Nanny get you ready."

Rosie's cries died down. She knew when she was beaten. She'd just have to submit but, as Nanny put on the enraged Rosie's hat again and wiped her eyes dry, she said sulkily: "You're horrid, Nanny, and I'm going to tell Daddy, when he gets home."

Nanny grinned: "All right , you just do that, but let's go for a nice walk now."

Rosie enjoyed their walks, best of all when they were accompanied by her little friend, Joan, whom she had met on their first scarey day of nursery school, at the venerable age of four. They were both feeling very homesick and took to each other from the start.

"Will you be my best friend?" Joan whispered, trying to swallow back the tears and be brave.

"Yes, and you can be my best friend too," Rosie said, brightening up. "I hate it here and I want to go home."

Joan nodded and her lips trembled: "So do I – I want my mummy." Rosie took her hand and held it tight.

"What is your name?" she asked. "Mine is Rosie."

"It's Joan Elizabeth, but my brothers call me Toddie."

"That's a lovely name – you are lucky," Rosie said enviously. She liked everything about this little girl. She was very thin, with hair as straight as a poker and she wore nice sensible clothing – a complete contrast to Rosie's finery which inevitably added fuel to the fire.

Rosie never suspected that Joan envied her too. She loved Rosie's chubby prettiness and luxurious apparel and would have liked to change places with her. Joan was a dear, gentle child, essentially loyal and loving. So began a close friendship, which was to last a lifetime.

*   *   *   *   *

Rosie's parents had a keen social conscience and she was taught, from an early age, to recognise the plight of the underdog. Although, in these prosperous times, life was predictable for the rich, for many the grinding face of poverty was ever-present. The slums were notorious for their rat-infested dwellings and the unfortunates, who lived in these hovels, had not any opportunity to better themselves. As you were born, so you died.

Rosie's father was a prosperous sugar refiner and did all he could to ease the lot of his workmen. His refinery was situated close to the docks so, when cargoes of raw sugar arrived from the West Indies, his lorries could conveniently pick up the consignments and deliver them expeditiously to the factory to be processed.

Even as a small child Rosie was interested in the business, which was often discussed at home. It seemed to fire her imagination. She would study the globe in the nursery and trace the route the ships would take from Trinidad. Her little finger would move slowly across the oceans and she would picture these merchant ships battling their way through Atlantic gales, buffeted and submerged in the troughs of the waves, but always surviving and bringing their precious cargoes safely to port for Daddy!

Sometimes, on wet days, she would happily sit in the nursery by the fire, drawing pictures of the factory with its massive oak gates open, showing the lorries being unloaded in the cobbled yard. Her pictures were action-packed with busy little figures running to and fro. Her father recognised her natural ability and carefully kept all her drawings, encouraging and praising her highly for her efforts.

As she entered her teens, her parents were faced with a big decision. They realised that, as an only child, she was inevitably being indulged and was leading too sheltered a life. It was time for her to strike out on her own and become more independent. After much deliberation they agreed that she should go to boarding school. She couldn't believe this awful thing was really happening to her – leaving her parents and being parted from her beloved pets and her best friend, Joan. But, in spite of her protests, she was packed off as her parents were convinced that it was for her own good.

Hers was a traumatic experience, moving from a secure world of great comfort and affection to austere living, with plain healthy food, icy cold water for washing and fresh air in abundance! Now her cossetted life had come to an end.

For the first term she suffered horrible pangs of homesickness. She was desperately unhappy and was often tempted to run away – particularly when she passed the railway station on their interminable afternoon walks in 'crocodile'. She was deterred, however, by the uncertainty of her reception if she arrived home. For, in spite of her parents love for her, there was no nonsense and she feared she would be unceremoniously sent back to school and her second state would be far worse than her first!

The next term, happily, was better and she soon settled down and became adjusted to her changed circumstances, though she thought the food was awful – steamed fish, rice pudding and prunes, and definitely no breakfast in bed! But she quickly made friends and, in spite of the strict regime and inflexible rules and regulations, she had fun – anyway there were always the holidays to look forward to.

Music and art were her greatest interests. During this period she studied the piano and became an accomplished pianist – subsequently all her life she enjoyed an abiding love of music. She also made great progress in drawing and painting. The tuition was excellent and she developed a mature competence.

When her schooldays finally came to an end, she was sad to leave all her friends, but thankful to depart from the restrictive shackles of this Victorian establishment. Later on, however, she got her schooldays into perspective and appreciated her splendid education. She felt that the high standards and discipline, instilled in her, had been well worthwhile and stood her in good stead in the testing times of life ahead.

*　　*　　*　　*　　*

Rosie had now grown into a beautiful girl, very slim, with shapely legs and a voluptuousness which she shyly attempted to conceal. Her hair was a reddish gold and framed her oval face. Her expressive eyes were perhaps her most striking feature, being a very deep hyacinth blue, which reflected her every mood. Altogether she was a beauty.

Her parents had advanced ideas, believing in careers for women, which was unusual for the monied classes in the 1930's. They were determined that she would have a university education, the prospect of which she enthusiastically welcomed.

Her outstanding ability in drawing suggested to her father that she should study to be an architect. The local School of Architecture was then one of the finest in the country, so seemed a natural choice. She had the qualifications for entrance and was readily accepted.

She looked forward eagerly to the start of her new career and, when the first day of term arrived, she was up bright and early, determined to make a good impression.

As she arrived at the University and pushed open the double doors into the lobby, she was a litle nervous, but she subdued this feeling and quickly found her way to the first year classroom.

She hesitated a moment before walking in, glancing hurriedly into her small pocket mirror; then, after patting her unruly curls into place, she took a deep breath and pushed open the door.

She was unexpectedly confronted by a sea of young men's faces and was conscious that her entrance had caused a bit of a stir – all eyes were turned towards her and conversation had momentarily ceased.

She certainly looked enchanting standing there. Her colour was heightened by this sudden surprise; then the silence was dramatically broken by a low-pitched whistle, followed by appreciative murmurings. Feeling unusually self-conscious, she was most relieved to see two other girls sitting at their desks in the front row. The nearer one, a pretty blonde, stood up and beckoned her to come over.

"Hello, you must be Rosie Greenwood," she said cheerily. "Welcome to the class. We've been waiting for you to arrive. I'm Mary Mitchell and this is Pam Shaw."

"Hello, yes I'm Rosie. Is it all right if I join you?" she asked smilingly.

"Of course, please do, we've kept this desk for you. We're the only girls in the class, so we must stick together - all these men are rather overwhelming," Mary remarked with a giggle.

"They certainly are," Rosie said wryly, "I'm amazed that we're the only girl students here."

"It isn't a profession that women seem to go in for," Mary replied. "What made you choose it?"

"Well, I love drawing and I am interested in design and particularly interior decorating. What made you consider it?" Rosie inquired.

"Well, like you, drawing is my favourite subject, but also I feel that women are much better at designing houses than men. They are so completely impractical," she said scathingly, "so I thought I'd have a go at it."

"I feel rather the same way," Pam said shyly. "I think we three girls should be able to teach these superior beings a thing or two. They are already looking down their noses at us! They seem to think that architecture is a male prerogative."

They chuckled like conspirators and Rosie felt more at ease. They were soon chatting away, exchanging information about their previous schools and personal backgrounds. Pam was rather a quiet girl and had little to say, though her eyes were alive with intelligence. Mary was the talkative one, but Rosie liked them both. They were obviously the 'blue-stocking' type, dedicated to their career, but they were very friendly and Rosie felt sure that their tiny feminine circle would be a happy one.

* * * * *

The first few weeks flew by without incident and Rosie concentrated hard on her work. She was soon used to being surrounded by the opposite sex and before long the girls were taken for granted and an easy friendly relationship developed between them. Rosie was a gay, unrepressed girl, who brought gales of fun and laughter to them all. She met several amusing characters, whom she liked and already five of them had formed a 'gang', who were –

Max Parker (Parkie to all) a 6′4″ man of mammoth proportions, whose sad and soulful eyes seemed incongruous in his ugly, rugged countenance. He had a terrific sense of humour and gave the loudest guffaws of laughter Rosie had ever heard. A gentle giant, she thought. He called her 'Princess' and fell instantly in love with her.

Bill Simpson, a clergyman's son who, in spite of this fact or probably because of it, was a wild character. He drove a sports car like a maniac and two years later was killed in a head-on crash. Rosie's relationship with him was purely platonic – they were just good friends.

George Taylor – was nicknamed 'Brush' by the gang because of his unusual black hair which stood up stiffly like a wire brush. He was a rather cynical young man, very matter of fact, though quietly good humoured. He asked Rosie early on if there was a place for him in her affections; when she regretfully turned him down, he showed little emotion and never raised the subject again – he was a realist.

Finally, Ken Little, a jovial South African, clean cut and utterly dependable, made up the gang of five.

The five became inseparable, with Rosie the only girl in the party. They were fiercely loyal as young people are, and helped one another out with projects, though in the classroom and for outside lectures the trio of girls stuck together and were ever good friends; the two dedicated ones regarded Rosie's set with amusement. There was no ill feeling or envy of Rosie's evident popularity with the opposite sex for the two girls were mature and dedicated to their studies; in both cases their parents were making sacrifices for their further education and at this stage they had no wish for romantic diversions.

*　*　*　*　*

The first project of the term was an unusual one – to design and construct a habitable tent and then put it to the test.

A bizarre assortment of designs was produced, but nevertheless most of them proved successful. There were two failures, however, for the men, when on a wet and windy night, the test ended in disaster and a thorough soaking for the occupants.

The three girls had decided to combine their efforts on the project, christened by Parkie the 'Trinity Tent' and their design, on test, proved to be the most practical. They slept out in the tent and were completely protected from the elements. This was a triumph for the fairer sex!

After the completion of a work project, the band of five would invariably celebrate by having a day out. They never lacked places of interest to visit.

Sometimes they would take the elevated railway which stretched the whole length of the docks from Garston to Seaforth, affording an exciting panoramic view of the Mersey. It was fascinating to see the famous passenger liners berthed alongside and they had fun competing in identifying the numerous flags of merchant ships from all over the world.

The gang would often alight from the train at the southern end of the line and visit Chinatown, with its tiny shop windows full of oriental curios. Rosie was intrigued by the ever-smiling Chinese. They were a well-behaved little colony, giving no trouble , so in spite of their opium dens, they were left undisturbed and the police turned a blind eye on them.

A favourite place for tea was a dive called the 'Crocodile'. It was actually quite a respectable little café, but to Rosie, with the dark narrow stairway up to the tea room and the strange pictures of crocodiles on the walls, it seemed a daring place to visit.

The exciting atmosphere of these first days of growing maturity and the easy camaraderie between the five of them was a new and happy experience for Rosie – one of the most carefree she was ever to enjoy. She felt as free as a bird and could hardly believe that the door of her gilded cage had opened.

*　*　*　*　*

"Will you be my partner for the Student Union Dance?" Ken asked eagerly. He was anxious to jump the gun and get in first.

"Thank you, Ken, I'd love that," Rosie replied, thrilled at the prospect of her first university 'do'.

"I know it's a long way off, so don't forget you're mine for that evening – for there will be bags of unscrupulous predators trying to tempt you away," he said sceptically.

"Don't worry, Ken, you can depend on me," she replied, her face full of happy anticipation.

When the big night arrived she felt excited, for she was only seventeen and had led such a sheltered life up to then. She was a great party girl, but on these occasions had always been taken and brought back by the family chauffeur. This was her first experience of true independence and she welcomed it delightedly with open arms.

From the moment they arrived at the party, Rosie was besieged by young men wanting to dance with her. She was looking very svelte in a peacock blue dress, contrasting delightfully with her golden hair. She was flattered by the attention of several men in their final year – the 'gods' of the university, who usually ignored first year students, but even they could not resist her charms.

Her partner, Ken, didn't get a look in and soon resignedly took a back seat. Faithful old Parkie, who realised he had missed the boat, stood miserably on the sidelines with a hang-dog expression, watching and whenever possible cutting in on her but only for a few minutes, when she would be swept away by another admirer.

Towards the end of the evening she looked around for Ken and saw him propping up the bar, obviously bored and fed up. She was dancing with a strange, untidy young man who had cut in on her. He held her too close for comfort, so she decided to make a break for it.

"Excuse me," she said, trying to draw away, "but I must find my partner. I've had only one dance with him so far."

He held her tighter than ever, pressing his face close to hers and smelling strongly of beer, which didn't suit fastidious Rosie.

"Not now, my beauty, he'll damn well have to wait for you until the music stops," he said aggressively. His voice was slurred and she realized that he was the worse for drink.

"Let me go – you're drunk," she said, trying to push him away, but she was captured and, unless she made a scene, she would have to put up with him until the dance ended. Suddenly, to her great relief, he was grabbed by the scruff of the neck and she was freed.

There Parkie stood, towering above them, holding her partner helpless in a vice-like grip, his face contorted with rage.

"You leave her alone, you drunken scum," he threatened. "Skidaddle, or I'll throw you out of this joint."

"Take your filthy maulers off me, Tarzan," he replied scathingly. "She's not your partner, so shove off."

"We'll see about that," Parkie said menacingly as he tightened his grip on the student's collar and started to shake him like a terrier shaking a rat.

"Stop that, Parkie – let him go or you will kill him," Rosie pleaded, tugging at his arm.

"All right, Princess, I think he's had enough," Parkie growled as he loosened his grip on the youth's collar for a moment to see what his reaction would be.

The lout spluttered and all his truculence had vanished. He had obviously decided that discretion was the better part of valour; dissolving into the sea of dancers he was not seen again that evening.

Parkie put his arms protectively around her, steering her between the dancing couples at great speed – it was a quick-step. She was aware that he was shaking with fury and did not answer when she spoke to him.

After the music stopped, he took her arm and led her over to the bar.

"Princess," he said apologetically, "please forgive my anger, but don't ever dance with that lout again or I'll knock his block off."

"Now Parkie," she replied firmly, "I've no intention of doing so, but anyway I'm quite capable of looking after myself, so please don't take on the role of my protector." She felt her independence was being threatened.

"I was only trying to save you, Princess," he said. She knew he was hurt, yet she resented his interference. He treated her like a child and she realised that their platonic friendship was changing; this was the last thing that she wished to happen. Their relationship up to then had been a comfortable, happy one.

He knew he had displeased her and tried to put things right.

"I haven't even had the chance to tell you how divine you look tonight, Princess," he said in a placatory tone, knowing he had overstepped the mark.

She smiled reassuringly up at him – he was such a dear and she couldn't be cross for long. Anyway his Sir Galahad attitude was flattering.

"Thank you, Parkie, you look pretty snazzy yourself," and as she said this, she couldn't help noticing the unconcealed love and longing in his eyes.

Hardly were the words out of her mouth when Ken appeared at her elbow.

"Hello there, young lady, you're certainly the most elusive partner I've ever had! Now how about the last waltz with me?" He spoke with a faint note of accusation.

"Of course, Ken," she said ruefully. "I am sorry I've been so neglectful, but I seem to have been inundated with requests."

"Oh, there's no need to apologise, Rosie. I've been watching you and I've seen your frequent glances in my direction." He grinned indulgently at her and, as the band struck up for the last waltz, he swept her away in a somewhat old fashioned manner, holding her almost at arm's length, with an agonised expression of concentration on his face, afraid of stepping on her toes.

"I'm not much good at the 'light fantastic', Rosie, but I'm tickled pink to be dancing with the most attractive girl in the room," he said gallantly.

"Thank you, kind sir, I'm proud to be dancing with such a distinguished young gentleman," she replied with a scintillating smile. They were happy together for they were good friends.

As the dance drew to a close and the music stopped, Parkie was quickly at their side, obviously anxious not to miss an opportunity.

"Can I give you both a lift?" he asked eagerly. "I've parked the Green Goddess right outside for it's raining cats and dogs."

"Well done, Parkie," Ken applauded. "Is that all right with you, Rosie?"

"Of course, that's absolutely super," she said tucking her arm in Ken's. "Let's leave before the rush."

They hurried out of the hall and the three of them quickly piled into the front seat of the Green Goddess. Parkie was off like the clappers and it was a good job that Rosie's parents were in bed and did not hear the roar of their approach up the drive, terminating in the screeching of brakes at the front door.

"Goodbye, Parkie dear, and thank you for the lift. It's been a lovely evening and thank you for rescuing me from that drunk," she conceded kindly. "I'm sorry I was so cross."

"Goodbye, Princess, I'll forgive you," he said gallantly. "I only wanted to protect you – God bless the beautiful belle of the ball – you outshone all the rest."

Ken escorted her to the door in his usual courtly manner, delivering her home safely, as he had promised her parents. He kissed her lightly on the cheek.

"Au revoir, and sweet dreams, Rosie."

"Goodbye and thank you, dear Ken, I've had a lovely time," she said warmly, then quietly she let herself in and tiptoed upstairs. She had thoroughly enjoyed her first students dance. How pleasant it was to be back in her cosy room. She was soon curled up in bed. She snuggled down and drifted happily off to sleep without a care in the world.

This was a golden period in her youth. The gods had so far been good to her; they had given her, as a right, so much more than most people enjoy but what would she make of these privileges of beauty and talent and a loving family background?

* * * * *

The following morning, Rosie slept on late as it was Sunday and the whole household indulged in the luxury of an extra hour in bed. She was awakened by a light tap on the door and knew it was her breakfast arriving. Breakfast in bed was a Sunday morning treat and one that she thoroughly enjoyed.

Jane, looking fresh and pretty in a frilly white cap and apron, carried in the tray. She was the same age as Rosie, yet looked older. Her background of poverty had taken its toll. She was proud to be 'in service' – the only occupation open to her – and was thankful to be working for such a considerate family in a pleasant house with plenty of good food and 'everything found'.

"Good morning, Miss Rosie," she said cheerily. "I hope you've had a restful night."

"Yes, thank you, Janie," she answered sleepily. "I don't think I've turned over once. I've slept like a log."

Jane liked and admired her young mistress and, as she drew back the curtains, the light streamed in on Rosie's tousled head. She looked little more than a child, curled up in a ball under her fluffy eiderdown.

Rosie sat up in bed, stretching and stifling a yawn then, surveying her gleaming breakfast tray with satisfaction, lifted the muffin dish cover and saw her favourite thinly sliced toast, hot and oozing butter.

"Yum, yum," she said appreciatively. "It looks absolutely delicious – you do spoil me, Janie. You know exactly what I like."

"Is there anything else I can do for you, Miss Rosie?" she asked, always so willing to help.

"Just one thing, please Janie, could you bring Chi-Chi?" She adored her little poodle and loved having him with her.

"I'll go and get him, Miss," she said making her way to the door. A minute later the little dog came scampering into the room and leapt on to the bed, bouncing around like a rubber ball, almost delirious with joy, then finally he settled down beside her, cuddling up as close as possible.

Rosie lay back contentedly on her pillows and sipped her tea, happily contemplating the fun of last night and of the many new conquests she had made but none of them particularly interested her.

She felt a bit troubled by Parkie's obvious affection for her. He was a darling and she was very fond of him. She wouldn't intentionally hurt him for the world.

He was five years older than Rosie, having previously studied law then, realising that he had chosen the wrong profession, had been encouraged by his father to switch to architecture. For this he had a real feeling and a brilliant flair for design. Already his ideas were being noticed and his work highly commended.

She respected his obvious talent and felt inadequate by comparison. She believed her work would always be commonplace. She did not fit easily into this niche.

*　*　*　*　*

Professor Gibson had given them a project of designing a small dairy farm. They had three weeks in which to complete the programme and, as they were expected to make a model, they would have to work hard to finish the scheme in time.

Rosie felt unenthusiastic; farms had never appealed to her. She sat looking despondently at a blank sheet of paper on her desk, vaguely trying to map out an outline draft, but nothing seemed to materialise.

Happily, Parkie appeared from the back of the classroom with a broad grin on his face, obviously content with his lot.

"Hello, Princess, why are you looking so glum?" he asked.

"Parkie, I know nothing about farms and couldn't care less. I will have to do immense research before I can even start," she groaned. "I can hardly tell a sheep from a goat, and I loathe sloshing around muddy farm yards."

He gave one of his great shouts of laughter.

"Cheer up, Princess, it's a heavenly day, so why don't we pack in work and go over to the Wirral and to the Boathouse for a potted shrimp tea? We can discuss farms on the way and, if you're still worried, I'll take you to see a good friend of mine, John Mott. He has a dairy farm just outside Chester. It will appeal to you as it is quite immaculate and the project will be a piece of cake then!"

"That sounds a wonderful plan, Parkie. It would give us a flying start. I must admit your idea of playing hookey really tempts me, but aren't the others coming?" she asked tentatively.

"No, let's go alone, Princess. I've various things I want to talk to you about and it will be a more comfortable ride with just two of us."

She nodded, though she felt *a deux* could be tricky. She sensed Parkie might be leading up to some sort of declaration and she wished she could head it off, but inevitably it was bound to come sooner or later.

"I'll go and get ready,"she said. "I'll meet you at the front door in a few minutes."

She made her way to the cloakroom and put on her coat. It was a blue tweed one, almost the same shade as her eyes. She wound a blue and white striped scarf around her neck and hurried through the building, waving a cheery goodbye to Pam and Mary, who had already got down to work – it made her feel rather guilty, going off on a spree.

The Green Goddess was waiting outside at the entrance and, as she jumped in, Parkie started up the engine with a roar. The car seemed to leap forward, shuddering and rattling with power. It was his pride and joy, and he vowed that he would never part with it, even if it meant a diet of bread and water – it could come to that, for she was a big drain on his resources.

It was a lovely late summer day with the trees a riot of colour in the sunshine, yet a haze softened the background. Rosie experienced a great thrill, bowling along in the open car through the Cheshire countryside. They were good enough companions not to feel the need for conversation. Parkie took his driving seriously, changing gears frequently so as not to strain the engine, listening intently to every noise that emanated from it.

Presently he slackened his speed as they swung off the main road on to a winding country lane which led them to the Boathouse Café. It looked most inviting with its fluttering chintz curtains at the open windows overlooking the River Dee.

"Let's go for a walk along the front, Princess, and work up an appetite for tea." He drew in a deep breath, the air seemed so fresh after grimey old Liverpool.

"That's an excellent idea, Parkie." She looked around appreciatively. "It's wonderful here today and it will do us good to stretch our legs." They set off at a brisk pace along the river bank, hand in hand. It was a picturesque spot with its old world fishermen's cottages and small village shops overlooking the wide stretch of river – highlights danced on the water, like tiny stars scintillating in the brilliant sunshine.

Parkie looked down at Rosie and thought how sweet and lovely she looked. Her softly-rounded curves were so enticing but he had never made any attempt to touch or kiss her before. He was filled with a warm and shining happiness, feeling that this was the right moment for his declaration in such a perfect setting.

" Let's sit on the wall, Princess, there's a question I must ask you." He helped her up – she was as light as a feather. Her face looked sweet and calm in spite of her apprehensions. She suspected what might be coming – there was no avoiding it now. She must handle this in the kindest possible way.

The old stone wall, drenched in the sunshine, was warm to the touch and, as they sat together overlooking the far bend of the river, he put his arm around her shoulders. Her eyes were downcast as he started to speak. He gazed at her in a passion of tenderness and his voice shook a little.

"Now for the most important question of my life, Princess, and I think you may already have guessed what it is. I love you dearly – to me you're the most adorable girl in the world. I want to take care of you always. Will you marry me?" His last words were hurried and breathless.

Rosie raised her eyes, now profoundly troubled. Dear old Parkie, how could she hurt him? There was a lump in her throat and it was hard to hold back the tears as she struggled for the right words.

"Parkie dear, I am honoured by your proposal, but I'm terribly sorry I can't accept," she said sadly. "I am very fond of you, but really love has not yet entered my life."

Her words were a body blow – agonisingly he wished he had waited. He suspected he had been too precipitate. He looked at her intently. He felt he had been fooled by her poise and her mature physical beauty, for today she seemed very much a child. His voice was husky as he answered her.

"Well, Princess, I'll just have to wait and hope."

She felt bewildered and out of her depth and torn by a feeling of guilt. Had she cruelly led him on? The sun was warm on her face, yet a chill ran through her. She desperately wanted to console him, but didn't know what to say.

She looked up at him appealingly, her kind heart ached for him. "Parkie, we can still be friends, can't we?"

A wry smile lit his face briefly. "Of course, Princess, nothing could ever spoil that. In any case, I shall never say die and will always hope that you will change your mind – after all, you're still very young."

Rosie wanted to protest, but managed to refrain. She knew the bottom had dropped out of his world. They sat in silence for another long moment, then she put her hand on his shoulder and gave it an affectionate pat.

"Help me down now, Parkie, and let's go and chase those delicious shrimps."

Sighing deeply, he nodded, as he helped her off the wall. The close contact filled him with love and longing.

"At your command, Princess, we'll do that thing." His voice was flat with disappointment – the stuffing had obviously been knocked out of him. The sun had disappeared behind the clouds and the river now looked dull and turgid. The magic of the day was lost.

As they walked back, the spring had gone out of his step. He was obviously shaken and terribly upset. He tried to put on a brave face and, as Rosie slipped her hand into his, he gave it a reassuring squeeze, for he knew she was miserable too.

They ate their tea silently and without relish, most of the time discussing their farm project. After he had paid the bill, he got up dejectedly. His despair was abysmal.

"Princess, its getting chilly, so let's go home."

She agreed and sadly they returned to Liverpool almost in silence.

As Parkie stopped the car at the front gate, Rosie impulsively gave him a big hug, trying her best to jolly him out of his misery.

"Don't fret, Parkie dear, you'll meet someone far nicer than me one day and then you'll feel you had a lucky escape from your erring Princess."

But he was inconsolable – his heart ached intolerably.

"No, that's not possible. There'll never be another Rosie for me" and, as he looked at her loveliness, he knew that she would never be his – the hurt was almost more than he could bear.

She also felt a sense of impending loss and even began to wonder if she had misinterpreted her own feelings and actually loved him after all. They were very close and had terrific fun together, but little did she know how she would react when the right man came along and her passionate nature was aroused.

* * * * *

The subdued relationship between Rosie and Parkie was noticed and the band of five seemed less of a happy group. Parkie himself was quiet and his loud guffaws of laughter were seldom heard in the classroom any more.

He often sat beside her desk, looking at her with sad eyes. He seemed to be drinking heavily, something he had never done before. The four men went regularly now to the local pub in the early everning – Parkie was obviously consuming more beer than was good for him, drowning his sorrows in drink. He would invariably come back from one of these sessions a little the worse for wear, weaving toward her, then leaning over her desk staring at her drawings. She hated to see him in this state and on these occasions would feel a wave of protective tenderness towards him.

Sometimes, however, he seemed irritable, then he would be critical of her work. His own was suffering badly – in fact he had not accomplished anything at all and this really worried her, for she felt responsible.

One evening, when he walked unsteadily into the classroom, she thought she would have a talk with him and take him to task over his lack of application, but it was obviously the wrong moment.

As usual he stopped at her desk, swaying slightly and gazing wistfully down at her.

"I must say, Princess, you are looking very beautiful this evening," he declared in a muffled voice.

"Thank you, Parkie," she replied rather tartly. "It's more than I can say of you – your tie is all askew and you look dishevelled."

He made no comment, but attempted to straighten his tie and ran his fingers through his hair; then, glancing down at her drawing board, he saw the elevations of the farmhouse that she had just finished.

"My God, Rosie," he exclaimed aggressively. "What a horrible design – it looks like a public lavatory, tarted up. I see you need your old Parkie to keep you on the straight and narrow." He chuckled mirthlessly.

She gave him a long level look; she was stung by his unkind criticism and retorted sharply. "I am at least trying to get something done, which is more than you are. I still see only a blank sheet of paper on your desk."

His surly mood suddenly seemed to change and he was the kind old Parkie again. He gazed at her sorrowfully.

"I do apologise for my rude remarks, Princess – of course you're absolutely right. I'm just wasting my time." He looked thoroughly ashamed of himself.

"Please forgive me – I've been drinking."

He turned away without another word and left the classroom.

Rosie packed up her things early and went home. As usual, Chi Chi was sitting on the window ledge in the dining room, peering anxiously into the dusk, waiting for her return. When he saw her walking up the path, he jumped down and rushed to the front door barking madly. As she came in, the little white ball of fluff circled excitedly round and round her legs, until he was picked up and cuddled; then he gradually quietened down.

After hanging up her coat, with Chi Chi in her arms, she walked through into the drawing room, where her mother was sitting by the fire reading. Mrs. Greenwood guessed something was amiss, for Rosie had returned home early again and for several days had not been her usual happy self. Being a shrewd woman, she saw which way the wind was blowing. She hoped that Rosie would confide in her and, as they sat talking, this is exactly what happened.

"I'm feeling rather worried about Parkie, Mum."

"What is the trouble, dear?" her mother enquired, listening attentively to her.

"Well, he has asked me to marry him and I turned him down. He was terribly upset and since then he hasn't been himself – he's drinking far too much."

Her mother smiled sympathetically. "Darling, you must not worry. You are bound to break hearts. It's all part of the growing up process. I foresaw this with Parkie and I'm very, very sorry for him, but don't be too upset, he's not for you. When the right man comes along, you'll know it at once – you will have no doubts. Parkie will soon get over this, though it's a painful process for him. Why don't you work at home more in future? We could turn the old nursery into a study for you. I'm sure your father would be only too pleased to get you a desk."

"Oh, Mum, what a wonderful idea! Then I won't have to see him so often and he will have a better chance to get over his disappointment. It would also be most convenient when I have to work late." Her eyes sparkled at the prospect.

They spent the evening planning together and, when Rosie went to bed, she felt more like her cheerful self again.

*　*　*　*　*

The farm project was finally completed. Rosie worked at home for the last two nights, trying desperately to finish the papier maché model in time. She wasn't pleased with it. She missed Parkie's sage advice.

He seemed to have disappeared entirely from the university. All his drawing equipment had been removed from his desk and he had not attended any lectures for over a week. She thought it best not to ask about him – it was a sore subject.

The schemes had to be submitted early on the fateful day and displayed on the walls for constructive discussion between students and their professor.

Rosie could hardly believe her eyes when she saw Parkie's drawings, completed and carefully hung. His original style was quite unmistakable – his design unique in its utter simplicity. She was fascinated by his interpretation.

As she stood there studying it, she felt a light tap on her shoulder. She turned around and there he was, looking very pleased with himself, smiling broadly, just like the old Parkie.

"Well, you see, Princess, you were quite wrong – I finished it after all."

24

He looked quite smug, she thought.

"Parkie, it's wonderful," she said with a genuine delight. "Your design is really quite outstanding – but please don't look at mine, in comparison it's so ordinary." Then, as an afterthought, "I've missed your help enormously and I'm dreading what the Prof will say."

"Don't worry, Princess, I've had a good look and, although it's not my style, I think you will get a high mark."

"Oh thank you, Parkie, now I feel better," and she did in more ways than one.

When the Prof arrived, they all stood around listening intently to his comments and appraisal of their work.

Rosie was delighted when Parkie's scheme was highly commended and chosen as being the most outstanding. Her own was well received but she knew it was a solid, uninspired design and felt most dissatisfied with it. However, as Parkie predicted, she was awarded a good mark.

"Princess, how about all of us going to the 'flicks' tonight and having a meal out?" Parkie suggested. "We haven't had any fun for a long time."

Rosie looked up at him with shining eyes. "I'd love to, Parkie, that would be terrific. Do you think, if it's all right with the others, we could see the new Greta Garbo film?"

"Certainly, Princess, it's supposed to be a damned good film."

They all agreed and it was like old times with the five of them squeezed into the Green Goddess, seemingly without a care in the world. Parkie had obviously come to terms with the 'Rosie situation' and got a grip on himself again.

The Garbo Film,'Camille', was too sad for soft-hearted Rosie; tears ran down her cheeks and she wished they'd chosen something more light-hearted. Before leaving the cinema Parkie produced a king-sized handkerchief and helped to mop her up. "Come on, little one, it's only a story," but Rosie was inconsolable, once she started she could not stop. She spluttered tearfully, "I'm stupid – I'm always like this, but poor Camille really upset me."

"Niagara Falls have nothing on you," Parkie said humorously, "next time I'll bring a mackintosh." This made them all laugh and Rosie was soon her usual cheerful self again.

They went to their favourite Chinese restaurant for a meal and had a hilarious time trying to use chopsticks. Parkie's great guffaws of laughter rang out as before. The smiling Chinese waiters watched them indulgently, discreetly enjoying their fun. Altogether it was a happy evening, and as they drove Rosie home at an alarming speed, all she could do was close her eyes and hope for the best. As they raced along they sang some of the old music hall favourites at the top of their voices. She tried to quieten them down as they approached her house. Fortunately they had the sense to heed her warning – knowing Rosie's parents was a sufficient deterrent in itself.

*   *   *   *   *

Their next project was to design a cottage; it was an interesting challenge. She knew exactly how she wished it to be. She had the gift of accurate visual memory and years ago, as a child holidaying in Ireland, she had come across a simple fisherman's cottage, built on a rocky promontory overlooking a sandy bay on the wild Atlantic coast. She could still hear the haunting cries of the sea birds and the tranquil atmosphere of solitary peace had stayed with her. It had always been her dream cottage.

She sat quietly at her desk, deep in thought. She knew she should tackle it the architect's way, but the temptation of an artist was great, so she rejected the conventional approach and decided to work backwards, reproducing it as a picture first.

She got out her charcoal and sketched a very fine drawing.Her strokes were accurate and meaningful, with true economy of line. Then,hardly able to wait, she applied the colour skilfully, as she so vividly remembered it. The fluffy white clouds contrasted dramatically against a cobalt blue sky. The little white cottage was sturdily built, high above the beach, to withstand the wind and weather beating in from the Atlantic ocean. The bay in the foreground looked utterly peaceful, bathed in vivid sunshine – one could almost feel the warmth.

She was pleased with the effect, for it was just as she remembered it. Now she must apply herself and lay out an interesting and practical plan for the cottage.

2

A TALL handsome young man walked into the classroom. He stood for a moment in the doorway glancing around. He was smartly dressed in a brown sports jacket, with a cream shirt and thickly knitted tie. His face was still suntanned from a holiday in Greece. His dark hair was thick and crisply curly. He looked unlike a student, but in fact he was in his last year – one of the gods of the university; at this stage a great change seemed to occur, when the untidy arty young boys suddenly turned into serious, smart, young men.

He caught sight of Rosie and made straight for her desk. She was so absorbed in her project that she was quite unaware of his approach. He looked down at her drawing and was most surprised by the quality of her work; for a first year student it was impressive.

"Hello," he said. "I hope I'm not intruding."

She looked up with a far away expression in her vivid blue eyes; then, bringing herself down to earth with a bump, she smiled at him.

"Hello – I'm sorry, I was miles away – did you say something?"

"Yes, but I hope I'm not upsetting your concentration," he said apologetically.

"Not at all," she replied, smiling dreamily up at him. He thought what heavenly blue eyes she had.

"You must be Rosie Greenwood – I am Peter Dunbar and I'm in my final year here. I've been asked to look you up by a mutual friend – Richard Taylor. He told me a lot about you and said, among other things, that you were a smashing redhead." His eyes twinkled as he spoke.

Rosie felt herself blushing slightly; she hated this description, for her hair certainly was not red, it was a sparkling gold. She replied in a slightly offhand manner.

"Oh, he's a dim and distant cousin of mine. I haven't seen him for ages and I'm surprised that he even remembers me."

"Oh, he remembers you all right and is a great admirer of yours! We were both at Winchester and became very good friends, managing to survive the rather spartan life there. Wearing a hair shirt is said to be good for the soul and I must admit it didn't seem to do us any harm," he said ruefully.

"My school was the same: self-denial was very much part of the curriculum," she replied.

They both laughed heartily.

"It's nice to meet a friend of Richard's," she conceded, unbending a little, "though I must admit that in his younger days he was an awful tease and I used to steer clear of him – but he's always been a great favourite of my parents."

"How are you settling in?" he asked.

"Oh, very well indeed. I like it here very much and enjoy the work. As you see, there are only three girls in our year, so we're quite in demand and have great fun."

"Don't be so modest, you'd be in demand anyway."

She started blushing again and was furious with herself; he seemed to make her feel young and self-conscious. He noticed her heightened colour and thought it enhanced her beauty.

"I was wondering if you would have dinner with me next Saturday night?" he asked. "I'm a member of a small club in town, which is rather nice and they have super food."

She hesitated for a moment, trying to recall her various engagements.

"That's kind of you, but unfortunately I have a date that night."

He thought she looked disappointed which encouraged him to persevere and he felt surprisingly frustrated himself.

"Well, can we fix another time? I suppose you couldn't manage next Friday instead, which has the added merit of being one day earlier?" he asked eagerly.

"Yes I think I can," Rosie replied. "That would be great fun."

"Good, then if it's all right with you, I will pick you up at your home at about 6.30?"

"That will be fine. I shall look forward to it very much. You must meet my parents – they will be anxious to have news of Richard and won't mind my going out with a strange young man under these circumstances. They are very straight-laced, I'm afraid."

He smiled: "Quite right, but I only hope I pass muster!"

"I hope you will too," she said jocularly, and they both laughed.

They looked into each other's eyes. His were a golden brown, warm with a smiling expression. There was a subtle attraction between them, which made her aware of him as a man. She thought how very exalted and handsome he was, so different from the first year students, though a stab went through her when she thought of dear old Parkie. She hated to feel any disloyalty towards him, but there was no doubt that Peter Dunbar was rather special and all her other admirers paled into insignificance beside him.

He looked at his watch: "Oh dear, I must hurry off now as there is an important lecture I have to attend – goodbye, Rosie. Roll on Friday."

"I'll be looking forward to it," she answered with a delightful smile.

Rosie felt she was walking on air. She found it hard to concentrate – her mind wandered constantly during lectures, pre-occupied by exciting thoughts of this god-like creature, who had just entered her life.

She finished her 'dream cottage' with consummate ease. Everything seemed to fall into place and she was pleased with the simplicity of her plan.

It was a straightforward design without any frills; the main feature of the living room being a large rugged stone fireplace, suitable for burning driftwood and so placed as to heat the whole cottage. Parkie was most impressed with her presentation and became aware for the first time of her ability as an artist. His respect for her talent increased considerably.

Parkie's design was charming – a cottage situated in a clearing in the woods. It was ultra modern with windows stretching from floor to ceiling, so that the outdoors seemed an integral part of the cottage itself.

Rosie could imagine living there, observing quietly from inside the fascinating wildlife of the woods. She congratulated him on his originality. She hoped that, as he threw himself more and more into these exciting projects, she would become of less importance to him.

She finished early on Friday afternoon. A thrill of excitement ran through her and made her heart flutter as she contemplated the evening ahead with Peter. She had never felt quite like this before.

Meanwhile Peter was sitting in his bachelor flat, trying to work. These last few months were vital to him, for he was determined to get an honours degree. He recognised the danger presented by his meeting with Rosie and knew that he must play it cool and not get too emotionally involved, but the very thought of her stirred him as never before.

He felt restless and finally threw his work on one side, deciding to stroll along to the library, as there was a text book he needed; it was obvious that he was not going to settle down to any serious study that day.

His old M.G. was standing in the road outside the flat. He noticed how untidy it was inside, so started putting all the books in a pile on the back seat. He was fond of his car, but was very conscious of the fact that it was not in the same class as Parkie's Bentley. Yesterday he had seen it disappearing round the corner with Rosie's curly head much in evidence in the front seat.

After making a few discreet enquiries, he learnt of Parkie's devotion to her and this disturbed him considerably; he had experienced an unusual pang of jealousy – quite ridiculous, he thought, as he had spoken to her only once and could well be disappointed tonight, but in his heart he knew this would not be so, for unquestionably there was something very special about Rosie.

He dressed with care and looked extremely smart in a dark grey suit with a Bengal striped shirt and blue spotted tie. He left in good time, anxious not to be late. She had explained exactly where she lived, so he had no difficulty in finding the house.

He felt unusually hesitant as he rang the door bell and was admitted by a pretty young parlour-maid and taken into the drawing room to await Rosie. The room was elegant and beautifully furnished with fine antiques. A Bechstein grand fitted comfortably into an alcove; he wondered if Rosie played.

He stood nervously with his back to the fireplace, fiddling with his tie; his usual self-confidence had deserted him – only temporarily he hoped.

A few moments later Rosie appeared. She looked so enchanting that she quite took his breath away. She was wearing a filmy dress and coat in a lovely grey-blue. The dress fitted her like a glove, showing off the beautiful contours of her figure, yet they were discreetly disguised by the matching coat.

She approached him rather shyly with a sweet expression on her face. The blueness of her eyes was intensified by the colour of her ensemble. She was even more elegant than he had realised and, helpless, he knew that he was lost. She in turn felt the same thrill, his good looks and masculinity captivated her and, in those fleeting moments, they both instinctively knew their fate was sealed. She was the first to speak, and her voice sounded a little breathless.

"I do hope you found your way here all right, Peter?"

"Oh yes , thank you, your directions were perfect. I had no trouble at all finding the house – how nice to live in Sefton Park, it is so conveniently close to town, yet in many ways it's rather like being in the country."

She nodded. "Yes, we love it here – from the upstairs windows you get a splendid view of the lake and the Park is really a joy in the Spring and Summer; it's just a riot of colour with all the flowers in bloom and it is particularly lovely in blossom time."

"I believe the Park was laid out by a Frenchman, Edouard André – he was Gardener-in-Chief of Paris and he won the commission in open competition."

"Yes, that is so," Rosie replied, "and he certainly made a wonderful job of it. I often marvel at his vision. The brilliance of his concept, using natural scenic features, gives it a delightful informality."

They looked at each other with smiling eyes.

"Do sit down for a moment. Mother is anxious to meet you and talk to you about Richard. We haven't seen him since he went up to Cambridge, but when he was a little boy and his parents were living abroad, he spent many school holidays with us and we became very fond of him."

"Yes," Peter replied, "he told me how kind you all were to him when he was so desperately homesick – he's quite a chap now – standing six feet four in his socks and is a Cambridge rugger blue."

At that moment the door opened and Rosie's mother walked in. She was an attractive woman, dignified and slightly aloof, obviously wary of any young man, who was a possible suitor for her only daughter. Rosie introduced them.

"Mother, this is Peter Dunbar who is a great friend of Richard's," she said circumspectly. "They're both Wykehamists."

"How do you do", her mother replied, "It is very nice to hear news of Richard. We have known him since he was a baby, but recently seem to have lost touch."

"I expect Rosie has told you that we have been friends for years. He's a good chap and quite a brain, as well as being a fine rugger player," Peter said with enthusiasm.

"Yes, we heard from his people that he is doing well and enjoying himself up there. Do tell him that we would very much like to see him again, when next you meet."

"I certainly will," he replied. "He is most anxious to see you too, for I had special instructions to look you up, when he heard that Rosie was also at the School of Architecture."

"I believe you are in your final year now?" she asked him with interest.

"Yes, that is so, providing I keep my nose to the grindstone and get my degree," he said modestly.

Rosie chipped in here: "I've heard there's little doubt about that – you've got a terrific reputation as an egg-head."

"I don't know whether that's a compliment or not!" he retorted with a wry grin. He looked at his watch. "I have booked a table for 7.30, so I think, if you will excuse us, Mrs. Greenwood, we had better be off."

"Of course – I hope you have an enjoyable evening but, Peter, Rosie must be home by 10.30 at the latest," she said firmly.

"Now off you go and drive carefully."

Mrs. Greenwood felt uneasy; Peter was almost too good looking and Rosie was still so very young and inexperienced, she could easily be swept off her feet.

As they left the house Rosie chuckled. "My mother isn't really the dragon she seems. In fact she's an absolute dear, although on first acquaintance, I must admit, she's rather intimidating."

"I think she is very charming and quite right to vet your escorts so carefully. I feel flattered that she has entrusted you to me."

He helped her into the car and they were quickly on their way to town; by the time they reached the club they were conversing vivaciously, exchanging confidences as though they had known each other all their lives.

Peter had a quiet sense of humour which appealed to Rosie; she was quick to respond to it and she was so natural and unaffected that Peter felt completely relaxed with her.

The club was small and attractively appointed, and Peter was obviously well respected there. They had drinks at the bar, then the head waiter led them to a corner table on which was a lovely bowl of fragrant pink roses. She instinctively knew they had been chosen especially for her. She bent forward and closed her eyes. "Uum, what a marvellous scent," she said. "I absolutely adore roses, they're my favourite flowers."

"Your name-sake and so you should," he said with a grin.

He thought how lovely she was. He looked at her pretty mouth – a natural bow, soft and seductive, yet strangely vulnerable. He was deeply moved and it showed in his face.

"I'm glad you like them, Rosie – special flowers for a special girl!"

The meal was delicious, Rosie's favourite Lobster Newburg, but the culinary efforts of the club were rather wasted on them. They were so completely absorbed in each other and quite oblivious of their surroundings.

Peter was in terrific form – his quirky sense of humour had Rosie convulsed with laughter and, when he announced it was time to leave, she could hardly believe her ears. "Surely not yet?" she said in amazement. "We've only just arrived!"

"I'm afraid so, my poppet – we must go now, if we are going to get you in before curfew. The time has absolutely flown."

"I feel like Cinderella," she replied with a little sigh of disappointment, as she collected her things together, preparing to leave. Peter put his arm lightly around her shoulders and guided her between the tables to the exit. He felt very proud of her – she was so very lovely.

They arrived back at the house with five minutes to spare, but he escorted her without delay to the front door. He must not put a foot wrong.

"Good bye and thank you for a lovely evening," she said warmly "everything has been perfect." He gave her a light kiss on the cheek; her skin was as soft as silk – oh, how he hated leaving her.

"Goodbye, Rosie, we must do this again very soon."

It suddenly dawned on him that he had fallen deeply in love. He had never believed in love at first sight, but now he knew it could actually happen.

*   *   *   *   *

Rosie made a firm resolve that she must not allow her work to suffer by lapsing into day-dreams over Peter. She overcame the temptation to look up every time anyone passed the classroom door. He too was making a determined effort to keep his concentration, so they arranged to meet only at weekends until after his finals.

Her social life went on as usual; the band of five were still very close friends; having so many interests in common was stimulating and their relationship was a rewarding one. They generally went to the cinema together one night a week and this particular evening had decided to see Charlie Chaplin's new film 'City Lights' – it was a classic. Parkie brought the Green Goddess as usual to the front of the building and, as they started driving off, Peter came whizzing round the corner, just in time to catch a glimpse of Rosie sitting in the front seat between Ken and Parkie. She was looking most glamorous in a white curly sheepskin jacket and was smiling bewitchingly up at Parkie. A stab of jealousy ran through him and he felt thoroughly miserable. Parkie was already an adversary and what was all this 'Princess' nonsense? She was his and he would not share her with anybody. He was amazed how possessive he had already become.

When Rosie arrived home that evening, the phone was ringing and she rushed to answer it – she was sure it was Peter and was thrilled when she heard his voice at the other end of the line.

"Hello, Rosie darling, how are you?"

She thought he sounded subdued. "I'm very well, thank you, Peter – I've just this moment come in, but how are you getting on?"

"Not too badly, but I am missing you very much. I have kept my promise and have been working furiously all the week and made quite good progress; it's frightening though how much I still have to do, but, Rosie, I must see you this weekend." There was a sense of urgency in his voice. "Could you possibly come over and spend the weekend with us? I'm anxious for you to meet my father and mother."

Rosie hesitated for a moment. "Of course I'd love to come, Peter, but I don't know if my parents will approve; they won't consider we've known each other long enough yet."

"Don't worry about that, Rosie, I'm certain it can be arranged. I will get my mother to phone yours and fix it all up – they're sure to get on well together."

"All right, Peter, you sound very confident and, if you can organise it, that will be fine with me." He seemed more cheerful now.

"I've missed you dreadfully this week, Rosie; being separated from you has been absolute hell. The only compensation is that I've made great headway with my model village, but you should see my flat – there are buckets of papier-maché all over the place – it's almost impossible to move around; however, the worst is over now as most of the landscaping is finished. Have you got any good ideas on making realistic-looking trees?"

"Well, as a matter of fact I have," Rosie replied. "Only yesterday I gathered some heather from the garden and used sprigs of it dipped in a glue-like substance, which Parkie made up for me. I'm thrilled with the result – it looks like the real thing."

"That sounds interesting, Rosie; could you bring me over a sample this weekend?"

"Of course, that is providing I'm allowed to come. By the way, I've just finished a tiny model myself. We weren't required to make one, but it's so helpful seeing the three dimensional effect; it can also be shattering. The house I was planning looked fine on the drawing board, but awful in model form. I'll never be a brilliant architect," she said regretfully. "I just don't have the flair."

"That's stuff and nonsense, Rosie, your drawing is quite superb."

"Thank you, Peter, for your encouragement, but I get depressed when I compare myself with Parkie. Now he is a real genius. You must come and look at some of his work. I'm sure he will be famous one day in the Gropius, Corbusier class."

Peter gave no reply to this, remaining strangely silent and Rosie instantly sensed his displeasure. Oh dear, he's jealous, she thought, so changed the subject quickly.

"If our weekend plans materialise, will you pick me up or shall I drive over myself?" she asked.

"I will collect you, of course, Rosie. I thought about 3 o'clock and then we would be home in time for tea. I can hardly wait," he said fervently. "There are so many things I want to show you. If the weather is good, perhaps we could sail on Sunday morning?"

"That would be great fun, Peter."

"Well, be sure to bring over slacks and a warm sweater. We could take a picnic over to Hilbre Island, it's only a short distance and in my little craft, we'd be there in no time."

"You know I'm only a novice at sailing, Peter, so you'll have to show me the ropes," she chuckled. "My experience has been mostly confined to rowing a boat on the Park lake."

"Don't worry, Rosie, I know you'll be an excellent pupil."

"I must ring off now, Peter, as it's getting late and the family are waiting up for me. Goodbye, and I'll be longing for the weekend."

Rosie put down the receiver and hurried into the hall, shedding her coat and scarf on the way. Her mother and father were sitting in the drawing room reading. She thought they looked a picture of contentment. Her father put his newspaper to one side as she came in.

"Hello, Rosie, we've been waiting for you. Come and sit down and tell us what you've been doing today."

She bent over and kissed them both.

"I'm sorry to be late, Dad, but Ken, Parkie and I went to see 'City Lights'. It was terrific. Charlie Chaplin is so funny and yet so pathetic. You don't know whether to laugh or cry. Parkie knew though, his great shouts of laughter seemed to shake the cinema. I almost felt ashamed of him. Of course, I don't really mean that, he's an absolute darling!"

"Who was that on the phone, Rosie?" asked her mother.

"Oh, it was Peter Dunbar. He wants me to stay with them next weekend. Apparently his mother is going to phone you about it. She sounds a bit of a martinet. They live at Caldy and Peter's mad about sailing. He's a member of the local club and has a super little Uffa King, designed by 'the Fox' himself, of course. We're planning to sail over to Hilbre Island on Sunday morning."

Her father showed obvious surprise.

"I must say this all seems rather sudden. A week ago we had never even heard of this young man. Isn't he rather jumping the gun?"

"He's really very nice, Dad." She smiled beguilingly at him and he started to melt.

"Well, your mother seemed to like him and being a friend of Richard's is an excellent recommendation – we shall just have to wait until his mother phones and take it from there."

Rosie breathed a sigh of relief, sensing they would not oppose her. She stifled a yawn, suddenly feeling tired and drained after all the emotional excitement of the last few days and longing for the quietness of her own room.

"Do you mind if I buzz off to bed now? I'm feeling rather sleepy and I must be up early tomorrow morning – going to the flicks has put me behind with my work, but it was worth it."

"Yes, of course, you get off now, dear. There's a hottie in your bed and I'll bring you a Horlicks as soon as you're ready."

"Oh, thank you, Mum, that sounds scrumptious."

How lucky I am, she thought. I don't think I'll ever want to leave home – even to get married – well, unless it was to Peter. She sighed with dreamy pleasure. She knew she would feel very differently then. She picked up her darling Chi-Chi and carried him upstairs, settling him down at the foot of her bed and covering him with his own special blanket. She was always happiest when he was with her.

*   *   *   *   *

All her weekend arrangements had been made. Peter had done his stuff. Mrs. Dunbar had spoken charmingly to Rosie's mother and they had both expressed the wish to meet sometime. It turned out they had several mutual friends, so this was reassuring and the weekend was agreed, though in fact there were reservations on both sides.

When the day arrived, Rosie was very excited and bubbly. Her mother helped her to decide what clothes to take and, after trying on a great variety, she finally chose to wear a creamy wool dress with a charming Victorian gold locket – a birthday present from her father. Her mother thought she had never looked more beautiful. She possessed an inner radiance now, which was clearly reflected in her lovely eyes. There was no doubt that she was a girl of character, but she was still so young and inexperienced.

Her mother knew that this was no casual weekend visit, and sensed there could be danger ahead. She liked Peter very much, but wondered if he had been spoilt, because of his good looks, his superior intellect and the advantages of class and education. Had he too much going for him? He could be strong willed. Rosie must have plenty of time to get to know him before making any commitment.

Rosie was all packed and ready to go with plenty of time to spare. Chi-Chi, sitting close beside her, looked disconsolate. The minute the suitcase appeared, his tail drooped and his eyes grew mournful. Rosie hated leaving him, even for a night. She patted his soft woolly head and he looked up at her expectantly with hope in his eyes. Was she going to take him after all? She only had to say: "No, Chi-Chi, you can't come today" and Chi-Chi understood. His tail went down; he was crushed.

The front door bell rang, just as Rosie was adding the finishing touches to her appearance.

"Are you ready yet, Rosie?" her mother called up. "Peter has just arrived."

"Yes, Mum, I'm coming straight down." She took one last look in the mirror then, picking up Chi-Chi, hurried to meet him.

Peter was standing in the hall and there was no disguising the evident joy that they both felt - Rosie was sparkling with happiness and Peter could not take his eyes off her – they were in a world of their own.

"Hello, Rosie," he said with a catch in his voice, "you look lovely."

He seemed oblivious of her mother standing there.

"How nice to see you, Peter," she replied, trying to curb her excitement at being with him again. She was laughing and gay, but somehow shyer and more reserved than usual. A new maturity was apparent.

"I think we had better be on our way now, Mrs. Greenwood, as Mother is expecting us for tea."

"All right, Peter, but drive carefully and take good care of Rosie."

"Yes, indeed, and I will bring her back on Sunday afternoon."

Rosie kissed her mother goodbye, as Peter put her suitcase into the car then, waving excitedly, they drove off through the Park. It looked beautiful on one of the last days of summer. The trees heavily clad with foliage of so many different shades of green and the lake a-ripple sparkled in the sunshine.

Peter seemed quieter and more thoughtful than usual. He was almost afraid of his own emotions; they were so strong. His whole being longed for Rosie, he adored her and nothing must come between them. He patted her knee and told her how marvellous she looked and she smiled happily back at him.

"I wish we had time to wander in the Park together," she said almost wistfully. She felt strangely sad at leaving it today; she sensed that she was making a break from her happy, secure life.

"I would love to show you the Palm House, Peter, it is full of most unusual tropical plants and I wish we could walk around the lake and feed the ducks and swans. There is an interesting variety of ducks here at the moment"

"I'm afraid there's no time for it today, Rosie," he said reluctantly, hating to disappoint her, "but we must do it on another occasion. Ma is a stickler for punctuality and tea is always served on the dot of four, so we had better not be late. The old man will be there too and, although he backs up Ma, he's more relaxed and couldn't care less himself."

As they passed through the city into the Cheshire countryside, Rosie had never felt happier. Peter was such a good companion and they shared many interests. She found him desperately attractive and longed to be closer to him. She had never before experienced this feeling for any man and her whole upbringing taught her not to show this. She instinctively knew he felt the same way about her but he, in turn, behaved correctly and gave little indication of his all-consuming desire for her.

He glanced down at his watch, speeding up a little as he saw they were getting short of time. Then suddenly an awful thing happened . A young man opened his gate leading on to the country road and a little brown puppy came flying out. Peter braked violently and sharply turned the steering wheel to take avoiding action, but there was a sickening bump and the car came to a screeching halt. Without hesitation Rosie leapt out ahead of Peter and rushed to pick up the little bundle on the road. She sat down on the grass verge and listened for his heart beats, speaking soothingly to the little creature. There was a faint flutter and then all was quiet. She glanced up with tears in her eyes at the owner of the puppy, who was standing there looking helpless – he seemed a nice young man.

"I'm afraid he's gone", she said. She could hardly speak for the lump in her throat.

The young man turned to Peter: "You are not in any way to blame, sir."

"I am terribly sorry," Peter replied regretfully, "but I just couldn't avoid him. He tore right out in front of me."

The owner looked down at the pathetic little pup, lying so still in Rosie's lap, when only a few seconds earlier he had been careering round the garden, so full of life.

"Poor old fellow," he said remorsefully, "but don't worry, Miss, it was all my fault. I should never have opened the gate like that – I just didn't know Terry was behind me – don't you fret now."

"Rosie dear," Peter said kindly, "get up and sit in the car, while I sort things out." He took her arm and helped her to her feet.

"No, Pete," she replied. "I'm going to carry Terry back to the house first." Her voice broke – "The little darling, it's such a shame."

The three of them crossed the road together and went into the garden. She wrapped the puppy in her white scarf and laid him gently down on the grass in a quiet corner; then, bending down, she fondly stroked his little fluffy head. "He's such a pet," she said with a shuddering sigh.

"I will bury him in the garden," the youth said sadly, "but there's no need for you to wait." Then he saw Rosie's stained dress and his face creased with worry.

"Oh, Miss, your dress is all spoilt – I am sorry." She looked down with unseeing eyes. It seemed so unimportant.

"Don't worry about that, it will clean up," she said reassuringly. "I am only sorry for you – it's awful losing a pet."

"Well, if there is nothing more that we can do, we will be on our way," Peter said sympathetically, giving the young man a farewell pat on shoulder. "I know how you must feel – I've got a dog of my own."

They quietly took their leave, both badly shaken and feeling it was a blight on their lovely day. Rosie hoped this harrowing experience was not a bad omen for the future.

"We must try and forget this accident, Pete," she said, trying to put a brave face on it, "for it was certainly not your fault and was quite unavoidable."

"I know," he replied sighing deeply, "but I can't help feeling guilty. I love animals and I've never done anything like this before."

She put her hand lightly on his knee. "It's heart-breaking, but try not to feel responsible, for clearly the owner was to blame. He should never have allowed the pup to dash out of the gate."

They drove along without speaking for a few minutes until Peter finally broke the silence. He must try to restore their situation.

"I don't think I've told you about our pets at home. They're a very important part of our family. We have a little rough haired terrier called Joey – I know you'll love him, and we also have a ginormous black cat, Tim – he's the largest cat I have ever seen."

"How marvellous, I've always wanted a big cat – I'm looking forward to meeting Tim. Ours never grow large, however well we feed them!"

He glanced at his watch again. "Oh heavens, it's already four o'clock, we'll have to hurry."

He stepped on the accelerator and soon they were winding up a steep hill towards the house.

"If you look through the trees now, Rosie, you can just see our green roof, gleaming in the sunshine."

A few minutes later they were passing through the gates, down a tree-lined drive, which led them to the house. It had recently been built to Peter's design and it was certainly most impressive.

He had chosen a white rough-cast finish, with a steeply overhanging roof of green Cornish slate. The front door was of natural oak, with elegant Georgian brass furnishings. Flanking it on either side were two stone urns, full of a profusion of delicate pink and white petunias. Rosie thought it was one of the most attractive houses she had ever seen.

They jumped out of the car hurriedly and Peter pushed open the door for Rosie to walk in. The view from the entrance was breathtaking. A huge picture

36

window faced them, framing an attractively terraced formal garden full of colourful flowers and shrubs. Beyond this the ground fell steeply away into the enchantment of a wood. The contrast of this man-made garden and the natural woodland beyond was dramatic and Rosie longed to explore its leafy depths.

"Peter, how gorgeous this view is. I don't think I have ever seen anything lovelier. I'd like to look around the garden later on – it's so heavenly."

As she stood admiring the unusual vista, a door opened and standing on the threshold was a tall, good-looking woman, who had obviously been a beauty in her time, but at this moment she had a slightly displeased expression on her face.

"Peter, you're very late. Tea has been ready for over half an hour and I asked you particularly to be on time," she said petulantly.

"I'm sorry, Ma, but we had an accident. We ran over a little dog and killed it, I'm afraid. It was most upsetting – Mother, let me introduce you to Rosie."

Mrs Dunbar turned and at a glance saw this lovely girl with her blood-spattered frock and slightly tear stained face. She smiled, relenting a little and said quite warmly: "How do you do, my dear, you must have had an awful shock. However did it happen?"

Rosie smiled wanly.

"It wasn't Peter's fault, Mrs. Dunbar, he was driving quite slowly, but this little puppy darted out and it was impossible to avoid him."

Tears welled into her eyes again at the thought of the little mongrel, and she was also upset by their cold reception.

Mrs. Dunbar spoke more kindly. "I'm sorry you've had this nasty experience. Peter, take Rosie up to her room, so she can change her dress, and I will see if Cook can do anything to remove those stains. She's a marvel at that sort of thing."

"Thank you very much, Mrs. Dunbar, I'll be as quick as I possibly can – I'm sorry we are late for tea."

Mrs.Dunbar returned to the drawing room and stood gazing out of the window. She realised Peter was seriously interested in this girl. She was determined that he would not get tied to anyone until he was qualified and established comfortably in a practice, but she knew it was going to be hard to make him see reason where Rosie was concerned. She was such a child, yet had the dignity and poise of someone much older. In spite of her tears and somewhat crumpled appearance, her little face was beautiful. Grudgingly she had to admire the fact that the dog had been more important to Rosie than her own appearance on this first meeting with Peter's family.

Mrs.Dunbar, however, was a strong-minded woman and, although she loved her only son, she demanded a strict code of behaviour from him. He, however, dug in his toes when he felt she had overstepped the mark and was then quite obdurate. She sensed this would be the situation now – any discouragement from her would fall on stoney ground and be ignored.

A few minutes later they both appeared and they certainly were a well-matched couple. Rosie looked enchanting, wearing now a soft, coral pink, angora dress. She felt shy and nervous of this rather formidable woman, but tried not to show it. She sensed disapproval in the air.

Sitting on the rug in front of the fire was the enormous black cat of which Peter had spoken.

"Oh, this must be Tim and he is indeed a monster." She bent down and stroked his sleek black fur. He responded by opening his huge green eyes and, as she scratched behind his ears, started a steady purr of appreciation.

"Well, I see you've made friends," said Mrs.Dunbar. "Timmy is generally reserved, but he obviously likes you."

Rosie felt glad that she had at least gained Timmy's approval!

"You haven't met Joey yet, our little black and tan; he's out in the woods chasing squirrels, I expect. He never succeeds in catching one, thank goodness, but won't give up trying!" Peter said with a grin.

A young parlourmaid brought in the tea and helped to hand round the sandwiches and cakes. Peter smiled at her.

"Ethel, this is Miss Greenwood. I'm afraid we have kept you waiting to serve tea."

"Oh, that is quite all right, sir," she murmured. "I'm sorry to hear of your accident."

She looked curiously at Rosie without being observed. In the kitchen they were all interested; they thought the world of Mr.Peter and were bursting to know what his young lady was like. Even though nothing officially had been said, the whole household was aware that there was a radical change in him and all put it down to this weekend date. As she passed round the cakes and sandwiches, she watched Rosie closely and, on catching her eye, Rosie smiled warmly across at her. Ethel thoroughly approved of Mr.Peter's choice and, on her return to the kitchen, gave them all a glowing account of the girl-friend.

After the tea was wheeled out, they sat round the fire talking. Rosie was more relaxed now, though she suspected that she would never be really at ease here. There was a tense, hypercritical atmosphere in the house, so different from the warm, loving relationship in her own home.

"While I was waiting for you to arrive," Mrs.Dunbar said somewhat pointedly, "I was reading a magazine article on the Abdication of Edward VIII – I think you both might enjoy it. The author takes a strong line that the King was wrong to put his personal feelings before his duty to his country. Winston Churchill comes in for a drubbing too as the King's champion and for his advocacy of compromise. What did you feel about the Abdication, Rosie?"

She replied hesitantly, feeling she would be judged on her response.

"He was a great favourite of mine, when he was Prince of Wales, for he undoubtedly did a lot of good among the poor and particularly the Welsh miners. I was very sad to see him go, but I do agree that duty must come first, though it must be heartbreaking to give up the one you love."

"The issue is black and white as far as I am concerned, without any shades of grey," Peter said emphatically. "He inherited the exalted position of king, and king he should have remained. The man I'm sorry for is his poor brother who, quite unprepared, was thrown in at the deep end."

At that moment the door opened and in walked Peter's father, a tall impressive figure, thick set with dark penetrating eyes. "Hello, my dear," he said to his wife. "I'm sorry I am so late for tea, but it's that London train again." His face lit up when he looked across at Rosie. "Is this the very special young lady, who we have been hearing so much about?" he asked.

"Yes, sir, may I introduce you to Rosie Greenwood?"

"How do you do, Rosie, we are delighted to have you with us."

"How do you do, Mr.Dunbar," she said smiling shyly back at him, the delicate colour in her cheeks deepening.

"I have been looking forward to meeting you" she said politely.

He looked searchingly at her and his expression was kindly. She felt an instant liking for him. Peter and his father were very similar, but his mother will take much more knowing, she thought.

"Now let's settle down," he said, "for I want to hear about Rosie! You are studying architecture too, I believe, my dear?"

"Yes, Mr.Dunbar, I am just finishing my first year. I expect I will get through all right, but it's been hard going. I love the drawing part, but find it rather a technical subject."

"This is nonsense," Peter interjected. "She's done some marvellous work but, being a perfectionist, she is never satisfied."

Rosie was pleased by Mr.Dunbar's interest in her and continued confidently.

"I would have preferred to have studied music or art, but my father wanted me to get a degree in architecture and I couldn't disappoint him."

"I'm sure it was a good choice," he replied, smiling approvingly at her.

"Now, how about you, Peter. You have only a few more weeks to go before your finals?"

"Yes, sir, I'm fairly well ahead with my project, but I will have to put on an extra spurt now."

Mrs.Dunbar added her weight here.

"A first class honours is so important to you, Peter, particularly when you have been offered such a splendid job I don't think you should spare yourself in any way."

Rosie felt uncomfortable. She suspected that Mrs.Dunbar regarded her as an unwelcome distraction at this time and, in all fairness, knew she was probably right. There was a pause, then Peter and his father started to discuss other subjects. Mr. Dunbar looked grave as he spoke of the growing power of Germany.

"The occupation of the Rhineland is just the 'writing on the wall'. War now seems inevitable and the people of this country must wake up before it's too late. Hitler is building air-raid shelters all over the big cities and he's not doing that for fun."

"Our lethargy in this country is quite incomprehensible," Peter said.

Rosie took the initiative and quietly spoke up.

"I have just joined a first-aid class with the Red Cross and hope to qualify as an ambulance driver within the next few months."

"That's what I like to hear," Mr.Dunbar exclaimed. "We are painfully unprepared and need more people like yourself, who recognise the danger signals and will take the initiative."

She was pleased by his praise and felt more at ease.

Peter looked over at her. "I don't think I told you that I'm in the R.N.V.R. and at the first sign of trouble I shall be called up."

Rosie's heart missed a beat – her sudden new-found happiness seemed threatened. Could her bliss be torn away from her? Already the thought of separation from Peter was unbearable. He smiled across at her but her little face was pensive and she didn't respond.

"You're very serious, Rosie. Is it the talk of war?" he asked.

"Yes, the prospect is too horrifying to contemplate," she said with a shudder. Mr.Dunbar smiled sympathetically.

"Well, let us change the subject to a more cheerful topic. I believe you two young people are going to the Nicholson's tonight?"

"Yes, it's Peggy's birthday and they're having a few people in for dinner."

The grandfather clock in the hall solemnly chimed the hour.

"Oh, dear," Peter exclaimed, "I didn't realise it was so late. We must get ready – I expect you will need plenty of time to change, Rosie?"

"Yes, Peter, I'm a bit of a slow coach, so I think I should go up now. Please excuse me," she said politely, turning to Mrs. Dunbar, before leaving the room. Peter stayed behind for a moment for a word with his parents.

"Well, what do you think of my favourite girl?" He looked confidently at them both – he knew they could not disapprove.

His father spoke first. "I like her very much. I think she is a sweet intelligent girl and certainly very beautiful."

"Well, Ma, how about you?"

She hesitated for a moment, but knew she must be fair.

"She seems very nice, but she is so young, Peter, only seventeen. I hope you are not going to become serious about her yet. You must get qualified before you think of anything like that."

"Well, of course, but my finals are only a few weeks away, so try not to be unreasonable, Ma."

With those firm words he left the room, whistling as he bounded up the stairs to prepare for the evening.

Meanwhile, Rosie was sitting in her dressing-room, looking thoughtfully through her window at the view of the woods below. This was a unique house and it made her realise Peter's potential as an architect. Perhaps he had not Parkie's genius, but this house was comfortable and pleasing to the eye.

She looked around her room: the wallpaper was the palest green and the paintwork brilliant white. The bedspreads and curtains were of a matching material in various shades of green, with splashes of coral in a 'Bird of Paradise' design. The furniture was all white, custom-made and of great elegance. The bathroom was white too, relieved with the same green and coral theme in the towels and bathmats.

Rosie ran her bath water and, as she stepped in, saw her reflection in the full length mirror on the wall. She looked at herself intently, giving her figure a critical appraisement. She could see no faults. She was slim, yet rounded, with a tiny waist and a full voluptuous bosom. It appeared a contradiction to the child-like face and innocent blue eyes, which looked back at her. She wondered how Peter would react if he saw her now. Would he find her beautiful? Rosie was awakened at last, the child was still there but quickly disappearing and in her place a loving young woman.

3

THE DINNER party had been most enjoyable and Rosie had met several of Peter's close friends, all of whom she liked. It had started rather formally in Brigadier and Mrs.Nicholson's usual style but afterwards, when the young people were left to themselves, it became a most hilarious evening.

After dinner Peggy, the Nicholson's only child, was persuaded to sing, with Rosie accompanying her on the piano. They chose all the old favourites — everyone joined in with gusto and joyously they made the rafters ring.

Peter had planned to leave the dinner party early, so as to have some time alone with Rosie. They drove to the Yacht Club and parked on the beach close by. There was a full moon shining on the water, which was as smooth as glass — there seemed to be magic in the air. Peter gazed at her in a passion of tenderness as she snuggled up against him. Her soft femininity and delicate perfume filled him with an almost uncontrollable desire for her, but resolutely he pushed this to one side, putting up a verbal smoke screen to hide his emotions.

"Rosie, darling," he said, "let's talk about ourselves."

"Yes, let's," she said eagerly, "but you kick off first, Peter, I want to hear all your secrets." Then, resting her head on his shoulder, she snuggled closer, preparing to have a heart to heart talk with him.

"You know, Rosie, I'm very ambitious and I am determined to become a successful architect," he said earnestly. "I certainly hope to start a practice of my own before too long."

"I'm sure you'll succeed, Pete — your parents' house is absolutely super. It's so functional as well as being beautiful."

"I'm glad you like it — sometimes I feel it's a bit commonplace, but I was restricted by their wishes, which was rather frustrating."

"It's a splendid house, in perfect taste and, after all, one rarely has a free hand. I'd be thrilled if I could design anything half as good," Rosie said generously. "I know I'll never be much of an architect. I wish I'd gone to an Art School. I think I've more potential in that direction."

"I must say I've been most impressed by your drawing," he said, "but you'll succeed at design, little girl, if you try hard enough!"

"I hope so, Pete, but it must be wonderful to create something really beautiful, rather than the ordinary stuff which I turn out."

"Give yourself time, poppet, you've only just started. I do hope you've got over the shock of that accident this afternoon, Rosie. I think we're the same about animals and running over that little dog really upset me."

"I know exactly how you feel, Pete — we're twin souls," she said with a sweet seriousness, which he loved.

"Yes I think we are," he replied softly. He took both her hands and his voice was low, yet vibrant.

"Rosie, my darling, I know it is very soon to ask you, but will you marry me? I've loved you from the first moment I saw you."

Her face lit up with joy and she replied without hesitation.

"Yes, of course I will, Peter. We were made for each other."

They gazed deeply into each other's eyes, spellbound by the enchantment of this wonderful moment. Then, putting his arm around her shoulders, he drew her to him and kissed her on the lips. It was a gentle kiss but, soon aroused, they clung together in a passionate embrace and a strange exciting thrill ran through her. He was the first to draw away, afraid of his own strong emotions, for her trusting innocence touched him and his voice trembled as he spoke.

"Darling, darling, you tempt me far too much – you drive me mad – you are so lovely." She saw the sudden fire of passion in his eyes.

"I understand, Pete," she whispered breathlessly. "I feel the same about you. I wish we could be together always, day and night. I just can't get close enough to you."

She could tell him anything now – swept away by her emotions and overwhelmed by her first devastating experience of love.

Determinedly she forced herself back to reality. They certainly must not be late returning, otherwise she knew they would be in the dog-house.

"Pete," she said incredulously, "do you realise it's after midnight?"

"Yes, Darling, I'm afraid I do, the time has absolutely flown. I suppose we really must be making tracks for home."

They clung together for a final kiss, then he started up the car and reluctantly they left the enchantment of the moonlit beach behind them, winding up the steep hill towards the house.

On arrival, they quietly let themselves in. Everyone had gone to bed, but lights were left on for them in the drawing room and the fire had burnt low in the hearth. While they stood, seeking warmth from its dying embers, Peter put his arms around her.

"Darling, do you realise how very much I love you and how desperately I need you?" he asked urgently.

Rosie looked into his eyes adoringly.

"Of course I do, Pete, I feel the same. Everything is just perfect and I'm deliriously happy."

She kissed him on the cheek lovingly. "I hate to leave you but I must go to bed now, otherwise I fear your parents will disapprove and that will never do."

Unwillingly she slipped from his arms: "Goodnight, darling –sleep well and dream of me."

"I am sure I shall, Darling," he said, giving her a little squeeze.

She tiptoed up the stairs in case the family were sleeping but, on reaching her bedroom door, Mrs. Dunbar appeared on the landing in her dressing gown, obviously waiting up for her.

"I do hope I haven't disturbed you," Rosie asked anxiously. "We are rather late, I'm afraid – we've had a super evening, but the time went so quickly."

"I'm glad you enjoyed it, dear, now be off to bed and have a good night's sleep. I believe you are sailing tomorrow, so you'll be making an early start. I heard Peter asking Cook to pack up some sandwiches for your lunch."

"Yes, I believe we are sailing over to Hilbre and I'm looking forward to it tremendously, though I have a lot to learn."

Mrs. Dunbar smiled, "You have to be tremendously quick and agile in Peter's boat, but I am sure you will soon pick it up – sleep well, dear."

Rosie had an impulse to kiss her goodnight for, although she still found her formidable and knew there was a barrier between them, she felt that once the ice was broken, Mrs.Dunbar would unbend and Rosie so badly wanted to be accepted.

Rosie woke early the following morning; she had slept like a top. She lay in bed contentedly contemplating the exciting events of last evening. She felt ecstatically happy, she had no doubts now, she adored Peter and he adored her. They would marry and live happily ever after.

When her day-dreaming was over, she quickly jumped out of bed, eager to start painting a picture of the garden and woods as seen from her bedroom window. The light was perfect and, if the watercolour turned out well, she had decided to give it to Mrs.Dunbar as a farewell present.

She put on her dressing gown and slippers; and was soon sketching in a simple outline. Then, with deft strokes, she applied the colour. She was a fast worker and was pleased with the finished result. The picture had undoubtedly captured the enchantment of the scene. She signed it carefully, then meticulously wrote on the back "To Mrs. Dunbar, in appreciation of a perfect weekend."

She was just adding some final touches, when there was a light tap on the door and Ethel walked in with the early morning tea. She was most surprised to see Rosie perched on the end of her bed with a paint brush in her hand.

"Good morning, Miss Greenwood, I hope you had a good night's sleep?"

Rosie beamed up at her. "Oh, absolutely super, thank you."

Quickly she hopped back into bed as Ethel handed over her tray – Ethel thought she had never seen such a lovely girl, even her little bare feet were a treat. She would have plenty to tell Cook this morning, when she returned to the kitchen.

Rosie smiled at her and held up the picture for inspection.

"What do you think of my painting, Ethel?"

"My goodness, Miss Greenwood, you are clever. It's lovely and makes me feel I'd like to walk amongst the trees, they look so inviting."

"I'm glad you like it," Rosie replied, pleased with Ethel's response, for she felt the same about the woods and hoped she had succeeded in capturing their enticement.

She drank her tea hurriedly and was soon up again, donning her slacks and a vivid green polo-necked sweater and plimsolls. It was a perfect morning, everything was so cool and fresh. She was really looking forward to sailing in Peter's boat.

As she ran downstairs, he was waiting for her in the hall with a joyful expression on his face – she was his very own now.

"You look absolutely adorable," he said and kissed her good morning. "I love you in emerald green – it's such a perfect contrast with your hair and makes it look like a golden sovereign."

"You're looking pretty handsome yourself, Pete," she murmured appreciatively, and indeed he was; informal sailing clothes suited him.

He linked his arm in hers and led her to the dining room.

"Now let's get breakfast over quickly, Rosie. I can't wait for you to see my sleeky 'Silver Mist'. The weather is perfect for sailing today, just enough wind to make it interesting for a beginner."

They were soon at the Club with the sails of their boat hoisted. It was a 14-footer, clinker-built, with a very tall mast and was exceedingly fast in the water. Rosie loved the boat on sight with its elegant slim lines and immaculate trim. It was Peter's pride and joy. He guided them away from the jetty and put Rosie in charge of the jib. She knew just enough to get by and, as they joined the main stream, the wind caught the sails; instinctively she did the right things. She was exhilarated by the speed as they cut through the water and was soon lying out balancing the boat in a most professional manner; they tacked back and forth across the estuary and skilfully she changed her position from port to starboard, miraculously escaping a crack on the head from the boom. Peter was delighted with her progress and, as they reached the jetty at Hilbre, she jumped ashore and helped him secure the boat.

They sat together on the pebble beach eating their sandwiches, tired yet refreshed after their sail across from the mainland.

It was bliss, relaxing in the sunshine with the soft wind blowing gently up the estuary, idly watching the great variety of birds on the water's edge and listening to the pure ringing cry of the curlew, "Cour-li" — slowly delivered and remarkably liquid, embodying a long bubbling trill.

"Oh, Pete," Rosie exclaimed joyfully, "the call of the curlew does something to me. I wish we could stay here forever — if only I'd brought my paints across! Look at those gorgeous oystercatchers" and, as she spoke, there was a sudden dart of black and white plumage as the flame-beaked birds took off in a horizontal flight from the water, alighting on the gleaming mud flats in the distance.

"Hilbre is a great place for birds, Rosie, and particularly for waders on their migratory passage. At certain times of the year, this foreshore is an ornithologist's dream."

"Let's come again soon, Pete, for a whole day and next time I'll bring along my old knapsack and paint a picture of 'Silver Mist' for you."

"I'd like that, darling," he said leaning forward and playfully kissing the end of her little tip-tilted nose. Her hair glinted in the sunshine and she looked vital and alive, yet she had never quite lost the trusting qualities of childhood. To Peter she seemed so sweet and good and, through this, dangerously vulnerable.

They were silent for a time, both immersed in their own thoughts, until hesitantly Rosie brought up a ticklish subject.

"Pete, darling, I don't think we'd better mention our engagement yet. After all, it is still unofficial and, if we leave it until after the results of your finals are published, I think we will have a better chance of our parents accepting it. If we tell them now, I'm sure there will be violent opposition."

Peter frowned darkly. He wasn't going to take this lying down.

"I'll play along with them for a bit, Rosie my sweet, but it's our business, not theirs — they must not be allowed to interfere with our lives."

Rosie suddenly gave a little shiver. She hated the thought of any trouble with her parents. She ruffled his hair and smiled ruefully up at him.

"You mustn't be too impatient, darling. At least give them time to get used to seeing us together, for after all we've known one another for such a short time. But, oh Pete, like you I can hardly wait for us to get married." She laughed gaily . "It's all so terribly exciting! Let's have lots and lots of children — I thought about a dozen. I absolutely adore babies."

Peter looked at her with a startled expression. "Rosie, you're not serious, I hope? I would certainly like a son and a daughter, but that's enough for me. I will want your undivided attention, young lady, but with all those mewling and puking brats about, I could see myself being left out in the cold."

"Don't worry, Pete," she laughed, "we'll always be as close as clams," and she squeezed his hand and kissed him lightly on the forehead. He loved her innate gaiety. There was so much laughter in her.

If only time stood still, he thought, for already they must leave.

"Come on, Rosie my pet," he said, "we mustn't be late for tea again today, for this time there would be no excuse."

They packed up their kitbag and were soon beating back to the mainland. They arrived just in the nick of time, bursting into the house, laughing and full of the joys of Spring.

First love is wonderful, Rosie thought, yet so painful. Peter had just told her that, immediately after his finals, he would be going away for several weeks for his RNVR annual training. She felt devastated at this prospect and wondered how she could possibly live without him for so long.

Mr. and Mrs.Dunbar were obviously pleased with Rosie's going away present, and visibly impressed by her ability as an artist. They thanked her warmly and promised to hang the picture on the guest room wall. Their goodbyes were cordial, though there was again a gratuitous warning from Mrs Dunbar about Peter's finals and the necessity for his complete concentration at this time.

Rosie made it plain that she was concerned too, which helped to reassure them. Altogether it was a happy departure and a most successful weekend but, although they fully approved of Rosie, they felt she was far too young for marriage. Peter must wait.

*   *   *   *   *

Life went on as usual at the University, with Peter's finals looming up the following week. Much as they wished to be together every moment, they both accepted the fact that this would be wrong. Rosie took it more philosophically than he did; she still had the 'band of five's' company.

She had decided that, in fairness to Parkie, she must tell him of her feelings for Peter. It was a painful session but, as it was not entirely unexpected, he accepted the news stoically, only asking that they should continue their friendship. Rosie secretly wondered if this would work out. She very much hoped it would, for she was still very fond of him and had enormous respect for his ability. He was a great help to her with his ideas, which often lifted her work out of the commonplace into something rather special.

Today Rosie, Parkie and Ken had decided to take a trip to Southport in the Green Goddess, to view a new house that had just been built on the shore. It was completely round and the furnishing was causing the owner many headaches. Parkie knew him socially and had been asked to give some friendly advice. Rosie, being so interested in interior decoration, tagged along with them. She was anxious to see this ultra-modern house and was full of her own ideas.

As they passed Peter's door, she dashed in to tell him where they were going. He frowned and didn't look at all pleased, murmuring something about 'that damned fool design'. She thought it was rather churlish of him and, for the first time, a niggling doubt entered her mind. She was very much aware of his possessiveness. Friends were important to her happiness and she felt anxious, in case he might smother her with his desire to have her always to himself. Yet she longed for him, with a desperate longing and quickly closed her mind to any negative thoughts.

The fresh air and good company soon blew the uncertainties away and, when she returned home that evening, full of new ideas engendered by Parkie's fertile brain, a long, loving phone call from Peter put everything to rights again. He knew he had provoked her and was anxious to make amends.

"I shall be studying in my flat almost continuously until my finals are over," he said, "for there's so much at stake and I'm quite overwhelmed with work, but it's absolute hell not seeing you, darling" – he sounded desperate.

"I know, Pete, I'm going to miss you dreadfully, but finals are terribly important and we really mustn't meet until afterwards. Then whoopee! We can have a king-size celebration". She sounded on top of the world and he only wished he felt the same, but seeing her with Parkie was upsetting his concentration. There was nothing he could do about it, until they became officially engaged.

"Let's make a date now for dinner at the club on the last day of my exams," he suggested. "There will be lots to celebrate – the end of my University career and the completion of your first year – also it will be a last fling before my naval training."

"That will be something to live for", she said extravagantly. "I'm already counting the days, though the prospect of another separation from you is awful."

"Now, Rosie darling, be good, no more dates with old flames, and keep all your admirers at bay – just remember that you're mine."

"Not quite yet, Pete, but I'll bear it in mind," she replied with a teasing laugh.

He didn't quite like her answer, for he was totally obsessed in his love for Rosie – reason and caution played no part and he cursed her parents for their tough line against an early engagement, though he was determined to get round this.

When the long-awaited evening arrived, it was a joyful occasion, though tinged with tears because of the prospect of another immediate separation.

On parting, Rosie clung to him crying unashamedly and that night she scarcely slept a wink; she doubted if she could survive without him for three weeks – first love was a devastating experience for Rosie, especially as it seemed all goodbyes. However, as soon as his intimate, loving letters started to arrive, she became happy again, counting the hours and looking forward with joy to his return.

One morning, a few days later, Jane brought in her breakfast with the usual letter from Peter in his unmistakable, bold handwriting. Beneath it was a thick typewritten envelope, postmarked Plymouth. Rosie was intrigued and decided to open it first. She could hardly believe what she read. An almost unknown great aunt, virtually a recluse, who had lived in a Georgian House on Plymouth Hoe, had died, leaving her Welsh cottage to Rosie.

She was flabbergasted, light-headed with excitement. She just couldn't believe her good fortune. She had met the old lady only once. She had visited her on impulse a couple of years ago, while passing through Plymouth and, taking a chance on her likely reception, had boldly rung the doorbell. A tiny dignified old lady had answered the door and to begin with Rosie doubted whether she would be allowed inside; but after she had explained who she was and that she had only an hour to spare, her aunt was reassured that her privacy was not being seriously invaded and Rosie was invited in.

They had sat together in straight-backed Victorian chairs in the formal drawing room overlooking the Hoe, almost in silence, until by chance Rosie noticed a fine little water-colour of Snowdonia, tucked away in a corner of the room. She loved that part of Wales and had broken the ice by asking who the artist was.

"I painted it myself many years ago," her aunt replied. "You see I own a tiny cottage by Snowdon and in the past visited it frequently and did many studies of the surrounding countryside."

"How interesting," Rosie responded with enthusiasm, "for I adore that part of the world and painting is my greatest love. Would you like to see some sketches which I have brought with me?"

"Yes, I would indeed," her aunt replied and, as Rosie unpacked her knapsack, the old lady scrutinised every sketch with interest.

"You have a most original style, my dear – I like it very much. I feel you have a great gift which you must foster."

"Thank you, I am most encouraged by what you say. I love your work too. I have always been crazy about fine line and colour wash," Rosie replied with sincerity.

It soon became apparent that her aunt was most knowledgeable and had a deep appreciation of the arts. For this short period the old lady's reserve was swept aside and she communicated with Rosie as she had not done for years with any other human being. Before Rosie departed, her aunt asked her to write down her name and address. She had wondered why.

The recollection of this meeting upset Rosie. She blinked her eyes, keeping back the tears, wishing she had done more for this lonely soul, yet sensing that her attentions could have been unwelcome; enough that they had experienced together this friendly hour of common interest and shared a love of the beautiful Welsh countryside. She felt deeply touched that this little old lady had entrusted her with this treasured cottage.

She picked up the letter again and read it more carefully this time. It said that Miss Nightingale had not visited 'Apple Trees' for many years, but arrangements had been made with a nearby agent that it was always to be kept in order.

A girl from the village went regularly to light fires and keep the cottage clean and aired, and a local young man tended the garden. The keys could be picked up at Messrs. Thomas & Thomas in Bryngwrn village, if Miss Greenwood wished to look over her property – a woman of property indeed! It was like a dream, she couldn't believe it.

Breakfast and even Peter's letter were forgotten, swept swiftly on one side, as she jumped out of bed and flew down the stairs to tell her mother and father the joyful news.

Rosie just couldn't wait to see the cottage and her mother was equally keen, so they decided to drive over to inspect it the following day. Her father had communicated with the solicitor and the keys were to be handed over to Rosie. A sum of money had also been left to meet the cost of the established maintenance and daily help. Great Aunt Louise had thought of everything – bless her! Rosie was in her seventh heaven, but if only she could have thanked her for this munificent gift.

It was about an 80 mile journey and they planned to make an early start, so as to arrive at the local inn in time for lunch. Rosie in her excitement lay in bed the night before, unable to sleep, wondering what the cottage would be like and dreaming of establishing a studio there and even of the ultimate – installing a piano. That would be absolute heaven. She decided she had been born under a lucky star.

Her parents were pleased with her good fortune, but apprehensive, for Rosie was still so young and this gave her a measure of independence, not altogether welcome at the time. They were secretly anxious about her and were alarmed that Peter and Rosie had obviously fallen head over heels in love: it had all happened much too quickly.

Rosie had confided in her mother that she and Peter hoped to become engaged soon. Her mother was shocked and told her emphatically that her father would never consent to an early marriage and certainly would not be in favour of a long engagement. This all had an unsettling effect on their relationship, making Rosie less open, and a certain feeling of restraint developed between them.

* * * * *

Fortunately it was a lovely autumnal day for their visit to the cottage. The countryside looked beautiful with the leaves turning colour and glowing with brilliance in the sunshine. They thoroughly enjoyed the journey, both excitedly speculating on what 'Apple Trees' would be like. It seemed no time at all before they were approaching the little village of Bryngwrn, with its small shops, stocked with a miscellany of goods to meet the needs of its tiny community. The peaceful atmosphere of this small hamlet filled Rosie with a longing to be part of it.

They drew up at the village inn, a simple one-storey building, with a colourful picture of Snowdon on the flapping sign outside, painted proudly by a local artist. They decided to have lunch first, so as to leave the whole afternoon free for going over the cottage. As they entered the inn, they were both impressed by its old oak beams and welcoming fire. The dining room was small, with gleaming white cloths on the tables. The meal was a simple one, with the inevitable roast lamb and two veg, followed by Rosie's favourite 'Spotted Dick'.

She was impatient to get going, so they did not linger for coffee, but went direct to the local agent for the keys. He gave them the necessary directions to 'Apple Trees' and they set off with high hopes. As they turned a bend in the lane, they caught their first glimpse of the cottage.

"Mum, that must be it, doesn't it look enchanting?" Rosie exclaimed delightedly.

"It certainly does, and the setting is so pretty – it's a real dream cottage," her mother replied enthusiastically.

"Oh, Mum, I just can't believe that this dear little place is really mine." Her head was spinning with excitement. "Let's hurry on – I can't wait to see inside."

As they drew up at the front gate, Rosie leapt out of the car and stood spellbound, hardly able to believe her eyes. The front garden was neat and trim. The latticed windows sparkled in the sunshine and the old oak door looked sturdy and reassuring.

"Isn't it absolutely adorable, Mum? It seems so welcoming, almost as if it were waiting for us to arrive."

Her mother nodded. "I never expected anything as lovely as this, Rosie." She was in fact most impressed, almost bemused by its charm and beauty.

"Oh, Mum," she sighed. "It's just perfect. I still can't believe that Great Aunt Louise has left it to me." Her heart lifted with happiness. "I'll always be grateful and love her for it."

Her mother smiled. "She obviously took to you, dear, but you are a very lucky girl; it could not be more attractive – it's like a picture-book cottage."

Holding hands, they hurried up the path, joyfully sharing the excitement together. Rosie turned the key in the lock and opened the door and they peeped in with eager anticipation. It was equally charming inside: warmth and a scent of flowers filled the air. A beamed old fireplace, laid with apple wood logs, dominated the living room; this was set off by contrasting white walls, which were hung with water colours of local scenes. Rosie examined them with interest and emotion.

"Look Mum, these pictures were painted by Great Aunt Louise. Aren't they charming?"

"Yes indeed, they're delightful, Rosie. I love her delicate technique, it is most original."

They were in fine line with colours, pale and fragile. To Rosie's eye they had an ethereal quality, as though the artist had withdrawn to a land of make-believe. Rosie's concept of the Welsh countryside was essentially rugged, *à la Cézanne*, whereas Aunt Louise's was delicate in the extreme, almost wraith-like. Having met her, Rosie felt that this treatment was a personality reflection – an utter sensitivity, that prompted her to seek solace in the life of a near recluse; yet Rosie loved the pictures and felt they had enormous charm.

"Come and look at the kitchen, Mum," she called. "It's super!"

Her mother came through. "It certainly is," she replied, "and how immaculate too." It was small and spotless, with a well-scrubbed deal table and ladder-back chairs placed beneath the window. The view was delightful, looking over an orchard, full of apple trees, gnarled and twisted with age and, as a backcloth, the wonderful panorama of the Snowdonia range. Already Rosie's fingers itched to get at her pallet. She yearned to sit here and draw the mountains in their ever-changing moods. She would never tire of this view.

"Let's see the upstairs now, Mum," she said as she hurried up the polished wooden staircase to the rooms above. There was one large bedroom at the back of the cottage, furnished with old oak and delightful flowery chintz coverings and curtains. Through the window could be seen a heavenly view of Snowdon. There were two other small bedrooms, a bathroom, and a useful boxroom.

Rosie was pensive as she looked around. "I've made a resolve, Mum, never to change the character of 'Apple Trees' – I won't alter it at all. I feel I am only the custodian and Great Aunt Louise and I will always share it." She spoke with the idealism of youth.

"That's a nice thought, Rosie, but inevitably, in time, you will stamp your own personality on the cottage," her mother said, rather bringing her down to earth.

"I suppose you are right, Mum, but at the moment I don't want anything changed."

"It certainly doesn't need it, my dear, it's all so lovely, in fact I quite envy you," she said with a little smile. Rosie took her arm.

"Perhaps you and I can stay here together sometimes?"

"That would be nice, dear but, my goodness, it's nearly three o'clock already and we must be getting back or your father will be anxious about us."

"All right, Mum, I'll lock up quickly and then we can be off, but first let's have a quick look at the quaint little church at the end of the lane."

"Very well, Rosie, but we must not be long; the time has absolutely flown."

They walked down the road together, savouring the fresh air and enjoying the tranquillity of their surroundings. In the distance they heard the sound of a train whistle and the chug-chug of the engine pulling out of the sleepy country station.

The little Welsh church, Norman in origin, seemed an oasis of peace and solitude. A group of trees sheltered it from the east winds and a stone wall, built from smooth grey cobbles, surrounded the churchyard. The mellowed grave stones, set in the grass, many of them ancient and green with lichen, gave the scene an atmosphere of timeless peace. Rosie and her mother stood quietly at the gate, gazing in.

The trees, whipped up by a sudden breeze, rustled eerily and a strange feeling of apprehension and foreboding descended on Rosie. She gave a little shudder. But, as the sun broke through the trees again, she felt reassured. Of course she was imagining it all.

She took her mother's arm, glad of the close contact.

"It's time we left now, Mum; deserted churchyards are a bit creepy, don't you think?"

"Yes, I agree with you, particularly in the late afternoon, so let's hurry back, dear. I'd like to be home before dusk."

Rosie needed no urging, but when they reached the cottage again, she was most reluctant to leave. She patted the weathered old gate, "Goodbye 'Apple Trees'," she whispered, "I love you and will come back soon." Then, hurrying to the car, she jumped in and drove away.

The expected letter from Peter was awaiting her at home. It contained a great outpouring of love and impatience to be with her again. Rosie longed to reply to it and reassure him how desperately she was missing him too. After dinner that evening, she retired to her room and wrote a long epistle describing their visit to the cottage, which had turned out to be so enchanting. She drew clever little sketches of the different features, as well as an overall plan. By the time she had finished, she had covered ten pages and it was past midnight.

The days went by quickly enough, though life seemed empty without Peter, and Rosie no longer felt free to chat happily to her mother about him or talk of any future plans. Her parents both felt that she owed it to herself to go out into the world and gain experience before settling down and her father was determined that she should get her degree in architecture.

Her mother had misgivings about Peter. Although she liked him and thought that, in worldly terms, he was eminently desirable, he might prove strong-minded and forceful and this could be a possible source of unhappiness for her beloved Rosie.

4

ON THE day of Peter's return from sea Rosie was wildly excited. He arrived home late that evening, so they were only able to speak on the telephone. When she heard his voice, a great surge of joy ran through her. She could hardly contain her happiness. They talked on and on for over an hour, until Rosie heard footsteps overhead and whispered: "We really must stop now, Peter, I can hear my parents moving about. Goodnight, darling, it's wonderful to have you back. See you to-morrow." Then, after simulating a kiss, she hung up.

Peter was collecting her early the following morning to visit the University, which was still officially closed for the vacation, but possibly the exam results would be posted on the notice board. This was a time fraught with anxiety.

Rosie had a restless night, almost too excited to sleep and haunted by the fear that his results might be disappointing. She knew she had been a disturbing influence and felt sure she would be blamed by both families, and particularly by Peter's mother, if he hadn't succeeded in getting an honours degree.

After tossing and turning for hours, she finally dozed off and slept fitfully until morning, when she was woken with a start by Chi-Chi bounding into her room with hysterical barks and jumping on to her bed.

Jane stood waiting with the early morning tray until all the fuss had died down. Rosie felt much better now, her fears of the night had vanished. It would be wonderful to see Peter again.

"It looks a lovely day, Janie," she said, sipping her tea.

"Yes, Miss Rosie, it's bright and sunny, but there is a nasty bite in the air and there was a sharp frost last night. I believe you are expecting Mr. Dunbar this morning?"

"Yes, Janie, I am," she replied gaily and her face was wreathed in smiles.

"I must not linger in bed too long. Would you please run my bath for me, for I haven't much time."

"Yes, Miss Rosie, I'll do it at once."

Rosie took infinite pains with her appearance that morning. She wanted Peter to see her at her best.

She was downstairs, waiting in the hall, when his car drew up. He looked very handsome as he jumped out, deeply tanned from his time at sea.

He hurried up the steps, when he saw Rosie waiting at the open door, and his face lit up with joy. He flung his arms around her and pulled her close.

"Rosie darling, it's wonderful to be with you again, I've missed you dreadfully. I've felt like half a person without you."

"And I have missed you too, Pete – three weeks have seemed like a lifetime," she said with feeling.

He held her at arm's length, contemplating her lovely face. "You are looking even more beautiful than I remembered, sweetheart," and indeed she did look lovely, her vivid blue eyes shining with happiness.

Unfortunately Rosie's mother saw this uninhibited reunion. She felt they should have shown more restraint and, as they all walked into the drawing room, she was somewhat aloof, but nevertheless she spoke graciously to him.

"Welcome home, Peter, you are looking very fit and brown."

"Thank you," he replied with a smile. "We had marvellous weather at sea."

"Rosie tells me that you may get your exam results today – I wish you good luck."

"That is kind of you – we're anxious to know the worst, so we have decided to go straight to the University and see whether they are out yet."

"Rosie hasn't heard anything either about her own results."

"Come on, Pete, let's get going now," Rosie said impatiently, "The suspense is too awful." She just couldn't wait to be alone with him and didn't want to be held up, chatting to her mother.

"All right, Rosie, we'll be off. Goodbye, Mrs. Greenwood, and please excuse our hurrying away like this – do keep your fingers crossed for us."

"Yes, I certainly will but, Rosie, you phone me if the results are through."

"Of course, Mum, bye for now."

After the young people had departed, Mrs. Greenwood gave a deep sigh; intuitively she sensed trouble. Their obvious adoration for each other was disturbing.

She knew they would never wait until Rosie's coming of age, and it was unwise to expect them to do so. She was apprehensive because of her husband's strong views on the question.

The School of Architecture was still officially closed, but some conscientious students were in the classrooms, mugging up for the following term. Professor Bailey, a senior lecturer, came into the University most mornings during the vacation, so they decided to see if he was in.

Peter knocked on his door and, when he heard a gruff "Come in", he was distinctly nervous. Rosie's legs felt like jelly, for the results really would determine their future.   Peter looked tense as they walked into the study.

"Good morning, sir, I hope you don't mind our disturbing you, but I was wondering if any results are through yet?"

Professor Bailey, usually a somewhat formidable figure, seemed to unbend. He smiled at them quite warmly, then he got up and shook Peter's hand vigorously – an unusual display of enthusiasm.

"I'm glad you came in, Dunbar, for I'm delighted to tell you that you have achieved your ambition of a first class honours degree. Congratulations, and very good luck to you."

Peter's head seemed to spin with pleasure and relief; he and Rosie looked at each other with obvious delight.

"Thank you very much, sir, this is wonderful news. Now I will be able to take that job offered to me in London by Jonas Carr. They accepted me only on condition that I got an honours, so now I'm all set to go."

Professor Bailey turned to Rosie. "I think there should be congratulations all round – Miss Greenwood, you'll be glad to know that you've passed your first year with flying colours."

Rosie beamed. "Thank goodness for that. As I hadn't heard anything officially, I was beginning to get worried."

"Well, you two have good cause for celebration today," he said smiling benignly at them. "Get off now and enjoy yourselves."

Rosie and Peter needed no second bidding. They were both triumphant, running down the corridor, ecstatic with joy. A great burden had been lifted from their shoulders.

"Peter, we must telephone the families at once and tell them the good news; then I was wondering if we might drive down to the cottage. I can't wait for you to see it and we could easily get there in time for lunch."

"That's a marvellous idea, Rosie. I can't think of anything nicer."

They separated and did their individual telephoning.

Rosie's mother sounded delighted with the news, but guarded about their visit to the cottage, impressing upon her not to be late or her father would be worried, if she were not home before dark.

Mrs. Dunbar was obviously proud of Peter's achievement. His good job in London was now assured, but typically she impressed upon him that to establish himself in a firm of such standing would require complete dedication from the outset. He knew what she was driving at and was irritated. He didn't wish to be lectured but was determined that he would not allow anything to dampen his spirits on this day of all days.

The visit to the cottage was a great success. Peter loved it and was thrilled by Rosie's good fortune. They had a marvellous time together on this first visit. They lit a log fire and sat close together on the couch, content and at peace, holding hands and planning their future. Peter would be starting his job in London very shortly and neither of them felt they could face another parting – but Rosie knew they must.

"My parents are adamant that they won't give their consent to an early marriage – so we'll just have to wait, there is nothing else we can do."

"That's complete nonsense, darling," Peter said dogmatically. "Now listen to what I have to say. I've been talking to senior naval officers while at sea and they have not the slightest doubt that we shall soon be at war with Germany. Surely this is the strongest possible argument for us to share a little happiness together, while we still have the chance. I have thought it all over deeply and feel that, if our parents will not listen to logic, we must go ahead and get married and present them with a *fait accompli.*"

Rosie's blood ran cold as she listened.

"Oh Pete, we can't do that to Mum and Dad. They've always been so marvellous to me and, after all, they do have reason for their opposition, as I'm still quite young." She had been taken aback by his suggestion.

Even though her desire was as great as his, she wanted to be fair and didn't wish to be stampeded.

"Now Rosie, I know you're only a chicken but no longer a child. You're a responsible young woman with all the common sense in the world. Let's face up to it, if war is declared, all hope of our idyllic life together will vanish."

"Oh don't say that," she exclaimed. "It's a terrible thought."

There was a brief silence. She realised how strong-willed he was, but had to accept his logic. The prospect of war being so close certainly influenced her.

"You know there is nothing I want more than being married to you, Pete, but I do feel you're rushing things a bit."

He looked crushed, then, pausing for a moment, spoke in a more conciliatory tone.

"Well, darling, for a start couldn't we become formally engaged?"

Rosie looked relieved. "Of course, I'll come along with that, Pete, but I only hope Dad does."

He wanted to say: "To hell with Dad," but managed to restrain himself. "I'll think it over, Rosie, and we can discuss it the next time we meet."

They drove home in silence, absorbed in their own thoughts. The term would be starting again shortly and Peter's imagination ran riot, when he thought of Rosie at the University without him and surrounded by men, including the most threatening of them all, her precious Parkie, the genius.

On parting he held her close, caressing her soft golden hair. He felt a great tenderness towards her and, as he buried his face in her neck against her cool, scented skin, his desire for her was overwhelming. Delay was intolerable.

* * * * * * *

On his final Saturday, they had arranged to go to a cocktail party in his training ship, H.M.S. Eaglet, the headquarters of the R.N.V.R., which was permanently berthed alongside one of the Liverpool docks.

Peter was anxious for his fellow officers to meet his beautiful Rosie; he was very proud of her and dying to show her off.

On the evening of the party, he arrived to collect her, resplendent in his naval uniform, which emphasised his good looks. Rosie was wearing a delicate oyster-pink dress, which accentuated her fair loveliness and, as they left the house, Rosie's mother saw them off and thought they made a striking couple.

They drove into the city, then proceeded along the Dock Road; it was badly lit and deserted – not a very salubrious place at night and policemen on foot patrolled in couples. It was strangely silent after dark, so different from the daytime hustle and bustle of this thriving port.

As they turned into Prince's Half Tide Dock and drew up alongside H.M.S. Eaglet, they heard the soft strains of music from within. The officer of the watch saluted them smartly as they stepped aboard.

Peter led Rosie to the wardroom. She was excited about her first party in the ship, but felt a little shy and clung to his arm. He, in contrast, seemed to exude an easy confident charm and, as they walked in, there was a loud buzz of conversation – the party was in full swing. Rosie felt desperately young and unsophisticated and wished she had worn her little black dress which made her look older. There were many smiles of greeting for Peter, as they weaved their way through the guests to the captain and his wife for formal introduction.

"I would like you to meet Miss Greenwood, sir," Peter said proudly.

"Rosie, this is my commanding officer, Captain Hislop, and Mrs. Hislop."

"How do you do, Miss Greenwood, welcome aboard Eaglet. Now I know why Peter was shooting such a line about his girl friend!" he said with a twinkle in his eye.

Rosie just smiled, but wondered what Peter had been saying about her.

"Don't rise to that one, my dear," Mrs. Hislop said kindly. "We've heard so many nice things about you and you're just as charming as we expected." She turned to Peter and said, *sotto voce*, "I congratulate you on your choice – she's lovely."

Rosie felt more at ease and was soon chatting vivaciously with the captain – he was a great leg-puller and they got on famously together. Peter had difficulty in tearing her away to introduce her to the other officers.

He watched her closely as she talked to his friends: her face was animated and she undoubtedly made a deep impression. He felt a profound love for her and longed to have her to himself, away from all these admiring faces. She was, however, reluctant to leave so soon but, when he pressed her, she laughingly agreed and they departed early for dinner at the club.

The head waiter made them welcome and again there was an exquisite centre-piece of deep red roses on the table. She was thrilled, when she saw them, for she was sure they had been ordered especially for her.

As they waited for their meal to be served, they talked gaily of all the pleasant people she had met at the party that evening. Peter was obviously very popular in the ship and she was delighted by the warmth of their reception.

The food at the club, as always, was delicious. Everything with Peter was perfection – very different from the rough and tumble of the 'band of five' – with them there was no ceremony, yet she missed their informality. She was happy with them in quite a different way.

Peter held her hand as they sipped their coffee, and gazed at her lovingly. She was the perfect girl for him and now he would make his declaration.

"Rosie darling," he said solemnly, leaning across to kiss her lightly on the cheek – "This is one of the most important moments in my life." Then, with a flourish, he produced from his pocket a small elegant box, which he opened carefully, revealing a lovely solitaire diamond ring – it was absolutely magnificent and Rosie's eyes danced with pleasure and surprise. "Give me your other hand, my darling," he said, as he prepared to slip the ring on her finger.

She looked up at him adoringly, almost too overcome to speak. Then huskily she thanked him. "It's really beautiful, darling," and, as she held up her long fragile fingers to the light, the brilliant diamond scintillated like a myriad of stars. It looked perfect on her hand.

"Oh, Pete, I'm so proud of it," she said and kissed him lovingly on the cheek. She was sparkling with joy. "I have never been so happy, darling," but soon they must break the news to the family – she rather dreaded this and felt strangely troubled. She almost wished Peter had not sprung it on her.

"Let's be off now, Rosie darling," he said and his eyes were twinkling. "I have an overwhelming desire to kiss you and I can't wait much longer! It's a lovely moonlight night, so we'll park the car beside your favourite lake."

Rosie nodded almost shyly in assent; her whole being wished to be close to him. He was so desperately attractive.

The Park was beautiful under a full moon. They gazed up at the stars in the heavens and felt that the night was made for them. He took her face in both his hands and looked into her eyes then, drawing her towards him, kissed her long and passionately with a new intimacy. Her body, so incredibly soft, seemed to melt into his own. He stroked her lovely perfumed skin and her response was ardent, but soon she drew away. She was apprehensive of what was ahead of them.

"Pete, we had better go now. My parents will be waiting up for me and we have to break the news of our engagement and show them my gorgeous ring."

Rosie was right, but he wasn't looking forward to it.

"Yes, my sweet, I think we had better get it over." He groaned inwardly – he suspected there would be heavy weather ahead.

As they walked into the drawing room, Rosie's mother knew instinctively what had happened. She had dreaded this moment and, although she had tried to prepare her husband for this eventuality, she did not know what his attitude would be.

Rosie ran over and kissed them both, not in any way revealing her anxiety. She drew a deep breath: she must brazen it out.

"Mum and Dad, we have wonderful news for you. Peter and I have just become officially engaged."

She stood there smiling, determined not to give an inch, but she saw her words had caused grave disquiet.

There was a significant pause and her father's face clouded over. He stood up and faced Peter with obvious anger in his eyes.

"Well, I suppose as you've jumped the gun, young man, and it's all a *fait accompli*, we can only offer our congratulations but, as you well know, we consider Rosie is far too young to be tied down and we don't approve of long engagements anyway."

There was an awkward pause, but Rosie's mother relieved the tension by asking to see the ring. Rosie held out her hand proudly for both of them to inspect it and they were visibly impressed, when they saw how lovely it was. With a great effort her father pulled himself together.

"Well, this calls for a celebration and only champagne is suitable for such an occasion."

He left the room and a few minutes later returned. After popping the cork and filling the glasses, he made a little speech, difficult in the circumstances, but his wife was proud of him.

Raising his glass, he forced a smile. "Congratulations to my dear daughter, Rosie, and my prospective son-in-law, Peter, and our very best wishes for your future happiness."

After a sip from his glass, he shook Peter's hand and kissed Rosie, then he turned to his wife and, putting his arm around her shoulders, drew her to him.

"I only hope that you will be as happy as your mother and I have been."

She squeezed his arm in response. She knew he was deeply hurt. His darling Rosie had gone her own way, openly defying him; but the worst was not yet over by any means.

He was a strong-minded man and intended to make it perfectly clear what was expected of them in the future.

"Of course, Peter, we will not agree to an early marriage. We certainly will not give our permission until she is twenty-one — and Rosie, you know we want you to become a qualified architect; we've always agreed it is best for you to have a profession."

Peter cut in here, rather abruptly.

"There is no need for that, sir, I will always be able to keep Rosie in comfort and there will never be any question of her practising."

"Yes, I understand how you feel, young man, but we never know what life has in store for us."

Peter stiffened visibly.

"With respect, sir, I really think that is only our concern."

Her father reacted sharply to these words.

"Don't forget that the age of consent is twenty-one."

There was a prolonged silence and they realised that they had reached an impasse.

Rosie's mother again relieved the awkward situation.

"Don't let's quarrel about anything tonight. You know we are both delighted that you have found each other and all we wish for is your happiness."

"I appreciate your kind words, Mrs. Greenwood," Peter said more calmly. "I'm sure something can be worked out, and now I must be getting home as I have a mammoth amount of work to do before leaving on Tuesday."

Rosie walked with him to the door, holding his hand and looking a little troubled.

"Good bye, darling, drive carefully and I'll see you on Monday."

They kissed with restraint, knowing the opposition was strong.

Monday was their last day together, so they decided to visit the cottage again and really get away from it all.

Mrs. Dunbar had sided with the Greenwoods, emphasising that Rosie was far too young for marriage. Altogether there were dark clouds on the horizon and the thought of being separated again was heartbreaking. Peter had firmly made up his mind that this must not happen and was utterly determined to circumvent this chain of events in some way.

They planned to arrive at the cottage in mid-morning, as the girl from the village would be there cleaning and Rosie was anxious to meet her and to reassure her that there would not be any changes made.

The countryside looked beautiful. Rosie loved the filigree patterns of the branches of the leafless trees. The rolling green hills, dotted with white woolly sheep and the rugged contours of the mountains were a constant delight to her. This prompted the thought that, after Peter had gone, painting would be a consolation. She was fortunate to have this absorbing interest.

Even in the country they could not escape the alarming newspaper placards, with Hitler's name appearing conspicuously on them, always reflecting the threat of war. It made Rosie's heart sink with apprehension.

As they approached the cottage, they saw a plume of smoke rising from the chimney and, on pushing open the front door, came face to face with the help from the village. She was a young Welsh girl with large brown eyes and a most endearing expression – Rosie took to her at once and, in later life, could always recall this first meeting with Bron.

"I expect you are Bronwen?" she said with a warm smile. "I am Miss Greenwood and this is my fiancé, Mr. Dunbar."

Bronwen bobbed a curtsey to them both. She was an old-fashioned girl.

"I am pleased to meet you, madam," her round little face turned quite pink. Rosie instantly wanted to put her at ease.

"Thank you, Bronwen, for looking after the cottage so well – it's all as clean as a new pin and I do hope that you will continue to work here exactly as you've done in the past. As far as I'm concerned, there won't be any changes made, though I expect I shall visit the cottage from time to time."

Bronwen's face lit up.

"I'm so pleased, madam, for to tell you the truth I love this place and enjoy looking after it."

"I'm very glad, for I feel the same way about the cottage," Rosie replied. This was an instant bond between them and, from that moment there commenced an understanding, affection and mutual respect, which was to last a lifetime.

Before leaving, Bronwen made them coffee, setting it out daintily on a tray beside the fire.

They were blissfully happy together but, because of parental opposition a cloud hung over them and, if they conformed, they were likely to be frustrated for at least another three years. It was damnable, but Peter was determined to find a solution.

"I will get home as much as I possibly can, Rosie, but to begin with, it won't be often. I must make a success of my new job; it's important to both of us now, for it's your future as well as mine."

"I do agree, darling, you must make a good impression from the start."

She sighed. "I must apply myself too, for term commences next week. It will be awful up there without you."

Peter's face darkened as he thought of Rosie on her own – his rivals ever ready to pounce! He knew he couldn't tolerate this situation and the constant anxiety could jeopardise his efficiency as he started with his new company.

"Rosie, I don't see how I can possibly manage without you. Do you think there is any chance that your father might relent?"

"No, Pete, I'm sure he won't. He still thinks I'm a child and the prospect of my marrying really upsets him. Mother feels the same, so I know they won't give in. I don't know what we can do about it."

"This is a ghastly situation, it's just damned idiocy," he said. "You know, Rosie, as I suggested before, we could take the bull by the horns and go off and get married and then there would be nothing they could do about it."

She wished he would take a softer, more understanding line but basically she agreed with him. She looked thoughtful and hesitated before replying.

"I think I'd be willing to do that now, darling. My priorities have changed and, assuming we can surmount the age problem, I would go along with it."

Peter's face lit up hopefully.

"Would you really be prepared to take such a drastic step? Rosie darling, you're such a home girl."

"Yes, I really would, Pete, for you are everything to me and I feel my parents are being completely unreasonable, although I know that they want only the best for me."

Peter jumped to his feet with enthusiasm and picked her up, whirling her round and round.

"Whatever's stopping us? Let's find the nearest register office on our way home and see what the form is."

They were full of youthful optimism now, brimming over with happiness again. Their anxiety was all forgotten with this exciting new development on the horizon. Peter was impatient to get going.

"I think we should depart now, Rosie, and go to the inn for lunch. I don't know about you, but I'm ravenously hungry."

"Me too, Pete, but I do hate leaving the cottage. It seems just like home to me now. I have really grown to love it."

As if in answer the sun unexpectedly broke through the latticed windows. The whole cottage became live and radiant, as though in appreciation of its new owner.

After a quick lunch at the inn, they were directed to a register office in a nearby town. They set off in high spirits and quickly reached their destination. Peter went in alone and talked to a young man at the reception desk, who meticulously wrote down for him exactly what was required. Rosie's birth certificate was not mentioned, so they felt that they were in the clear. As she was resident in the area, everything seemed to be plain sailing and they drove away full of hope. On their journey home they made plans. First of all he had to find a place in London for them to live.

"Wouldn't it be super, if you could find a little mews house, Pete? I absolutely adore them."

"So do I, Rosie, but don't be too optimistic, it may not be easy; but keep your fingers crossed and you can be sure that every spare moment I'll be on the hunt for one. As soon as I find something, we can finalise our plans."

Rosie edged up closer to him. Her thoughts wandered to the joys of being his wife. She couldn't care less about giving up architecture. She felt she wasn't a career girl anyway. She longed for marriage, children and a home of her own.

As well as being a housewife, she would have plenty of time for music and painting, and they would have lots of animals. Her heart ached, as she thought of leaving Chi-Chi behind, but he was happy with her parents and much better left there.

On reaching the house Peter stopped the car for a final farewell. It was no good prolonging the parting.

"Look after yourself, my darling, and don't you worry: we'll soon be together again."

Rosie felt comforted by his assurances.

"I hope so, Pete, it will be awful without you."

After a long lingering kiss she broke away and ran up the drive to the house. She was close to tears, but collected herself and, just before he disappeared from sight, she turned and blew him a last kiss.

She decided before going to bed to make a desperate attempt to change her father's mind. She found him in his study, writing letters at his desk, but he proved to be as adamant as ever, saying he would not give her permission before she was of age. All her arguments in favour of an early marriage were shot down in flames. He made her furious by stressing that she was too young and didn't know yet what she wanted, and that she needed to know Peter much better over a longer period of time – also, from Peter's point of view, it was not good. All his concentration should be focused on his new job and getting well established with his company. She felt that this was Mrs. Dunbar speaking.

This was the final straw and she lost her temper and told him that she refused to be treated like a child – she must live her own life as she saw fit. She stormed out of the room and miserably prepared for bed.

Presently her mother came in to see her. She was kind, but still supported her husband's viewpoint, though she tried to comfort Rosie.

"Don't worry, my dear, the time will soon fly by and, if you really love one another, it will all be worthwhile – later on you'll be thankful that we didn't allow you to be so precipitate."

Rosie had softened somewhat and, after her mother had kissed her goodnight, said, "Tell Dad I'm sorry I was so beastly tempered, but I still stick to my guns. I know he is wrong."

"Very well, dear, I'll convey the message to him. Sleep well and don't think about it any more tonight."

"Goodnight, Mum, and sweet dreams."

Rosie tossed and turned all night. She was thoroughly miserable. She no longer had any doubts. They must go ahead and get married secretly. Finally she drifted off to sleep, only to be tormented by frightening nightmares.

The next day at breakfast Rosie was very subdued. Her mother thought she looked pale and was worried by the dark shadows under her eyes. Chi-Chi sat quietly beside her, sensing there was something wrong. When she had finished her tea and toast, she picked him up and went to sit in the morning room by the fire – close to the telephone. She felt torn apart by her two loyalties and for once all her *joie de vivre* had deserted her. When the telephone rang, Rosie gave an unaccustomed start but, as soon as she lifted the receiver and heard Peter's voice, everything seemed to fall into place again and she felt happier and more confident.

"Big surprise, Rosie! I'm catching the evening train," Peter said.

"Joy oh joy!" exclaimed Rosie.

"Can you meet me at the Adelphi for lunch – say at 12.30?"

"Of course, darling, I'm as good as there!"

When she walked into the hotel, Peter noticed how pale she was. Her sparkle seemed to have deserted her. He kissed her tenderly and they sat down together at a quiet table and ordered drinks. Rosie told him of her frustrating talk with her father the night before.

"Peter, do find us a house as quickly as possible and then we will get married at once – it's quite unbearable being separated."

"Are you sure, darling? You won't mind missing a white wedding with all the trimmings?"

"No, Pete, that is unimportant. All I want is to be with you."

They spent most of the afternoon planning their wedding. If all went well they would spend their honeymoon at 'Apple Trees'. Just before leaving the hotel Peter made a pressing request.

"Rosie, promise me that while I'm away you won't have any dates. It would drive me quite demented if I thought you were going out with any of the old crowd." He spoke with a slight note of accusation.

Rosie hesitated and looked away.

"You'll have to trust me, Peter, otherwise our whole relationship breaks down. I don't want to make any promises which I can't keep and, when the term starts again, we'll be working on some joint projects. I just cannot stand aloof. Anyway, if our relationship is as strong as it should be, we must both have confidence in each other's fidelity."

Peter had to agree, but secretly he was seething with jealousy. He must have Rosie exclusively to himself and until then he would not have any peace of mind. They had a sad parting, but all their plans were made and they could only hope that everything would work out as they intended. She felt desolated as the train pulled out of Lime Street station.

5

AFTER PETER'S departure Rosie had another sleepless night. She felt sick at heart and desperately lonely without him. She almost wished she were back in the old days, before they had ever met, carefree and quite unemotionally involved. When the first morning light showed through the curtains, she was thankful the night was over.

She gloomily went down to have her breakfast, a very different Rosie from the cheerful girl that her parents knew. They both secretly wondered if their uncompromising attitude had been the right one. They were disturbed to see her so despondent.

"What are your plans for today, Rosie?" her mother asked.

She looked up dejectedly. "Oh, I was thinking of finishing some work before the term starts," she replied, but she sounded less than enthusiastic at the prospect.

"Why don't you leave your work until tomorrow, dear? We could have lunch in town and go on a shopping expedition instead – you could do with some new winter dresses."

Rosie brightened up – she thought this sounded far more fun and needed no persuading to go along with the idea. As her father left for business, he slipped a five pound note into her hand.

"Buy something nice for yourself, Rosie. What about that set of oils and portable easel we saw the other day?"

"Oh thank you, Dad, I'd love that. It would be so convenient to carry, when I go away." In saying this she felt desperately guilty, knowing what the circumstances of her next trip would be, and her eyes were downcast as she kissed her father goodbye.

She glanced briefly at the morning paper while finishing her coffee. Displayed on the front page was a menacing picture of Hitler, standing high upon a rostrum, silhouetted against the skyline, his arm outstretched in the customary Nazi salute. Before him paraded an impressive display of military might. An awesome force of heavy tanks, guns and armoured cars, followed by a great turn-out of goose-stepping troops, marching with the utmost precision. The stadium was packed with a sea of faces, cheering sycophants frenziedly returning their Führer's salute. Here was the writing on the wall! Rosie shuddered.

Ominous rumours were leaking out of Germany, revealing the Nazis' extreme anti-semitism. Rosie had always been in sympathy with the Jewish race, for she admired their native talent, particularly in the field of the arts. She respected them for their industry as well as their inherent family loyalty, and this latest round of persecution filled her with horror. A cold chill ran through her and she closed the paper hurriedly.

"I'll get ready now, Mum," she said. "It's ages since we've been shopping together and it will be fun." She was glad to have something that would take her mind off these atrocities and also distract her from her loneliness. In spite of this inauspicious start, they enjoyed the day out. They arrived home, loaded with parcels, including a new outfit that her mother had generously bought her, and also the artist's equipment, which she had coveted. Rosie felt brighter and more like her old self again. She was of a cheerful disposition and nothing could keep her down for long.

As they walked into the house, the phone was ringing. She dashed to answer it, praying that it was Peter, but she was disappointed. It was her old school friend, Sue, who wanted to meet her for lunch the following day.

Rosie welcomed the invitation for she urgently needed to confide in somebody and Sue was the ideal person. She was a sympathetic listener and a good ally. Rosie felt better now, it would be a relief to talk things over with a trusted friend. She told Sue to prepare herself for a long session, as they had a lot to discuss. Sue was obviously intrigued and promised to be early.

It was a pouring wet day, dark and thoroughly depressing. Rosie donned her vivid green raincoat, which looked refreshingly cheerful in such weather. As she walked into the restaurant, several young men, reading their newspapers, lowered them and looked with interest in her direction.

Sue was already there, sitting at a corner table. She waved and beamed at Rosie as she approached. Sue was a very pretty blonde, with round, blue, innocent eyes and a slim, elegant figure. She was generally in high spirits and great fun to be with.

"Hello, Rosie, how are you old thing? You look a bit down in the mouth," Sue observed, studying her friend closely.

"Oh, I'm all right, Sue, though I do have problems which I'd like to talk over with you – you're always so full of good northern common sense."

"I don't know about that," she replied with a broad grin, "but I'll do my best to give sage advice – before the oracle pronounces, here's the waitress, so let's order and then you can spill the beans!" she said light-heartedly.

When the waitress had left, Rosie's saga commenced.

"You know that Mum and Dad won't hear of Peter and me marrying until I'm twenty one, which is in three years time. Well, Sue, we just can't wait. We're mad about each other and, now that Peter is working in London, life without him is just not worth living. It all seems so pointless."

"Well, what can you do about it, old thing? I'm sure they won't change their minds."

"I know they won't, Sue, so be prepared for a shock. We've decided to run away and get married. It's all arranged – it's going to take place in Wales, from the cottage."

"Rosie, you don't mean it?" Sue gasped. "I'm quite astounded at your daring and I can't imagine how your parents will react. This *grande passion*, which you and Peter share, is something I haven't experienced yet! I must admit that I feel doubtful about it all, but do tell me more." So Rosie carried on.

To begin with, Sue was apprehensive about the whole scheme and was reluctant to subscribe to it but, after discussing all the pros and cons, she agreed that, under the circumstances, a runaway marriage was perhaps the only solution.

They chewed over the plans like two conspirators, their eyes sparkling with excitement. They decided that Sue would be a witness at the wedding. She and Rosie would go to the cottage together for the wedding weekend, as Rosie would never be permitted to stay there alone; this was the perfect answer.

"Suppose the registrar asks for your birth certificate?" Sue questioned. "They'll never marry you, if they discover you are only eighteen."

"I know," said Rosie with a worried frown. "Peter has been to the register office and the certificate was never mentioned, so it should be all right. The bans of course must be published."

"But, Rosie," Sue interjected. "You look awfully young. I don't know how you'll get away with it."

"I'll sleek my hair down, wear something chic and sophisticated and smoke a cigarette in that long green onyx holder of mine."

Both girls roared with laughter. They felt like partners in crime and , as they separated, they were in the best of spirits.

The next week flew by, as term had restarted and Rosie concentrated hard on her work. Peter wrote every day and so far he had not found them a house. He was utterly miserable without her and spent all his time hunting for somewhere to live. He was starting work the following Monday, taking the place of a young man, who was leaving to study in America under Frank Lloyd Wright.

When Monday morning loomed, Peter felt a little apprehensive. He dressed carefully and left the small hotel, his temporary abode, with plenty of time to spare, determined to make a good impression. He got there before the office was open and had to wait about outside. Fortunately Mr. Jonas, the boss, was the next to arrive and, as he unlocked the door, he remarked that it was a good omen for a new recruit to be early. Peter liked this gruff, reserved man and respected his reputation as an excellent administrator and brilliant architect.

The office soon filled up and Peter was given a desk next to Dick Simmonds, the man he was replacing. He was most helpful and took Peter under his wing, explaining to him the general routine.

He asked Peter to have lunch with him at a pub around the corner. They got on famously and, over a glass of beer and a sandwich, Peter told Dick of his housing difficulties and showed him a picture of Rosie.

"She looks an absolute honey," Dick exclaimed.

"You're bang on there," Peter replied. "I hope you meet her before you depart."

"I hope so too," Dick said and then came out with a surprising proposition.

"Why don't you rent my little house? I had intended to keep it on, but I can't really afford to do so with an expensive one in New York as well – you would be ideal tenants and I know you'd look after it."

Peter looked eagerly across at him.

"That sounds quite a possibility, do tell me more about it."

Dick grinned disarmingly.

"Well, it's central and in very good nick. Downstairs the accommodation consists of a small sitting room with a dining alcove, plus the kitchen and a minute garden at the back – very secluded. Upstairs it has two tiny bedrooms and a bathroom.

Peter's excitement showed in his face.

"It sounds exactly what I'm looking for. When would it be convenient for me to come and see it?"

"Well, how about tonight? We can go back together straight from the office. It will only take a few minutes to show you around."

"That would be splendid, Dick, the sooner the better as far as I'm concerned. I am getting rather desperate as everything I have seen so far has been hopeless."

Peter was delighted and found it difficult to keep his mind on his work that afternoon – the hours seemed to drag.

They left the office together, took the Underground and then had only a short walk. As they approached a terrace of large Regency houses, Dick pointed out the cottage. It was built originally for a coachman and had been converted into a most desirable dwelling. It was very attractive with a bright blue front door, window boxes and a small patch of garden at the side. Peter could hardly believe his eyes – it was just what he and Rosie had dreamed of.

Dick opened the front door into a tiny hall. There was an interesting spiral staircase ahead, leading to the upstairs landing. The floors were all closely carpeted in dark grey and the walls were a delicate pearl grey throughout. Dick led him into the living room which, to Peter's delight, had an open fireplace. He envisaged sitting there with Rosie on winter evenings before a blazing fire, and could hardly contain his excitement.

At the far end of the room was a small dining alcove with Scandinavian table and chairs. On the wall was a picture of a gorgeous blue Persian cat with enormous orange eyes, looking most regal and wearing a glittering coronet; this supplied a touch of humour to the room, which amused Peter. The kitchenette was small and, beyond that, a door opened on to a patch of grass with a single laburnum tree and an inviting rustic seat beneath it. He and Rosie could sit there on warm summer evenings, having a drink before dinner, with the hum of the London traffic in the background – what bliss!

The upstairs was simplicity itself. There was one double bedroom, spacious yet attractively furnished, suitable for a bachelor – undoubtedly Rosie would change all this. The other room was used as a studio, full up with pots of paint, drawing boards and easels – just right for Rosie.

Peter was quite overwhelmed by his good fortune.

"Can we really have it?" he asked eagerly. "It's exactly what we want and I promise that we'll look after it well for you. Rosie is absolutely immaculate."

"That's fine, old chap – now how about a glass of beer while we discuss the business side?"

"Thank you, Dick, I'd like that."

They sat with their drinks, debating the pros and the cons, but the financial side was arranged without difficulty.

"I think it should be a personal understanding between us, Peter – a gentleman's agreement."

"I go along with that wholeheartedly," Peter replied, looking into Dick's trustworthy, open face.

"Well then it's a deal," Dick said with a broad grin. "I shall like the comforting thought of you both living here looking after the place for me."

The two young men shook hands on it. They both knew their rather unorthodox arrangement would work.

In the next few weeks they became close friends and, as Dick was due to leave for New York shortly, Peter was anxious for Rosie to meet him. Her parents were coming to London to see a show and would be staying overnight at the Mayfair Hotel. Rosie persuaded them to take her with them. It was arranged that she would spend the evening with Peter, while they were at the theatre.

After their month's separation, they both wondered how it would feel to be together again in such different circumstances. Rosie was ready early, impatiently waiting in the lounge for Peter to arrive, her eyes glued to the revolving doors; she was looking as beautiful as ever but more mature. No longer did she look the child with unruly curls. She was dressed with a simple, expensive elegance. Since being parted she seemed to have developed into a svelte and sophisticated young lady. Peter noticed the difference the instant he saw her and her reaction was exactly the same about him. The good looking student she had known, was now a smart young professional man who had gained immensely in confidence. He led her over to a corner couch and they sat there holding hands. His voice shook a little as he spoke.

"Rosie, I don't know how I've lived without you for these last few weeks – it's been absolute purgatory. The only thing that has made it bearable has been my work, which has been all-demanding. I really haven't had a minute to myself. Everything is going well as far as my job is concerned and I just can't wait for you to see 'our house'. It's right up to your specification."

"Oh, Pete, you have been clever; it seems almost as if the gods are smiling on our machiavellian plan," she answered mischievously.

"Don't speak too soon, Rosie, we're not married yet – though I must admit everything is going remarkably well at the moment."

He ordered drinks and Rosie held his hand tight – the horrid, aching loneliness, which she had felt during his absence, had now gone.

When the drinks arrived, Peter raised his glass and with a twinkle in his eye declared: "Let's drink a special toast to our 'Rosie' future" – they both laughed merrily as they clinked glasses. Then, not to be outdone, Rosie replied with an impish grin: "And may our love bloom forever."

"Well said, my clever little one!" He chuckled, "I'm sure that together we'll make a splendid team."

He was delighted when Rosie told him of the arrangement she had made with Sue. He was fond of Rosie's special friend and thought it a splendid idea to have her with them on their wedding day.

Presently he glanced at his watch and quickly jumped to his feet.

"Rosie, we must go at once, if we're to see Dick at seven."

They downed their drinks and hurried to the entrance, where the commissionaire hailed them a taxi and they were soon caught up in the mêlée of the busy West End traffic.

Rosie found the London atmosphere stimulating. She loved the theatre as well as the art galleries and was thrilled by the availability of concerts and ballet.

"Oh, Pete," she exclaimed, "it's so heavenly being with you again and I'm dying to live in London." She sighed with dreamy pleasure. "Life is so tremendously exciting here."

He looked intently into her eyes.

"Rosie dear, I hope you always feel that way. I will try my best to make you happy, but I have a sombre side to my nature too and I hope it never causes you unhappiness."

Rosie looked surprised, for he always made her laugh.

"Why, Pete, you've never told me this before and I've certainly never seen this other side of you."

"I'm afraid, young lady, I've kept it under cover, but occasionally it rears its ugly head." He said this in a jocular manner and Rosie didn't take him too seriously. She stared reflectively at him for a moment, then quickly dismissed the idea from her mind.

"We're nearly there now, Rosie, so start looking out – it's just around the next corner."

She spotted the little house at once from his description – it was perfection, with its simple brick facade, enhanced by colourful window boxes. She turned to him with shining eyes, she was overjoyed.

"Oh, darling, it's absolutely super," and, as he paid off the taxi, she stood gazing with delight at their future home – this was the sort of town house she had always wanted.

Peter gave a sharp rap on the elegant dolphin knocker and almost immediately the door was opened by Dick, his burly figure filling the entrance. When he saw Peter, a broad grin spread across his kindly face.

"Hello, old chap, how nice to see you, please come in – welcome to your new home!" He was obviously thrilled to see them.

"Dick, let me introduce you to Rosie, my bride-to-be," he said proudly.

"Hello, Rosie, I've been hearing so much about you, it's lovely to meet you at last." He grinned at Peter. "You were right old chap, she is a beauty!"

Rosie smiled up at him divinely and they were instantly friends.

"I've heard a lot about you too and I'm delighted we've finally got together," she said warmly. "I'm quite overcome by the charm of your little house."

"I'm glad you like the look of it. What about a Cook's tour of inspection before we have our drinks? I warn you it's tiny, like a doll's house, and this will only take a minute."

"Yes, please, I'm dying to see it," she said eagerly and her excitement was reflected in her starry eyes as she gazed around. The little house exceeded her wildest dreams. It was perfect for the two of them.

When they returned to the living room, she was obviously thrilled.

"Oh, Dick, it couldn't be nicer," she pronounced gaily and unexpectedly she reached up and kissed him on the cheek.

"Steady on now, Rosie," Peter remonstrated good-naturedly. "Remember your kisses are only for me."

They all laughed and, while they sipped their drinks, there was plenty of banter between them – Rosie felt that she had known Dick for years.

After a delicious supper, they settled down by the fire and listened to records and browsed through books, mostly on modern architecture.

When Dick showed them a recent publication of Frank Lloyd Wright's brilliant new designs, Rosie exclaimed quite spontaneously: "Oh, what joy, I'd love Parkie to see these, they are most exciting and right up his street."

The sudden frown on Peter's face did not escape her.

"Who is Parkie?" Dick asked.

"Oh, he's an old flame of Rosie's," Peter replied in an off-hand manner.

"You'd like him, Dick," she said almost defensively. "He's brilliant on design and the most outstanding student in our year."

It all passed off quite well, but Rosie was aware of tension – she'd have to watch it. Peter obviously resented Parkie.

They sat eagerly discussing their plans for the future. Dick was full of enthusiasm for working in America with such a prestigious firm. It was a golden opportunity for him. Rosie and Peter told him of their secret wedding plans.

"It's all so exciting," she exclaimed joyously. "I feel over the moon with happiness," but when Peter spoke of the strong possibility of war a shiver ran through her.

"If war breaks out, Dick, of course Rosie won't stay here alone, so we'll just have to close up the house and post on the keys to your father."

"We mustn't dwell on that nasty possibility," Dick replied cheerily. "It will probably never happen."

The evening seemed to fly by. The little house rang with laughter and it already seemed like home to them both. They left glowing with bonhomie.

Peter was anxious to have her to himself again and even a taxi ride was better than nothing. He held her close, eager to kiss her, wishing the journey would go on for ever, but they were soon back at the hotel.

He hoped desperately that the Greenwoods would be late out of the theatre, but they were already there waiting, sitting in a quiet corner in the hotel lobby. They greeted Peter effusively; they were obviously pleased to see him.

"You are looking very fit, Peter, how is the new job going?" Mr. Greenwood enquired with interest.

"Splendidly thank you, sir. I seem to have fitted into the organisation quite well."

"Where are you living now, Peter?" Mrs. Greenwood asked with a smile.

"At the moment in a small hotel off Russell Square, but I've had an enormous stroke of luck. One of the young architects in the office is being transferred to New York and has agreed to let me rent his marvellous little mews cottage – it is absolutely perfect. Rosie and I have just been over there."

"It's a dream of a place," Rosie said rather awkwardly. There was an uncomfortable silence , for the Greenwoods could see the possible implications of this development. Then Rosie's mother skilfully changed the subject and, although the atmosphere was strained, they didn't discuss the matter any further.

When the time came for Peter's departure, they all walked with him to the swing doors. The Greenwoods shook hands warmly with him. Peter and Rosie had to be content with a demure kiss.

That night, as Rosie lay in bed, she thought carefully of her future and felt well content. Apart from her deception of her parents, everything seemed idyllic. It wouldn't be long now before they would be blissfully happy together for always. Peter was the man of her dreams.

*　*　*　*　*

The scene was all set for the wedding. Rosie told her parents that she and Sue were going to 'Apple Trees' together for a weekend. They put up very little resistance, as it was beginning to dawn on them that Rosie must in future be given more freedom.

She packed carefully, taking rather more than was necessary for a few days visit, concealing an extra suitcase in the back of the car. Her heart ached as she held Chi-Chi close to her for a final goodbye. He gazed reproachfully up at her. He sensed that he was being left behind again. She looked around her familiar room with a sharp pang of regret. This was the parting of the ways and the full impact of it struck her forcibly. She was leaving the security of her childhood and stepping out into the unknown.

She quietly closed the door and ran downstairs. Her eyes were full of tears. She mustn't let her mother see how upset she was. She hesitated outside the breakfast room for a moment, afraid of showing her distress and giving the game away. Then, having collected herself, she popped her head hurriedly around the door.

"Goodbye, Mum, I must fly now or I'll be late meeting Sue at the station."

Her mother fortunately was immersed in the newspaper and oblivious of Rosie's agitation. She looked up only briefly, blowing her daughter a farewell kiss.

"Goodbye, darling. Have a nice weekend and drive carefully. We'll see you on Monday."

Rosie swallowed hard, not able to reply to this, but said instead: "Take good care of Chi-Chi for me" and then, without a backward glance, she hurriedly left the house. She jumped into her car and was quickly away.

Before leaving the park she drew up under the trees, giving herself time to regain her composure. After wiping her eyes and powdering her nose, she felt better. Tomorrow she would be with Peter again and with any luck for the rest of her life – there would be no more separations. She felt a warm glow of happiness at this prospect.

Sue was waiting for her at the entrance to the station. She waved exuberantly and a broad grin spread across her face as the sports car drew up beside her. She jumped in with obvious excitement, throwing her suitcase on to the back seat.

"Hello, Rosie old thing, how are you feeling?" she asked. Her eyes were laughing and she was full of fun.

Rosie smiled a little uncertainly as she weaved her way through the busy station traffic.

"What a relief it is to see you, Sue – at the moment I feel pretty awful, having just made the break from home. I only hope Mum and Dad won't take it too badly. I have a nasty feeling the Dunbars will never forgive us. You know how sticky Mrs. D. always is."

Sue tried her best to be reassuring.

"Don't worry, Rosie, they'll soon see sense and, once the deed is done, they're bound to accept it. To insist on your waiting for another three years is quite unreasonable."

Rosie nodded and smiled ruefully.

"I do hope they finally see it that way, but thank you, Sue, for bolstering me up. I feel better already" – and she really did, with confident Sue beside her.

They were quickly clear of the city centre and approaching the busy industrial outskirts. As they passed Cammell Lairds, the mammoth gates were open, giving them a fleeting glimpse of the ship-building complex of this giant company. Rosie loved the industrial north. She was a northerner born and bred and this heartland of activity fascinated her.

Presently they were driving through Port Sunlight, the hub of Lord Leverhulme's huge soap empire, its garden city suburbs delightfully landscaped with open grassy spaces and trees. The houses were substantial and attractively designed – a new concept of living for factory workers. Such enlightened thinking was well ahead of its time and attracted a splendid work force, loyal to this progressive enterprise.

Soon they were clear of the built-up area, away from the congested traffic and into the open country, heading for North Wales. It was a cold crisp day and the sunshine filtered mistily through the trees. The two girls were quiet as they drove along, both immersed in their own thoughts, but it was a harmonious silence. Sue was sensitive of Rosie's feelings and she could imagine how mixed up she must be now, all at sixes and sevens. Her heart leapt as she thought of handsome Peter and the excitement and drama, which surrounded these two glamorous people. She only wished that she knew him better. He was certainly a 'knock out', but she had a niggling feeling that he might not be easy to live with. He was so sure of himself and obviously used to his own way, but he certainly loved Rosie, of this she had no doubt.

Sue finally broke the silence.

"I'm longing to see your cottage, Rosie dear, you know you really are a fantastically lucky person – everything seems to fall into your lap."

She said this without the slightest trace of envy. She was genuinely delighted with Rosie's good fortune. She was an exceptional girl, understanding and generous of spirit.

"Thank you, Sue, but let's hope my luck holds! I'm longing to show you the cottage. It's a sweet place and I'm sure you'll love it, but you can judge that for yourself. We shall soon be there."

They went straight to the village inn for lunch and, on arrival, were warmly greeted by the proprietor, who took a lively interest in these 'city folk'. Sue loved the old world simplicity of the place and its spotless cleanliness.

As they sat in the dining room, waiting for their lunch to be served, Bronwen appeared at the table. She was obviously pleased to see Rosie: her face glowed with pleasure. She bobbed a little curtsey when introduced to Sue.

"Everything is ready at the cottage, Mam. I've polished all the furniture, the beds are made up and I've lit the fire."

"Thank you, Bronwen, I'm sure it all looks lovely," Rosie said appreciatively.

Bronwen blushed with pleasure. "Yes indeed, Mam, it does. I'll be in tomorrow and, if you want me at any other time, just knock hard on our cottage door. Gran's always there, but she's deaf."

"Thank you, Bronwen, I'll be in touch with you in a few days," Rosie smiled warmly as Bronwen shyly took her leave. It was evident to Sue that a nice understanding had developed between them

They hurried through their lunch, impatient to get going and, on leaving the inn, they linked arms and ran down the front steps, giggling like a couple of schoolgirls. They got into the car and were quickly on their way, driving along the quiet country lane towards the cottage.

"Look across the valley, Sue," Rosie said excitedly, "You can just see 'Apple Trees' in the distance. Isn't it adorable?"

Sue screwed up her eyes and caught a glimpse of the cottage nestling between the trees.

"It looks absolutely gorgeous, Rosie, right out of this world," she replied almost in awe. "But drive on, I'm most impatient to see the inside."

"I'm longing to see it again myself, " Rosie added as she speeded up, and a few minutes later they were drawing up at the front gate. They jumped out and ran down the garden path; they were both so eager that they found it difficult to get the key into the lock quickly enough.

When they stepped inside, everything looked snug and lovely. The room was warm and glowing, with a log fire burning merrily in the hearth. Sue gave a little gasp of delight.

"It's fabulous, Rosie, a dream of a place." Her eyes were shining as she spoke.

"I'm going to christen it 'The Enchanted Cottage', for the way you inherited it was like a fairy tale."

"Yes, indeed, I still can't believe it's really mine; it seems too good to be true, but God bless Great Aunt Louise!" she said with feeling.

After a whirlwind tour of inspection, they finished up in the kitchen and Rosie put the kettle on.

"Let's unpack quickly and then come down and have a cup of tea – I'm dying for one. How about you?"

"Yes please, Rosie, but I'll make it when you're ready – after all I am the bride's maid!

"Good old Susie," she cried gaily as they dashed upstairs with their suitcases. Rosie closed her bedroom door and sat pensively by the window. She loved the view. She could look at it all day long, with its changing moods and colours. At this moment the sun was out and the shadows on the hills were deeply etched. The mountains appeared remote and majestic in the background, their summits swathed in cloud.

The room was delightfully gay, with white walls and pretty blue floral curtains and a matching bedspread. The old oak furniture was handmade and simply carved. She was secure and happy here – it seemed perfect for her wedding night.

"Oh Pete," she whispered, "I can hardly wait!" She was filled with a deep yearning for him. She loved him totally and passionately and knew that her love was fully returned.

There was a light tap on the door and Sue's beaming face appeared.

"Shall I make the tea now, Rosie dear?"

"Yes please, Sue, and then I must write that letter to Mum and Dad. It's horribly on my mind."

She hurriedly finished her unpacking, then she ran downstairs to join Sue by the fire. They sat drinking their tea and reminiscing about their schooldays. It seemed only yesterday that they had been wearing gym slips, giggling together as teenagers; now, here they were, two glamorous young women embarking on this great adventure.

They were true friends, completely at ease together. They never had to measure thoughts or words, for they knew that on no account would there be any censure or criticism.

After tea, Sue took out the tray to do the washing up, leaving Rosie in peace to start her fateful letter.

She sighed deeply as she commenced.

Dearest Mum and Dad,

When you get this letter, I shall be married to Peter and I hope that the news will not come as too much of a shock to you. We love each other dearly and feel that we must grasp our chance of happiness while we can, for it seems that war is now inevitable and it could well deny us any future together. We do beg you to see our point of view. Please try to understand and forgive – for without your understanding we will not have any peace of mind.

I shall always be grateful to you for a childhood of absolute bliss. I could not have had two more wonderful parents.

We are staying at the cottage this weekend, then returning to London on Monday night. Our address there is, 1a Wellington Mews, Knightsbridge, S.W.7.
I am sure we are doing the right thing, so please don't worry about me.
With heaps of love and kisses,

From your
Rosie

She remained sitting by the fireside, staring into the flames. It was growing dark outside and in the dimly lit room the firelight cast strange and mysterious shadows on the walls and ceiling.

For one dreadful moment, she wished that none of this had happened. She longed to put back the clock to her serene and uncomplicated childhood days.

*   *   *   *   *

Rosie woke up slowly, stretching and yawning in her delightfully comfortable feather bed – it was so soft, like being enveloped in a cloud. She opened her eyes and gazed anxiously out of the window. She was instantly reassured. The sun was shining and the sky was blue. The only sound was the sweet trill of the birds and the occasional bleat of a sheep from afar – it was a perfect wedding day.

She lay still, contemplating this great event in her life. A thrill of excitement ran through her as she thought of Peter. He was the most desirable man in the world and being his wife would be sheer heaven. A runaway marriage, though exciting, was fraught with anxiety – so many things could go wrong.

She was relieved when she saw Sue peering round the door with a steaming cup of tea, beaming with youthful exuberance and loudly humming the 'Wedding March'.

"How does the beautiful bride feel this morning?" she asked breezily.

Rosie sat up. She smiled, then a slight frown clouded her smooth brow as she leant forward and took the cup.

"I'm fine, thank you, Sue, but this is just what I need to buck me up," she said gratefully sipping her tea. "Do sit down for a moment and let's have a natter. I'm feeling terribly excited, but a bit worried – particularly about this under age business. Wouldn't it be awful, if they refused to marry us? I just couldn't go on living without Peter."

"Don't get cold feet, Rosie dear, you won't have to. Peter was confident and I am sure it will go off like a dream. Now drink your tea while it's still hot and I'll go down and get breakfast ready. I'm afraid there is no time for gossiping this morning. Time marches on and we mustn't be late."

"You really are a brick, Susie, and the finest morale booster in the world; I could never have managed without you."

Sue blew her a kiss as she closed the door and hurried downstairs. She was determined that everything would run smoothly and that there must not be a last minute rush.

They had arranged to meet Peter at eleven that morning at the register office, so both girls went up to get dressed immediately after breakfast, though they were tempted to linger over their coffee and talk. Bronwen was coming in later to do the tidying up, so the chores could be left to her.

When Rosie came downstairs, all ready for their departure, Sue was waiting in the hall below. She gave a little gasp of admiration.

"Rosie, you look absolutely gorgeous. I think Peter is a very lucky man." Her eyes filled unexpectedly with tears. Was he good enough for darling Rosie?

She did look breathtaking — her face reflected her inner radiance. She was wearing a simply-cut cream wool dress, which emphasised her shapely figure, and over this a light mink jacket and small matching pill box hat. Her hair curled softly round it.

Rosie smiled, pleased that she met with approval.

"Thank you, Susie dear, you look lovely too. Your dress and coat are stunning. I adore cherry — it always looks so cheerful, like its owner!" She tucked her arm warmly in Sue's. "I think it's about time we left now for, although it's the bride's prerogative to be late, I'd rather not keep Peter waiting."

They smiled happily at each other as they sallied forth for the great occasion. They looked supremely confident, though secretly they were both a trifle apprehensive. Rosie was thankful to have stalwart Sue beside her.

Peter was there when they arrived, looking as usual self-assured and debonair, but his face lit up when he saw Rosie and they were instantly in each others arms, quite oblivious of any onlookers. After a few seconds he released her and stood back gazing at her with obvious delight.

"You look simply adorable, Rosie, you've never looked lovelier."

"Thank you, Pete, you look smart and handsome too."

Her eyes did not leave his face — his words filled her with joy, but she did wish he would say something nice to dear, loyal Sue, as well. She felt Sue was being left on the sidelines, but he only had eyes for his bride and after all it was their day — Sue would understand.

Before the ceremony took place, they were ushered to a desk nearby. The chief registrar was waiting for them and beside him was the young clerk, whom Peter had consulted on his original visit. The registrar greeted them pleasantly, shaking hands and smiling unctuously. He shuffled the papers on his desk and Peter, with a sudden flash of perception, sensed trouble and braced himself.

"First, may we have the young lady's birth certificate, sir?"

Peter kept cool, but the words were like a bombshell.

"I'm afraid I haven't it with me," he replied calmly, determined to bluff it out. " We were certainly not told that it would be needed."

There was a significant pause. The registrar raised his eyebrows and stared doubtfully across at them.

"Well, that is an essential document which we must have, or alternatively a letter of consent from her parents. Otherwise how do we know that she is twenty-one?"

Peter looked suitably indignant and, with a flash of arrogance, produced a piece of paper from his wallet and handed it over.

"Your clerk here wrote down for me what would be required and, as you see, there is no mention about a birth certificate."

Rosie's heart was thumping and she had turned rather pink, but she tried hard to look relaxed and nonchalant. Sue squeezed her arm in encouragement, which helped her confidence.

The registrar studied the paper carefully, then looked up disapprovingly at the youth beside him.

"Thomas," he said with irritation, "you forgot to add to your list the most important document of all."

Poor Thomas blushed to the roots of his hair and, with downcast eyes, mumbled his apologies.

There was silence for a moment, then the older man looked at Peter with a worried expression on his face.

"Well, as the fault is ours, in fairness to you both we must not hold up the ceremony. We will have to take your word for it that she is over the age of consent." They all breathed a sigh of relief; then the little party followed the registrar to the inner room, where the marriage ceremony was to take place. It was a nerve-racking incident and they were all thankful when Peter finally slipped the slender platinum ring on Rosie's finger and they were really man and wife. They later agreed that it had been a sticky moment, but all three of them had carried it off with great aplomb – thank heaven for dear, forgetful Thomas, he'd certainly made their day.

"My God that was a close shave," Peter exclaimed as they walked jubilantly out into the sunshine. Their spirits were high as they hurried across the busy street of the small market town to the County Hotel opposite.

"I need a stiff drink for my nerves after that," Sue said, roaring with laughter.

"We'll soon fix that, Sue, for I badly need a snifter myself," Peter replied.

He had arranged for them to have a private sitting room. It was warm and comfortable with a bright fire burning in the hearth. A table was set in the bay window with the usual centrepiece of dark red roses, as ever conveying Peter's message of love. When Rosie saw them, her face lit up with joy and she smiled radiantly. "Oh Peter, I just can't believe that we are really married. I'm deliriously happy."

"So am I, my darling little wife," he replied giving her a bear hug, then lifting her off her feet and swinging her around.

"Steady on, Pete, you're making me seasick!" It was a truly joyous occasion and Peter's quick wit kept the girls highly amused; peals of laughter filled the room.

The lunch was excellent and the little County Hotel, without doubt, had done them well. After they had finished their delicious repast Sue, with a mischievous smile and glass in hand, stood up and like a toastmaster called: "Pray silence for the one and only bridesmaid" – the champagne had been good and she just could not suppress a girlish giggle. "It is my happy privilege to propose a toast to the handsome groom and his very beautiful bride, my dear friend Rosie. God bless you both and I wish you all the happiness in the world." It was an emotional moment and Peter was quick to reply.

"Thank you, dear Sue. My wife and I," he said proudly, "could not have had a more delightful bridesmaid, so I give us the toast of Sue, coupled with the name of our absent friend, forgetful Thomas, without whom this happy occasion would never have been possible."

They all sipped their champagne and laughed hilariously. 'Forgetful Thomas' had made their day.

The time flew by so fast that they had to make a dash for the station to catch Sue's train, which was due to leave in ten minutes time. They bundled her aboard, without a moment to spare, with lots of hugs and kisses. "Goodbye – take care of yourselves and have a good time," Sue called out – the whistle blew and with a jolt the train was off.

Sue waved vigorously out of the window until the two figures disappeared from sight. She had a lump in her throat and felt curiously flat now that all the excitement was over. She sat back in her seat and closed her eyes, going over in her mind the thrilling events of the weekend. It was all wonderfully romantic.

She prayed that life would treat Rosie kindly and hoped that she had not given her bad advice – but anyway she knew that nothing would have stopped their marrying. They were mad about each other and were determined to go ahead.

Meanwhile the newly-weds were driving back to the cottage, still quite unable to believe that they were really married, for it had all been so easy after all. Just a few words and the deed was done.

As they passed the little church at the end of the lane, Rosie put her hand on Peter's arm.

"Let's stop, darling, and go in and say a little prayer and then I shall feel that we are properly married."

"That's a good idea, Rosie," he said lovingly patting her knee.

He slowed up and parked the car by the gate. The sun was warm and the churchyard silent. The only sound was the crowing of a solitary cockerel in the distance. They walked hand in hand through the lych-gate, up the gravel path to the ancient oak door. It pushed open easily, their footsteps echoing on the smooth slate floor.

On the chancel was a plain gold cross, with a soft background of blue, on which white and gold arum lilies were skilfully embroidered – it was old and beautifully worked. Above this, the stained glass window cast a roseate glow in the setting sun. As they knelt down at the altar, the utter stillness of the tiny church gave Rosie an eerie feeling and she shivered.

"Let's go home, Pete," she whispered, holding his arm close. "I have a creepy sensation. I don't know why, but I had it before when I came here with Mum – almost a premonition of disaster and yet I love this place."

He too had a strange foreboding, but concealed it. He bent down and kissed her.

"Silly old thing, Rosie, this isn't the day for spooky thoughts but, if that's how you feel, let's be on our way."

They let themselves quietly out of the church and, by the time they reached the cottage, it was all love and laughter again. Rosie thought she had never felt so happy.

They stood for a moment at the gate, gazing at their little home. The cottage had an air of waiting expectancy. Peter pushed open the gate, then suddenly swooped down and boisterously picked up his new bride. She gave a squeal of surprise, as he ran up the path with her, laughing uproariously. In his strong arms she seemed as light as a feather.

"I must carry my beautiful bride over the threshold," he said, smiling joyfully and covering her face with kisses.

She clung to him lovingly as he put her down in the hall.

"We're home now, darling," she whispered softly, "and I'm divinely happy – you are the most exciting and wonderful man in the world!"

"You're right there, Rosie," he replied facetiously and I only hope that I shall always be worthy of my beautiful little wife." Then she suddenly noticed a wicker basket outside. It had a large envelope tucked under the handle, addressed to Mrs. Peter Dunbar.

"Whatever is this?" she asked. "It looks most mysterious."

"Pigeons," he said facetiously as he carried it into the sitting room, putting it down by the fire.

She tore open the envelope and read it aloud – "I am the first young Dunbar and my name is Biscuit." Eagerly she released the toggle fastening and lifted the lid. Out jumped the most adorable ginger kitten that Rosie had ever seen, fluffy with marmalade stripes and an enormous blue satin bow around his neck. His large amber eyes looked up at her quizzically.

"Oh, Biscuit," she cried with gladness. "You're adorable" and tears of joy clouded her eyes as she picked him up, hugging him like a baby. He would take the place of her darling Chi-Chi. She looked tenderly across at Peter.

"I know he must be a present from you, darling, and you couldn't have given me anything nicer, he's an absolute joy."

Peter chuckled. "Rather an unorthodox wedding present, but I really thought it would please you, my little sweetheart."

She rushed into his arms and clung to him with delight. Biscuit, being squashed between the two of them, flattened his ears in alarm and gave a protesting 'miaow'.

"Oh, Biscuit darling, I'm sorry," she said, smoothing his ruffled fur and scratching behind his ears until he finally responded with a steady purr of appreciation.

"Put another log on the fire, Pete darling, for pussy cats love to be snug. I will go and make us some tea and bring him a saucer of milk at the same time."

Very soon she was cuddled up on the couch beside Peter, gazing into the dancing flames. Biscuit was curled in a ball at their feet, dozing contentedly by the fire. Life was very sweet.

"Pete, you are a darling, being so thoughtful. Having Biscuit makes all the difference. Our enchanted cottage seems like a real home now." It had a special essence for Rosie – a haven in which she felt secure and protected.

6

THE SUN streamed through the bedroom window forming diamond patterns on the wall. Snowdon could be seen clearly in the distance. The purple range of mountains stood out in stark relief against a vivid cobalt sky.

Rosie lay gently cocooned in Peter's arms. She snuggled closer to him and was filled with a deep contentment. Their love-making had been ecstatic – a coming together of their innermost selves, with a depth of passion exceeding anything that either of them had ever dreamed of. They were as one now. It had been a breath-taking experience. She anticipated with eager excitement their increased intimacy. She wriggled closer, trying gently to wake him up. Dreamily he opened his eyes and gazed at her wonderingly, his face alight with love.

"My darling little wife," he said with a catch in his voice. "I can hardly believe you are really mine now. You're the most adorable girl in the whole wide world and last night was pure heaven."

She smiled shyly back at him. "It was for me too, Pete darling" – then she said with an impish chuckle, "I just can't wait for more," sliding her hand over his chest and pulling him closer to her. He kissed her again and again with a mounting passion, filled with the ecstasy of physical happiness and overwhelming desire to possess her once more.

It was the middle of the morning before they woke up for the second time. The windows were open and the curtains drawn back. The sweet pungent mountain air filled the room. Peter was the first to make a move.

"How about a nice cup of tea, darling?" he asked with a boyish grin as he bounded out of bed, pulling on his dressing gown.

"That would be gorgeous," she replied, yawning and stretching sleepily. "Good old Pete! I hope you will always go on spoiling me like this."

He bent over and ruffled her hair. "Of course I will, my little enchantress. I will ever be at your beck and call," he said teasingly.

By the time he arrived back with the tray, she was sitting up in bed with her curly hair tousled and her eyes sparkling. He thought how seductive she looked. He was thrilled to see her all mussed up. She was so utterly desirable and he knew with conviction that his feelings for her would never change. He felt a twisting of the heart – the bitter sweet pain of love, an overwhelming adoration of her which shook him by its intensity.

Biscuit had followed him upstairs and, with a little miaow, jumped on the bed beside her with a heavy plop and, as she stroked him, he purred away steadily, expressing his approval. She poured some milk into a saucer which he eagerly lapped up, then fastidiously he cleaned off his whiskers with his tiny paws before curling into a ball and going to sleep. He was already quite at home.

"I think it's about time we got cracking, Rosie dear, as we're going out for lunch. I don't know about you but I'm absolutely famished!"

"Yes, Pete, so am I – it won't take me long to get ready, if I hurry."

She was soon lying in a brimming tub, full of foaming bubbles, lazing in the warmth of the water; then making up for lost time, she jumped out and dressed quickly.

As she waited for Peter to appear, she took Biscuit for a tour of inspection around the garden, so that he could get used to the new terrain. He wandered nervously in and out of the bushes, cautiously examining every nook and cranny, sniffing appreciatively at a large cluster of catmint which he had discovered, but he never strayed far away from her.

After he had indulged his curiosity, she carried him back into the cottage, hugging him close. She put him in his basket near to the fire. "Go to sleep, Biscuit," she said, stroking his fluffy little body. "We won't be gone long."

She and Peter set forth, hand in hand, at a brisk pace towards the 'Mermaid Inn' which was situated in a nearby village and reputed to have excellent food.

It was warm, almost an indian summer. The meadows were speckled with daisies and the trees still heavily clad with golden foliage. The country air was a tonic to them both. It brought the colour to Rosie's cheeks and intensified the blue of her eyes.

They took a short cut through the fields, scrambling up the paths and making their way between the gaps in the stone walls, finally descending into the village. They were in high spirits when they arrived at the 'Mermaid' and were ravenously hungry after their exertions. It was a dear little stone pub on the village street. Peter had to stoop to enter the low-beamed doorway and there was a fire blazing in the open hearth to welcome them.

"Isn't this a super pub, Rosie? It must be very old, about 17th century I should think. Look at the thickness of the walls."

"Yes, they're at least two feet thick and built of stone, quarried locally at Llanberis, I expect. I'm so glad that we came here," she said as she bent over, warming her hands by the cheerful blaze. "This place is very snug."

The innkeeper, who was a burly dark Welshman, appeared; he guessed at once that they were a honeymoon couple – they had a special aura about them and he wanted to make them very welcome.

"Can I take your order, sir?" he asked with a pleasant smile, handing Peter the menu. "There isn't a great deal of choice at this time of the year, I'm afraid, but our speciality is Lancashire hot pot and pickled cabbage."

"That sounds absolutely yummy," Rosie said. "It makes my mouth water, so that is my choice. How about you Peter?"

"I'll have the same. I love these old traditional dishes. Will you bring me a pint of bitter please – what would you like to drink, Rosie?"

"I'm very thirsty, so a ginger beer shandy would be just the ticket."

"Would you like it in here by the fire, sir? The dining-room is a bit big just for two. I can set it up on a small table for you."

"That's a splendid idea," Peter replied. "It will be much cosier here."

They were soon eating their lunch with the room all to themselves as the holiday makers had all departed.

The hot pot was superb, with a crispy potato topping, served in individual earthenware dishes – followed by home-made apple pie and cream. Needless to say they did full justice to the meal.

When the landlord returned he found them sitting by the fire, holding hands like two love birds, so he felt that his suspicions were confirmed.

"We did enjoy our lunch," Rosie said enthusiastically. "It was delicious."

"It was a meal fit for a king," Peter endorsed as he paid the bill.

"Thank you, sir, our hot pot is always a great favourite."

"We absolutely love it here and we'll certainly be back for more!" Rosie said with a smile as they left the inn.

On their return journey, after an upward climb through the fields, they stood on a hill top, gazing down at the cottage from afar. It looked delightfully cosy, nestling among the trees, with a wisp of smoke rising from the chimney. Rosie sighed deeply: "How sad that this is our last day, Pete. I hate the thought of leaving. We seem in a world of our own here, away from all the harsh realities of life."

"I agree with you there, darling, particularly when I think of returning to the grindstone once more."

For the first time she consciously thought of her parents and the shock they would have tomorrow when the post arrived. It seemed like weeks since she had left home, whereas in fact it had been only a few days. She must dismiss these disturbing thoughts and not let anything spoil their magic, for they had been truly blessed, but soon she would have to face up to the situation.

"Come on, Pete," she cried provocatively. "I'll race you back to the cottage." And, laughing gaily, she went tearing off down the hill with Peter in hot pursuit. When he caught up with her, he pulled her down on to the soft grass, showering her with kisses. No other woman had ever moved him in this way. His heart beat with an unfamiliar intensity.

"Oh Rosie darling, I do adore you," he said, shaken by the depth of his own emotions. "I can hardly wait to get you home." He helped her to her feet.

"I can still win," she called teasingly, as she challenged him and dashed off again, racing down the lane and arriving at the front door breathless and convulsed with laughter, just beating him by a whisker.

That evening they sat close together by the fire in their dressing gowns, with the curtains drawn, closing out the onset of early darkness. Rosie looked sweet in a white fluffy gown with furry white slippers.

"You look like a little bunny, Rosie," he said affectionately, patting her hand. "In fact I may call you 'Bunny' in future."

"Very well, Mr. Rabbit," she said with twinkling eyes and they roared with laughter. He loved her infectious gaiety."

"You know, Pete, you're just perfect for me. I think I'll call you 'Perfect Pete' in future."

"Plese don't do that, Rosie," he said and he really looked troubled. "You must not put me on a pedestal. I'll only have further to fall. You know I'm full of human frailties!"

"I haven't noticed them so far, PP, so tell me what they are."

He laughed. "I don't want to reveal my deep, dark secrets yet, young lady – but beware!"

He cuddled her closer to him – first love was truly wonderful.

They had their supper on trays in front of the fire, talking non-stop. They were both excited at the prospect of their new life together in London. The little mews house was a thrill to have, but they would never form the same attachment to it as they had to 'Apple Trees'.

"Rosie darling," he said, stifling a yawn, "let's go to bed now, for we have a busy day ahead of us and I'm almost asleep – this warm fire makes me drowsy – so, my sexy puss, you can't tempt me again tonight."

She held him close. "Don't worry, Pete, I'm exhausted too – but isn't it all heavenly?" – her little face radiated happiness.

"Yes, my darling, it is. I love you to distraction and wish we could be alone here always."

Holding hands, they ran upstairs, leaving Biscuit settled in his chosen chair by the fire; they were asleep, entwined in each other's arms, as soon as their heads touched the pillow.

* * * * *

They were up early the next morning, preparing for their departure. Biscuit was put in his basket under protest, in case he was nervous and tried to escape.

When everything was finally stowed away in the car, they stood at the gate looking wistfully back at the cottage, which had provided them with such a perfect retreat for their first blissful days of marriage. They both felt sad. Would they ever share such complete happiness again?

"It's awful leaving here, Pete, it has all been so wonderful," Rosie said with tears in her eyes.

"I know, poppet, it makes me sad too. It's been a perfect honeymoon, but now that we're married there's nothing to worry about, so cheer up, my sweet."

They were quiet as they drove along the peaceful country lane. Peter held her hand for she was still pensive, upset that their blissful interlude was over. She held Biscuit on her knees in his wicker basket, talking reassuringly to him.

Later on they regained their high spirits, for they had so much to look forward to. Rosie finally ventured to lift the lid of Biscuit's basket. To begin with he peered out cautiously with ears flattened then, as he got used to the motion of the car, he made a bold jump and perched precariously on Peter's shoulder, digging in his claws and refusing to move, his wild eyes mesmerised by the passing scenery and the traffic flashing by.

"Ouch Biscuit, that's painful. Can you move him Rosie?"

"OK, Pete," she answered, carefully dislodging his claws, but he soon jumped up again.

Some of the leaves had fallen from the trees and formed a golden carpet. The sunshine filtered through the branches, making intricate patterns on the ground. Snowdon stood serene in the background.

Rosie had a sudden urge to record this transitional scene. She pulled out her sketching block and, in spite of the bumping car, outlined a rough study, making notes on colours for future reference.

"I will paint a picture of the Welsh countryside for you tomorrow, darling, as a permanent reminder of our perfect honeymoon." She felt most excited at the prospect and could hardly wait to start.

"I would love that, Rosie, but remember you're a housewife now and you've got a very demanding and hungry husband to feed!"

"I won't neglect you," she said in jocular tone, "but I must find time for painting too – for, after you and my parents, it's the most important thing in my life."

"That's all right, Rosie, but remember I come first. You're mine now and I don't want to share you with anybody or anything."

She laughed indulgently. "Don't worry, Peterkin, you won't have to."

The journey passed quickly. Peter was a fast, though careful, driver and Rosie felt completely relaxed with him. As they approached the outskirts of London, they were slowed down by the congestion of traffic returning after the weekend break.

They drove slowly through Hyde Park, being held up by a troop of the Household Cavalry on their way to the ugly old Knightsbridge Barracks. How striking they looked in their magnificent uniforms, riding on their perfectly groomed horses. Their shining helmets and breast plates glinted in the low angled light.

Rosie thought London, with all its old traditions and pageantry, was a stimulating place in which to live, but, as they turned out of the park gates into Knightsbridge, her peace of mind was shattered when she read on a hoarding the succinct words – 'Hitler threatens Austria'. Her heart sank; was this to be the next crisis? A dark shadow seemed to cloud the day.

"Did you see that placard, Pete, about Hitler's threat?" she asked apprehensively.

"Yes, I just caught a glimpse of it, darling, but it's no good worrying, as there is nothing we can do to change the situation. At least we must be thankful that we have Chamberlain as Prime Minister. He is no war-monger and will do his best to keep the peace."

"I hope to God he manages it. I've got a terrible dread of war." But as they turned the corner into the crescent and she saw their little house, she jumped for joy and all her worries vanished.

"Isn't it adorable, Pete? Look at your new home, Biscuit."

She lifted him off Peter's shoulder, turning his reluctant head towards the house, then she popped him back in his basket for safety, though he protested violently when she shut down the lid.

They were soon indoors, exploring their new home; it was warm and snug and they were thrilled with it all. When Peter opened the refrigerator door, he found a bottle of champagne awaiting them with a warm message of congratulations from Dick. "What a lovely welcome for us," Rosie exclaimed happily.

"Yes, how super – good old generous Dick! It's just what we need to revive us after a long journey. Let's crack the bottle now, Rosie, then have an early supper and get to bed."

"That's a good idea, Pete," she said, "for we will have to be up bright and early in the morning. I'm going to miss you dreadfully, while you are at work."

After a simple meal, they went to bed and were asleep almost at once; they didn't even turn over until the strident sound of the alarm clock rudely awoke them the following morning.

* * * * *

On the Monday when Rosie was expected home, her father and mother were having breakfast, engrossed in the daily papers. The news was disturbing and the probability of a world war seemed greater than ever.

Mrs. Greenwood had just finished reading a sickening article about the harassment of Jews in Nazi Germany, with a strong suggestion that Hitler's ultimate aim was the complete extermination of the race. There were shocking pictures of elderly Jewish men and women being forced to scrub the pavements, with the word 'Jude' conspicuously displayed on their backs and now regarded in Germany as a symbol of shame. The photographs and stories were horrific, and Rosie's mother turned over the page with a feeling of revulsion.

There was a light tap on the door and in walked Jane with the post. She handed the letters on a salver to Mr. Greenwood, who separated them, passing over those addressed to his wife.

"My goodness, there is one from Rosie," he said with surprise. "It's addressed to both of us, so you'd better read it aloud to me."

She hurriedly tore it open, feeling full of apprehension. She knew something unusual had happened. Her voice trembled as she read the letter. When she had finished, there was a dead silence in the room, broken only by a coal falling on the hearth. She bent forward and pushed it back. She hardly dare look at her husband and, when finally their eyes met, she saw his expression of bewilderment. His darling child, the apple of his eye, was defying and deserting him like this.

Then his mood changed to one of anger and, raising his voice, he exclaimed: "How dare the young puppy do this to my daughter – anyway the marriage is not legal. She is under age and I will have it annulled."

His wife left her chair and went over to sit beside him.

"Dearest, you would never do that to her, you love her far too much. Try not to feel so hurt. We know she is too young and immature to marry, but Peter is a nice person and things could be very much worse."

He pushed his chair away with such force that it fell over backwards.

"Do not communicate with them in any way," he said vehemently. "They can manage on their own now. After all we have done for Rosie, she can find out for herself what it is like being without us. It won't be long before she discovers on which side her bread is buttered. I will instruct the bank today to stop her dress allowance. Now, Elizabeth, remember that this is my wish and, if you defy me, I shall consider it an act of disloyalty."

When he left the room, she felt completely shattered. Rosie was their life and to cut her off like this was like severing a part of themselves.

After a few moments she calmed down. She knew her husband well. He was much too kind and forgiving a person to maintain this attitude for long and particularly with his darling daughter.

Now she had the horrid task of speaking to the Dunbars. She only hoped they would not put the blame on Rosie. She would try her best to make them accept the situation and not judge the young people too harshly. In her heart of hearts she felt that Peter and Rosie had a certain amount of right on their side and she longed to communicate with them. This she would never do without her husband's consent. He had been hurt enough and another act of disloyalty from her would finish him.

* * * * *

Rosie hated seeing Peter leave for the office each morning – it was a new experience for her to be in the house alone and one which she did not relish. There was, however, plenty to do and not being at all domesticated she had much to learn. She buckled down with her usual enthusiasm and it wasn't long before she developed a flair for cooking, which she found fun. She took great pride in her little house and always kept it spick and span.

She gave Peter a terrific welcome when he arrived home each evening. There was always a bright fire burning and a meal ready for him. She studied a Cordon Bleu cookery book and was most adventurous in her choice of dishes – he loved her enterprise, but best of all he had her undivided attention, which was so essential for his happiness. Providing he had her to himself, he was perfectly content.

Every morning she rushed to the front door as the letters dropped through the box but, as the days went by without any word from her parents, their silence became a real heartache. Perhaps they would never forgive her. She longed to show her mother their little home – she was so proud of it and wished to demonstrate what a good housewife she had become. She began to feel lonely and bereft. Peter sensed she was missing them and tried his best to keep her from fretting, though he resented the fact that he alone was not enough for her.

They went to the theatre at least once a week, generally having to queue for seats in the 'gods', and they regularly attended concerts at the Albert Hall; but Rosie's days were lonely ones, cut off from her old carefree, happy life. She often thought of the 'band of five' – now four – and wondered if they missed her.

*　　*　　*　　*　　*

One afternoon, feeling lonely and for the first time in her life bored and restless, Rosie decided to visit the National Portrait Gallery. An exciting new exhibition had just opened with some of the leading artists of the day contributing.

She took the tube to Trafalgar Square and sat idly on the edge of the fountain for a few minutes, watching the pigeons being fed. It was a bright crisp November day and she enjoyed being at the hub of this great metropolis, listening to the continuous hum of traffic around her.

An old tramp, his gnarled face weather beaten and incongruously wearing a battered bowler, was throwing down bits of bread from a screw of newspaper. He was surrounded by plump pigeons which in their excited turmoil fought for morsels that he cast in their midst. His rheumy old eyes sparkled as he distributed his largesse – this was obviously a daily ritual with him; he was perhaps enjoying the act of giving in his own humble way.

She sat pensively observing him, wondering if he slept in the crypt of St. Martin's as many tramps did. Then she wandered over the square and crossed the road, entering the gallery and was soon completely absorbed.

She was fascinated by the diversity of the excellent studies from which she gained inspiration. They made her itch to return to her own canvas. She loved especially the work of James Gunn, which was almost photographic in style – yet his were brilliant studies, which reflected dramatically the individual personalities of the sitters. They were alive and seemed to speak to her from their frames.

She had lost all track of time and, to her great consternation, she suddenly realised that she could not get home before Peter. She hailed a taxi, encouraging the cabbie to drive like a Jehu – but they were frustrated by the congestion of the traffic and, when she finally arrived, Peter was already there, impatiently waiting for her. He was obviously put out and looked as black as thunder.

"Where the hell have you been, Rosie? The house is freezing and nothing is ready. I have been worried to death about you."

She looked at him askance and swallowed hard before she replied: "I'm sorry, Pete, but I went to that new exhibition at the National Portrait Gallery and got so carried away that I forgot all about time."

She felt guilty, but hurt by his bullying attitude. Was she always supposed to be waiting for him, at his beck and call? Perhaps she had spoilt him. Her lips trembled which he noticed and he quickly softened his approach.

"Never mind, poppet, let's go out and have a meal. We could try that new Chinese restaurant down the road – you're such a wizard with chopsticks."

She cheered up visibly and he was soon his loving self again – but the incident left a scar and after this she was always careful to be home when he arrived. She did not like these restrictions for she was essentially a free person.

*   *   *   *   *

After a few weeks of marriage, Rosie started to feel decidedly off colour, especially in the mornings. Peter was worried; it was all so unlike Rosie but, when she became worse and was even sick and dizzy during the day, he insisted on phoning Dr. Kennett, the local doctor, who had been so highly recommended by Dick. He was a conscientious man and promised to call that morning. He was anxious to do his best for them as Dick had given them a terrific 'write up'.

He was a tall, thin, aesthetic young man and Rosie liked his serious approach, but was amazed and disbelieving when he told her she was probably pregnant.

"That isn't at all likely," she exclaimed, "for we have been married for only a few weeks and I couldn't possibly be feeling ill already."

"You're wrong there, Mrs. Dunbar," he said with a kind smile. "Some sensitive people feel unwell very soon after they conceive – anyway, time will tell."

"How exciting, I never imagined it could happen so quickly."

He took away a specimen and told her that he would be able to confirm one way or the other in about a week and, in the meantime, she must take it easy.

Rosie hesitated about telling Peter the news until she knew something definite. Her sixth sense told her he would not be pleased. When he came home that evening, after kissing Rosie he immediately asked: "What did the doctor have to say?"

"He doesn't really know but he thinks it could be a virus – I'm feeling better now."

"Thank heaven for that. I've been worried about you all day," he said with relief.

She was able to eat her meal as usual that night, so he was reassured that all was well again. Nothing must happen to his Rosie.

The week passed slowly. She could hardly wait to hear the result of the test. She longed for a baby, yet her feelings were confused. Her father's warning words were not forgotten, and the threat of war seemed to have increased. She was sure too that Peter would regard it as a mixed blessing. He was certainly not ready to share her with anyone yet, but oh the delight of having a baby of her very own – it seemed the most exciting thing in the world to her.

She tried to keep Peter at arms length and their love-making was subdued – nothing must harm the baby, if she were indeed pregnant. He was patient, putting the change down to her illness, but he painfully missed their previous gay abandon and could not understand this new, withdrawn Rosie.

Finally the eagerly-awaited phone call came and she was told that she was indeed pregnant and could she call at the doctor's that morning. She was in a whirl of excitement, but how she longed to have someone with whom to share the joyous news.

She gazed into every pram that she passed on the way to the surgery and was enchanted by the babies. She had always wanted a big family, but for the first time realised how strong her maternal instincts were. This would be the most important and fulfilling experience of her life.

After an examination in the surgery, Dr. Kennett confirmed that all was well and the baby was due in early July. He smiled kindly at her as she returned to his office for a talk. She looked such a child to be pregnant and her huge blue eyes held a dreamy happiness that he did not wish to dispel, but in spite of this he sounded a warning note.

"Now, Mrs. Dunbar, everything is all right, but I do warn you that you must be careful for the first few months as you have a badly tipped uterus, which could cause a miscarriage in the early stages. You should not exert yourself too much and I would advise no marital relations until at least after the third month – by that time you will be much more secure. I do stress, however, that you must lead a normal life, but take only mild exercise and watch your diet, then all should be well. Are you both pleased about starting a family?"

A worried expression came into her eyes and a little sigh escaped her.

"I haven't told Peter anything yet. I wanted to make quite certain about it first. I'm sure he'll be pleased, but he probably would have preferred to wait. I think he likes me to himself."

They both laughed.

"A perfectly natural feeling for a young husband. Now let me know, if you have any problems. I live only around the corner from you, so I can easily pop in to see you on my way home in the evening."

"Oh, thank you doctor, that gives me such a reassuring feeling."

She shook hands warmly with him, leaving the office with emotions of both joy and foreboding.

After his words of warning she was almost afraid to walk home. She was terrified at the prospect of losing the baby, but she remembered his advice about exercise and determinedly pulled herself together – she must not become neurotic. If only she could talk to her mother and have the comfort of her family around her – as she thought of this it was hard to hold back the tears. Would they ever relent and get in touch with her? She missed them dreadfully and not being able to share this experience with them was a terrible disappointment.

That afternoon she prepared a special dinner for Peter and herself. She bought fresh flowers for the table and a bottle of wine. She lit the fire early and dressed carefully. Now she was going to be a mother, she felt more responsible and decided she must be a more dignified person.

As soon as Peter arrived home he sensed a subtle change in her and when, as usual, he swept her off her feet and whirled her boisterously around, he noticed a drawing back.

"Careful, Pete, you're making me dizzy."

"Aren't you well again, darling?" he asked anxiously. He thought she looked pale. "Sorry if I was too exuberant, but I was so thrilled to see you that I'm afraid I got carried away."

She kissed him warmly. "Don't worry, I'm all right, Pete, and I have been longing to see you too. I've organised a special dinner for us tonight – Chateaubriand, which I know you love, and a nice bottle of claret to go with it."

"It sounds perfect, darling." He was delighted by her culinary endeavours. "I'll just go upstairs and wash my hands – I will only be a minute and then we can have a drink. I've something interesting to tell you."

They were soon settled by the fire. This was the best part of the day for them both.

"You're looking especially glamorous tonight, Mrs. Dunbar," he said, "in fact very seductive," and the ardour was evident in his face – "but first let me tell you my good news. The old man called me in this morning to say that he is using my plan for the new housing estate they are going to build at Ealing – it's quite a feather in my cap, being such a new boy."

"Congratulations, that's wonderful, Pete," she said, positively glowing with pride. "I'm absolutely delighted, but not at all surprised. I thought your plan was a super one. The houses are both practical and of a good design; in fact I would like to live in one myself. May I come and visit the site the next time you go up? I would be so interested."

"Of course, my poppet, we'll definitely arrange that for one day next week."

"Now, Pete, it's my turn. I have something thrilling to tell you too."

"Good, but let me pour us another drink first."

She waited until he settled down again then, drawing a deep breath, took the plunge.

"Pete, it's so exciting I hardly know how to start. I've been to see Doc. Kennett today and I'm pregnant – isn't that absolutely wonderful?"

Her face was radiant with happiness and, as he looked at her, an awful feeling of jealousy possessed him. He fought to control it and forced a smile on his face but Rosie, with a sinking heart, knew it to be contrived.

He quickly mastered himself.

"That's really wonderful, darling – I hope it will be another little Rosie and that she is as sweet as her mother. This is certainly an occasion for celebration. Let's drink to her, shall we?"

The icy fingers around Rosie's heart relaxed a little. They clinked glasses and, as Peter's shock wore off, he became more himself again. He soon started planning for the arrival of the baby and talked of turning the studio upstairs into a nursery.

After their delicious dinner they sat down and exchanged ideas for the new room.

"Let's go and buy a cot tomorrow, Rosie, and that will inspire us and we can build the room around it." He warmed to the project.

She looked worried. "Pete, I haven't told you the bad part yet. Doc. Kennett says I must be very careful for the first three months, as there's a definite risk of my miscarrying, and buying a cot so soon might be tempting fate. He has also banned our love life for that period."

Peter's expression changed. He looked furious, scowling heavily. The full realisation of what this baby entailed struck him forcibly and he was eaten up by jealousy. He reacted strongly.

"I'm afraid we'll have to disregard this unpleasant advice, Rosie, for I've no intention in the world of giving up our fun."

Rosie looked at him with a horrified expression – her face paled. Was this really Peter speaking? It seemed unbelievable. For the first time she saw him in a different light – it was all unflattering. He was utterly selfish.

"You selfish beast," she shouted. "I never dreamed you'd be so awful."

She burst into tears then ran out of the room, slamming the door behind her.

She felt terribly alone and sensed that in future, instead of their happy carefree relationship, a strain would be building up between them.

7

PETER TRIED to make amends, but a barrier had built up between them. Rosie was not feeling at all well and her spirits were low. His egoism had left a scar. She feared their close relationship would never be quite the same again – she felt uncertain of him. He was not the knight in shining armour that she had first imagined; she was disillusioned.

She tried to be the same warm, loving girl and took great pains to give him his usual welcome home each evening, but in bed at night she determinedly kept herself aloof. Nothing must harm the baby and Peter must be prepared to make sacrifices too. He desperately missed their former intimacy and, when some weeks later he drew her close to him, she called him a selfish beast. He was shocked by her reaction and after this left her severely alone. He threw himself into his work, which was demanding, and consoled himself by believing that Rosie's behaviour was only a passing phase.

The war clouds were gathering fast. Czechoslovakia was Hitler's latest target; he demanded incorporation into the Reich of the predominantly German-populated areas. There was little doubt that this would be the next country to be swallowed up. Hitler's greed for power was insatiable.

Air raid shelters were being dug in the London parks and there was talk of gas masks being issued. It struck terror into Rosie's heart, when she thought of the baby she was bringing into the world – how right her father's warning had been. She already loved and feared for this unborn child as it stirred within her.

They were approached by a Jewish organisation, asking if they would be willing to give a temporary home to Jewish nationals fleeing from Germany. She and Peter talked it over and Peter, knowing how deeply Rosie felt for them, came along with the idea. She was pleased that he was willing to inconvenience himself and their relationship improved in consequence.

Their first arrival was a young girl called Edith, who had just completed her doctor's training in Stuttgart. Her English was perfect and she was soon to be placed in one of the London teaching hospitals. Edith and Rosie took to each other from the outset and even Peter admired Edith's stoicism. She was a tiny girl, only five feet tall, but with the heart of a lion. She had left behind in Germany her parents and younger brother, Gerhardt, for they had all begged her to escape while she had the opportunity. She hoped fervently that, once she was established in England, they might find a way of following her.

Edith spent most days at the Jewish centre during which she was interviewed and carefully screened. Hitler at this time was allowing some Jews to filter through, on condition that they sent back to Germany certain information needed for the war effort. If they failed to do so, reprisals would be taken against their families left behind.

One evening after dinner Rosie and Peter were sitting by the fire listening to Edith's harrowing stories of the pogrom in Germany. She sat huddled in her chair with a haunted expression in her eyes and spoke in a low monotone, as if afraid of showing any emotion.

"This reign of terror against the Jews at home is quite horrifying," she said with a shudder. "The dreaded Gestapo generally strike after dark, and the fear of a visitation from their henchmen is a very terrible thing. They hammer on the door often in the dead of night, then burst in and, with trumped up charges, arrest the innocent victims, who are never seen again. We don't know what becomes of them, but dreadful stories are leaking out."

"It's too awful to contemplate," Peter ejaculated in a shocked voice. "We read a certain amount about these atrocities in the newspapers but it is unbelievable that in a so-called civilised society such dreadful occurrences take place."

Edith nodded, then carried on in the same expressionless voice, as if compelled to get it off her chest. "The night before I left home there was a ghastly incident in a house across the street. Nazi thugs broke in and two children, little more than babies, were brutally separated from their parents and flung screaming into a truck. The distraught parents fought like tigers to save them but they were knocked insensible and dragged into a separate vehicle. When the grandparents tried to intervene, they were unmercifully assaulted and kicked down the stairs – their only crime was being Jewish," Edith said brokenly.

Peter spoke in a husky voice, "I don't know what to say, Edith, to comfort you. It is quite inconceivable that a nation can condone such depravity – it's like returning to the dark ages." He was filled with compassion for her.

Rosie's heart ached, she just couldn't speak – it was too awful to contemplate. She groped for Peter's hand and held it tightly, their own differences paling into insignificance. He put a protective arm around her shoulders, knowing how she felt and they became closer than they had been for weeks.

They were sitting quietly, having been stunned by these horrific disclosures, when suddenly the silence was broken by a loud 'rap-rap' on the front door, alarming in its urgency. They were momentarily startled, then brought back to reality. Thank God this was England and there was nothing to fear. Edith was the first to get up.

"You both sit still and I'll answer it," she spoke firmly. She always tried to be as helpful as possible in return for their hospitality. They heard the front door opening and the sound of excited voices in the hall and then there was a dead silence. Peter sprang to his feet in alarm and flung open the door; he saw a tall young man standing there, his face a mask of suffering as he held tiny Edith in his arms. Hysterically she was clinging to him, her head buried in his chest, desperately repeating over and over again: *"Gott sei dank – Gott sei dank – ein segen!"* (Thank God – Thank God – you're safe.)

Suddenly becoming aware of Peter's presence they pulled apart and, with tears of joy running down her cheeks, Edith introduced the haggard youth: "This is Gerhardt, my brother," she gasped, "he's managed to escape – I can't believe it." His poor anxious face was unshaven, his clothes dishevelled. "Welcome, Gerhardt," Peter said in astonishment, vigorously shaking his hand. "Thank heaven you've made it." It was a moment charged with emotion.

"I've been very lucky," Gerhardt replied in a choked voice, doggedly struggling for composure.

"Come inside and get warm," Rosie said kindly, taking his arm and guiding him to a chair by the fire – fleetingly she caught the frightened expression in his eyes. It was that of a hunted animal and made her blood run cold.

"You are safe here among friends," she assured him. "Sit down and relax. You look exhausted. Peter will get you a drink."

He sank gratefully into a chair and closed his eyes momentarily. Edith sat on the floor beside him, her head resting against his knee. She was still unable to believe that her adored young brother was actually safe and sound. "How did you manage to get away," she asked, "and how about Mama and Papa?"

"Oh Edie," he answered brokenly, "I had to leave them. They begged me to – Mama went down on her knees and there was nothing more I could do for them. I was being watched by the Gestapo and it was only a matter of time before they picked me up, so I left after dark and travelled to the border in easy stages. I took a chance there by bribing a frontier guard with my gold watch and he allowed me to ski across the border to Switzerland. I think he was secretly on our side."

"Thank God for that but, Gerhardt, how were Mama and Papa when you left them?"

Gerhardt was overcome with emotion and broke down completely as he spoke. "More than anything in the world they wanted us to be safe, Edie, and they promised that they would do their utmost to follow," but Edith shook her head despairingly.

"I know that will never happen – the defeat of Germany is the only way of ending this nightmare," she said hopelessly. For the first time Rosie felt that she would welcome a war, for this inhumanity must be stopped at all costs.

* * * * *

Gerhardt was a trained engineer and it was only a few days before both he and Edith were placed. Rosie hated to see them go and, when Peter arrived home that evening, her tear-stained face worried him. She seemed so despondent, very different from the carefree girl he had married. He wished with all his heart that the baby was not on the way.

That night in bed, Rosie told him how miserable she felt and how much she missed her family. He deeply resented her dependence on their love, but concealed his feelings. He must get in touch with them. He felt now they had been proved right in forbidding Rosie to marry so young. War seemed inevitable and the added responsibility of a baby was madness at her age. Yet their delirious first few weeks of love had been perfection, a never-to-be-forgotten experience, but would it ever be quite the same again?

The next day he wrote to her mother and father, telling them of her pregnancy and how unwell she was. He ended by urging them to come and see her, as she was missing them dreadfully. He was sure that they would respond to this, for they adored their only daughter and they surely would relent.

He left the office early that evening, calling in at the toy department of Harrods on the way home. He wanted to be the first to buy his child a toy and he thought it would please Rosie and make her feel that he was looking forward to the baby's arrival.

He saw at once exactly what he wanted. A giant furry teddy bear with an enormous red and white spotted bow around his neck and a jolly expression in his shiny button eyes. He was sitting with a family of smaller bears around him. Peter smiled to himself and, without even enquiring the price, said he would have the teddy bear.

When he arrived home and Rosie saw it, her face lit up and for the first time in weeks she laughed and was her old self again.

"What a splendid Teddy, it's the largest I've ever seen!"

"I just couldn't resist him in Harrods. It's our first present for 'Junior' and his name is Mr. Smith."

"How do you do, Mr. Smith," she said shaking his paw.

He sat between them on the couch and they solemnly conversed with him. They decided he was a brainy bear; consequently his opinion was frequently sought. He answered "yes" or "no" by a nod or turn of the head and, when he held a strong opinion, he banged his paws vigorously on the table in front of him.

That night they were close again. "You know, Rosie, I'm as proud as Punch that we're having a baby, but when you first told me I couldn't help being anxious – you're so young."

"Not all that young," she answered defensively.

She was partially reassured by his words, but knew this was not a completely true explanation, for his possessiveness manifested itself more every day. He wanted her undivided attention at all times and even resented her knitting baby clothes, telling her it was better to buy them. Yet they loved one another deeply and she cuddled close up to him and found his nearness a great source of comfort.

*   *   *   *   *

Rosie lay down every afternoon and that day she felt dull and lethargic. She longed to put up her feet; the weather was hot and muggy and the little house felt airless. She dragged herself upstairs to bed.

She washed her face and hands and put on a light dressing gown. She caught a glimpse of herself in the mirror and thought how pale and apathetic she looked. Her blue eyes were shadowed and her sparkle had vanished.

Her painting had been neglected for some time. Housekeeping and preoccupation with pregnancy seemed to have been all-demanding. As she looked out of her bedroom window and saw the little laburnum tree in full blossom, she had a sudden desire to paint its golden flowers, hanging so daintily in such great profusion. After the baby was born she would really get down to painting again – she was cheered up by this exciting prospect.

She sighed deeply as she curled up on the bed, drawing the ever-present Biscuit close to her. She lay still, conscious of the movement of her child. She loved to feel this new life within her – little flutters like fairy fingers. They were so completely as one. She almost wished the baby could remain in her womb, postponing the inevitable parting.

She must have dozed off for a moment, but was woken up by a knock on the front door.

"What a nuisance," she thought. "It's probably the milkman wanting to be paid."

She crawled out of bed, putting on her slippers and making her way carefully down the stairs. They were steep and, when she reached the hall, she felt rather sick and dizzy. She opened the door, almost in a daze and for a moment could hardly believe her eyes, for there on the threshold stood her mother and father. She stared at them incomprehensively. They were gazing anxiously at her – this pale, forlorn girl in her cotton wrap. Could this be their happy, vivacious Rosie? They were manifestly shocked and in a flash their disapproval vanished, leaving only an overwhelming concern for her.

Rosie flew into her mother's arms in floods of tears and for several moments clung to her sobbing inconsolably; then, turning to her father, she hugged him warmly. She was overjoyed to see them, everything would be all right now.

"It's heaven to see you both," she gasped. She was all choked up and it was hard to speak. "Come into the living room and sit down."

They followed her in, almost afraid to trust themselves to answer.

"It's marvellous to see you again, Rosie," her mother said huskily. "We've missed you dreadfully." How had they managed to live without her for so long? It had been foolish – nothing but stubborn pride.

They sat together in the small cosy room, feeling enormous relief at being reunited again. A great weight had been lifted from their shoulders – they felt almost light-headed. To Rosie it seemed quite unbelievable that they were really here beside her in her own little house.

Her mother was the first to gain control of her emotions.

"Peter wrote and told us that you haven't been at all well, Rosie, and I must say you are looking very pale and much thinner."

"I haven't been too good, Mum," she said, "but I am better now that you are here."

She dried her eyes on a large pocket handkerchief which her father had provided, then, pulling herself together, she managed a wan smile.

"Would you like a cup of tea, I'm sure we could all do with one?"

"Yes please," her mother replied with gusto. "That's a marvellous idea, but I will get it, Rosie. You stay here and talk to your father."

"Can you manage on your own, Mum?"

"Oh yes, I'm good at finding my way around other people's kitchens."

"There's a chocolate cake in the red tin next to the tea caddy. I made it myself," Rosie said proudly.

As Mrs. Greenwood left the room, Rosie's father sat down beside her. He thought how tired and drained she looked. It hurt him dreadfully; she was so unlike the happy girl who had left home a few short months ago. He took her hand and looked searchingly at her.

"Rosie, everything is forgiven and forgotten now, so there's nothing to worry about – we're all good friends again."

She nodded and her eyes were full of tears.

"Tell me why you are looking so dispirited, Rosie."

She hesitated before replying. "I don't really know why, Dad, but I haven't been well and I've been very lonely here in London without you and Mum. You know about the baby, of course." She said this with a wry smile, looking down at her conspicuous outline. "The doctor warned me that I could easily lose it, which is an awful worry, but I'm well past the critical stage now. Peter has been marvellous to me, but I don't think he's pleased about starting a family so soon." A sigh escaped her and she bit her lip. "I expect he's right, with the threat of war and everything, but it would be lovely if he felt the same way as I do about it."

"And how is that, my darling?" her mother asked, as she walked through carrying the tea tray.

"Oh, I want a baby more than anything else in the world," Rosie replied. Her face softened and she looked radiant as she spoke. Her mother felt uneasy. Rosie longed for this child almost too much.

They chatted happily over their tea, exchanging news and catching up on the months of silence that had been lost between them. Then Rosie, bursting with pride, showed them around her little house. They thought it was lovely and were quietly impressed and amazed that she managed to keep everything so immaculate, for at home she had never been the least bit domesticated.

"We are staying at the Mayfair for a few days, Rosie. Can you and Peter have dinner with us tonight?" her father asked.

"Oh, we would love that, Dad. We have so many things to tell you and it will be a nice change from cooking for me."

"Good," he replied, "we'll expect you about seven."

"Well, I think we'll be off now, dear," her mother said , "and then you'll have time for a rest before Peter gets home. Don't hurry tonight, there is no rush – it doesn't matter if you are a few minutes late. We will wait in the lounge for you."

Rosie kissed them warmly goodbye and, as she closed the door, was amazed how much better she felt – it was a transformation. She sang as she ran up the stairs. She felt lighthearted and at last free from worry. The awful estrangement was over. She was the bubbling and ebullient Rosie once more. She lay down again, curling up beside Biscuit and was soon asleep. Peter was surprised when he came in and found her still lying there, looking so serene. She sat up in bed, beaming at him and holding out her arms.

"Pete, just guess what happened this afternoon?"

He kissed her and with a twinkle in his eye said, "Your mother and father have been here."

"Right first time, Pete. I know you wrote to them – it was good of you. I feel much happier now. I was so lonely and cut off before."

His arms were around her, so she did not see his fleeting expression of jealousy, but he quickly controlled himself."

"When am I going to see them, Rosie?" he asked. "I want to have a long talk with your father."

"We're meeting them for dinner tonight at the Mayfair, if that is all right with you, darling?"

"Yes of course, that will be terrific fun, though this first meeting since our marriage may be a little strained."

"No, Pete," she reassured him. "They have completely forgiven us and refuse even to mention the past. They don't want it to be brought up again."

She jumped out of bed and gave him an extra hug. "Oh, isn't it marvellous, Pete, being part of a family once more?" Her eyes danced. "The baby will soon be arriving, and with Biscuit and of course Mr. Smith, everything will be perfect."

Peter looked reflectively at her, the expression in his eyes unfathomable.

"It's wonderful seeing you so cheerful again, Rosie, but surely it should be possible for just the two of us to be happy together. To begin with it was utter bliss."

Rosie sensed the warning signs.

"Of course it still is, Pete. My most precious moments are with you alone, but we mustn't become self-centred and exclude the outside world, otherwise our horizons will recede."

"Wise Rosie, the sage," he said enigmatically. "Perhaps you are right, but remember, my darling, you are mine and fundamentally I resent sharing you with anyone."

Rosie refused to be denied her new happiness and said laughingly, "Silly old Pete, we are made for each other and that will never change."

As they walked into the lounge of the hotel, eyes were turned in their direction. They were undoubtedly a most handsome couple. Her mother and father gave a sigh of relief as they saw Rosie. She looked very different from the forlorn little waif, who had answered the door to them that afternoon; yet there was a frailty about her, a vulnerability which had never been there before.

Mr. and Mrs. Greenwood rose to greet them, shaking hands cordially with Peter, leaving no doubts that bygones were bygones. He responded with equal warmth, kissing Rosie's mother on her soft cheek and thinking what an attractive woman she was. He had recognised, at their very first meeting, an infinite depth of character. She was the pivot of the family – he liked her father too. He was a kindly, sensitive man, devoted to his wife and daughter, but deep down Peter felt he was a rival for Rosie's affection.

Their reunion dinner went very well. They were all at their best, determined to mend any bridges and to re-establish a good relationship. They returned to the lounge for their after-dinner coffee and sat comfortably together in a corner of the room, remote from other guests and able to talk naturally without being overheard.

There was so much news to catch up with and Mrs. Greenwood made a point of taking a great interest in Peter and the progress he was making with his work. He was able to give a good account of himself and was flattered by the interest which they showed in him. Rosie was bubbling over with enthusiasm about 'Apple Trees' and how much she loved it. They all enjoyed the story about the arrival of Biscuit and the latest addition to the family, Mr. Smith, the brainy bear.

"Well, Peter, how do you feel about the prospect of being a father?" Mrs. Greenwood asked. She realised it was a loaded question, but was anxious to see what his reaction would be – she didn't expect his uncompromising reply.

"Well, to be perfectly frank, I feel this is the wrong time to start a family, as I'm convinced that war is imminent – but we will just have to make the best of it."

Rosie drew back, hurt and uncomfortable. Her mother looked at him directly and he knew he was being censured.

"Rosie will inevitably have to bear the brunt," she replied, "but of course you both went into this with your eyes open."

He tried to dispel the acrimonious note he had introduced into the conversation.

"Naturally we don't regret anything and I am hoping so much for another little Rosie – that would be delightful."

Her father chipped in. "I'm afraid, young man, you'll have no choice in this matter."

Mrs. Greenwood tactfully changed the subject to safer ground, but her heart ached for Rosie. She thought of the joy that she and her husband had experienced, when they knew their child was on the way and how thrilled they had been with their baby daughter; but perhaps, when Peter became a father, his attitude would change.

During the next few days Rosie and her mother had the most exciting time, shopping for the baby's layette. Only the best was good enough and the exquisite hand-embroidered clothes, which her mother bought for her first grandchild, gave Rosie tremendous pleasure. They looked like doll's clothes to her and she could not believe that her baby's limbs could possibly be small enough to fit them.

One afternoon Rosie and her father, who had similar interests, visited the Wallace Collection together. They liked the small intimate display of antique furniture and Rosie as ever was drawn to the pictures. She enjoyed studying at leisure the old masters and their various techniques. She particularly liked Frans Hals' 'Laughing Cavalier'. It was a masterpiece of expression and she spent a long time studying it. After this visit she decided to try portraits herself. She hoped to persuade Peter to sit for her – he would make an excellent subject. His dark handsomeness and classical features would be most paintable, but his eyes would be tricky. They were so changeable, sometimes with a quietly amused expression and at others supremely aloof and withdrawn.

On the last evening they spent together, Rosie's father suggested that she should come home with them for a few weeks to be 'fussed over'.

"Oh, I couldn't possibly leave Peter," she demurred. "Whoever would cook for him?"

Surprisingly Peter agreed with her parents. "I can cook for myself, poppet, I'm not helpless you know and it would do you the world of good. I can easily look after myself for a week or two." Rosie hated the thought of leaving him.

"I shall miss you dreadfully, Pete, but, if you are sure you can manage, it would be lovely to see everyone again. I will take Mr. Smith along to keep me company!"

*　*　*　*　*

She was thoroughly spoilt at home and being with Chi-Chi again was an absolute delight. Poor Chi-Chi, instead of giving her his usual uproarious welcome, hung back though wagging his tail vigorously. Rosie was surprised at his behaviour, but suddenly the penny dropped. Chi-Chi was alarmed and resentful of the presence of Mr. Smith. Without more ado, she turned and dumped the teddy bear in the cloakroom and closed the door. Instantly Chi-Chi was his usual self again, quite overcome with joy to see her. He leapt into her arms, smothering her with kisses and barking hysterically.

She went back to the University one morning, to meet all her friends. It seemed so strange to see them sitting at their desks or talking in groups. Nothing appeared to have changed since she left, yet now she felt remote from them – on the outside looking in. Ken Little was the first to notice her, standing at the door. He hurried to greet her and she was soon surrounded by the old crowd, all delighted to see her again and anxious to hear her news, though Parkie seemed shy and withdrawn. She sensed he wanted her on her own and soon she managed to break away from the others. He had one urgent question which was very much on his mind.

"Are you really happy, Princess?" he asked, looking searchingly into her eyes. She realised that he was still concerned for her.

"Oh yes, Parkie, and I'm thrilled about the baby." This was obviously embarrassing to him, so she quickly changed the subject to something less personal.

"We love our mews house and find living in London fun. We have regular tickets for the Proms and go to the theatre at least once a week. The last show we saw was Agatha Christie's 'Mousetrap'. You know how I adore thrillers. Remember the one we saw together at the Royal Court? You practically had to hold me down in my seat, I was so terrified!" They both laughed and now it was Rosie's turn to ask questions. "Enough of me – now, Parkie, most important of all, how are you?"

"I'm all right, Princess," he said seriously, "but I still miss you and I fear I always shall, but so long as you're happy that is all that matters. My mind is more at rest now. As for my work, it is going well and I'm grateful to be doing something I really enjoy. I shall always be indebted to my father for this. How long are you staying, Princess?"

"Oh, only for a few more days. It's lovely to be home again with the family and I'm getting thoroughly spoilt."

"That's what you deserve, my dear."

There was a sad melancholy in his voice which touched her.

"God bless you, Parkie," she replied warmly. "You're very sweet to me – I want you to know you have a very special place in my affections."

Impulsively she reached up and kissed him then left abruptly. She felt terribly sad; he was such a dear, so kind and considerate. For a moment a disloyal thought crossed her mind. If it had been his baby, he would have been over the moon with happiness, but she quickly dismissed this feeling. Peter was the only man for her.

She was meeting Sue for lunch at their usual restaurant and they arrived simultaneously. Their exuberant greeting caused a few frowns from elderly ladies at nearby tables. It was wonderful to see her again and they were both bursting with news. As soon as the lunch was ordered, Sue turned to her with a broad grin on her face.

"Now, Rosie, tell me all about it from beginning to end and don't leave anything out!"

Rosie chuckled . "I just don't know where to begin – but first and foremost I'm expecting the baby in July. It must have been conceived at 'Apple Trees', probably on our first night there. Isn't it wonderful, Sue? It makes the cottage a very special place for me."

"I knew that it was an enchanted cottage, but what does Peter feel about it?"

Rosie hesitated before answering, not wishing in any way to let him down, but feeling she must confide in somebody and Sue was the only possible person.

"He's not pleased, Sue. He pretends to be, for my sake, but he really only wants me to himself. He doesn't even like me to paint any more, as it draws my attention away from him."

Sue frowned. She had a feeling of disquiet, for Rosie was gifted and her talent must not be stifled – she felt she must speak out.

"You'll have to put a stop to that, Rosie. If you let him get away with it, he'll only get worse and worse."

"I am trying to, Sue, but it isn't easy. He is good to me in every other way. After all, nobody is perfect – not even me!"

They both laughed, but they were more subdued. Sue felt disturbed – somehow she wasn't surprised. She always suspected he would be like this.

"I was so relieved, Rosie, when I heard your family had finally relented; they really took much longer about it than I expected."

"Sue, I was absolutely miserable until they did. You know they were right in a way when they said I was too young for marriage. However, I'm managing well on the domestic side and Pete says I'm a marvellous cook. Do come and stay for a night before the baby arrives; we've got a spare bed in the studio, which we have now turned into a nursery, and we would both love to have you."

"I will try, but Ronnie and I are seriously thinking of taking the plunge ourselves and getting married in the autumn. I'm very busy collecting my trousseau together and mother'is all excited, planning a large wedding for us. It's supposed to be the bride's day, but I would say it's more the mother's wouldn't you?"

Rosie nodded, "I feel rather sad when I think of the pleasure I denied Mum, particularly as I'm the only child. I suppose I really should have waited."

"I don't see how," Sue said staunchly, "you were completely swept off your feet – no longer of this world – so don't blame yourself, Rosie."

"I think you're right, Sue – I was a bit pixillated." They both laughed merrily and it seemed like old times.

"I must be off now, Rosie dear, but it's been marvellous seeing you and we'll meet again soon – take care of yourself and particularly that godchild of mine," she said giving Rosie's stomach a discreet pat.

Charles, their elderly chauffeur, was waiting outside for Rosie and he drove her through the city at his usual steady pace. He took the route down the dock road, which was a hive of activity. Many ships were alongside and bull-necked dockers, with their muscles bulging, were busily unloading the cargoes. The streets were congested with lorries and horse-drawn vehicles.

The hooves of the powerful animals were slipping and pounding on the wet cobbles.

It was disturbing to see the poverty here and Rosie felt guilty in her luxurious car, protected by money and privilege. As they slowed down at a corner, she saw a pitiful sight – a thin little boy with legs like sticks, his bare feet muddy and blue with cold. His head seemed too large for his body, supported by his poor scraggy neck – obviously he came from stock which for generations had been nurtured on inadequate food.

He stared wistfully into the car. Rosie knew she would never forget his woeful expression. Her heart ached for this pathetic little waif. She quickly wound down the window and threw out half-a-crown – a veritable fortune to him. She just caught the look of incredulity as the coin landed at his feet, before the car drew away.

When she arrived home, instead of having her usual afternoon's rest, she took out her oils and started recording on canvas this tragic scene. The poignancy of the picture, which she had commenced, upset her so much that she decided to put it away and dismiss it from her mind – little did she realise the stir that this picture would create in later years, after she had brought herself to complete it.

The day soon arrived for her departure – she hated to leave her parents. They had been so good to her and had given her a much-needed break. She knew she would miss them sadly, but was thrilled at the thought of being with Peter again. She only hoped that her added dimensions would not be off-putting!

8

THE WEEKS before the birth of her baby were happy ones. Peter was most considerate and Rosie tried to make him realise that he was the most important person in her life, as indeed he was.

Her peace of mind was inevitably disturbed by the fear of war, which inexorably drew closer. Air Raid Precaution and Civil Defence offices were appearing all over the country. The realisation had dawned that there was an urgent necessity to provide protection for the people against bombing. An 'Anderson' Air Raid Shelter was designed and made available for use of the civilian population. It was a corrugated iron structure, to be erected in the garden and could accommodate four to six people.

Rosie's father had a special shelter built in the basement of his home. It was equipped with bunk beds; picks and shovels were also provided in case the occupants had to dig themselves out. The contractor, who did the reinforcing, claimed that, if the house were to collapse on top of it, the shelter would withstand the strain – reassuring words, but somewhat hard to believe.

If a state of emergency should arise Peter, being in the naval reserve, would be called up immediately and it was arranged that Rosie would leave London at once and take the baby to 'Apple Trees'. It was a dreadful thought, but they were both determined to make the best of the present and let the future take care of itself.

Peter came home one evening full of enthusiasm. He had decided to take Rosie away for a week's holiday, before the baby arrived, and thought it would be fun to go to Paris. They had never been abroad together, so it was a real adventure.

"We're not going to do it on the cheap, Rosie, we'll spend some of that money put on one side for buying a house. Let's do it comfortably."

He was armed with brochures and, after poring over them for most of the evening, they decided to take the boat train across, being the most comfortable and convenient way to travel and least strain on Rosie.

"We'll make this into a second honeymoon, darling, and stay at the Ritz."

"That will be marvellous," Rosie replied, and her eyes sparkled at the prospect. She had been to the Ritz before and particularly loved the elegant spacious bedrooms and balconies overlooking the Place Vendôme; it was a glamorous place in which to stay and convenient for the shops and art galleries.

"If it's anything like our first honeymoon, it will be perfection," she said dreamily.

"It will be even better, my poppet, though regretfully we'll have to be more circumspect," he said looking down obliquely at her added dimensions.

They both needed the break and did not lose any time in preparing for the trip and indeed only three days later they were checking into the hotel.

They were blessed with marvellous weather and Paris reflected as ever its springtime magic. They loved to wander hand in hand in the Tuileries, with the trees bursting into new leaf or to potter among the bookstalls on the Left Bank. They became very close again, their relationship warm and loving.

They made frequent visits to the Louvre and the Jeu de Paume. Rosie just could not see enough of the Impressionists, whose work she adored. She studied their techniques and colours and longed to start painting again. Peter preferred the old masters and particularly the precision of the Canelettos, drawn with such infinite detail, which particularly appealed to him as an architect.

Their exciting shopping expeditions in the Rue de Rivoli and the Place de l'opéra were fun and Peter bought her filmy nighties and negligées – very French, for when her pregnancy was over. "I can hardly wait for you to wear them," he said impatiently – he longed for their intimate relationship to be restored.

"Oh Pete, how I long for it too," she sighed audibly, "but the time will soon pass and then I can wear your provocative Frenchie frillies!"

Maxim's was a 'must' and the following day they had a delightful lunch there, enjoying the usual impeccable service. Their elderly waiter was intrigued by this young English couple – the girl, so obviously *enceinte,* but so very lovely, and the handsome husband's attentive devotion to her touched the Frenchman's romantic heart. On leaving they were bowed out with courtesy and deference.

In the evenings they ate in small intimate restaurants on the West Bank and visited well-known Parisian night spots, taking in the spectacular production of the Folies Bergère – Parisian entertainment at its gayest. The scantily-clothed figure. "I hope these glamour-pussies are not too tempting, Pete?" she asked saucily.

"Well, I must admit they are a bit," he said teasingly, "but I have eyes only for you, my poppet, so there is nothing to worry about."

On their last day they had tea and delicious cream cakes at a café, sitting in the sunshine on the Champs Elysées, watching the passers-by and feeling relaxed and sublimely happy. Never for a moment did they imagine that before very long German soldiers would be sitting on these self-same chairs and Paris would be held firmly in the Nazi grip.

The week had passed all too quickly and they were soon back in their little mews house, happy and pleased to be home again. Peter's inspiration had achieved its objective and the break had done them a world of good.

Rosie settled down contentedly to wait for the birth of her baby and, when one night she experienced aches and pains, she tried to ignore them and get off to sleep again as the baby was barely due. Peter she knew was very tired, so she did not want to disturb him unnecessarily. However, as the niggling pains developed rapidly into something much more severe and at regular intervals, she shook Peter awake. "I'm sorry to disturb you, darling, but I think we'd better get to the hospital as quickly as possible. I may have left it rather late." He leapt up instantly in alarm – the dreaded moment had arrived.

"You should have woken me earlier, darling, you are a silly billy." He dressed himself hurriedly but was all fingers and thumbs. "Are the pains very bad, sweetheart?" he asked as he tried to help her get ready, but she could scarcely reply. The pains were now so agonising and at such short intervals that it was difficult to get her dressed. He managed somehow or other and was soon bundling her into the car, which he drove to the hospital as fast as he dare. Inwardly he was worried to death about her and the ordeal she must undergo.

Rosie was silent, enveloped in a world of suffering, trying her best to stifle her groans for Peter's sake, but involuntarily they escaped her. Once, in respite, she managed to gasp: "Oh Pete dear, it's awful, but don't worry, I'll be all right." Then as the pains unmercifully broke over her again, she was lost to all conscious thought. She must just hang on.

As they drew up at the emergency entrance, strong reassuring arms helped her from the car. She gasped goodbye to Peter and, as she was led away through the double doors, she looked back at him with a pathetic wave which tore at his heart-strings. He'd never let her go through this again. He was filled with an overwhelming love and compassion for her.

He sat in the waiting room, prepared for his night's vigil. His mind was in a turmoil – all he could think of was his darling Rosie's agony, and fear for her safety haunted him. Hours seemed to pass as he paced the floor and once a muffled scream made his blood run cold. The night dragged on interminably, interrupted occasionally by a young nurse bringing him a cup of tea, which he gulped down gratefully. Each time he questioned her, but she knew nothing, until finally she was able to report that Rosie was in the delivery room and it should be all over soon. Shortly after this, a pleasant sister came in with her face wreathed in smiles.

"Mr. Dunbar, I believe?"

Peter stood up and nodded dumbly. She saw what a state he was in.

"Now you can relax, sir, for I have good news for you – you have a splendid eight pound baby boy."

"But how is my wife?" croaked Peter. His voice seemed to have deserted him and his face was gaunt in the dim light of the room.

"She is doing very well indeed, though a first baby is not easy. She is asking for you so, if you will wait for a few minutes, you can go in and see her."

His head reeled, he could hardly believe the good news after his hours of torment. He managed a smile, but it was hard to respond properly.

"Would you like to see your son first?" she asked kindly.

Peter pulled himself together. "Yes please, sister, that would be wonderful." And his face suddenly lit up with relief, pleasure and excitement.

She led him down the corridor to an ante-room, where he put on a white coat and mask. He waited there until she brought the baby to him, resting the small bundle in his arms; then she discreetly disappeared, leaving him alone to welcome his son into the world.

At first he was terrified of dropping the child and awkwardly he tried to support the little wobbly head, which seemed perilously insecure – then becoming bolder, he examined the minute hands and feet; they were so astonishingly small, with nails like diminutive pink shells.

He was fascinated yet repulsed by this morsel of humanity. How had he and his beautiful Rosie produced this crumpled scrap? For a moment he was distressed, unable to relate himself to this ugly mite, who was of his own flesh and blood.

Unexpectedly the baby's face screwed up and, turning scarlet, started to cry with a loud, lusty wail for one so small. Peter instinctively tried to comfort the infant, rocking him gently. He put his finger in the baby's pink creased palm and was thrilled when the tiny fist tightened around it and the crying ceased. From that moment Peter loved his son. The strength of that love and pride was a revelation to him.

When the sister returned, father and son were as one. She knew the miracle had occurred, as she had hoped it would. He handed her back the baby, then started off down the corridor to see his beloved Rosie.

She looked deathly pale and exhausted – yet triumphant. The small bridge of freckles across her nose stood out starkly. Her deep blue eyes were ringed with shadows.

"How are you feeling, my darling?" he asked in a passion of tenderness, for she looked little more than a child lying there. "Was it too awful?"

She smiled bravely back. "I'm fine now, Pete, but it was pretty bad and I fear I won't have the courage to go through this again."

"Thank God you are safe," he said, "that is all that matters. I've been almost demented with worry about you, but we have a wonderful son and I'm very proud of him."

He sank down on the bed beside her and gently kissed her forehead. She squeezed his hand lovingly.

"You don't mind that it is not a girl then?" she asked.

"Of course not, darling, every man wants a son. Perhaps we'll have a 'little Rosie' next time." Brave words, but secretly he hoped this would be their last.

He felt strangely different with her, for she was now a mother and had assumed another role. She was no longer exclusively his. In future he would have to share her. A wave of apprehension ran through him as he lay his head against her shoulder, seeking reassurance. She patted his dark head and murmured softly: "Darling, darling Pete, I do love you," and tears of emotion squeezed out of the corners of her eyes and ran unheeded down her cheeks. He wiped them gently away and stood up. She was exhausted and he must go now, though he hated to leave. He longed to lie beside her in the comforting solace of her arms.

"Darling, you are tired out and you must go to sleep. I'll be off now and will be in to see you early this evening."

She smiled lovingly up at him – poor darling, he looked so pale and dishevelled after his night's vigil. He bent down and kissed her cheek, then tiptoed out of the room, feeling strangely disorientated.

After the door closed, she turned gingerly on her side. She felt sore but liberated and at peace. All was well and her ordeal was over. The thought of her tiny son filled her with a blinding joy and overwhelming love for him. She closed her eyes and quickly fell into a deep and dreamless sleep.

Rosie was kept in the hospital for ten days. She was happy there, in spite of feeling tired and drained. She could not feed the baby herself and this came as a shock and disappointment. The doctor warned her that it would take some time to get her strength back, for the birth of her child had not been easy.

Her mother and father came to London the next day to see her and were delighted with their grandson. Peter rushed in from the office each evening and his arms were always full of flowers. She longed to see him and tried to make herself look as glamorous as possible for his visits. Motherhood suited Rosie: imperceptibly she had matured and her beautiful eyes held a new softness.

They had engaged a nurse to stay for three weeks after Rosie's return from the hospital and she proved to be a wonderful girl, taking full responsibility for the baby and making herself generally useful.

Rosie and Peter had plenty of time to themselves and she made a point of lavishing as much affection as possible on him at this time.

After a great deal of thought, they finally decided to call the baby Richard Peter Dunbar, which was soon foreshortened to Ricky. Peter was delighted with his son and each evening, on his return from the office, he would bound up the stairs to the nursery to spend a little time with him before he went to sleep.

Rosie dreaded the nurse leaving. She was still far from well and began to feel apprehensive about taking full responsibility for the baby. It emerged that she had good reason for her forebodings – no sooner had the girl departed than Ricky, up till then a happy and contented child, became fractious, crying for long periods during the day, but in the evenings, after his nine o'clock feed, he howled the house down. Rosie suspected that somehow she had departed from the established formula and the new one was not suiting him, and being so inexperienced she worried irrationally.

Peter insisted that Ricky was getting spoilt and that she must leave him alone to cry it out. She knew that Peter was resenting the extra time she was spending with the baby, but she just could not bear to leave him upstairs on his own, sobbing his heart out. She adored the child and even the slightest upset was a torment to her.

One terrible evening Ricky started to howl, just as they were sitting down to a late supper. Peter had worked on at the office and returned home tired and tense. She felt exhausted too and every cry from the baby reacted on her.

"You leave him alone, Rosie," he said irritably. "You are turning him into a spoilt brat; pretty soon our lives won't be worth living."

Rosie tried to remain calm and keep her temper. "Don't be silly, Pete. Ricky has always been so good and I really believe a baby only cries if there is something wrong."

"Well, for God's sake do it my way for once, Rosie, and stop fussing; he'll soon give up when he finds you don't go running to him."

"All right, Pete, I'll leave him alone until we've finished our meal," she said, trying to be placatory .

She gritted her teeth determined to ignore the screams from above; her nerves were taut, stretched almost beyond endurance. As soon as supper was over she could stand it no longer. She opened the dining room door and listened carefully. She thought his cries sounded fainter – different from his usual piercing howl. She brushed roughly past Peter, now completely oblivious of his censure, and flew up the stairs, convinced that something had gone wrong.

She rushed into the nursery and was aghast at what she saw. Somehow or other Ricky had turned over on his face – it was buried deep in the pillow, and he no longer had the strength to raise his head, having exhausted himself crying.

Frantically she picked him up. He was blue and convulsed through lack of oxygen. She patted his back and held him close until gradually his breathless sobs quietened down to a faint whimper, being comforted and reassured by his mother's presence. She kissed his downy little head and tears ran down her own cheeks. She was quite distraught. Looking up, she saw Peter standing framed in the doorway with a heavy scowl on his face.

"You are absolutely ruining this child," he began but Rosie, for the first time ever, screamed at him, beside herself with rage and anxiety.

"You leave us alone; if I hadn't come up when I did he would have suffocated – his face was buried in the pillow. Can't you see how blue he is?"

Peter looked closely at the baby and was obviously alarmed, but he would not climb down and still obstinately tried to force her to put Ricky back into his cot. "He's all right now – just put him back and let's have our coffee," he said, giving an impatient shrug, though he did feel a twinge of conscience.

She went for him like a wildcat defending her young. Her eyes were blazing.

"I'm his mother and I will do what I think best for him – now leave us alone. I don't want to see you again tonight."

She slammed the door in his face and noisily turned the key in the lock.

She slept fitfully on the spare bed, close to Ricky, tossing and turning until the early hours of the morning when, exhausted, she crept downstairs and made herself a hot drink. She could hear the first faint chirps of the birds outside, then finally comforted she dozed off. She was woken up by the door opening and Peter tiptoeing in with an early morning cup of tea for her. She sat up and took it from him. He looked rather sheepish and repentant, as he gazed into the cot at his sleeping son.

"Is he all right now, Rosie?" he asked. "I'm sorry about last night – I was completely in the wrong."

She looked back at him stonily. "Yes, but don't ever give me any more of your advice. A mother's instinct is always best and, if anything had happened to him, you would never have forgiven yourself and neither would I."

After this episode Peter interfered less, but a certain resentment started to build up between them. Fortunately Rosie's mother and father came down to see them again on a flying visit. They thought that Ricky was the image of Peter and this quietly pleased him and somewhat relieved the tension in the household. Mrs. Greenwood didn't think that Rosie looked at all well and suggested that a long weekend at 'Apple Trees' would do them both good – perhaps Miss Phillpots, the nurse, could come back for a few days and take charge of the baby.

Peter thought this was an excellent idea – how wonderful to have Rosie to himself again. He immediately started making plans. Time off from the office would not be a problem, as he had done a great deal of extra work for them recently. Before speaking to Rosie about it, he telephoned Miss Phillpots and, to his relief, she agreed to return for a few days, as there happened to be a gap between her cases.

Rosie was delighted when he told her what he had arranged. She had an appointment with her gynaecologist the following week and this one should be the last. She hoped she would get the 'all clear' from him to resume their normal married life. Peter was champing at the bit and she knew he'd had rather a rough time of it. Somehow she felt guilty, though it certainly hadn't been her fault.

Their plans were all made for leaving after her doctor's appointment. Rosie hated being parted from Ricky, but he would be in good hands. They both needed to get back to their old loving relationship and 'Apple Trees' seemed the ideal setting for this. However, much to Rosie's dismay, the doctor told her that as she had been so badly torn they should wait another week or two.

She felt she hardly dare tell Peter and only broached the subject when they were halfway there. She tried to speak casually.

"By the way, Pete, the doctor insists that we still must wait."

"Is that idiot interfering in our love-life again?" he asked aggressively.

"The doctor is right, Pete, it is still too soon."

His disappointment was intense but, after driving along in silence for a few miles, he managed to snap out of his black mood.

"Sorry if I was short with you, Rosie. It's wonderful being here with you again."

"That's all right, Pete – let's forget it."

When they arrived at the cottage it was so heavenly being there that all the unpleasantness was forgotten and they became more like their old loving selves once more.

After their long drive they were tired so they quickly prepared supper, which they had on trays by the fire, and went early to bed. That night there was a full moon and they did not draw the curtains, so that they could enjoy their favourite view. They were surprised and enchanted to see what a dramatic difference – almost unearthly – this lunar brilliance made to their familiar scene. The utter silence, which had descended, was pure balm after the ceaseless hum of London traffic. Rosie felt relaxed and happy again.

Peter held her close in his arms, her soft loveliness was an unbearable temptation, and he was at his most persuasive.

"Darling, you're still the most desirable girl in the world and I want you so badly – this waiting is absolute purgatory. Don't you think that fuddy-duddy specialist of yours is being over-cautious?"

Rosie hated to refuse him, knowing how upset he would be. Foolishly she acquiesced, but it was a painful unsatisfactory reunion – endurance for Rosie and frustration for him. Finally he drew away from her.

"Damn babies and pregnancy," he said almost viciously. "They just about spoil everything – they're not worth it."

She promptly turned over, hurt and disillusioned by his utter selfishness. She closed her eyes and tears silently ran down her cheeks. She knew she would never forget these unforgivable words. He had broken the spell – the wonder of the birth of their firstborn. Presently he touched her on the shoulder.

"Sorry, Rosie," he said miserably. "Of course I don't mean it."

She lay unmoving, tense and angry. "Oh yes you do, you care only about yourself. You've shown yourself up in your true colours again and spoilt everything."

He didn't reply but just turned over, engulfed in his own misery.

He woke with a start the next morning, appalled by his behaviour and when he looked at Rosie, still sleeping, her face pale and tear-stained, he suddenly realised what she had gone through in the past few months and how it had changed her; he had been no help at all. He gathered her into his arms, so full of remorse. "Rosie darling," he whispered, "please forgive me, but I love you so desperately that I lose all control."

She seemed remote and listless, without emotion, refusing to discuss what had happened between them the night before. "Forget it," she said, "your idea of love, and mine, are rather different, but I don't want to talk about it any more." She sipped her early morning tea and impersonally discussed their plans for the next few days. However hard he tried to explain, she refused to be drawn.

There were repairs to be done to the cottage before the winter weather set in and Peter decided that, under the circumstances, he had better get on with them. Rosie had a crying need to insulate herself from her troubles and the only way she knew how was with her paint brush.

She packed up her painting equipment and, without consulting Peter, wandered off down the lane and did not return for several hours. He was deeply hurt by her independent line, but dare not say anything. She was brighter when she came back, though still subdued for the normally ebullient Rosie.

That evening they sat on the couch together by a roaring fire, Peter's arm around her shoulders, discussing the worsening international situation. Then he changed the subject to the more pleasant topic of the picture which Rosie had painted that morning. "I'm most impressed, Rosie, by your latest picture. You really have achieved a striking effect with those golden autumn leaves glowing in the sunlight. I think water colours are your best medium."

"I'm glad you like it" – she was pleased with it too. She always seemed to accomplish her best results when under emotional stress. It was almost a process of exorcising herself. Now she felt in better heart.

A few days later they left the cottage with a feeling of sadness, for this stay had not been a happy one. Their acrimony had passed, but Rosie was less acquiescent – their roles had subtly changed. Peter's dominating authority had been undermined and Rosie's judgement proved sounder. From now on he trod more warily, particularly where Ricky was concerned.

*　*　*　*　*

September 1938 was a month of crisis, with Chamberlain flying for a third time to meet Hitler and Mussolini in Munich. He was determined to avoid war at all costs. This time he was supported by Daladier, the French Prime Minister.

After long and arduous negotiations Chamberlain's objectives were mostly conceded and the Munich Agreement was drawn up, in the process of which Czechoslovakia was sacrificed. It stated that Britain and Germany would never go to war again.

Chamberlain flew back to England in triumph, flourishing his scrap of paper. "Peace with honour – peace in our time." He genuinely believed he had come to terms with Hitler. There was a general feeling of euphoria in the country as the moment of peril had seemingly passed – but this was short-lived. Czechoslovakia had been betrayed. The best that could be said of the agreement was that Chamberlain had bought time for Britain to prepare for the conflict ahead. From this point the war effort gained momentum.

The months passed by quickly and Ricky was growing into a chubby little boy with a sunshine personality. He was a most affectionate child and loved both his parents, but Rosie he adored. Peter was never demonstrative in front of her but when alone with him they had fun. He would pick Ricky up and throw him high into the air and, on catching him, would give him a huge bear hug. Ricky would chuckle with delight; he looked forward to this game and his nature was such that, even if Peter showed impatience and irritability with him at other times, he bore no resentment.

Rosie was delighted that affection had developed between father and son and encouraged it all she could, but she still had reservations about Peter's jealousy, which would blaze up if he felt Ricky was getting more attention from her than he was. As time passed by, however, she and Peter became closer again, for they still loved each other dearly and, with so many interests in common, they had a stimulating relationship.

An atmosphere of crisis was again building up in the country. Intensive pressure was now being inflicted on Poland. Hitler was claiming that he must have *lebensraum*, or more living space, for Germany's increasing population – Poland and the Danzig corridor must be absorbed. It seemed certain now that this would be his next objective, with Czechoslovakia used as a springboard for his assault. Already a formidable force of German troops and tanks was massing on the Polish border. The Allies had guaranteed the integrity of Poland by treaty, so it seemed that Britain would soon be plunged into another great war.

This country, which has not been invaded for nearly a thousand years, would be in dire peril; but in times of danger the British people stand firm and are fearless – indeed a formidable foe.

The reserves would be called up first, so Peter had packed his bag in anticipation and, when the telegram finally arrived from the Admiralty one Saturday morning, he was not surprised. Rosie was horrified. The thing that she dreaded most had actually come to pass. He had opened the envelope and glanced at the wording, then handed it to her. She quickly read the orders then, blinking back her tears, she flew into his arms.

"Oh, Pete darling, this is awful, I can't bear you to leave us. We'll be lost without you." As they clung together, he kissed her tears away and stroked her curly head.

"Keep a stiff upper lip, Rosie darling, that's all any of us can do – being away from you will be absolute purgatory for me." He felt heart broken at leaving her yet, as a man, he instinctively responded with eager excitement to this call to arms. This was what he had been trained for.

"Rosie, you and Ricky must leave London at once for 'Apple Trees'," he said urgently. "Never mind about this house for, if war is declared, they'll probably bomb the hell out of it anyway. I'll write to Dick at once."

Rosie shivered, as she looked around their dear, familiar home.

"All right, Pete, as soon as you've gone we will pack up and leave."

"No darling, I've been thinking it over and, if we start preparing at once, we can depart simultaneously on Monday morning. When I leave for Chatham, you can set off for Wales."

Rosie nodded in agreement. Her lips trembled.

"Let's do that, darling. I can't bear the thought of being here alone after you have left." She was close to tears again.

He tried to comfort her. "Don't get too upset, darling; there's still a chance that Hitler might back down; it's hard to believe that he'll run head on into a world war."

But this time she knew the die was cast. She pulled herself together – she must be stoical.

"We had better get going right away, Pete, there's an awful lot of sorting out to do in a very short space of time."

As she began her frantic packing, she had a feeling of complete unreality – could this really be happening to them – this awful separation and her loved ones all in danger?

On their last night together they lay closely entwined in each other's arms, and dawn was breaking before they finally drifted off to sleep. They had to be up early that morning to get the car all loaded up with their belongings and, of course, Biscuit and Mr. Smith.

Peter wore his naval uniform and Rosie thought how handsome he looked. There was a lump in her throat as she saw Ricky, his little face all smiles, holding out his arms for Peter to pick him up and put him into the car – she saw a trace of tears in Peter's eyes, as he hugged his son goodbye.

"Take good care of Mummy for me, old chap – I'll see you soon." Ricky looked up at him – a little worried now, sensing a sadness in the air.

When they said their own private goodbyes, they were very close. In their final embrace, Rosie whispered: "Come home safely, my love." Then she jumped into the car, her eyes brimming with tears, not risking a backward glance in case she broke down. She accelerated madly and in a minute they were turning the corner into the park, out of sight of their little house. She knew she would never see it again – another chapter of her life had ended.

9

SUNDAY 3rd September 1939 was a glorious day, warm and sunny with cloudless skies. It seemed to hold a special quality. One of those rare and perfect days, remembered so vividly by all, for an utter tranquillity seemed to pervade the beautiful countryside; there was a stillness in the air. Rosie could faintly hear the church bells ringing in the distance. It seemed good to be alive – yet this never-to-be-forgotten day was to be indelibly engraved on the memory of man, for the horror and unbelievable suffering that was to follow in its wake.

There had been an early broadcast on the wireless, announcing that the Prime Minister would speak to the nation at 11.15 that morning. The world waited and hoped, but it seemed certain that war would be declared, for two days earlier Germany had unleashed her military might and had brutally invaded Poland, whose integrity the Allies had guaranteed.

Rosie sat waiting with her hands tightly clasped, gazing out of the window at the beauty all around her. She wished to drink in this undisturbed peace while she still could, before the shattering reality of war was thrust upon her. It was coming up to the time, so she switched on the wireless in anticipation and sat quietly by the fire for the announcement.

At 11.15 the Prime Minister, Mr. Neville Chamberlain, was introduced by Alvar Liddell, the B.B.C. newscaster, and gravely he addressed an anxious and waiting nation.

"I am speaking to you from the Cabinet Room at Number 10 Downing Street. This morning, the British Ambassador in Berlin handed the German Government a final note stating that, unless we heard from them by 11 o'clock that they were prepared at once to withdraw their troops from Poland, a state of war would exist between us. I have to tell you now, that no such undertaking has been received and consequently this country is at war with Germany."

Rosie shuddered as she switched off the set. Her face was drained of colour, she was horrified at the news. She bent down and lifted Ricky out of his play-pen, holding him very close to her as if to protect him, terrified by the possible consequences for her child. Whatever would become of them all? She was desperately worried about Peter at sea and her parents would be in considerable danger too. Liverpool's dockland and its giant shipyards would be a major target for German bombers. Her world seemed to be crumbling around her, all because of the actions of one man, this megalomaniac and evil genius, Adolf Hitler. His duplicity was indisputable, his appetite for fresh conquests quite insatiable.

It was, however, in a way almost a relief that the uneasy peace was over – the tension in the country for the last year had been hard to bear and the constant appeasement of this monster disturbing and distasteful to all. War had to come and now the country could at least get at the throat of its enemy.

Almost immediately the strident screaming of an air-raid siren shattered the peace and quiet. Oh God, she thought, it has started already. Ricky looked anxiously up at her, his blue eyes wide with apprehension at this unfamiliar noise. She managed to smile reassuringly back at him, though her heart was thumping madly.

She swept him into her arms and picked up Biscuit too, awakening him from his peaceful sleep by the fire, and ran with them to their prepared cubby-hole under the stairs – the only place offering any protection in the cottage. She had a queasy feeling in the pit of her stomach, as Ricky's happy, trusting little face smiled up at her gleefully – now thoroughly enjoying what he thought was a game. She kept up the pretence as best she could, but silently she prayed for his safety.

She waited, straining her ears for gunfire and explosions, but all was quiet and, about ten minutes later, the all-clear sounded – it had been a false alarm. She sighed with enormous relief as they left their refuge and returned to sit by the fire. Many thoughts and fears filled her mind. She wondered what part she could play in the war-effort. Tomorrow she would go down to the local Red Cross office and tell them of her previous training. Perhaps there would be something useful she could do.

She was startled by the urgent ring of the telephone. She jumped up to answer it and was delighted to hear her father's strong, reassuring voice at the other end of the line.

"Hello, Rosie dear, are you all right? I hope Chamberlain's announcement wasn't too much of a shock."

"No, Dad, I quite expected it," she replied calmly, determined not to show her anxiety. "We've just had an air-raid warning here, but nothing happened, thank goodness. How about you?"

"Yes, we had one too, I think it must have been a false alarm." He laughed grimly, "preparing us for the shape of things to come perhaps! They're just putting up the barrage balloons here – they look most impressive, like miniature airships. They should be good protection against low-flying aircraft."

"I'm reassured to hear that," Rosie replied. "I'm really worried about your both remaining where you are. I only wish you and Mum could come and stay with us here."

"I wish we could too, Rosie, but the factory must be kept going – sugar is an important commodity in a war and I wouldn't dream of deserting the men. Your mother absolutely insists on staying here with me. I've tried hard to persuade her to leave, but with no success."

"I think she's right," Rosie replied. "She would never have a minute's peace without you."

He paused for a moment. "Now for the most important question of all, how is that grandson of mine getting on?"

Rosie laughed. "He's fine and quite enjoying the excitement; he thinks it's all a game."

"Excellent, well keep your chin up, my dear, and take good care of yourselves. Don't worry about us, Rosie, we'll be all right in our shelter – we'll keep in regular touch with you by telephone."

"Goodbye, Dad, give my love to Mum – it's been lovely talking to you."

Thoughtfully she replaced the receiver. She felt comforted and not so alone, but her heart ached for Peter; the worry and uncertainty of the future didn't bear thinking about.

Rosie quickly settled down in the cottage and she was grateful for the safety it afforded them. Ricky flourished in the country air and had just started to take a few faltering steps. She was thrilled and longed to share the excitement with Peter. She wrote him loving letters each day, telling him how lonely she was without him and recounting his son's progress. She was relieved that Biscuit had settled down so well in the country, changing from a cosseted city cat to an outdoor one, revelling in the wide open spaces and eagerly exploring his old hunting grounds.

After a few weeks had passed and there had not been any air raids, a great sense of relief, as well as anti-climax, filled the country. People were gradually adjusting to wartime conditions. Groping their way about in the blackout became almost second nature to them and, with gas masks always slung across their shoulders, they seemed ready for anything and their spirit and morale were high. This phoney war, as it was called, fooled nobody. It was just a lull – the real testing time was yet to come.

The grim annihilation of Poland, which had so swiftly taken place, left little doubt of the horrors in store. The gallant Poles were an inspiration in their life and death struggle, fighting with meagre equipment, fanatically trying to stem the tide of German military might. Heart-rending stories were coming through of the brave Polish cavalry, with their hopeless, burning patriotism, riding to their inevitable death against the German tanks.

Desperate messages were being sent from Poland, appealing for military aid, yet Britain was powerless to respond, as she virtually had not adequate means even to defend her own homeland.

The war at sea was immediate and disastrous. On the night of 3rd September, a German U-boat torpedoed the outward-bound liner "Athenia" with heavy loss of life. It was an ominous portend of things to come. U-boats commenced to take a heavy toll of merchant ships and, by the middle of November, 60,000 tons of British shipping had been sunk by the deadly magnetic mine.

On 17th September 1939, the old British aircraft carrier, "Courageous" was torpedoed in the Bristol Channel with a loss of over 500 officers and men.

Scarcely a month later Mr. Churchill, now first Lord of the Admiralty, announced the sinking of the battleship "Royal Oak" in Scapa Flow – the main anchorage of the Home Fleet. The nation was stunned that it had been possible for a U-boat to penetrate the supposedly-impregnable defences and still escape undetected. It was a remarkable exploit of skill and daring by the enemy and another mortal blow for the British, whose pride in the Royal Navy was so much a part of their national heritage.

*   *   *   *   *

Bronwen came in for a few hours every morning. She was an absolute brick. She adored Ricky and was like a second mother to him. Rosie had no qualms about leaving him in her hands. Rosie was taking an extra course with the Red Cross and also had a part-time job driving a mobile canteen. She visited outlying sites and coastal airfields, taking along tea and cigarettes and various other supplies – it was like a small mobile shop.

She was very popular and, as her van arrived, she was quickly surrounded by officers and men, all eager to talk to her. She was invariably cheerful though, after reading of fresh disasters at sea, it was often hard to keep smiling.

Peter was serving as first lieutenant in a minesweeper on the east coast convoy run, guarding and shepherding into port merchant ships with their precious cargoes of essential supplies for this beleaguered island.

He wrote regularly; reading between the lines, she knew he was having a tough time, desperately short of sleep and in constant danger from U-boats, mines and bombing. His letters sounded strained and, although time after time he said how much he missed her, he rarely mentioned Ricky, which seemed unnatural and upset her. She longed for them both to share their son. He was such a darling child. He looked very like his father but, instead of dark brown eyes, he had Rosie's vivid blue ones. They were most expressive, kind and thoughtful.

She drew a few simple studies of him with emphasis on his eyes, wishing to capture the expression she loved. But somehow it saddened her for he did not seem to be quite of this world. She worried about him constantly – living alone made her almost fanatical about his safety. Bronwen didn't help as she was just as bad and, when his grandparents came to see him, they were even worse, justifying themselves by saying he was unspoilable and that they had never known a better baby. He was a completely happy little chap and warmly returned all the love and affection that were showered upon him.

One dreary morning in early December, Rosie woke up feeling listless and depressed – perhaps it was the weather. The mist hung low over the trees and the distant view of Snowdon was completely obscured by cloud. Her ever-growing anxiety for Peter's safety gnawed at her, particularly as a letter was long overdue. Her usual gaiety had gone; there seemed nothing worth doing – it was like living in a vacuum. She thought of her painting, but even this disturbed her. She doubted whether she had any real talent – she feared it was all an illusion that she had created.

Ricky was still asleep so, putting on her cosy dressing gown and bedroom slippers, she wandered down stairs to make some coffee, stopping by the piano for a moment and idly playing her favourite 'Für Elise'; but today its haunting refrain seemed an irritation to her. She felt disillusioned with herself for not becoming a better pianist. Jack of all trades, master of none, she thought.

Restlessly she put a log on the still-warm embers of the fire. It flickered, then crackled and flared up cheerfully. She huddled up in a chair, sipping her coffee. The warm drink was soothing and she began to feel more herself again. How selfish she had become, worrying about her own personal interests, when there was so much at stake – this ghastly war still to be won, but oh how she missed Pete! Her need of him had been bottled up for too long and was the cause of her constant frustration.

She remembered with painful longing their perfect honeymoon, under this very roof – her awakening, when her passionate nature had emerged and the joy they had shared together had been something out of this world. Could they ever become so ecstatically happy again?

Her thoughts were disturbed by the sound of Ricky's stirring above, then his voice calling down to her. She bounded up the stairs and pushed open the door. "Hello darling," she said delightedly, "how is my Ricky?" – his little face was flushed with sleep and he smiled sunnily up at her.

"Mum, mum, mum," he answered as she gathered him into her arms; she felt such an overwhelming love for him that all her previous frustrations disappeared. Rosie was indeed essentially a mother. She hugged him close as she carried him into the bathroom and he responded lovingly, holding her tightly around the neck, with his warm cheek pressed against hers.

She ran the bath water and popped him in with his favourite little toy, which he called 'Dadip' – the nearest Ricky could come to saying 'Daddy's ship'. It was a cheerful little craft which could not be sunk and, as she soaped him, he banged happily away at 'Dadip', chuckling as it bobbed up again and again. As she squeezed a sponge full of water over his curly head, he screwed up his eyes, squealing and laughing merrily – bathtime was always a joyous occasion.

Today their game was interrupted by the telephone ringing. Rosie hurriedly wrapped him in his fluffy towel and ran downstairs to take the call. As she said 'Hello', there was crackling on the line and the sound of money falling into the coin box at the pressing of Button A. At once Peter's voice came through, loud and clear.

"Hello, Rosie my darling, how are you?"

She could hardly speak, she was so overwhelmed with relief and excitement.

"Oh, Pete, I'm fine, but thank God you're safe; it's wonderful to hear your voice again."

"And yours too, darling. I'm in Aberdeen at the moment and have a week's leave. I'll be with you tomorrow morning, arriving on the 9.30 train. Will you meet me?"

"Of course, Pete darling, how absolutely marvellous. We'll both be there."

Then the line seemed to go dead. Rosie replaced the receiver with a feeling of ecstatic joy and relief – he was safe. Laughingly she whirled Ricky round and round, dancing and singing "Hooray, hooray, Daddy's coming home, Daddy's coming home!" Her happiness was so infectious that he clapped his little hands and joined in the merriment, gurgling with laughter.

When Bronwen arrived, Rosie was bubbling over with excitement and could hardly wait to share her good news.

"Bron, Mr. Dunbar has just phoned us from Scotland. He has a week's leave and will be here tomorrow on the early morning train."

"Oh Mam, I am pleased – we can give up worrying about him for a bit" and her round little face beamed with evident pleasure and relief. "What a difference he'll see in our 'cariad bach'. He wasn't walking or talking when Mr. Dunbar left, and now he's a regular little chatterbox, bless him."

"You seem to understand him better than any of us, Bron – it's still all double Dutch to me and I don't know what his father will make of it."

They both laughed merrily, happy at the prospect of tomorrow's reunion.

"Should I run round to Mr. Jones, the butcher, Mam, and see if he'd let us have a piece of Welsh lamb off the ration? I'm sure he'd do it for a service man on leave and particularly for Mr. Dunbar."

"Oh please, Bron, that's a wonderful idea – you really are good to us."

Affectionately Rosie squeezed her arm. She was the salt of the earth and her loyalty to them as a family touched her deeply.

"When you get back, Bron, we'll clean the cottage from top to bottom. I want everything to be perfect for his homecoming."

"Yes indeed, Mam, I'll only be away for a few minutes and then we can start."

There was nothing that Bron liked better than this – she loved cleaning and polishing, she was a real home-maker.

Shortly she returned in triumph, with a small leg of lamb, wrapped in newspaper, carefully concealed in the bottom of her shopping bag. Mr. Jones was cautious of his reputation in the village and any favouritism could be frowned upon; he had also slipped in a good marrow bone to make little Ricky some strengthening soup. He adored the child and invariably hurried to the doorway of his shop, if he saw them passing by, waving cheerfully, his ruddy face beaming. Confidentially he had told Rosie that he would never let the 'little un' go short.

Rosie decided that she would have a special hair-do for Peter's homecoming, so Bronwen stayed on that afternoon, looking after Ricky and doing some cooking for the 'returning hero'. She made him one of her special chocolate cakes which he always enjoyed, *gâteau à la Bron,* as he called it, and she also made several of his favourite fruit pies. When Rosie returned, a lovely aroma filled the cottage and the small larder was groaning with delicious home-baked food – Bron had generously helped out with the rations.

Rosie looked lovely, Bron thought, as she hurried back into the cottage – her arms loaded with yellow and white flowers to add a touch of sunshine to the rooms. Her hair shone like gold and her vivid blue eyes danced with happiness – her anxious look had vanished.

Smiling excitedly, she produced a red, white and blue bow for Biscuit. "Look, Bron, this is for 'the patriot' to wear," she said as she tied it round his neck. Then, sweeping Ricky into her arms, she twirled him round and round until dizzily they collapsed on the couch together, almost sick with laughter.

"I'd be a bit careful, Mam, if I were you, for he's just had his tea and might throw up."

"Oh Bron, I'm so excited, I can hardly contain myself," Rosie exclaimed.

"She's still a child at heart," Bron thought. She often worried about her mistress for, although she liked Peter and thought him more handsome in his naval uniform than any film star she had ever seen, there was a certain reserve about him which she could not understand.

The next day Rosie was up bright and early, putting the last finishing touches to the cottage. She dressed Ricky in a new romper suit – a present from his Granny. It was a lovely shade of deep blue which matched his eyes, and he looked absolutely adorable in it. She was longing for Peter to see him for, during his absence Ricky had changed from a baby into a chubby little boy. Then she got herself ready with special care and was pleased with her reflection in the mirror. Living in the country had given her rosy cheeks, which were most becoming.

Finally, she put a match to the fire, which blazed up promisingly. She left Biscuit curled up in his favourite chair, wearing his colourful new bow; she felt satisfied that everything looked as smart and as snug as could be. She banged the front door and, with Ricky safely ensconced in his push chair, she walked briskly along the winding country lane to the station. She could hear the train puffing and chugging along in the distance, and they arrived just as it pulled into the platform.

Two burly farmers were the first to alight and then Rosie saw Peter, in his naval uniform, stepping down at the far end of the platform. Even from a distance she could see he looked tired, drawn and considerably thinner. She ran with the push chair like lightning towards him and flew into his arms with an overwhelming warmth. He held her close and she was stirred with love and longing for him and felt an immense relief that he was safe. Finally they drew apart.

"You're looking marvellous, Rosie – absolutely blooming !" he said with his old humour. "It's wonderful to be with you again and being in the country is absolute bliss. It's what I badly need just now."

"Oh, Pete, we've longed to have you back – I can hardly believe that it's really you!" She gave him an extra hug.

"It's me all right, but I'm not so hot. I'm horribly short of sleep," he said ruefully.

She thought how hollow-eyed he looked. "Poor old Pete – it must be awful," she said sympathetically, linking her arm through his as they walked out of the station, pushing Ricky ahead of them. The ticket collector, having witnessed their reunion, smiled broadly at them as they passed through the barrier. He thought they were a nice little family.

Ricky, feeling neglected, kept turning his head around to look at this strange man, who was walking so close to his mother and who had so far ignored him completely. Rosie was painfully conscious of this too.

"Well, what do you think of your little son, Pete? He's grown so much since you left – I've been longing for you to see him."

Peter looked down at his child, wishing to show an interest in him, yet still eaten up by his old jealousy. Why hadn't Rosie come to meet him alone? Finally he lifted Ricky from his push-chair and gave him a peremptory hug and kiss.

"He certainly has changed," he said in an off-hand manner. "He's quite a big bundle now."

Rosie didn't like his curt reply at all. She felt terribly disappointed at his reaction and instinctively drew away. He quickly returned Ricky to his push-chair and took no further notice of him. Rosie felt thoroughly miserable – she couldn't have Ricky ignored like this, so unwisely she pursued the subject.

"You know, Pete, he can walk now and talks quite a lot, which is a great achievement at his age."

"Oh yes, I'm quite aware of that," he laughed with derision. "You see your letters have been almost exclusively devoted to his progress."

"That's not fair, Pete," she said sadly. Her heart ached, nothing had changed – she recognised all the old danger signals. What a way to start a leave! The sun had disappeared behind the clouds; a cold wind blew up and the country looked bleak and forbidding.

She changed the subject hurriedly. Peter was obviously over-tired and over-strained, and the long night journey would not have helped. She held his arm close as they walked along silently, but their spirits soon revived when they pushed open the cottage door and saw the blazing fire and dear Biscuit sitting so placidly beside it. Peter went straight over and stroked him affectionately then, with a deep sigh, sank heavily into the chair beside him. He looked up at Rosie a little sheepishly.

"The cottage looks lovely, darling, and so do you. Country life seems to suit you."

"Thank you, Pete, for those kind words; would you like a cup of coffee right away? You look exhausted."

"That would be nice, Rosie, I can barely keep awake," he said apologetically. "I'm horribly short of sleep. We've been doing watch on, watch off, for weeks and it's finally caught up with me."

He closed his eyes for a moment, looking utterly weary. Rosie quickly put on the kettle, then started to attend to Ricky's needs. This was usually his playtime and he looked up at her expectantly, but today this couldn't be so. She put him in his play-pen, surrounded by toys and popped in Mr. Smith for company, and then she hurried back to the kitchen to make the coffee, from the largest bottle that Camp produced.

Ricky couldn't understand her lack of attention and was upset by this strange man, who was studying him so closely. Suddenly he started to cry for his mother with heart-broken sobs. After a minute of this Peter, scowling heavily, rapped his hand on the side of the play-pen and shouted harshly, "For God's sake, Ricky, shut up!"

Rosie flew back with the coffee and picked him up, trying to hide her distress. Being in his mother's arms quickly comforted him and he stopped crying at once. He looked at this stranger with puzzled eyes – nobody had ever shouted at him like this before.

They sat opposite one another sipping their coffee, with Ricky still in her arms. Peter glanced across at Rosie. She was obviously still upset, but he felt uncontrollably irritated.

"Shouldn't he be in bed now or something?" he asked.

"No, he shouldn't," Rosie snapped; her face was flushed and her blue eyes were blazing. "He has only just got up and actually it's his playtime – perhaps it is you who should be in bed" – then in a slightly more conciliatory tone, "Why don't you go up and have a nap and come down at lunchtime?"

"Only if you come too," he snapped back, reacting abrasively.

"Well, that's impossible, I've got to look after Ricky and anyway there's the lunch to cook."

"Where is Bronwen? Can't she come in and do these things?"

Rosie's eyes were bright with unshed tears.

"Yes, of course she can, but I thought it would be nicer to spend our first day alone together as a family, but I was obviously wrong."

Peter, seeing her hurt, felt thoroughly ashamed and realised he had overstepped the mark – he must try to curb his jealousy and irritation.

"I'm sorry, Rosie darling, I'm behaving like a bear, but I'm completely drained, please forgive me. I'll do as you suggest and have a sleep until lunchtime."

He ambled slowly up the stairs and Rosie heard the bed creak and groan as he almost fell upon it, kicking off his shoes, but not even removing his jacket.

She sat motionless with Ricky on her lap, stunned with disappointment; then, pulling herself together, she hurriedly dressed him again in his unnoticed new romper suit, popped him into his push-chair and ran over to Bronwen's with him. She knocked on the little cottage door and Bron's anxious little face appeared at once.

"Hello Bron, could you possibly take care of Ricky for me? He's a bit fractious and Mr. Dunbar is absolutely exhausted" – then, almost apologetically she added: "They've got to get used to each other again."

She felt all hurt and broken up inside and Bronwen knew it. Kindly she took the child from Rosie.

"Don't worry, Mam, I'll look after him until Mr. Dunbar is rested. He can stay with me for as long as you wish."

*　*　*　*

Peter's leave was not a success. Rosie felt that she was seeing him in a new light and it was not a favourable one. He appeared a self-centred man, spoilt and demanding. He, in turn, felt a deep sense of injustice over the way he was being treated. Here he was, fighting for his country and, when he came home, his wife paid him scant attention. Ricky's demands always had to be met first and even Biscuit's needs seemed to come before his own. He was of course exhausted and saw everything out of true perspective. Their love-making lacked all spontaneity and sadly they had lost their blissful closeness.

Ricky was no longer feeling happy and secure and would start crying during the night for no particular reason and Rosie would leap out of bed in sheer panic. Ever since he was nearly suffocated in his cot in London, she could not rest for a moment unless she was certain he was all right.

The weather was cold and bleak, so they stayed indoors most of the time. Rosie did a few pencil sketches, but even this displeased Peter, so she left him alone reading and spent a great deal of time in the kitchen. She could at least provide good food for him and he would benefit from the rest. Rosie was wretched at this turn of events. She tried to show him affection and not be too hurt by his unfair attitude, but Ricky's sad little face haunted her.

They both resolved to make the last day together a success, but unhappily it was not to be so, for Ricky had caught a cold and was far from well. She felt she dare not lift him up when he started to wail, as she knew this would be frowned upon, so she just prayed he would stop crying of his own accord. When he did not, Peter got up from his chair and gave him a resounding slap and shouted angrily: "For Christ's sake belt up, you spoilt brat," then, turning to Rosie, said irritably, "It's about time a little discipline was introduced, otherwise he will rule this household."

"Don't ever do that again, Peter," she said sternly.

She was thoroughly incensed that he should strike a child and particularly one who was unwell. She picked Ricky up and his little body was convulsed in sobs; nobody had ever hit him before and his secure world seemed to have turned upside down. She hugged him and wiped away his tears and, ignoring Peter completely, swept past him and carried Ricky upstairs to his cot. He was hot and flushed, so she gave him a baby aspirin and stayed with him, gently stroking his head until, comforted, he finally fell asleep.

She returned to the living room where Peter was still sitting sullenly in his chair. He leant forward as she approached but, before he had a chance to say a word, Rosie spoke up. A bitter smile played around her mouth.

"You should be ashamed of yourself, treating your son the way you do. You show no real interest in him and your horrid jealousy completely ruins our family life. I'm convinced that our marriage will break up, if you continue to behave in this unkind way." She paused for a moment, fighting back her tears. "I warn you, I'm not prepared to jeopardise Ricky's happiness for you, particularly as you have made it abundantly clear that you don't love him. He's certainly not a spoilt brat and, when you're not around, he is as good as gold."

She expected him to defend himself but, to her surprise, he remained silent. His face looked grey and his eyes sunken deep in their sockets. For a moment she felt sorry for him, but only fleetingly.

"I think it would be best if you returned to your ship today. Ricky is far from well and I don't intend leaving his side until he is better."

Peter got up slowly from his chair and looked at Rosie long and hard.

"I'm sorry I slapped him. I know I shouldn't have done so, but my nerves are pretty stretched. You are wrong, Rosie, when you say I don't love him. I do, and have done from the moment he was born. Remember though, that I warned you I would never want to share you with anyone or anything and this still applies." There was a brief silence before he carried on. "I'll go up now and pack, and I'll soon be out of your way."

Rosie turned her back on him and did not answer. There was a lump in her throat, when she remembered how excited she had been at the prospect of this leave and what a dismal failure it had proved. Her heart ached, but she could not excuse his callous behaviour.

He went upstairs and hurriedly packed his bag; then he tiptoed into the nursery and looked down at his sleeping son; as he touched his flushed little cheeks, Ricky opened his eyes and gazed up at him and unexpectedly gave him a most enchanting smile – it was a 'Rosie' smile. Peter knelt down and, taking Ricky's chubby little hand in his, whispered: "Forgive me, son," then kissed him gently on the cheek and quietly left the room.

Rosie was in the kitchen, washing up the breakfast dishes as he came down and stood beside her. She hardly turned her head.

"Goodbye, Rosie, I'm sorry about everything." Then, in a muffled tone, "Please forgive me. I am not myself."

She ignored his plea entirely. "Goodbye, Peter, and good luck," she replied stiffly.

He gave her arm a squeeze, but did not attempt to kiss her and she just continued with the washing up, until she heard the cottage door slam behind him. Then her self control, so tightly held in check, broke down and she was sobbing uncontrollably.

She sank into a chair, her head buried in her hands, her elbows resting on the kitchen table. She stayed like this until, worn out with crying, she dragged herself upstairs to the lonely bedroom and, lying exhausted on the bed, soon drifted off into a troubled sleep.

*   *   *   *   *

The first few days after Peter's departure were agonising ones. Rosie waited eagerly for the postman each morning, but nothing came and she missed his letters very much. She felt she had no defence against the terrible loneliness that engulfed her. To make matters worse, Ricky's cold turned to bronchitis and he needed careful nursing to get over it. She was worried sick about him and, until his temperature was normal, she would not leave his side.

She longed to get back to her driving job again and knew that, if she were out and doing something useful, it would all be more bearable. Bronwen helped to share the burden. The bond of affection between the two of them was strong and Bronwen treated Ricky as if he were one of her own. Although nothing had been said, she knew there had been trouble and her heart ached for Rosie.

As soon as Ricky was well again, Rosie returned to work. It helped to take her mind off her troubles. They had missed her and she was given a warm welcome at all the out-lying sites that she visited. As soon as her mobile canteen drew up, she was surrounded by officers and men, who were homesick, and bored by lack of enemy action.

116

She was often asked out to dinner by hopeful young officers, but she always turned them down. She had no wish to become involved and, unless a definite break were made with Peter, her sense of fairness would not allow any flirtations. She did, however, become friendly with a captain in the Royal Artillery, Stewart Clarke, whom she had known as a child in Liverpool. They had gone to dancing classes together and their parents knew one another. He was engaged to a charming girl and only wished for a friendly relationship; this suited Rosie, as there were no complications. He often called at the cottage to see her. Ricky loved his visits and, to Rosie's chagrin, called him 'Daddy'.

He had a red spaniel called 'George', which he always brought along with him and which, strangely enough, got on well with Biscuit. It seemed a case of love at first sight for, on George's first visit, he bounded straight over to the cat and covered his face with affectionate lolloping licks. Biscuit was incensed at the time, but finally grew to enjoy this treatment and they became good friends.

One afternoon Rosie was sitting on the rug beside Ricky; they were playing together with his building blocks. Grandfather Greenwood had given them to him and they really were a marvellous present — made in Scandinavia and large enough and sufficient to erect a substantial little house, just the thing for the son of an architect. Ricky's great delight was to build himself a wall and then knock it down. This he did with whoops of joyous laughter.

"Bang, bang, Mummy," he would shout just before the demolition and her cue was always: "No, no Ricky, don't do it!"

He was almost sick with laughter as he ignored her plea and, with a swing of his arm which almost toppled him over backwards, the bricks came tumbling down.

To-day their favourite game was interrupted by the friendly creak of the front gate and, as Rosie looked up, she saw Stewart approaching along the path with George in tow. She ran to the door to let them in, a welcoming smile on her face.

"Hello, Stew, how nice to see you. Do come in and have a cup of tea."

"That's very kind of you, Rosie, but this time I can't stay long. I've just come to tell you that I've been posted overseas."

"Oh, Stew, we shall miss you," she said sadly and her face fell. "You're always such cheerful company, but whatever are you going to do with George?"

"Well, Rosie, that's partly why I'm here today." He spoke hesitantly and his face creased with worry. "I wondered if by any chance you might like to take the old fellow? I can't bear to have him put down and there are very few people with whom I would trust him."

She smiled reassuringly. "Of course, Stew, we would simply love to have him. We're all so fond of animals and he will be great company for us. I was in fact thinking of getting a dog myself and George is such a dear."

His brow cleared. "Well, that's all settled then, Rosie. I can't tell you what a relief this is to me. It's going to be hard parting with him, but there's no alternative. Do you think I could possibly leave him this afternoon?" He smiled shyly. "I've brought his basket, plus biscuits and dog food with me, just in case you'd accept. To be quite frank, I'd like to get it over; it is extraordinary how fond one can get of an animal."

"Of course, Stew, bring in all his clobber, while I make you a quick cup of tea."

Rosie was soon back with the tray, but there was none of the light-hearted banter today; they were both subdued. She knew how he hated parting with the dog, so didn't prolong the visit, saying she must get Ricky's supper ready. It was the kindest way.

She walked down the path to see him off. She felt sad and depressed, but tried to cheer him up.

"Goodbye and good luck, Stew, and don't worry about George. I will take very good care of him." She kissed him lightly on the cheek.

"God bless you, Rosie my dear, and thank you for everything. I shall be thinking of you."

He closed the gate without a backward glance and hurried to his car. She sighed deeply as he left — she hated all these horrid partings. She wondered if she'd ever see him again. How thankful she would be when the war was over, but it had hardly started yet. The only real enemy action so far was at sea. This phoney war, so called, was demoralising for everybody — not knowing what to expect or what action to take.

Many of the evacuees, who had been sent to the country, hated it; they were drifting back to the cities, their parents deciding to take a chance on the possible dangers ahead. There had been a few air raids on small country towns, with only minimal casualties. However, nobody was under the illusion that they would escape. It was only a matter of time before Hitler's fury would be unleashed against them.

After several weeks a letter arrived from Peter, just a couple of pages with very little news. He mentioned again lack of sleep and freezing weather. He hoped they were both well, but the tone of his letter was cool. Rosie's heart ached; it was so different from the pages and pages he used to write to her, full of love and longing. She was suffering from a painful sense of guilt about him now. Supposing he was killed, how would she feel then? Exactly whose fault was all this trouble between them? She knew it must be partly hers, but was reluctant to shoulder much of the blame.

10

PETER, who was first lieutenant of the minesweeper M57, was having a very tough time at sea. He was still exhausted by lack of sleep and the strain of being constantly alert to danger was taking its toll. To make matters worse, the bitter east winds seemed to cut through his now-slender frame like a knife; but nevertheless M57 was a happy ship. The commanding officer, Lieutenant Commander Roy Buckland, R.N.R., was a veritable dynamo of a man. His decisions were incisive and, in an emergency, the ship's company had complete confidence in him.

It was heartbreaking every time a merchant ship was sunk, for the naval escorts felt a personal responsibility for the safety of each ship in the convoy. Their concentration was never relaxed and their senses were keyed up, almost to breaking point, to anticipate any threat to their charges – a cruel torture for men starved of sleep.

Peter turned out of his bunk for the middle watch on the fatal night of 28th February, 1940. The captain, after hours on the bridge, had returned to his cabin, with standing orders that he was to be called instantly if any emergency arose. It was cold, pitch dark and very foggy, and all sounds were curiously muffled. The concealment afforded by the fog was illusory; both officers and look outs never relaxed, straining their eyes to ensure that there was not a predatory wolf skulking in the midst of their flock, for with such a large convoy, in bad visibility, they had constantly to be on the *qui vive.*

Creeping along the east coast they were making for Harwich, where the ship was putting in for minor repairs. Peter had made his plans for these few days. He would go straight to the local hotel, where he would luxuriate in a steaming hot bath, sleep the sleep of the just and eat and drink whatever took his fancy. He did not intend to contact Rosie. He was too exhausted and the strain was remorselessly sapping his vitality. He contemplated these rest days ashore with pleasurable anticipation. He stood on the bridge with eyes skinned for trouble, his ears alert to any sound of danger, and counting the hours until they would reach port.

In the meantime, under the cover of the blanketting fog, a small flotilla of E-boats was stalking the convoy, steeled in readiness to make a tip-and-run attack, as soon as the visibility was good enough. When the moment came, they closed in rapidly to 400 yards, fired their torpedoes then, with the benefit of their full forty knots, turned and withdrew for home across the Channel.

Only one torpedo was to score a hit. Flashing through the water like a giant fish, without a whisper of warning, it struck the ill-fated minesweeper M57, penetrating and exploding with a tremendous impact amidships on the port side.

The ship shuddered and Peter was flung sideways into the wing of the bridge. He lay dazed for a moment in a huddle on the deck. His head had crashed against the starboard bulkhead and temporarily he had blacked out. His senses, however, quickly returned, as a deafening explosion from the vicinity of the engine room rent the air and huge tongues of flames shot up, soaring and twisting into the night. He saw it all with a vivid intensity, as he dragged himself to his feet, shocked into activity.

The terrible groans of the wounded, and the screams from those trapped in the scalding agony of the engine room, resounded in his ears – those poor devils! Sickened with horror, he stumbled across the bridge to fire the distress rockets then, lifting the cover from the voice pipe, he hoarsely shouted: "Captain, sir," but there was no response, so he repeated it louder – but there was still no reply.

Peter took charge, his face grey with fatigue and anxiety. He turned urgently to a seaman at hand: "Woods, go down to the captain's cabin at the double and see if he is all right. I can't get any reply from him."

Woods was soon back looking white and shaken. "The captain's cabin is a blazing inferno, sir. He must be dead. The Damage Control Party are there."

"I feared so," Peter replied resignedly, knowing there was nothing further he could do, now he must take over.

Already the stern was awash and submerging rapidly. Amidships there was a cloud of escaping steam hissing as the ship sank lower in the water.

Standing beside Peter was Chris Macleod, a young R.N.V.R. officer, full of courage and daring. The force of the explosion had flung him against the binnacle, but he soon collected himself, finding his first experience of enemy action stimulating, yet frightening in the extreme.

"Chris, have a look around the upper deck, I can't see a bloody thing with all this smoke about – come back quickly and let me know the score."

"At the double," Chris replied, his senses now fully recovered from the stunning blast.

He dashed off and in the darkness collided with Dusty Miller, the gunnery officer, who was struggling to his feet, having been blown across the deck when the torpedo struck. He was obviously in a bemused state.

"Are you OK, Guns?" Chris asked.

"Yes, I'm a bit shaken up but I'll be all right in a minute." Chris left him propped up against the bulkhead and completed his tour of inspection as best he could. The upper deck was a complete shambles. On his way back to the bridge he met Tom Watson, the navigating officer, who came staggering out of the chart house in a dazed condition, bleeding profusely from the head and obviously no longer *compos mentis.*

"Come with me, Pilot, I'm on my way back to report. The bastards have finished us – next stop the 'oggin," he said grimly – but he got no coherent reply. It was heavy weather propelling Watson up the now-inclined and slippery deck but they arrived on the bridge, panting and exhausted by their efforts.

"It's quite hopeless, Number One," Chris reported. "There are two bloody great holes that we can do nothing about. There is a large fire out of control 'midships and she's taking in water fast – Pilot here is not so hot either."

"So I see and it's as I thought," Peter said grimly. "She's sinking fast by the stern – now go down and make sure the secret communications and books have been destroyed and report back to me as soon as you can."

Without warning there was another shattering explosion and the ship shuddered again ominously then settled lower in the water – she had obviously broken her back.

Peter had to act quickly. He went to the tannoy and in a calm, yet authoritative voice gave the final order, repeating it several times.

"D'you hear there? D'you hear there? Abandon ship – Abandon ship – every man for himself."

Then, after a final glance around, he said: "Let's get going, Chris, there's nothing more to be done here and she's sinking fast. I'll help you with Pilot."

"Thank you, Number One, he's a bit of a handful." The two men left the bridge supporting the navigating officer between them, slithering down the ship's ladder on to the deck below, which was awash with oil.

Utter chaos and confusion reigned, just like a terrifying nightmare. The bows were now at a crazy angle. A few dark figures were emerging from between decks, struggling to keep a foothold. Carley floats and life rafts were being pushed overboard by a petty officer, skilfully organising a party of men.

Peter noticed a young rating, little more than a boy, hanging on to the ship's rail, with a stunned, vacant look on his face. As the blow had struck, he had been on his way to the bridge with mugs of cocoa – he could not comprehend what had happened.

"Don't waste time. Get going, son. Inflate your lifejacket and jump for it," Peter shouted above the din. The boy looked hesitantly down into the pitiless blackness below, but obey orders he must.

"Aye, aye, sir," he said, and after hurriedly blowing up his lifejacket he leapt overboard, disappearing into the night. Chris Macleod was the next to go, supporting Tim Watson.

"I can look after Pilot," he said to Peter, putting his arm around the bewildered man. "Come on Pilot, let's go."

"The best of luck to you," Pete called as they plummeted into the sea together, and were swallowed up in the intense darkness below.

It was only a matter of minutes now before the ship would go down. Peter took a final look around at the broken hulk – the good old warhorse, writhing in her death throes. There was no sign of life anywhere – it was an eerie experience being alone in the dark, with death all around him.

He took a deep breath and jumped; as he hit the murky waters, he was temporarily stunned, but the icy cold shocked him back to activity. He started to strike out, away from the ship, as fast as his ebbing strength allowed, looking frantically around for his shipmates, but he could see nothing in the swirling fog.

He was in dire straits now, waterlogged and struggling for air through his oil-clogged mouth and nose. His chilled limbs could no longer readily respond to the urgent messages from his brain to keep going. It was a desperate struggle and it seemed his number was up. Was he to be left to die alone in this unfriendly sea? His thoughts were only of his beautiful Rosie. Would he ever see her again or was he destined to drown, swallowed up by this murky blackness?

He was only semi-conscious now, but vaguely he became aware of the faint sound of splashing oars close by – unless it was a cruel hallucination. He managed a stifled cry: "Ahoy, there," – and eerily out of the fog a dark shape loomed above him. The next thing he knew he was being hauled bodily out of the water and tumbled roughly inboard.

He lay back gasping for breath, until the helping arms of his shipmates dragged him to a sitting position. He looked into their oil-blackened faces. "Thank God for the navy," he croaked, then spewed up a stomach full of oil and sea water – this seemed to clear his head. He raised himself painfully and gave the command, "Pull away like hell before the next explosion."

When it came it was small and muffled, just a last futile protest, as the ship was swallowed up into the depths of the ocean.

He must have lost consciousness, for the next thing he knew he was lying on the deck of a merchant ship, covered with a warm blanket, and being revived with a tot of brandy. He asked a rating if there were many survivors.

"Only a few, sir. She went down so quickly that we could not get near."

Peter lay quietly, thankful to be alive; apart from a very sore head, he seemed all right. He wondered about his brother officers, and could not dismiss from his mind their splendid captain, respected by the whole ship's company – God rest his soul.

He was suddenly aware of someone hovering beside him and glancing up he saw the stocky figure of his friend, Chris Macleod, looking as buoyant as ever.

"Are you all right, Peter?"

"I'm fine and glad to see you, old fellow, but what happened after you jumped?" he enquired.

"I was picked up from a Carley float" – a haunted look crossed his face. "I'm afraid Tim Watson was lost. He was covered in oil and just slithered from my grasp and disappeared. I did my bloody best," he said remorsefully.

"That goes without saying – the chaos was appalling," Peter looked around at the few survivors lying close by. "Do you know if any more have been picked up, Chris?"

"I believe not," he replied – "many were caught below."

Peter knew he would never forget the agonised screams from the engine room – those good men, trapped in a fiery, steaming inferno but, for his own sanity, he must not dwell on such thoughts.

The merchant ship's medical officer, after a perfunctory examination of each man in turn, had them quickly transferred to the sick bay for cleaning up and temporary dressing. When the ship reached Dover they were all conveyed to the nearest naval hospital. Peter by this time was in fair shape, but was kept there for forty-eight hours to recover from the blow on his head, and also from shock and exposure. He was thankful for these few days of recuperation. Then, to his great relief, he was granted fourteen days survivors' leave.

He had no inclination to join Rosie in the country. He wanted to be away from all that domesticity and, when Chris Macleod suggested a few nights in London at the Savoy, he jumped at the idea.

He telephoned Rosie from the hospital and just caught her as she was hurrying out to her job.

"Hello, Rosie dear, how are you?"

"Very well, Pete, but where are you calling from?"

He felt deflated at the lack of enthusiasm in her voice. "I'm in Dover and have two weeks' leave. How about coming up to London and joining me at the Savoy for a few days? It would be a complete change for you."

There was a significant pause. Their strained relationship made it hard for her to reply.

"I think it would be better if you came here, Pete. I work every morning now and I can't take time off without at least a week's notice."

"Surely they can make exceptions?"

"No, I'm afraid not, Pete. After all there is a war on!"

He laughed ironically. "Yes, I am aware of that, Rosie. In fact I'm on survivor's leave at the moment."

"Oh I am sorry, Pete, are you all right?" Her voice sounded anxious now.

"Yes, I'm fine. I'll be home in a few days – just forget about London."

She felt guilty, but there was nothing she could do about it.

"I really would like to have joined you, Pete, but at such short notice it is virtually impossible."

"Don't worry, I'll see you soon and don't bother to make any preparations for me – goodbye, Rosie."

He banged the receiver down, uncontrollably upset and jealous. He felt sure it was that perishing son of his again.

In the meantime Chris Macleod had made arrangements to meet his special girl friend at the Savoy Hotel and asked her to bring along an attractive partner for his pal. Casually he mentioned this to Peter, saying that they would have a good evening together. Peter readily fell in with the plan. He felt reckless and badly needed a diversion to blot out the horror of the last few days. To hell with Rosie, he thought: she's a dead loss.

When they arrived at the hotel, they received the usual warm welcome extended to service officers. Peter was taken up to one of the Savoy's most luxurious bedrooms, overlooking the river. The comfort of it was sheer heaven by contrast with the sparseness of his old cabin aboard ship.

The enormous bath in the over-sized bathroom appealed to him particularly. He quickly shed his uniform, which the valet took away for pressing, and was soon lazily soaking in the tub. The warmth of the water had a soporific effect on him and he now wished he could spend the evening quietly alone; but, as his thoughts inevitably strayed back to the grim loss of his ship, he knew a few drinks would do him good. Reluctantly he forced himself to get out and dried himself off on an enormous fleecy white bath towel.

As he walked through to the bedroom, his bare feet sinking into the thick piled carpet, he was struck by the king-sized bed. Surely this must be the bridal suite. If only Rosie were here! He needed her desperately; the thought of her lovely softness beside him was almost more than he could bear. For the first time he realised how deprived he had been. The unrelenting tension, that filled life at sea, had temporarily driven physical desire out of him. Now it had returned and Rosie was hundreds of miles away. A wave of bitterness and anger swept over him.

He dressed hurriedly, determined to have a good evening without her; let her get on with it.

He had arranged to meet Chris at the American Bar which was crowded with service men, some with their wives and sweethearts. There was a convivial buzz of conversation going on.

Since the outbreak of war, the British reserve had been overcome and a wonderful new spirit of friendliness and informality had developed within the country – a comradeship engendered by the need to pull together as one against the common enemy.

As he glanced around, he quickly saw Chris sitting at a centre table, laughing uproariously, accompanied by two gorgeous girls, both in Wren officers' uniforms. He felt strangely disorientated and light-headed by this sudden change of circumstances – from the grim realities of war at sea, culminating in disaster, to this scene of light-hearted gaiety and glamour.

Chris stood up as he approached and, with a welcoming grin, clapped him enthusiastically on the shoulder. He was an attractive young man, of medium height, with rugged good looks and a lively personality, full of fun and laughter.

He admired Peter particularly after the way he had calmly assumed command of the M57 following the disaster.

"Hello, Peter old boy, how nice to see you; take a seat, but first let me introduce you to the girls. This is Maudie, my number one sweetie-pie, and her friend, Babs – ladies, here is my gallant shipmate, Peter Dunbar."

"Hello," he said, brightening up. He felt flattered by their warm reception. The girls were anxious to meet this Adonis, who had been so graphically described to them by Chris, and they were not disappointed. They smiled and looked thoroughly pleased with Peter in the flesh.

Maudie was a tall slim girl, with sloe-like eyes and a smooth olive complexion. When she smiled, her teeth were dazzling white and she wore vivid red lipstick. Quite a dish, Peter thought. Babs was a complete contrast. She was smaller and more shapely, with blond hair, worn in a page-boy style. Her eyes were blue and heavily lashed and her vivacity was evident from their first introduction. She was a goer indeed. Immediately her eyes held Peter's; it was obvious to him that she found him attractive. Generally speaking she was not his type, but tonight she suited his mood and, after a couple of stiff drinks, he felt that more so than ever.

They had booked a table for dinner in the restaurant below and, as they walked down, the band was playing 'The White Cliffs of Dover', which really tugged at the heart strings. After the meal was ordered, Peter asked Babs for a dance and, as she stood up, he noticed with interest her curvaceous figure. The severely cut uniform seemed to accentuate her femininity. They danced well together and she pressed herself close to him with her blond head nestled into his shoulder. He loved the fragrance of her. She was fresh and very seductive and he found her disturbingly attractive.

Their meal was good for wartime London though there was little choice but, after the monotony of shipboard fare, it was delicious. The wine was excellent and altogether theirs was a jolly party. They exchanged partners once or twice, and Peter liked Maudie immensely. She was a girl of great character and obviously devoted to Chris. She had eyes for no-one else.

"What do you think of Babs?" she asked, as they danced their first waltz together. "I hope I made a good choice of partner for you. I don't know her well, but she is certainly attractive and always great fun at a party."

"You couldn't have done better, Maudie," he replied. "I'm thoroughly enjoying myself; after the life we've been leading at sea, this is terrific."

"Chris tells me you have a lovely wife and baby son; where are they living now?"

"We have a cottage in Snowdonia, which is an ideal retreat for them," he replied. "Yes, Rosie is very beautiful, but being a mother is everything to her and she's disinclined to leave our son for a moment."

Maudie sensed the tacit criticism and she always defended her own sex.

"You know I think she's quite right. If you take on the responsibility of a child, then it should be your first priority; but that's just my own personal opinion and I know most husbands wouldn't agree with me."

Peter was irritated with her for a moment and all his previous *joie de vivre* deserted him but, as they joined the others and another bottle of wine was ordered, his mood changed again. The orchestra struck up the 'Lambeth Walk'. They all leapt to their feet and, with great abandon, danced it together as a foursome. There was an atmosphere of forced gaiety, a desperate desire for pleasure, lest it be snatched away.

After dinner, Chris and Maudie disappeared for the rest of the evening, obviously wanting time alone together. Peter was pleased to have Babs on her own; she seemed more bewitching every moment.

"Come on, glamour girl, let's go up to the bar again and have another snifter and you can tell me all about yourself. I know you are a great party girl, but I want to hear much more."

He took her hand and steered her rather unsteadily up the stairs towards the bar. He had already indulged himself pretty freely, which was quite out of character for Peter. He felt reckless and his guard was down.

They took a corner table and, after the drinks arrived, he knocked his back in almost one gulp, then put his arm affectionately around her shoulders.

"Now, Babs, my little sex kitten, tell me about yourself."

She looked at him coquettishly and laughed, showing her even white teeth and the tip of her little pink tongue.

"There isn't really much to tell, it's all rather dull," she sighed. "I've made a disastrous marriage and I'm lumbered with a baby I didn't really want. Fortunately my mother takes good care of him for me, so I'm more or less foot loose and fancy free. My philosophy at the moment is 'Gather ye rosebuds, while ye may,' for who knows what may happen tomorrow?" She looked deeply into his eyes; he was the most attractive man she'd met for years.

"Well, I'm not going to argue with that; none of us knows what is in store and it's a damn good thing we don't," he said with obvious feeling. "So the best of British luck to you!"

She drew closer to him.

"Now, Pete, it's your turn to tell me your life story — I'm all ears."

He looked at her beautiful, yet shallow little face, and did not feel inclined to confide in her. He shrugged and felt a twist of conscience.

"I really don't have much to tell either. I'm married and my wife and son, Ricky, live together in the country. Rosie is a dedicated mother, so I'm generally the odd man out — just a spare part; but let's leave it at that. Now how about another drink?"

"That's a good idea, Pete."

His voice was slurred now and, as he drank another whisky, his judgement was dulled and all his inhibitions gone. He asked the leading question she was waiting for.

"Are you staying here tonight, Babs, or going back to the Wrenery?"

"I haven't really decided yet, but reservations say there's a small room, without bath, that I can have, if I want it."

She looked searchingly up at him and he replied rashly, burning his boats. "Why bother, I've got a wonderful room — I think it must be the bridal suite — overlooking the river. It has a king sized bed — I shall be lost in it alone. Would you consider coming to share it with me? You know you're a most seductive girl and a poor sex-starved officer like myself would be delighted if you would join him."

She smiled knowingly and he knew in a flash that she had planned this from the start; but he didn't care — to hell with Rosie, she'd brought it on herself. She had neglected him and he felt amply justified. He needed fun and laughter and, most of all, oblivion.

It was bitterly cold, as Peter came out of the Embankment entrance of the Savoy and walked slowly along beside the Thames. He looked at the river flowing, still and silent, and groaned inwardly as he thought of the emptiness of last night's experience. He felt tainted and sick at heart. His conscience agonised him. In his drunken stupor he had been disloyal to his beautiful Rosie and he knew she had not deserved it.

He thought of the utter perfection of their first love-making; the spiritual and physical quality of their blending together as one. For once he considered the fact of having conceived a child so quickly. This seemed a precious gift in itself – a natural blessing of their union. Why had he not seen it that way before? He had discarded this pure gold for dross. Why had he done it?

He forced himself into self-analysis. In his weakness he had really sought to punish Rosie – trying to make her experience his agonies of jealousy – to pull her bright spirit into the shadows. Impossible, thank God, for Rosie was Rosie, essentially loving, but one thing he had learned about her – she was strong and would fight for the happiness of her child like a wild cat. It was primeval and he could never win against this – so his thoughts ran on. He was determined once and for all to rationalise his confused thinking and not let his emotions blind him.

Would he really want her any different? Would he have loved her as much, if she were less maternal, putting her own pleasures before her responsibility for their child? Babs was a good example of this; her selfishness appalled him.

His thoughts turned to Ricky, as he had last seen him, and his heart ached. Even after his unkind treatment, the little face had looked up at him smilingly – 'a Rosie smile'. The full recognition of his feelings for his son struck him forcibly and undoubtedly, if Rosie had shown any indifference to the child, he would not have tolerated it.

He knew that he could not live with her again without a confession of his unfaithfulness. They had solemnly promised that they would always be honest with each other, agreeing that, if either were to stray, they must have the courage and integrity to confess to their misdeed. He at least must honour this promise, whatever the consequences, or surely his would be the ultimate betrayal.

He squared his shoulders with resolve and quickened his pace. His mind was made up. He must catch the first train.

11

THE JOURNEY from London had seemed interminably long, yet it had given Peter plenty of time for deep thought. He felt he understood himself better now – a touch of humility had entered his soul.

He sat huddled in a corner of the cold, draughty railway carriage, idly watching the smoke from the engine drifting past the window. He was thankful that he was near his destination at last, for now he could see the familiar snow-clad peaks of the Snowdon range in the distance. He gazed dejectedly at the view. The mountains looked cold, remote and forbidding. The colours were hidden by the absence of sun on this bleak grey afternoon.

The train was starting to slow down, so he gathered together his few belongings in readiness. As it pulled into the tiny country station and came to a juddering halt, he jumped out, surprised to find that he was the only passenger alighting.

The platform was deserted and the gusty March wind was piercingly cold. The rotund little figure of Mr. Jones, the station-master, was waiting to take his ticket. It was too cold for standing around talking today so, after a cheerful quip, Mr. Jones quickly scuttled back to his office, where a bright fire blazed in the small black grate. As Peter passed by, he already had his feet up again puffing away at his pipe.

There was no welcoming committee for Peter today. No vivacious Rosie with sparkling eyes, running to meet him, her beauty breath-taking, captivating his heart. It was like this after a separation. Her loveliness in reality always far surpassed his recollection of her.

He hunched up his shoulders against the cold, shivering as he trudged along the country lane, now so familiar to him. There was not a soul about. Rain was in the air, for the gulls had come inland, wheeling overhead with their strange eerie cries. Their white wings showed up brilliantly against the background of the leaden sky. He noticed the hawthorns already budding and the woolly hazel catkins in the hedgerows, which Rosie loved to gather for the cottage – Spring would soon be here and this thought lightened his spirit.

It was tea-time and already dusk was falling. There was quite a gale blowing up now. As he reached the brow of the hill and looked up across the valley, he saw the cottage comfortably nestled amongst the trees; there was a warm glow from the flickering fire, radiating through the downstairs windows. His heart leapt with joy, home seemed to be beckoning him. He hastened his step, hardly able to wait to see his family.

Inside, it was almost time to draw the blackout curtains, but Rosie was reluctant to do so. It was nearly Ricky's bedtime. He was playing contentedly with his toys on the rug and a cheerful log fire crackled in the hearth. Rosie was busy, knitting socks for the troops – a job she hated, but it seemed the patriotic thing to do. Biscuit was sinuously curled up on her lap, now quite accustomed to the clicking of the needles. George, as usual, was lying sprawled at her feet, twitching and dreaming of the Elysian Fields no doubt.

She heard the gate give its usual creak and wondered whoever it could be on this freezing afternoon. George sprang up, barking furiously and, as she heard footsteps approaching up the path, she laid aside her knitting and deposited Biscuit on the rug. She heard the handle turn, then suddenly the door burst open by the force of the wind outside, filling the cottage with an icy blast.

There on the threshold stood Peter, now struggling to close the door behind him. Rosie could hardly believe her eyes, for she hadn't expected him for several days yet. His face looked drawn and grey with a heavy weariness. He looked years older. She ran towards him with a feeling of overwhelming concern. He gathered her into his arms, holding her so close that her face was buried deep in his greatcoat – she could hardly breathe.

"Oh, Pete," she gasped," how lovely to have you back again." He was reluctant to let her go, but finally she broke away with a laugh.

"You're almost suffocating me – come and sit down by the fire, you're freezing."

She took his coat and led him to his favourite chair. He sank into it, gratefully stretching out his long legs in front of him.

"Oh, Rosie darling, it's wonderful to be home again."

He looked around at the snug cottage, as though he just couldn't believe his eyes. She sensed a great difference in him; he was kinder, less abrasive. Something had changed him, leaving him vulnerable, and he needed her – that much she understood.

"Whatever happened to your ship, Peter?" she ventured to ask, yet dreading his reply. He looked at her with haunted eyes.

"It was sunk by an E-boat – torpedoed 'midships – there were only a few survivors."

"How dreadful, Pete." She was shocked into silence for a moment. "The captain?" she asked with concern.

"He's a goner, Rosie – I've lost a real friend there."

"What a ghastly experience for you; no wonder you look so weary, but thank God you're safe. Just sit and relax and I'll make you some tea."

"Thank you, darling, that sounds wonderful."

When she returned from the kitchen, he was sitting with Ricky on his knee and it gave her much pleasure to see them so close – she was struck by how very alike they had become. Peter was giving him big bear hugs, accompanied by life-like growls. The little fellow was chuckling with glee, his eyes alight with excitement, obviously happy and content to be with his father again. George, the latest addition to the family, was at his feet – they had already made friends.

As she handed him a cup of tea he looked up and smiled appreciatively at her.

"Darling, I can't tell you how wonderful it is being with you and the family again."

She noticed that Ricky was no longer excluded – it seemed that the rift between them had been healed. For her part she was more than ready to make it up. She had been heartbroken by the turn of events.

She could vividly imagine what he had gone through, losing his ship and brother officers – she felt very sorry for him. He had always written so warmly of the good comradeship between them all. It had been a happy ship.

"Was the sinking very dreadful, Pete, and were you in the water for long?" she asked.

"Yes, the whole episode is like a nightmare," he replied wearily. "I'll tell you all about it another time, but at the moment I'm trying to forget it – I'd much rather hear about what you and Ricky have been doing." He looked at her latest picture, standing unframed above the fireplace. "This portrait you've done of Ricky is the living image of him. You have a tremendous talent for portraits, Rosie. You know I'm very proud of your achievements."

She flushed with pleasure, she was astounded at his praise – how he had changed! He seemed himself again, the old loving Peter, the young man she had first married.

She saw him blink his eyes wearily. She knew he was exhausted and emotionally drained. She felt full of remorse for not meeting him in London, when he had needed her. Ricky had fallen asleep in his arms by the warmth of the fire and he gazed down at his son's flushed little face with unmistakable devotion.

"He's growing so handsome, Rosie, and I feel enormously proud of him."

"And so you should, Peter Dunbar, for he looks just like you and that's good enough for anyone."

Their laughter mingled, as they looked deeply into each others eyes, and the love light was there between them, just as in their courtship days. Rosie's heart leapt ecstatically; she crossed over and knelt beside him, pressing her soft cheek against his.

"I do love you, darling – thank God you survived. By the way, how long a leave have you got?"

"Well, I have thirteen days left now" – a shadow seemed to cross his face – "but, Rosie, they're giving me a shore appointment for a time at Chatham Barracks. I shall hate not being at sea with a war on; it almost seems like funking it, but this time I have no choice."

"Pete, you've more than done your bit already and you badly need a respite; I'm thankful for one too – what a relief it will be not having to worry about you. Oh Darling, I'm so happy. I haven't felt like this for months."

Her face lit up with an expression of unutterable joy, but he did not respond – she had an uneasy feeling inside her. She drew back and looked at him searchingly. It gave her a shock, for there was no happy response. His sad, anxious eyes looked back at her, now full of remorse and even shame. He drew a deep breath.

"Rosie darling, there's something I've got to tell you and I only hope to God you can forgive me."

Her heart started to race madly – she dreaded hearing what he had to say. Strangely she had anticipated something like this and now she wanted to postpone the moment – to have time to pull herself together.

"Let me put Ricky to bed first," she said quietly. She lifted the warm little body from his arms and held him close to her, carrying him asleep up the stairs. She quickly had him tucked up in his cot. He looked at her drowsily, as she bent down to kiss him, and he was asleep before she left the room.

She was reluctant to go downstairs yet, so she tiptoed over to her own bedroom for a moment. It had always been a refuge to her. She looked out of the window at her favourite view, but today there was no reassurance there. It looked bleak and comfortless. All her happiness had vanished once more.

She did not sit next to Peter on the couch, but on the chair opposite. She sat very upright, her face drained of colour; in contrast her eyes looked like two dark anguished pools of blue. Peter felt a wave of compassion for her and was filled with a terrible pang of remorse. In all conscience he had hurt her enough without this. How could he bear to tell her?

"Rosie, you know we made a pact together – under all circumstances we would be honest with each other?"

She nodded, dumb with misery.

As he carried on, his voice was husky and hesitant.

"We both agreed that any hidden deceit between us would undermine our relationship and that, however serious the consequences, we would stand by this decision . Well, Rosie, I have come face to face with this." There was a long pause and Rosie waited for him to carry on. "Last night I betrayed you. I slept with another woman. She was nothing to me and the experience was completely without meaning."

Rosie drew in her breath sharply; she felt choked as though everything was closing in on her. She raised her eyes to his. The shock of his betrayal and his weak, contemptible behaviour shattered her.

"But why, Peter, why? Surely you would not deceive me so casually without reason?"

"There was a reason – I had far too much to drink last night and I needed you so desperately and, when you refused to come, I felt you had failed me. You know my weakness. I was consumed with jealousy, convinced that again I was being relegated to second place; it almost seemed an opportunity to pay you back and give you a dose of your own medicine. I am deeply ashamed, and I know I have been absolutely wrong – what I did was quite unpardonable." His voice was thick with emotion. "Please, Rosie, try to forgive me."

She slowly turned to look at him – her eyes were blazing – she let the contempt show in her expression. It seemed impossible to believe that, after their own perfect love-making, he could be tempted into such a sordid affair. A deep flash of jealousy ran through her and sceptically she wondered just how pleasurable it had really been. Could she ever trust him again? Yet he had been honest with her, generously taking all the blame. She gave him credit for this. With great effort she spoke.

"The blame is not entirely yours. I know I should have joined you in London, and would have done so, if our relationship had been right."

She spoke coldly now. "I'd rather not see you for a day or two. I want time to think everything over on my own. Why don't you go and stay with your parents? There is a seven o'clock train you can catch tonight."

It was a cruel response, driving him out in the cold again, but he deserved it.

He nodded dumbly. "All right, Rosie, if that's what you want, but please, darling, try not to feel too badly about me. I adore you and couldn't live without you." His voice broke.

Rosie got up quickly from her chair and her eyes flashed. "Well, perhaps in future you'll have to. I don't take kindly to cheats."

Then, putting on her sheepskin jacket and calling George, she was out of the cottage like lightning, banging the door behind her.

The icy wind stung her face, cutting cruelly through her, but she welcomed the discomfort of it. Somehow it lessened her inner pain. She walked briskly for a mile or two, battling against the wind, determined not to return until Peter was out of the house. Her mind was in a turmoil. He had spoiled everything between them – sullied their relationship – it could never be the same again. There would always be this wound, this betrayal, which would be with her until the day she died – nothing could expunge it.

*   *   *   *   *

After Rosie returned from her lonely walk, she let herself quietly into the dark and silent cottage, with George trailing close behind her. Before taking off her coat, she ran anxiously upstairs to see if Ricky was safe. She had never left him on his own before and she had been worried in case he should wake up and need her – but her fears were totally groundless: he was sleeping peacefully.

Her heart twisted painfully as she saw in the half-light that Mr. Smith had been propped up in the corner of the cot by Ricky's feet. Peter had put him there and she knew instinctively that he had been worried too about leaving his son alone.

The cottage was cold and she shivered as she hurried back to the fire and threw on some extra logs. They crackled and blazed up furiously with the sparks flying up the chimney. The dismal wail of the wind sweeping down the valley was an eerie sound and penetrated through the cracks and crannies of the old cottage.

She curled up in her usual chair, kicking off her shoes and tucking up her feet – she looked little more than a distressed child, coping with grown-up problems. Biscuit jumped up beside her, demanding attention, repeatedly rubbing his head against her shoulder and purring like a little steam engine.

"Oh Biscuit, dear Biscuit," she cried dejectedly. "Whatever shall I do?" – and as she gathered him up in her arms she burst into a flood of tears. She felt shattered and, for the first time in her life, completely insecure; for in spite of their ups and downs she had always been confident of Peter's unfailing devotion to her and now he had destroyed her youthful ideal of ever-faithful love.

She was tortured by agonising pangs of jealousy. The horrifying thought of Peter's intimacy with this other woman was quite unbearable. She wondered what the girl had been like – perhaps more beautiful and much more fun than herself.

Since becoming a mother she knew she had changed from being a gay, carefree, fun-loving person into a responsible parent, but she was the same warm, passionate girl, whom Peter had married and she still found him extremely attractive.

Her own mother had warned her that she must always put her husband first, but she had ignored this advice and become primarily a mother not a wife. She blamed herself for this, with heart-aching regret, but it had been Peter's uncontrollable possessiveness that had really upset their lives; yet as she pictured him as he was now, having suffered so many horrifying experiences in fighting for his country, she felt she should have shown him more patience and consideration – there were faults on both sides.

She was pulled in so many directions that no clear cut answers came to her. She knew she still loved him but, although he appeared to have learnt his lesson, a leopard never changes its spots. Could she bear to continue living with him and overlook his unfaithfulness? This was the question that haunted her. After much soul searching, she thought not. She could survive without him, if she must – yet nothing would ease the pain that filled her and the deep disappointment that their wonderful dream of perfect love had turned to ashes.

It was getting cold, for she had used up all the wood and the embers of the fire were now grey and lifeless. She felt emotionally drained and very much alone. She dragged herself up the stairs to bed, carrying Biscuit with her for companionship. He snuggled up to her and they lay curled up close together all night.

The next few days seemed endless to Rosie, yet she hoped Peter would not hurry back, for she was not ready to face him yet. In his absence an even deeper resentment was building up inside her. She had sorted out her feelings and had come to the conclusion that he was an arrogant man, who had taken over her life and spoilt it by his green-eyed jealousy – not even able to share her with his own son. She was no longer prepared to give up all her interests and centre her life entirely around him. She was essentially a free person and liked to stretch her wings and was not willing to accept the confines of life which he had laid down for her. He could have all the girl-friends he wanted and good luck to him!

The following day the wind had dropped, but the rain was torrential. Rosie had been visiting remote coastal RAF sites; heavy mist hung over the airfields and visibility was down to a few yards; however, in spite of the weather, most of the officers and men came drifting out of their huts for a cup of tea, if only to see her bright smile and have a chat. These young pilots, rearing to go, found this enforced inactivity absolute purgatory. She had tried to cheer them up but it was hard going and she was thankful to be on her way home again.

As she pushed open the front door, her hair a mass of curls and her cheeks pink from the cold, she felt a sense of warm security. George gave her his usual exuberant welcome and Ricky, who was in his play-pen, shouted excitedly "Mummy, Mummy" and held out his arms to her. She rushed to pick him up, kissing him hungrily and he responded by winding his little arms around her neck and putting his cheek close to hers. As she looked over his shoulder she jumped, startled to see Peter standing by the kitchen door. Her eyes widened with surprise, but there was no warm welcome for him this time.

"Hello, Rosie," he said hesitantly. "Here I am again, turning up like a bad penny." He obviously felt ill-at-ease, uncertain of his reception.

"Hello," she replied coldly: "What time did you arrive?"

"I got here a couple of hours ago, so I told Bron she could go home and I'd look after Ricky. I hope that was all right?"

She nodded in agreement.

"We've had a good time together, old chap, haven't we?"

Ricky was all smiles and wriggled out of Rosie's arms and ran unsteadily to his father, clinging on to his trouser leg for support. Peter picked him up and threw him high into the air, catching him as he fell.

"More, more," Ricky pleaded, almost beside himself with laughter.

"That's enough for a bit, old fellow, I'm out of breath."

He turned to Rosie: "You look drenched, darling, would you like me to make you a cup of tea?"

She realised he was trying to please her, but he wouldn't get round her like this.

"Thank you," she said in an off-hand manner. "That would be nice, but first I'll go upstairs and change – I'll be down in a minute."

His heart sank as he wandered into the kitchen and started preparing the tea. He realised his absence had not improved the situation. She looked cold and unforgiving – he felt quite hopeless. He loved her so very much and he cursed himself again and again for his folly – would he never learn, or was it too late – had he already lost her?

They sat silently together in front of the fire; the atmosphere was tense. Ricky was asleep now, snugly tucked up in his cot, and all the chores were done except for one thing more. Rosie slipped away for a moment, having decided to make up the spare bed in Ricky's room. She was not going to have Peter sleeping with her.

When she came down again, she told him she'd moved his gear into the nursery and the bed was ready. He was staring gloomily into the fire and he did not answer her. His face looked ashen and Rosie noticed that his hands were shaking. She felt a sudden pang of anxiety for him, but it was no good procrastinating. She had to tell him her decision now. Her voice shook a little as she started to speak.

"Peter, I've decided I can't stay married to you. There are many reasons for this and it's no good discussing them, but that girl – she'd always be there, like a spectre between us."

There was a deathly silence in the room, broken only by the ticking of the clock and the faint hiss of damp logs in the grate.

She continued: "I know now that I was too young and immature to marry. I was just a child and was blinded by your good looks." She choked a little. "You were my knight in shining armour, but now I know that it is what's inside that really counts."

He raised his head and looked bleakly across at her. She was shocked by his ravaged face and anguished eyes. He spoke slowly and deliberately – every word seemed an effort.

"Rosie darling, please don't say such things. We couldn't separate. We're part of each other. That girl – it meant nothing at all – she was just a tramp. I hated her afterwards and despised myself more. You know I adore you – far too much, that's part of the trouble."

She lashed out at him now, her face flushed with anger. "Don't be such a hypocrite. If you loved me so much, how could you ever contemplate sleeping with another woman?" She laughed caustically: "You really don't think I'm as naïve as that, do you?"

"Rosie, you just don't understand how it was – it had absolutely no significance, you must believe that." He paused. "But what about Ricky? You couldn't think of separating us now; a normal child needs a father and, after a bad beginning, we are now great pals and he enjoys being with me." He had a strong point there – one that she had agonised over and she could not honestly refute it. Denying Ricky anything hurt her, let alone his father's love.

He rose to his feet wearily and crossed over to where she was sitting. He knelt down beside her, holding her close to him and burying his head against her shoulder. She tried to draw away, but he held her tightly, in a last desperate appeal.

"Rosie, Rosie, don't treat me like this. You and Ricky are all I've got and, if you ever left me, I wouldn't want to go on living. I know I've behaved abominably, but at least I've been honest with you. Surely this in itself demonstrates my integrity, as far as our relationship is concerned?"

"Yes, I'm glad you told me, Peter," she answered more calmly, "but everything now seems spoiled and sullied between us."

Her face was stricken and there was an awful silence in the room again.

"Please forgive me, Rosie darling," he said brokenly, "and for God's sake give me another chance."

Suddenly a paroxysm of uncontrolled sobs shook him – they seemed to be tearing him apart. She could hardly believe this was happening to her self-possessed Peter. She put her arms around him. She couldn't stand this terrible distress, this agony of mind, it was too cruel.

All her love for him flooded back like a warm tide. He seemed like a child to her now and, as she patted his dark head, so like Ricky's, she said softly: "Shush, shush, everything will be all right. I won't leave you. We'll try again." All she wanted now was to comfort and reassure him – anything to stop this heart-rending grief. Her arms tightened around his shoulders and she realised how thin he had become – she was shocked and would have forgiven him anything at this moment, as a wave of compassion swept over her.

That night they slept together in the double bed, locked in each other's arms, both drained by their emotions – so different from the carefree young people, who had slept there only months ago, then so confident and full of joyful promise.

* * * * *

Rosie was given a week's leave and she made a point of dedicating herself entirely to restoring Peter's well-being and shattered nerves. She cooked him all his favourite dishes and soon he looked less thin and gaunt. They went out for long walks together, much to George's delight; even Biscuit sometimes accompanied them, tracking stealthily in the hedgerows and occasionally popping his head out of the undergrowth to show them that he was still there. Ricky loved this and his eyes danced with excitement as he watched out for Biscuit's appearance.

The weather had changed and Spring suddenly burst forth. The cottage garden was a delight – full of daffodils and narcissi. The apple orchard was enchanting, the trees covered with new green leaves and their branches tipped with deep pink buds, until suddenly one morning there was a miracle – the trees, like a bride, wore a delicate mantle of pale pink blossom.

Peter seemed utterly content just to be with the family. He and Ricky had great fun together and their obvious affection for each other was a joy to Rosie. Sometimes in the evenings when Ricky had gone to bed, Peter would ask Rosie to play the piano for him. He found it soothing and she carefully chose pieces she knew he would enjoy. He often asked her for Elgar's *Salut d'amour*, a sentimental study, that the composer had written for his beloved wife. It was one of Peter's favourites.

Once she would got out her sketch book and ask him to sit for her. He liked to watch her slim, delicate hands at work. She did some brilliant pencil drawings of him and long afterwards, when she came across them, she understood the extent of the strain he was under at the time. His thin face, haunted eyes and the droop of his shoulders were reflected in every study.

The first bombs which had started to fall, mostly on small towns on the south coast, were no doubt a warning of what was to come. Yet this long lull gave the British people ample scope for their unfailing optimism. The air-raid sirens sounded twice in the village on consecutive days, intruding on the blessed quiet of the countryside. Once they heard the ominous sound of German planes passing overhead.

Rosie was out shopping in the village the morning that Peter's orders came through and, when she returned with their meagre weekly rations, he met her at the door, relieving her of her parcels. She noticed he looked strained and worried again.

"Hello, poppet, my confounded orders have just come through – I have to report at Chatham Barracks on Friday. I'm joining the staff as a divisional officer. I hate the prospect of a shore appointment."

Rosie's face dropped: "Oh dear, that is awful. I've been hoping and praying that we'd have longer together, but I'm thankful that you're having this spell ashore. You really need it, Pete; although you're much better, you still look a bit peaky."

"Nonsense, Rosie, I'm quite restored again but this job at Chatham makes me feel like a drop-out." He looked thoroughly disgruntled, yet he knew that he and Rosie needed more time to heal the breach.

They still slept together in the big bed, but it was obvious that her passionate desire for him had gone, yet she wanted to be close. He knew that he must not pressurise her, but it was a strain, his need for her was strong. Would things ever be right between them again? – only if he were given more time to restore her confidence in him.

"Rosie, why don't you and Ricky come down to Chatham with me? I've been thinking it all over; I can easily get digs for us there and then we could at least be together for a month or two until I get another sea appointment. I hate to miss a day of Ricky's childhood. He's growing up so fast now and this precious time can never be recaptured."

She knew he was putting on the pressure. She hesitated for a moment before replying – her face looked troubled.

"I'd love to do that, Pete, but it would be foolish to take Ricky into a potentially dangerous area. Yesterday it was reported on the wireless that there had been a bomb attack on Chatham docks."

Peter brushed this argument aside.

"I would get us digs in the Rochester area, which is above the town and miles from the docks and any military installations. After all, nowhere is really safe these days and even here a stray bomb could get you. I personally think we ought to stick together as a family for as long as possible."

She was in a dilemma; she hated to refuse him again, but undoubtedly Ricky was safer here. She thought it over for a few moments before replying, then came out strongly against the idea.

"No, Pete, I think it is too much of a risk to take."

He dropped the subject like a hot cake, but there was a feeling of tension in the air again and he couldn't mask his deep disappointment.

The following day, being Peter's last one at home, they decided to have a picnic lunch in Penrhyn woods, across the hill from Bryngwrn.

"I'll get the grub ready, Rosie, while you do the rest," Peter said zestfully.

"Good, I'll tidy up the cottage a bit and get Ricky dressed," Rosie replied with enthusiasm.

It was a lovely spring morning, warm and sunny; there was a general feeling of reawakening and hope in the air.

"Let's make it a super day – a day to remember," said Rosie, smiling radiantly up at him as they set off hand in hand together. "I've brought my pastels and I want to try doing a family group, providing you all have the patience to sit still for me."

"We'll do our best, darling, but I can see George is going to be a problem!"

"He always gets terribly excited, but he will soon calm down," Rosie replied.

George was dashing down the lane ahead of them, barking hysterically. He loved these family outings.

"Did you notice that Biscuit was scouting around the cottage garden before we left, and then mysteriously vanished?" she asked. "Well he's keeping pace with us under cover of the trees.

"Yes, I've been watching him," Peter replied. "He's stalking us in the undergrowth."

Ricky in his push chair was intently looking out for 'Bic' too. His sharp, intelligent eyes never left the hedgerow and, whenever he caught a flash of ginger, he shouted excitedly: "Bic here – Bic here!"

As they entered the woods Peter swung Ricky up on to his shoulders. "Gee-up, Neddy," he shouted as he jogged him up and down like a bucking bronco. This was Ricky's favourite game and he was almost sick with laughter as he dug in his heels. "More Dada, more," he implored until Peter was finally all in.

"That's enough, old chap, Neddy's run out of steam," he said lowering Ricky to the ground.

George plunged ahead of them, his excitement renewed by all the strange scents of the woods, determined to track them down.

Rosie followed more sedately with the picnic basket, revelling in the beauty of the forest. Everything was so verdant and fresh. Clusters of primroses and violets, now in profusion, carpeted the grassy banks, and the fresh green foliage was such a delight – a wonderful reawakening of nature.

Presently they found a clearing in the trees – it was dappled with sunbeams. "This is a lovely spot, Rosie, let's have our lunch here," Peter said, sitting down on the soft springy turf as if to test the veracity of his statement.

"Yes, this is perfect; help me to spread the rug, Pete, and I will arrange all our clobber."

"How about having lunch straight away, Rosie? I'm absolutely famished and I'm sure Ricky is too."

Rosie smiled. "We must wait for a minute, for one member of the family is yet to come," she said with a twinkle in her eye.

"All right, but not for long, all that lovely grub is too tempting," Peter said skittishly as he expectantly eyed the picnic basket.

Rosie lay down on the rug, closing her eyes and listening to the country sounds. An early bumble bee, awakened from hibernation, circled round the hanging furry catkins above her head, contentedly humming away.

It was only a minute or two later, when she heard a rustle in the undergrowth beside her, then a discreet miaow as Biscuit quietly revealed himself. Ricky pointed excitedly and gave a squeal of delight as he saw Bic's large amber eyes peeping through the long grass: "Bic, here, Mummy, Bic here."

Rosie sat up at once. "Now that we're all present and correct, let's unpack the food and see what delicacies are in store for us. I must admit I'm ravenous too – the sandwiches look delicious, Pete, and I see you've even put in a nice juicy marrow bone for George!"

He made them all laugh for, after a good old chew, he carefully buried the bone, obviously keeping it for another occasion.

After they had finished their lunch and were replete and drowsy, Rosie quickly produced her pastels and started to draw. She worked rapidly and it was not long before the study was completed and she stood back, well satisfied with the result.

"Can I see it now, Rosie?" Peter asked.

"Yes, of course. It's a new approach for me, almost primitive in style – all the colours are bright and Biscuit, with his ginger stripes, seems to dominate the picture – I'm rather pleased with it."

Peter studied it closely. "I like it very much, Rosie, it's fun and unusual. Ricky looks nice and I don't look too bad. George seems utterly relaxed, so soft and floppy and Biscuit is perfect – it's Biscuit to the life!"

Rosie liked the simplicity of the picture. Her experiment had come off. "I'm pleased with it myself," she said delightedly. "I think I've caught the mood of the moment. It will be a permanent record of this lovely day we've spent together as a happy little family."

"We'll have many more of them, Rosie," Peter said quickly, as though there might be a doubt.

Peter's last night was a sad one. When he and Rosie were in bed he did his utmost to persuade her to join him in Chatham with Ricky. He used all his persuasive powers, but she was adamant that she wouldn't risk it. She felt miserable for him and terribly guilty. Was she making the same mistake again?

That night they made love for the first time since his return. It was a travesty of what had been before – there was no point in pretending otherwise.

Peter was heart-sick: "Darling, why can't we be the same as we used to be?" he asked despairingly. "I love you so dearly – don't you want me now, Rosie?"

There was a long silence, as she lay in his arms, quiet and tense.

"I can't help it – that girl, she's still between us. I think she always will be."

"Oh don't, Rosie, don't," he pleaded. "I've told you it didn't mean a thing. Darling, I don't want to make excuses, but you have no idea what I've been through – the sinking of the ship, the horror of it. The screams – I couldn't stop hearing them, the icy water and choking black oil. I can't talk about it yet, but one day I will and you'll understand. I needed you so desperately then, Rosie, and when you turned me down I felt utterly rejected."

His voice broke – it was almost a sob again. Suddenly she was clinging to him, weeping distractedly for them both, for surely they had been victims of cruel circumstances. They lay together all night in each other's arms and he rocked her tenderly until she fell asleep.

The next morning she agreed to join him in Chatham.

12

PETER did not waste any time in finding a place for them to live. He started making enquiries at once and was told of Mrs. Neal, a middle-aged widow, living in Rochester, who might possibly provide a temporary home for them. He made an appointment at once to see her and they liked each other on sight – an instant rapport was established between them.

Mrs. Neal had long felt that she must make a contribution to the war effort and, as her house was far too large for one person, helping this nice naval officer and his family seemed the complete answer. Her husband had been a ship's engineer and had been killed a few years earlier in an accident down at the docks and she hadn't any children. She welcomed the thought of the little boy and even the dog was acceptable. She was touched by Peter's obvious devotion to his family and his urgent need to find somewhere for them to live for this short period while he was on shore duty.

The house was substantially built, the end one in a terrace. It was immaculately kept and Peter felt that Rosie would be happy there. Mrs. Neal agreed to let them have two bedrooms and also her best front sitting room. The house was warm and comfortable and Peter knew he had indeed been lucky to find such a nice place.

It was arranged that Rosie and the family would arrive the following weekend and he hastily phoned her with the good news. "Rosie, I've had a bit of luck. I've found marvellous digs for us in Rochester – with a Mrs. Neal. She is a widow and a very nice person and the accomodation is good. I know you'll like it and get on well with her."

"That's wonderful, Pete, but what is the house like?"

"It's very nice indeed – spick and span and Mrs. Neal is an absolute dear."

Rosie sounded quieter than usual. "That's good, but I'm still worried about bringing Ricky. He's so safe in the country and I hate deserting Biscuit."

"Biscuit will be all right with Bronwen and there's nothing to worry about here. We're miles from the docks and it's perfectly safe. It will be wonderful when we are together again."

So very much against her natural instinct Rosie was persuaded to join him in Chatham.

The day of Rosie's departure arrived all too soon. She packed the car with meticulous care. There was so much to take for a child, and even George needed his basket – his own little domain. The sun was brilliant that morning and the garden was now in all its glory, full of spring flowers and blossom – she just hated the prospect of missing the enchantment of the coming months at home.

Bron came running out of the cottage with the last bulging package, full of the inevitable bits and pieces essential for a family. Her earnest little face looked concerned, she was upset that they were leaving.

"Don't worry about anything, Mam. I'll take good care of the place while you are gone and I'll see that Biscuit is well fed. When he's lonely, he always comes miaowing at my back door."

"Thank you for everything, Bron. I know he'll be all right with you. I think we have all we need but, if not, I'll drop you a line and perhaps you'll send it on. I've left our address on the kitchen table under the milk bottle."

Ricky was sitting contentedly in his car seat. He loved any sort of expedition.

Bron ran around and gave him a cuddle and a big kiss.

"Goodbye, my little 'cariad bach'. I'm going to miss you dreadfully, for you're the sweetest baby in all the world." Her eyes were anxious and full of tears. "Oh, Mam, do come back soon and don't stay if the bombing gets any worse, but I know you must be with Mr. Dunbar, poor man, after all he's been through."

"Goodbye, Bron, we won't be away for long and au revoir 'Apple Trees'."

She said this wistfully for she hated leaving. Then, with a last farewell wave to Bron, she was accelerating down the winding lane, past the old church and through the village into the open country.

The journey was long and Rosie was thankful when they eventually arrived at their destination. As they pulled up outside the house she thought how neat and clean it all looked, with spotless white curtains at the windows. She sat back in her seat, resting after the strain of the drive; manoeuvring through the dense traffic around London and the busy roads through Greenwich hadn't been easy.

She saw Peter bounding down the steep steps. He looked much better – so vital, and his face lit up with pleasure to see them. Her forebodings all flew out of the window as she jumped out of the car to greet him and he hugged her close; they were both obviously thrilled at being together again.

"Hello darling, how wonderful to see you. Did you have a good journey?"

"Not too bad, Pete, but it's a long way and I do feel rather weary."

"Come in and relax. Tea is all ready for you."

George was panting with excitement at seeing his master and was leaping about all over the back seat. Ricky sat patiently awaiting his father's attention, his thoughtful blue eyes full of eager anticipation. When his door was opened he spontaneously held out his arms to Peter and, as he was carried up to the house, he hugged his father tightly. Peter felt strangely moved by this genuine show of affection.

Mrs. Neal was waiting in the hall to greet them. She had watched their arrival and was touched by their obvious delight at being reunited. She felt she had done the right thing in providing them with a home.

As Rosie came up the steps, Mrs. Neal thought what a lovely-looking girl she was, and Rosie took to her on sight. Instantly her heart went out to this kindly, middle-aged woman.

"Hello Mrs. Neal," Rosie said warmly, "it is so good of you to share your home with us; we very much appreciate it."

"I'm very pleased to have you here, my dear, for I'm on my own now and I've plenty of room for you all. What a lovely boy," she said, patting Ricky's little head – he looked at her solemnly for a moment, weighing her up, then gave her a beautiful smile and affectionately held out his arms. She swept him up and hugged him and from that moment on Ricky could do no wrong in Mrs. Neal's eyes.

They soon settled in happily together, establishing a routine that suited them all. Mrs. Neal adored Ricky, she had never known a child so sweet and loving. Her life had been empty since her husband's death and now suddenly she had a ready made family. Fortunately she liked animals and, provided George stayed in his basket and didn't jump up on to her best front room suite, she was more than content to have him.

She was a very good cook and gave them meals separately in their sitting room, on a stout old oak table in the window. Rosie was happy and comfortable here, but she was most apprehensive of Ricky's safety. The bombing seemed to be hotting up all over the country and she told Peter that she was worried and wondered if they should return to Wales but he wouldn't listen – he was adamant that they were as safe there as anywhere.

A few nights later, however, they were having their supper when the siren started wailing – it was such an eerie, frightening sound. Almost immediately the anti-aircraft guns were in action and the thunder and vibration from them seemed to shake the house.

Peter grabbed Ricky and put him hastily under the table, then unceremoniously pushed Rosie after him. George, who was terrified by the noise, quickly joined them, shaking all over, but Ricky seemed quite unperturbed, imitating the boom-boom of the guns. He grinned up at his mother, enjoying what he thought was a lovely game, but all Rosie could do was to hold him tight and wish with all her heart that she had not brought him away from the safety of Wales.

It was again a tip and run raid on the docks and soon they heard the drone of enemy aircraft overhead, returning from their deadly mission of destruction; shortly afterwards the all-clear sounded. Peter tried to be jocular, but was inwardly rather shaken.

"It's safe to come out now, Rosie, so let me help you up and we can finish the rest of our meal" – but she scrambled out on her own, with Ricky in her arms. Peter was trying to appear confident, but he already had doubts about the wisdom of bringing them here, yet he was too stubborn to admit it.

"You know, Rosie, we are quite safe up on the hill – we're well clear of the dockyard," he said, trying to justify his decision, "and there is nothing here on which Gerry would waste his bombs."

"I hope you're right," she replied coldly, but she was beginning to think that she had been very foolish to give in to him and was already contemplating an early return to Wales.

The next day was lovely and warm, so Rosie and Mrs. Neal, who had become good friends, decided to take advantage of the sunshine and, with Ricky and George, go for a walk to explore the district.

It was so very different from her beloved Wales, but Rosie enjoyed the change of environment. She was a thoroughly adaptable person, who could find interest and happiness wherever she happened to be. She was particularly interested in the City of Rochester, with its many historical and literary associations; indeed Dickens had spent part of his life here, and she was keen to visit his house – the 'Bleak House' of the novel.

She was most anxious to see the Norman cathedral, so they decided to make this their first objective. They could not go inside with George in tow, so contented themselves by walking around the outside, admiring its two famous doorways, especially the western one which was unique with its highly decorative carvings of exceptional beauty.

They loved the tranquil atmosphere of the close and, after their cursory inspection of the cathedral, they sat on a seat contentedly soaking up the sunshine, talking and fussing over Ricky.

"Not having any children of my own has been a great sorrow to me and particularly now that I am widowed and all alone," Mrs. Neal told Rosie confidentially.

Rosie patted her hand in sympathy. "You know the old saying, Mrs. Neal, that children are a mixed blessing and, although Ricky is everything to me, I often wish we had waited until after the war before having a baby. I worry about him constantly and never have any peace of mind."

"I can understand that, my dear, but you must try not to think that way. He is such a lovely boy and you should enjoy every minute of his childhood." She leant forward and stroked his little face and he beamed back at her.

"You certainly have a special place in Ricky's heart," Rosie said sincerely "and you have had from the very beginning. You seem almost like another grandmother to him."

"How nice of you to say that, Rosie, for I really love the child and he has brought sunshine into my life. I've been very lonely since my husband died."

"I'm so glad we have helped, for you have been marvellous to us – even befriending our exuberant George," she said giving his head an affectionate pat. "You don't know how I grateful I am to you."

"Bless you, my dear. You know I'm very attached to you all."

"And we are to you," Rosie answered sincerly.

"I think we should go now, it must be nearly Ricky's tea-time and soon he'll be getting hungry and crochety, and we don't want our little angel to lose his halo!" Mrs. Neal said with a wry smile.

On their return journey she pointed out the borstal institution, from which the bad boys had been removed and which was now used by the navy for training sailors.

"The thick-walled cells make natural air-raid shelters and, as the building is such a conspicuous target, it's just as well," she remarked.

Rosie's heart dropped, for here was a naval target in Rochester itself, to say nothing of the A.A. guns around there. She felt that Peter had deceived her by not revealing this obvious danger, but she did not say anything.

As they approached the house, their next-door neighbour, Mr. Timms, was clipping his privet hedge. When he saw Ricky, he waved; his wrinkled old face as brown as a walnut was wreathed in smiles. His only son had been killed in action early on in the war. He had been in the merchant navy and his ship had been blown up by a mine in the North Sea.

Mr. Timms was very interested in this little family, but his poor wife found it painful to see Peter in his naval uniform passing her window each day. She had so far been unable to bring herself to speak to any of them, but her husband gained comfort from talking to Peter and often spoke of his son and the circumstances of his death.

As they reached the house, Mr. Timms laid down his shears and came through the gate toward them. "Well, how is my young feller to-day?" he asked, chucking Ricky under the chin. Ricky beamed delightedly back at him, clapping his hands and shouting "Timm, Timm, Timm."

"It's Mr. Timms, Ricky," Rosie corrected.

"No, let him be, he's my boy and clever to know my name." He was obviously delighted.

"Would it be all right if I took him in and showed him to the missus? I think it might do her good and give her something else to think about."

"Of course, Mr. Timms," Rosie replied warmly. "We'll leave him with you while we go and get tea ready."

"Thank you, my dear, that's good of you. I'll bring him back presently," he said as he carried Ricky triumphantly into his house.

* * * * *

Peter was home each evening about 5.30 and they all had high tea together; then Mrs. Neal put Ricky to bed. This was at her own request and, knowing how much she loved the child, Rosie agreed to the arrangement; secretly she missed this time with her son, but she must not be selfish.

She and Peter enjoyed their quiet evenings together by the fire, discussing events of the day and the changing war situation. There was no denying that things were going badly, though everyone still confidently talked of victory and would never concede for a minute that Britain could possibly be defeated.

The phoney war was abruptly ended when Germany savagely attacked Denmark and Norway. Denmark had succumbed almost at once, but the Norwegians hung on, fighting a losing battle with desperate heroism against hopeless odds. Their appeals for help from Britain had been answered when a naval and military force was sent to Norway, but they could not match the strength of the Luftwaffe. Within three weeks British troops were forced to withdraw. Altogether it was a disastrous campaign and this defeat was a shattering blow for the Allies.

Peter felt he should be taking a more active part in the war effort and was restive. He loved being with his family, though his relationship with Rosie was still strained. The beauty and closeness of their love-making had not returned – spoilt by the memory of the Savoy incident. He wondered if this skeleton in the cupboard would ever go away. He felt guilty and frustrated being on shore duty, especially with the rapid deterioration of the war situation. He longed to be back in the thick of it again, yet he dreaded leaving Rosie until their loving relationship had been properly restored.

Following the Norwegian reverse, the Luftwaffe next savaged Holland and Belgium – things were going from bad to worse.

Neville Chamberlain, having lost the confidence of his own party and with public opinion very much against him, had resigned his premiership and now in this dark hour he was succeeded by the old war horse, Winston Churchill. When this courageous, dynamo of a man addressed the House of Commons for the first time as Prime Minister, he made one of his most indomitable wartime speeches. His every word was received with wrapt attention.

"I would say to the House, as I said to those who have joined this Government, I have nothing to offer but blood, toil, tears and sweat"... which proved to be all too true for there was still worse to come and further disasters occurred in quick succession.

Germany's mighty panzer tank force was now unleashed and turned its attention on France and, by the simple expedient of skirting the northern limit of the Maginot Line, they drove a dangerous wedge between the allied armies. Belgium quickly capitulated, leaving the left flank exposed and France was soon *in extremis.*

Despite the gallant efforts of the British Expeditionary Force, there was no alternative but to fall back to the Channel coast and evacuate the troops. Here a miracle was performed on the beaches of Dunkirk where the soldiers, exposed and harried by air attacks from the deadly Stuka dive bombers, were picked up under the very nose of the enemy.

The navy was supported by a miscellany of craft of every description – a veritable armada, from merchant ships down to the smallest pleasure boats, manned by brave civilian volunteers. They set sail from England with grim determination, regardless of the danger, to cross the narrow strip of water to rescue and bring home their fighting men. In all 338,000 British and Allied troops were ferried across the Channel, but the extent of the loss of arms and equipment was great and could be ill-afforded at this time.

This episode will go down in the annals of history as a glorious retreat – in his praise of this supreme effort Winston Churchill, the realist, nevertheless reminded the nation that we had in fact sustained a serious defeat.

It was only a matter of days before Italy declared war on Britain.

The final blow, however, was struck when France capitulated and Paris was occupied by triumphant, goose-stepping Germans, without a shot being fired. It was quite unbelievable that such a thing could have happened to this gay and lovely city, and it seemed only yesterday that Peter and Rosie had been sitting contentedly in the sunshine on the Champs Elysées.

Now Britain really stood alone and Churchill, preparing the country to defend its island home, made his second stirring speech to the House of Commons. The nation listened with baited breath and hung on to his every word.

"We shall not flag or fail. We shall go on to the end. We shall fight in France, we shall fight on the seas and oceans, we shall fight with growing confidence and growing strength in the air; we shall defend our island, whatever the cost may be. We shall fight on the beaches, we shall fight on the landing grounds, we shall fight in the fields and in the streets, we shall fight in the hills; we shall never surrender."

As Rosie and Mrs. Neal listened together to this speech on the wireless, Rosie felt petrified. "Oh, Mrs. Neal," she said pitifully, "I should never have had Ricky – it frightens me how much I love him and, if those Nazis land here, goodness only knows what might happen to him. I've heard terrible stories about their brutality to children."

Mrs. Neal's eyes filled with tears and she put her arm round Rosie. "Try not to worry, dear. We're all in this together and with Mr. Churchill as leader we shall win. Those Nazis will never get a foothold in this country."

Rosie made up her mind there and then that, despite what Peter said, she would no longer be lulled into a sense of false security by him. She would take Ricky back to Wales the following week before the Germans came, for the south east was the front line now. She started to make preparations and the first thing she did was to write to Bronwen.

She would not tell Peter yet – she knew that he would do his best to talk her out of it.

13

IT WAS a beautiful, warm sunny day and, in spite of the alarming news, life had to go on, so Rosie decided to walk into Chatham to buy the week's rations and any other extras that she could find, to eke out their meagre wartime fare. She had not yet broken the news to Peter that she and Ricky were leaving shortly but decided that she would do so that evening.

It was a long walk downhill into the town and the climb back would be difficult with parcels to carry, so she chose to take the empty pram along. She had left Ricky safe in his playpen and, in spite of George's entreating glances, she hardened her heart and left him behind too.

It was good to be alive despite the gloom and as she set forth her hair glistened like gold in the sunshine. She looked slim and lovely and far too young to be a mother. A number of servicemen smiled at her with admiring glances as she passed them by, and there was the occasional wolf whistle from cheerful sailors, with their swinging bell-bottom trousers.

Chatham was best known for its naval barracks and dockyard, but generally it was an undistinguished though bustling little town, full of small shops. Rosie's favourite was a gallery which had a good stock of artists' materials so, after doing the food shopping, she intended to have a browse around and lay in a stock of paints and canvases. She had decided to paint a picture of Mrs Neal's house as a goodbye present, for she was intensely proud of her home and Rosie knew this would please her. She dreaded breaking the news that they would be leaving, for Mrs. Neal loved Ricky like a child of her own, but perhaps she would come and stay with them at the cottage from time to time.

As she walked along she was deep in thought, considering how to handle the painting. The house, 'Silver Birches', was the end one in a terrace of thirty. It was a typical L.S. Lowry setting – high up with steep steps leading to the front door. It was built of grey stone and the gable end was cobbled, which was most unusual in this part of the country. There was a pretty swathe of grass in front and delicate silver birches softened the somewhat harsh landscape, with its rows and rows of terraced houses. Rosie was looking forward to starting the picture. She felt it could be an unusual study with clean lines and a vivid contrast between the spotless white paintwork and the sombre grey walls. She had decided to employ the dry-brush technique, using very little water and building up the thickness of the paint. She wanted this to be a very special present, as she had become fond of this lonely woman, who had welcomed them so warmly into her home.

She started humming as she strolled into the town, feeling more confident and happier. She was always content when she had a project under way. She decided to hurry with the food shopping, so as to leave plenty of time for searching around for art materials, but she had no sooner parked the pram outside the grocer's shop than the dreaded wail of the air raid siren was heard.

These were always testing minutes of threat and her instant reaction was to race back home to Ricky. Without hesitation Rosie seized the pram and started running up the street which was crowded with early morning shoppers who were alarmed and rushing uncertainly in all directions, some colliding with the pram and retarding her progress.

It was only seconds later that she heard the broken throb of aero engines above, followed by a shattering barrage of anti-aircraft guns, which was terrifying in its sudden impact. Then there was the dreaded sound of bombs whistling down and ending in a deafening explosion nearby, which seemed to split her eardrums, shaking the ground and leaving Rosie stunned yet miraculously unharmed.

She stood stock still for a moment, paralysed by the shock, then she started to run frantically again, with only one thought in her head – to get back to Ricky. She rounded the corner that led up the steep hill to Oswell Terrace, now alive with running figures.

A booming voice from a megaphone started blaring out repetitively for all civilians to take cover. She ignored this command, in fact it failed to register with her at all, until a burly A.R.P. warden grasped her arm and marched her brusquely into a nearby shelter, pushing the abandoned pram to the side of the road.

"You're not allowed on the streets during a raid, Miss; you must wait in here for the all clear to sound."

But Rosie was distraught and determined to escape.

"Let me go," she implored, "I must get back to my little boy, please let me go."

"Whereabouts do you live?"

"At the top of the hill – Oswell Terrace it's called."

"Don't worry, he'll be all right up there, they're only attacking the dock area," he replied confidently. "Everything on the hill should be safe enough."

The shelter was full of silent people with apprehensive expressions. The curtained opening was pulled to and Rosie was aware of the tension that each individual was feeling. It was airless in there and crowded to full capacity, stifling and claustrophobic. A little old woman with anxious eyes tugged at her arm for comfort.

"I've left my poor cat at home, sitting by the fire. He's twenty years old and he's all I've got. I always put him in the cellar as it's quieter there, but today I didn't; I left him sleeping upstairs, not wanting to disturb him." She sighed deeply. "Somehow you don't expect anything bad to happen when the sun is shining."

Rosie gave a sympathetic response but her thoughts were focused only on Ricky.

"Your little boy isn't on his own, is he?"

"Oh no, Mrs. Neal, the lady we live with, is looking after him, but I must get back."

There was desperation and a touch of hysteria in Rosie's voice. The terrific barrage of anti-aircraft guns shook the shelter to its flimsy foundations. Then an enormous explosion, obviously close by, rocked the ground and everyone flinched at the terrifying nearness of the blast.

After the shock waves had passed and the roar of tumbling bricks and plaster died away in a slow rumble, the heavy drone of engines was heard again overhead. Everyone waited quietly with bated breath for the next explosion – the silence was broken by the terrified sobs of a child in his mother's arms; the young mother's face was tense with anxiety as she tried to calm him. Rosie's heart went out to her but she was filled by a terrible dread for her own child. When the next explosion came, it was further off, higher up the street. All breathed a sigh of relief. People started to whisper among themselves, trying to gain reassurance from one another.

Rosie wondered where Peter was. He must be in the thick of it but instinctively she knew that he would be all right. It was Ricky who mattered and she must not waste any more time getting back to him. She edged closer to the opening and, while the warden was preoccupied in calming down a hysterical young woman, Rosie slipped unnoticed out of the entrance, thankful to be in the fresh air once more.

She ignored the now-overturned pram, swept on to its side by the force of the blast, and started running up the steep hill as fast as she could, her breath coming in gasps and sobs. The devastation frightened her and, as she stumbled over piles of debris, the clouds of brick dust brought on terrible spasms of coughing.

She saw with horror that a group of houses on the corner had been completely demolished, evidently by a direct hit. An ambulance screeched to a halt by her side and the stretcher bearers jumped out to assist the rescue workers, who were digging madly. It seemed unlikely that anyone could be left in there alive, but their efforts were unflagging and, as she passed, she saw them lift a mutilated body from the wreckage, which they quickly covered with a blanket and transferred to the ambulance.

She was forced to slacken her pace, the shock of what she had seen and the exhaustion of running had taken its toll — her heart was fit to burst. She sank to her knees on the broken paving stones for a rest and at this moment the welcome wail of the all clear sounded. With a certain measure of relief, she dragged herself up and started climbing the hill again, ploughing her way through loose rubble and broken glass, hurled from the shattered windows on the street, but she never slackened her pace — an inner fear drove her on.

She was nearly at the top now, only the corner to turn and then the terrace would be in sight. As she made the final last effort she heard an ambulance bell clanging, and both ambulance and a heavy rescue tender had swung into the street, accelerating fast and quickly overtaking her.

At first glance the terrace of houses seemed intact but it was only as she drew nearer that she saw the horror that confronted her — a sight indelibly engraved on her mind with a terrifying clarity that was never to leave her.

She blinked her eyes unbelievingly, for the end house in the terrace no longer stood there. It had been freakishly sliced away from the rest, as if by a blow from a giant meat cleaver; she looked up and saw the familiar pink roses of their bedroom wallpaper standing in stark relief against the house next door. Nothing else was recognisable, only the devastation, piles of bricks and rubble — the pathetic remains of Mrs.Neal's beloved home.

Terror overwhelmed her and her breath came in great spasmodic gulps, as she dragged herself towards the smoking ruin. A squad of workers, scrambling amongst the wreckage, was digging furiously. She heard one say that a damaged Heinkel, rapidly losing height, had dropped its bombs before crashing a few miles further on.

She started to scrabble amongst the broken beams and bricks, frenzied like one possessed, not sparing herself, extracting anything movable, completely oblivious of her torn and bleeding hands. As one of the A.R.P. squad approached she managed a hoarse croak: "There's a woman and a child buried under here." Then her strength ebbed away and blessed unconsciousness took over.

The next thing she knew was having brandy forced through her clenched teeth and faintly hearing a voice as if from a great distance.

"You've done enough luv, come and rest." Swimming before her eyes was the kindly face of a middle-aged woman in Red Cross uniform, but Rosie struck out wildly, fighting against the restraining arms that held her. "Let me go, my little boy is trapped under there."

As she dragged herself to her feet again, still struggling to get free, she heard one of the workers shouting for help.

"Come over here all of you, there's someone buried under this rubble."

She stumbled towards the voice and saw with horror an arm protruding from beneath a pile of masonry. Joining the others, frantically she pulled off the debris piece by piece, until the head and shoulders of an elderly woman covered in brick dust was revealed. Poor, dear Mrs. Neal, her grey hair streaked with blood, her face deathly white, frozen in a mask of shock.

Rosie tenderly smoothed the hair back from her forehead and wiped the dust from her face, then the stretcher bearers, not wanting to lose a moment, carried the body swiftly away, struggling and scrambling for footholds in the loose debris.

Rosie resumed her frenzied digging with phenomenal strength, drawn miraculously from some hidden inner source. It seemed an eternity before they came across the familiar old oak-table – still intact and standing firmly on its castors – their only refuge. She gave a little cry of desperation as she tugged wildly at it and, with the help of the others, they lifted it clear.

There was Ricky, her darling, lying among the rubble. His little face was mercifully untouched, cherubic in its innocence. His expression was peaceful and serene, so pale and angelic against this stark background of devastation. George was lying dead close beside him and his teddy, Mr. Smith, face down in the dust.

Rosie in her insane grief picked up the little body. It seemed to have no weight or substance any more. She studied his face carefully – it was content, as if in a deep sleep. She sat on a pile of bricks clasping her son close to her, rocking him gently back and forth. Of course this was only a nightmare and he was just sleeping; presently his eyes would open.

The rescue team withdrew sorrowfully, leaving her undisturbed. She closed her eyes for a moment to shut out the grim reality that surrounded her, until she felt the touch of a hand on her shoulder and, looking up, saw Mr. Timms bending over her, stricken by grief and pity.

"Let me help you, my dear," he said shakily.

"Mr. Timms," she whispered, "we're all right, but please take George and Mr. Smith to a safe place." He nodded, his face was creased with pain as he turned and gently picked up the limp body of the dog and the begrimed favourite teddy. He carried them to his own garden next door and laid them carefully down on the grass, then he returned to Rosie.

"Come to the ambulance now, my dear, your child must be taken to the hospital," but Rosie would not move. She held her little son in her arms with a vice-like grip and, when a Red Cross worker tried to separate them, she strongly resisted.

"He is all right," Rosie whispered, as she smoothed back his hair. "Look at his face, he is just sleeping."

At that moment a car came tearing along the street, screeching to a grinding halt beside the ambulance; the door was flung open and out jumped Peter. He stood for a moment, unable to believe his eyes, incredulous and appalled by what he saw. Then he started running frantically towards them, stumbling and crashing through the wreckage.

He knelt beside Rosie, cradling her and his dead child in his arms. His horror was so overwhelming that he was struck dumb by shock – there was only the agonised sound of his heavy breathing beside her. Then gently but firmly he lifted Ricky from her arms and this time she did not resist. With stumbling steps, picking his way slowly through the ruins, he carried the little body to the ambulance, laying him gently down and, after one final agonised look, he turned away.

Mr. Timms, his head bowed and with a hand on her shoulder, was standing close to Rosie. He helped her to her feet and quietly led her to his house. Her limbs were heavy and she walked with great effort. She seemed to be in a trance-like state, utterly spent by her endeavours. Mrs. Timms was waiting for them at the door and she took Rosie's arm and guided her to a chair by the fire. Then Mrs. Timms bathed her bleeding hands and tried to comfort her. She made her a cup of sweetened tea to help combat the shock and, with brimming eyes, persuaded Rosie to drink it.

"There, there, lass, drink this now," she coaxed. "It will make you feel better," but Rosie did not answer, she just gulped it down like a child. She seemed hardly conscious of what was going on around her and, when Peter returned after spending a few minutes talking with Mr. Timms, they left silently together and her face was still blank and expressionless.

Peter took her to a small hotel in the centre of town, so that she could lie down, but after a time when she still seemed unaware of her surroundings, he sent for a doctor. It was an elderly man who eventually came, exhausted by his own rescue efforts, but he talked compassionately to Rosie as gently he bandaged her damaged hands and gave her sedatives to calm her and take the edge off her suffering. She was, however, completely oblivious of the terrible happenings of the day – she was quite numb. She had pushed the unbearable memory away into her subconscious – she sensed only a blankness, as if she were living in a vacuum until, with a horrifying flash, it all came back to her when she heard the doctor ask if the child had been taken to the mortuary. Then she knew.

"Oh God," she silently prayed, "not Ricky, not Ricky." Something in her seemed to snap as her mental anguish tore at her agonisingly and unmercifully. She rolled over with hands clenched tightly under the pillow, her eyes closed, her whole body racked with grief.

The doctor left sadly, feeling helpless and inadequate in face of this tragedy, though realising that this was just a foretaste of what was in store for so many. Peter sat beside her on the bed, suffering intensely, but keeping in check his own unbearable grief. He held her close to him, trying to provide her with a little comfort, but suddenly she broke away, her spent body showing almost superhuman strength.

"Now you listen to me" – her voice was hard and cutting. It was a stranger's voice bereft of tears. "Your selfishness has killed our child. You insisted that we came to this death trap, just for your own gratification. I will never forgive you or live with you again."

She tore her wedding ring savagely from her agonisingly painful fingers and, with all her force, threw it across the room.

148

"Rosie, Rosie, don't say that," he pleaded. "We need each other desperately now and without you life would have no purpose – I could never carry on alone."

"Well, that is your choice. I no longer want to live with you again."

Then with these bitter words she slumped back on the pillows, all strength and resistance drained from her, as mercifully the sedatives drugged her into unconsciousness.

Peter carefully covered her with an eiderdown and sat down on the bed beside her, lightly holding her bandaged hands. His darling Rosie who, only a few short months ago, had been a gay carefree girl and now he had brought her to this.

The guilt he felt was horrifying; would his conscience ever be at rest again? He looked searchingly at her and saw how much she had changed. Her eyes were sunken, her face paper-white and stricken. He felt an overwhelming surge of pity for her, submerging his own sorrow in a way that he would never have believed possible.

As he thought of his son he recalled what a disciplinarian he had been in the early days and deeply regretted it; after all Ricky had still been only a baby. He had been far too stern and cursed himself for it. He remembered how the child had always come back with a smile and, under all circumstances, had given him a ready affection. He had been a darling child and the loss of his son was pure agony to Peter. Tears coursed down his cheeks, as he laid his face against Rosie's hand; she stirred and, as she woke into this nightmare world alone with him, she found she couldn't bear to look at him – it was too painful.

Her voice was low and hoarse as she spoke: "Peter – the funeral – I would like Ricky buried in the little churchyard at Bryngwrn. Can you arrange it? We want only the family."

"Of course, Rosie, he will be at peace there." His voice broke and he could not carry on, yet there was so much he wanted to say. Her eyes were closing again.

The doctor had told him that she would sleep on for hours after the strong sedatives he had given her and the immense physical effort she had made. Peter hated to leave for holding her hand was his only solace, a link between them, which he feared to break, otherwise the tenuous threads of their relationship might be completely severed. But he must go now, for there was much to be done. He stood up wearily and, bending over, kissed her lightly on the forehead.

"Oh Rosie, Rosie darling," he implored: "Please, please forgive me. You're all I have. I can't exist without you." This time she did not stir, so gently withdrawing his hand, he slipped away quietly.

*   *   *   *   *

The little churchyard at Bryngwrn was dappled in morning sunshine and the birds sang joyfully in this quiet sanctuary. The countryside lay peaceful and serene in the glow of a warm summer's day – so blessedly remote and untouched by the horrors and the grim realities of war.

As the tiny coffin was lowered into the ground, Rosie gazed down at it, her anguished eyes like two deep pools of blue, her face pale and expressionless. She knew now that this place was intended for her son; it was predestined and this explained the strange uneasy feeling that she had experienced in this

149

churchyard on her first visit, gravely disturbing, yet with a strong spiritual quality.

She felt that he would rest peacefully here in this quiet green valley where he had spent most of his short life – not even two summers long. He would always be nearby and she could never leave the cottage now; it would be her home. She seemed to stand aloof – a tiny figure clad in black. Peter at her side seemed utterly remote. He realised that for her he did not exist. Their parents were trying to draw comfort from each other, but Rosie's mother never let her eyes wander from her daughter's frail little figure.

Standing unobtrusively alone, hidden by the trees, was Bron, stricken and quite unable to believe that in the few short months of separation this terrible tragedy had occurred. She quietly mourned the little boy, whom she had loved so much, and her heart was wrung with pity for Rosie.

As the earth fell upon the coffin, Rosie quietly and with dignity turned and slowly walked away, disappearing alone through the trees towards the cottage. Her mother watched her with despair. She knew that there could be no human comfort for Rosie – only God could give her spiritual strength to overcome this terrible grief.

Peter stood alone now; he seemed stunned, so publicly rejected by his wife and, although he watched her walk away, he did not make any attempt to follow. Rosie's mother drew nearer to him, her warm heart aching with sympathy for this broken young man. She linked her arm through his and held it close to her.

"Peter, my dear," she said softly: "I think we should all go back to the cottage now to join Rosie. She will be waiting for us."

He looked at her blankly. "Yes, I suppose so," he said in a hopeless voice, "but she has no time for me now."

She squeezed his arm. "Rosie is still in a state of shock. When she gets over this, she will see things differently. Try not to worry, Peter, time is a great healer. Let's catch up with the others, my dear."

Peter swallowed hard, trying to control his emotions. "Thank you for your understanding – I'll never forget your kindness to me of all people."

* * * * *

The dusty sunlight flooded the room, tracing pale criss-cross shadows on the carpet of the now-silent cottage. Their parents had departed, leaving Peter and Rosie alone.

Rosie's mother and father had been first to go, heartbroken that they could not do anything to relieve their daughter's anguish and shocked by the obvious chasm that had developed between her and Peter. They had striven hard to conceal their deep distress at the loss of their adored grandson, who had indeed been the centre of their lives, but the strain had been too much for Mrs. Greenwood and she had broken down as she kissed Rosie goodbye.

The Dunbars had left shortly afterwards, anxious to be on their way before dark, for air raids were a very real threat now. They were profoundly saddened by this tragedy, but they had never forgiven their son for his runaway marriage and both felt that he had brought this upon himself. Peter was conscious of their censure and missed the understanding and comfort that he so badly needed at this ghastly time in his life. Rosie's parents had been so very different, showing him kindness and affection without a hint of blame. Their concern for Rosie was, of course, paramount but their sympathy for him was sincere. Indeed, they could hardly bear to contemplate his suffering and the onerous guilt that lay so heavily upon his shoulders. They hoped and prayed that Rosie could find it in her heart to forgive him.

During this time dear Bron, as always a tower of strength, had prepared a light luncheon for them all. She had not consulted Rosie or bothered her with questions, but just plodded along on her own, doing her very best. Her earnest little face was troubled and Peter, seeing this, even in his own distress, had gone into the kitchen and put his hand on her shoulder in gratitude. They both understood – words were unnecessary, but Peter tried: "Thank you, Bron," he said in a choked voice then he fled from the kitchen fearful of breaking down. Then Bron left, closing the back door silently behind her and walking through the fields towards home, her large brown eyes a blur of tears.

Alone together now, Peter and Rosie sat tensely staring into the fire, carefully avoiding each other's eyes – how cruel fate can be, in so short a time their bliss so rudely shattered. Her adoration of him had turned to angry indifference. She felt she hated him now as she sat there silently analysing his behaviour. He had been so stubbornly determined to have everything his own way and through this he had murdered their son. She was finished with him and could not bear to have him sitting here in her cottage.

Peter was the first to break the awful silence.

"What are your plans for the future now, Rosie? You can't possibly remain here on your own."

She sat forward in her chair with blazing eyes.

"Oh yes I can and I will. This is where I intend to stay, close to Ricky. This is my home and I shall never leave it." She drew in her breath sharply: "I would be grateful if you would go now – for good – I never want to see you again – this is absolutely final."

He looked at her intently, as if memorising her every feature. Then wearily he stumbled to his feet. His face was a mask of suffering as he spoke his final words to her.

"Goodbye Rosie, my darling – you will always be that to me. Please believe me, I meant no wrong. I was just trying to bring us close together again. If you should ever need me, I have a sea-going appointment now in M.T.Bs. You can always contact me through the Admiralty."

He turned blindly and, with unsteady gait, reached the cottage door. He picked up his cap and, without a backward glance, closed the door quietly behind him and was gone.

The silence in the cottage was quite intolerable, but Rosie had made up her mind that she would stand on her own feet without the support of any other person. She had decided, positively and finally, to survive alone, but her agony of mind that night tested her endurance almost to breaking point. When the first light of dawn appeared in the sky and she heard the tentative chirp of a lone bird beneath her window, she was still on her knees beside her bed, but she knew she had won – nothing could ever be as bad again – she had survived this first awful night.

Sue arrived unexpectedly a few days later and, in quiet despair, pleaded with Rosie to leave the cottage but it was all to no avail. The two girls wept together, for Sue loved her little godson and the shared grief gave them both a measure of comfort.

Rosie promised to get in touch, if there was anything she needed, so Sue had to be content with this — but her heart ached with compassion as she left Rosie, alone now, so changed by death, sorrow and heartbreak.

*   *   *   *   *

In the weeks that followed, Britain's fortunes were at their lowest ebb. The danger of invasion was increasing daily and everyone waited with oppressive anxiety for the deadly onslaught from across the Channel. The loss of vital arms and equipment, sustained at Dunkirk, was serious and the vulnerability of the defending forces was all too apparent; yet the morale of the country was sustained by the inspired leadership of the prime minister, Winston Churchill. There was no doubt the British bulldog was showing his teeth and would fight to the death.

Rosie drove her mobile canteen as a full time job now, visiting outlying coastal airfields and military sites. She had volunteered to join the Red Cross unit as an ambulance driver, in either Liverpool or London, and was waiting for her transfer to come through.

The full force of the Luftwaffe was now directed against England, with recurrent raids on the south coast spreading to the southern counties and penetrating deeper each day. Rosie's one desire was to be in the thick of it, hoping that this would steer her thoughts away from her irreparable loss.

To the outside world she seemed composed, but she was still numbed by the shock, yet her inner grief, seemingly kept well under control, was in fact tearing her apart. Sometimes she raged against the cruel fate that had taken Ricky from her and denied her the joy of watching him grow up. She often day-dreamed about him, wondering what he would have been like as a young man and always pictured his maturing into a kind, warm, lovable person. At such times she tried hard not to show her distress — she was not the only one suffering in this terrible war.

Children were being hurriedly evacuated from the cities to the greater safety of the country. It was a pathetic sight to see them gathered together in small groups on the railway station platforms; even little tots were sent, complete with gas masks and name labels pinned to their coats. The poor parents, seeing them off, tried hard to keep a stiff upper lip despite their feelings of despair. Some of the older children were cheerful, regarding it as a great adventure, others were heartbroken, sobbing and clinging to their mothers, not wanting to be parted from them.

In the air the Battle of Britain was raging fiercely, being fought out between the two adversaries for daylight supremacy. Fighter pilots were a race apart, men prepared daily to risk their lives for freedom, and fighting a very personal war against terrific odds.

They were ready for anything, completely undaunted by the enemy's great superiority of numbers. Often a handful of Spitfires or Hurricanes would take on a force of fifty or sixty Messerschmitts, cutting through their formation and scattering them — weaving, turning and dodging the tracer bullets, grimly determined to do or die. These gallant young pilots, so conspicuous for their daring, were the nation's heroes.

Dog fights in the sky were a regular occurrence now: this life and death struggle was watched by civilians with bated breath from below, marvelling at the fearlessness of these brave young men, friend and foe alike.

More and more raids were being directed at airfields, including surprise attacks on grounded planes, which had not been given sufficient warning to get airborne. Rosie had been in such a raid recently. She had been sitting in her mobile canteen, just about to leave, when suddenly Heinkels had swept in from the sea, diving out of the sun and raking the airfield with their machine guns; then returning again and again to bomb the runways.

She had felt little fear and had remained quietly in her driver's seat, deciding to take her chance where she was – then quite unexpectedly the car door was wrenched open by a young officer, who grabbed her arm roughly and dragged her out, unceremoniously pushing her under the vehicle and quickly following after her.

"Whatever's the matter with you, my girl; are you trying to commit suicide?"

She found herself looking into the kindly, honest face of a young pilot, his grey-blue eyes strongly reminding her of her father's. She smiled at him: "Thank you for rescuing me, Sir Galahad," she said breathlessly. "I was probably foolish to take the risk."

Before he could reply to this, there was the rising scream of another bomb descending and he drew her to him, burying her head in his jacket for protection. It must have landed close, for the explosion was deafening. After the dust had settled, she looked up at him and managed another smile – he felt instantly drawn to this beautiful girl, so cool under fire, who seemed almost oblivious of the danger around them. There was another loud scream of diving aircraft and the sharp rat-a-tat of machine gun fire, followed by the sound of aero engines receding into the distance.

"Are you feeling all right?" he asked, looking anxiously down at her.

"Yes, I'm fine," she said, disentangling herself from him and putting a little distance between them.

"I think the all clear will be sounding any minute now, but let's stay here until it does, just in case they return."

She nodded in agreement. She felt safe and happy here with this pleasant young man. She knew she could trust him and was reluctant to break away before she need.

"Thank God that most of the squadron were in the air," he said fervently. "'In fact I think they may all have got off. I only hope that the ground personnel have not suffered."

She glanced at his uniform and saw his wings and asked: "Are you attached to this squadron?"

"No, I'm only visiting here. I come from Biggin Hill."

At that moment the all clear sounded and they crawled out from under the vehicle, half afraid of what they would find.

The runways were full of gaping holes. 'Operations' was intact and the officers' mess was still standing. Close by a bomb had landed, covering a Spitfire with dust and rubble; another Spitfire, undamaged, was gleaming nearby in the sunshine – the only two of the squadron not airborne. The pilots of these planes were already running towards them and there was a general hive of activity as the working parties were preparing to mend the runways.

Rosie and her pilot stood together for a moment, feeling slightly dazed and there was only time to take a cursory look at each other when the public address system stridently summoned: "Squadron-Leader Scott report to the C.O. immediately."

"That's for me, I'm afraid, so I must go." With a smile and a quick salute, he rushed off.

She knew there was nothing that she could do to help, so she had better get out of the way as quickly as possible. She drove hurriedly off the airfield, feeling thoroughly demoralised and very much alone.

What a futile thing war is, she pondered; yet at the start she had been filled with a patriotic fervour and a conviction that the cause was right. Now she knew nothing could justify this senseless killing. Even some of the fighter pilots admitted that they had respect for the bravery of their faceless enemy, whom they were engaging. What an awful world to live in, she thought; then she realised that she felt a little shaky and would be glad to get home.

As she walked into her solitary cottage, the quietness of it struck her like a blow and she was filled with a great lonely sadness. She saw Ricky as he had always been, sitting in his playpen, waiting for her with his arms outstretched, eager to be picked up. She remembered his warm little body, affectionate and loving, as he clasped her round the neck with his cheek close to hers.

She sank into a chair, tormented, the knife twisting in the wound. Tears flowed down her cheeks and she knew the ultimate pain of her suffering was now with her. Her silent tears turned to frantic sobs that tore at her unmercifully and uncontrollably – on and on, until the soft summer darkness had fallen in the valley – the only glimmer of light in the room came from the smouldering logs. All her strength had ebbed away, leaving her limp and lifeless, like a rag doll.

She picked up Biscuit, who was curled up on the rug and, without even switching on the lights, stumbled up to bed. She lay down, still fully dressed, pulling the eiderdown over them both and instantly fell into a deep sleep.

My Special Date — R.A.F. 1942

"How about a date?" Geoff asked,
"will tomorrow evening do
in the Bull's Head at eight?
We'll all be there,
Bill, Dickie and his mate.
We are not on duty,
so the earlier you come
the better, my beauty."

The ancient pub all dark,
with not a chink of light,
except the treacherous moon
mercilessly shining bright.
I opened the screened door
to quite a different scene —
the bar crowded with R.A.F. blue,
some navy and khaki too.

I see them quietly sitting there,
drawn together in a corner,
no longer gay and debonair.
Mothers' sons, just boys, yet giants
quaffing their pints of beer,
with ashtrays ladened,
no outward sign of fear.

They rise unsteadily to their feet,
with faces tired and drawn.
Gone is their usual *joie de vivre.*
I feel an instant stab of fear,
and ask them: "Why is Geoff not here?"
Their eyes averted to the ground
answered me without a sound.

Then Bill spoke up with studied calm,
"I'm afraid old Geoff has bought it,
silencing the guns at Brest;
he struggled to keep airborne,
my God he did his best,
but he ended up in the drink,
his Spit riddled with holes
and we saw him sink."

I hid my sorrowing face from them,
but no tears must be shed
for this gallant young pilot, my hero.
We cannot even bury our dead.

B.B

14

ROSIE AWAKENED early the next morning with a feeling of complete exhaustion. She was drained and lifeless. She wearily dragged herself up to a sitting position and looked listlessly through the window at the calm majesty of the mountains; then she gazed slowly around her room and was shocked as she saw herself in the dressing-table mirror. Was this really a reflection of her – this dishevelled, haggard young woman with red swollen eyes and without a trace of beauty? Her hair lay damply close to her scalp. How could she come to look like this? Her pride was stung – with an effort she got up, careful not to disturb the sleeping Biscuit.

She ran a deep, hot bath and lay back, relaxing in the warmth. It was restful and comforting and eased her aching limbs. She felt somewhat better now, for she realised that she had been through a deep emotional crisis. She had drained the cup of misery dry.

As the bath water got cooler, she stepped out and wrapped herself in a large luxurious bath towel. Then she vigorously rubbed her hair dry, until it returned to its usual vibrant mass of curls. She bathed her eyes over and over with icy cold water and finally they were soothed and almost back to normal again. Then, taking freshly laundered clothes from her drawer, she quickly dressed and felt and looked more like the old Rosie.

She must hurry now and get breakfast over as she had three calls to make that morning at outlying sites. She knew her visits gave pleasure to the men and many of them talked to her about their wives and families.

The morning was an uneventful one and, as she returned to the cottage, she realised how much better she was feeling after her emotional outburst of the night before. Everything seemed more bearable and she was able to cope with life again. Perhaps her wounds would eventually heal.

It was a lovely warm day, so she quickly made herself a cup of coffee and a sandwich, which she ate sitting on the front doorstep, enjoying the sunshine. She thought of George, who had always sat there with her. If only he had been spared, what a comfort he would be now. She yearned for another animal and would get a dog as soon as the war was over. George II, she thought and, in anticipation, a little warmth entered her chilly heart.

She seemed to doze off for a moment, lulled by the drowsy sound of bees, busily collecting their precious nectar and soothed by the soft cooing of doves on the roof. Suddenly she was disturbed by the creak of the gate and was surprised to see a tall, slim Air Force officer approaching up the path. His face seemed vaguely familiar, then she realised who he was. He was the man who had rescued her the day before. She put her tray to one side and stood up, smoothing her hair back and smiling at him.

"Hello, how nice to see you again," she said, the delicate colour in her cheeks deepening. "I'm sorry that I didn't have a chance of thanking you properly yesterday for taking such good care of me."

He looked at her seriously for a moment, then his face broke into a disarming smile.

"There is no need to thank me for that, it was my pleasure, but you'll be wondering why I'm here. After the raid yesterday, when all the clearing up was being done, a gold locket and chain with a photograph of a little boy inside was

159

found in the deep grass, close to where we were sheltering. I thought it was probably yours, so I volunteered to bring it along."

Rosie's hand went quickly to her neck and she was amazed to find that the locket was missing. She was astonished that she had not noticed it earlier, as it was one of her most treasured possessions. She flushed with surprise and relief as he produced it out of his coat pocket and handed it over to her.

"Oh, thank you," she said gratefully as she quickly snapped it open making sure that her favourite picture of Ricky was safe, but as his dear little face smiled back at her, a large lump came into her throat; the pilot noticed the sudden flicker of pain that showed in her eyes.

She closed it slowly and looked up at him. "I can't tell you how indebted I am to you – perhaps for my life yesterday and my precious locket today." Her voice was husky as she carried on. "You see the picture inside is of my little son, Ricky, who was killed in an air raid a short time ago."

He felt shocked and words seemed inadequate. "I'm deeply sorry," he said sympathetically. "War can be so very cruel."

There was a pause as Rosie pulled herself together, then she raised her eyes. "Come in and have a cup of coffee – it's all piping hot on the stove."

"I'd love to," he said and followed her into the cottage, looking around appreciatively at the comfort and quiet good taste of the room.

"Do sit down by the fire, I'll only be a moment."

While she was away, he studied her book-lined walls with interest. She obviously had catholic tastes, but he noticed particularly that books on art and music predominated.

She soon returned with the tray and sat down opposite, handing him over a cup of coffee.

"Do you realise that I don't even know your name yet?" she said in a jocular tone.

He stood up abruptly. "I'm sorry, I should have introduced myself earlier. I am Benjamin Scott and I know that you are Rosie Dunbar. They told me this at the airfield and how to find your cottage."

"Well, how do you do, Benjamin Scott, I'm delighted to meet you."

"And I sincerely return the compliment, Rosie Dunbar."

They chuckled together, then he sat down again in his comfortable chair.

"What a heavenly cottage this is. The setting and tranquillity is absolutely tremendous – I could never tire of looking at that fantastic view!"

He got up and walked to the window.

"Have you lived here long?"

"An aunt left it to me about five years ago. I simply adore it and shall never leave."

"Never is a long time," he looked at her enquiringly. "I suppose your husband is in the services?"

"Yes, he is in the navy" – she paused, then added "I think he's in M.T.Bs." Her voice shook a little. "We have separated and I don't hear from him any more." She was surprised that she had volunteered this information. It was the first time that she had told anyone. Her tongue seemed to be running away with her.

"Ricky, my son, is buried in the little churchyard just down the road from here; so, you see, that is why I say I shall never leave."

She looked up at him and he saw the bleakness in her lovely blue eyes and felt an overwhelming pity for her. She seemed so young to have gone through so much. His concern showed in his kindly face and Rosie felt warmed by his sympathy. She smiled at him and they were both suddenly conscious of an obvious mutual attraction. They were very much *en rapport.*

"I seem to have monopolised all the conversation, now tell me about yourself."

He hesitated for a moment. "There's nothing much to tell. I'm 22, unmarried and, like you, all alone in the world. My mother and father were killed in an air raid six months ago." He spoke quietly and she knew he was still upset by their loss. "It was a direct hit on their house. The old man was a doctor in the west country, and I intended to follow in his footsteps. In fact I had just completed my first year of medicine at Edinburgh University, but when the war broke out I joined the R.A.F. My parents, poor dears, were so worried about me, especially as I was an only child and it is ironical that they should have bought it first."

Rosie noticed the 'first', but did not comment on it.

"Yesterday you told me that you are stationed at Biggin Hill. Are you flying back today?"

"Well, no, I've been given two weeks' leave after a rather hectic time on ops. As I hardly know Wales at all and the country is so lovely, I thought of tarrying a while. I hoped to find a comfortable bed and breakfast place and have a good look around. I've already made up my mind to climb Snowdon."

"That will be fun," she said enthusiastically. "I have done it many times: it's heavenly, but quite tough going."

"My goodness, you must be a rugged sylph," he said, looking at her slim figure with surprise.

"My appearance is deceptive," she replied with a smile. "I'm really quite strong and keep myself in good trim by taking long walks. There are so many lovely places to see around here."

"I suppose you wouldn't care to come with me, as my guide, to climb Snowdon?" he asked hopefully. "It would be so much more fun than going alone."

He waited anxiously for her reply. She looked across at him, frowning slightly, obviously undecided – then her spirits suddenly rose and she thought 'why not?' After all, Peter had completely let her down and in reality her marriage was finished.

"I would enjoy that very much," she replied after a brief pause. "Would tomorrow suit you, as I have a day off, and we will need a whole day for the trip?"

"Splendid! What time shall I be here?" he asked eagerly.

"I should think about 9.30 – then we should be up at the summit by lunchtime. I'll make some sandwiches and coffee for us."

His face broke into a boyish smile. "I haven't looked forward to anything so much for years."

She liked his enthusiasm and was glad to please him – he was such a dear.

He stood up and she realised how tall he was – at least 6′ 4″ – however did he fit into the cockpit of a Spitfire?

"I'd better be off now, as I want to visit one or two bed and breakfast addresses and try to get fixed up somewhere for tonight. Thank you very much for the coffee and for your company. This is the first time I've felt at home anywhere since my parents were killed." She sensed his loneliness and was deeply sorry for him; he in turn understood how she was feeling. "I'm sure you must find this cottage very lonely on your own, don't you?"

"Indeed I do. If it wasn't for my great love of painting, which absorbs much of my time, I think I would be quite lost."

"I didn't know you were an artist," he said with interest. "Are those your water-colours on the wall?"

"Yes, they're mostly local scenes; it's a wonderful area for subjects to paint, the scope is quite fantastic."

"I'm mad about art myself," he said. "I'm most impressed by your work. I love your delicate style and your draughtsmanship is superb."

"Thank you, kind sir, it's always encouraging to be appreciated."

"Have you ever exhibited your paintings?" he asked.

"Yes, some have gone to a nearby gallery and, I must admit, they have sold very quickly, but I never like to part with any of my work. Each picture seems to have a bit of me in it and, if I dispose of too many, there won't be any 'me' left!"

They laughed as she opened the cottage door and they walked out into the sunshine together. The garden was a riot of colour and fragrance which seemed to reflect its owner, he thought – even the name was appropriate. He jumped light-heartedly into his car and was quickly away, waving as he went – there was happiness in the air again.

That evening his thoughts never left her. She was the girl of his dreams – enchantingly beautiful, sensitive, talented and brave as a lion. He had no doubt that he had fallen head-over-heels in love. His might be a short life – he was convinced of this – but she was the girl for him.

Rosie slept better that night than she had for months and awoke much refreshed. She jumped up hurriedly, feeling full of enthusiasm and, after dressing, made their sandwiches and filled two flasks with coffee. It was a lovely day, clear and bright – a mauve shroud enveloping the mountains made her yearn to paint them – her old interests were reviving. She was really coming to life again.

She ran gaily up the stairs to change, glad to be out of her drab uniform. She put on her climbing rig and took great pains with her makeup. When she had finished, she looked at herself in the long mirror and was rather pleased with her reflection.

Presently she heard the sound of a car approaching along the country lane and drawing up at the gate. She stepped eagerly out of the house, slamming the door behind her and ran up the path with a welcoming smile. For the first time Ben was aware of the real Rosie. Her eyes were sparkling and he saw the full radiance of her beauty.

"Hello," he said, as she jumped into the car. "You bowl me over; you look so lovely, particularly in that shade of smokey-blue; it matches your eyes."

She felt pleased; it was nice having someone interested in her. "Thank you, Ben, you look pretty dapper too. Did you find a B and B place all right?"

"Yes, a jolly good one in the next village. They've given me a key, so I'm a free agent and can come and go as I please."

"That's marvellous," she replied. "I am glad you are fixed up."

"Now, Rosie, where do we go from here? Remember you're the guide and I need directions."

"Of course, Ben – I planned our route last night and have decided that we'd do best to start from Llanberis, which is the easiest path to climb. We will follow the railway track up to the summit and have lunch when we get to the top."

They were soon at the tiny station in Llanberis and, after parking the car, started their climb by the side of the railway track. To begin with the grass-covered slopes were easy but, as they progressed, the going became steeper and rockier. Ben, who was mechanically-minded, was fascinated by the rack and pinion railway. It had been completed in 1896 and had proved a huge success, transporting tourists to and from the summit – but today they seemed to have the mountain to themselves.

They felt exhilarated by the cool morning air and an easy relationship had already developed between them, even though they had known each other for such a short time.

Ben stopped frequently, as he had yet to develop his climbing legs; he already felt that on the morrow he would be very stiff after his effort. Rosie admired his dogged determination and welcomed these breaks, which gave them time to absorb the grandeur of Snowdonia. She identified each mountain peak for him and told him about the indigenous flora and fauna. They kept their eyes skinned for the rare feral goat, which occasionally could be spotted in the more mountainous regions, but today there was no sign of one. He was fascinated by her local knowledge and avidly listened to all she had to tell him.

It was harder going as they approached the steep precipice of Clogwyn ddur Arddn; they took the track which skirted the edge of it. Looking down from this great height, they were overawed by the sheer drop to the valley below, with its tiny tree-fringed lakes and white cascading waterfalls – all in miniature.

"How are we progressing, Rosie?" he asked breathlessly. "I'm afraid that I'm already beginning to run out of steam, yet you're still hopping around like a little mountain goat! I don't know how you manage it."

He looked at her with obvious admiration and she grinned back at him.

"You're doing all right, Ben. I should say that we're about halfway there now – Snowdon is 3560 feet high and I think we're making pretty good time for a couple of amateurs."

"My God, Rosie," he gasped, "have we still so far to go? I don't know if I'll ever make it to the top. I'm puffing like a grampus already."

She laughed. "Come on, lazy, of course you will – per ardua ad astra!"

"Fair enough, now you've put me on my mettle, young lady," he said, gritting his teeth and starting to climb again, obviously determined to take up the challenge and not be beaten.

As they neared the summit, the way got steeper and rockier, and the loose scree made the going hard and more perilous. Ben was completely taken by surprise when Rosie, bubbling with laughter, suddenly shouted: "I'll beat you to the top, Ben," and with great agility proceeded to do so. In spite of his aching limbs, he was a very close second, and, as he clambered up behind her, hemanaged to muster a triumphant: "Hooray, we've made it – three cheers for Sherpa Rosie!"

"Four cheers for good old Ben," she replied. "You've done marvellously. I'll make a mountaineer of you yet!"

Still puffing, he put his arm around her shoulders, then in silence they surveyed the stupendous panorama of wild mountains, high passes and craggy peaks which unfolded before them.

"I love this spectacular, rugged scenery — it is quite awe-inspiring."

"I know," she said, "it's rather like being at the top of the world, faraway from the problems of mice and men." She sounded wistful.

It was blowy and quite chilly in spite of the bright sunshine, so they didn't tarry there for long.

"Let's be off now, Ben, to my special place for lunch. I'm absolutely famished and dehydrated."

"Lead on, my little sherpa," he replied with gusto, "I'm ravenous too."

They descended from the summit and were soon comfortably settled on a stretch of soft springy turf with an outcrop of rock behind them. It was as warm as toast out of the wind and they quickly pitched into the sandwiches and coffee, which tasted delicious after their exertions.

When they had finished, they sat quietly in their sheltered nook, feeling relaxed and happy, enjoying the magnificent view stretching before them. Ben was filled with a deep contentment. He had a sudden urge to take her in his arms and kiss her, but decided this was not the moment.

"The Welsh call Snowdonia 'The eagles' resting place,' Ben, though in fact there are no longer any eagles around here."

"What about that chap hovering over there, Rosie?" he asked. "Surely that is one."

Rosie raised her head, screwing up her eyes in the sunshine: "Oh no, that's a buzzard," she replied, "though it does look a bit like an eagle. There is a great variety of rare birds in these parts, including choughs, kites and ring ouzels; fortunately wildlife is respected around here."

In due course they both lay back and closed their eyes, enjoying the warm sunshine on their faces. After a time Ben turned on his side and surreptitiously gazed at Rosie. Her skin was the colour of peaches and freckles powdered her nose like gold dust. Her generous mouth looked soft and vulnerable. She slowly opened her eyes, sensing that he was looking at her and a delightful smile broke over her face.

"That's not fair, inspecting me while I'm asleep."

"You look adorable, Rosie, asleep or awake."

He leant forward and impulsively took her hand. He looked at her long slim fingers and almond-shaped nails. "You have the hands of an artist, Rosie." Then he noticed her damaged fingers and his expression quickly changed. "Whatever has happened to give you these deep scars, Rosie?"

She drew her hand away almost violently then, looking down at her clenched fist, she suddenly burst into tears. "I don't want to discuss it, Ben." He pulled her close to him and waited for her composure to return. She soon dried her eyes, but she was pathetic and forlorn. His heart ached for her.

"Rosie dear, please tell me about your beautiful hands. I'm sure it will be a relief to confide in someone — someone, who loves you."

At these words she raised her eyes and searched his honest face. She knew what he said was true and that she could utterly trust him.

Her troubles came tumbling out — her bitterness towards Peter — his possessiveness and jealousy from the beginning, spoiling what could have been an idyllic marriage — his unfaithfulness — finally his selfish insistence on moving his family to a danger zone, for his own gratification, this tragic decision that led to the death of their little son.

164

Ben was utterly shattered by her story and heartbroken for Rosie – yet he could understand how she would be hard to share with anyone.

They walked silently down the mountain together, hand in hand, both deep in thought. What could the future hold for them?

Ben had a strong premonition that he would not survive another tour of ops. A fighter pilot's life-expectancy at this stage of the war was three weeks. He was terrified for Rosie – he cared nothing for himself. She was the one who mattered.

She clung tightly to his hand and his love for her was overwhelming. Somehow things must be left right for her. He thought of Peter and curiously had no animosity toward him. He felt that he understood this awkward, headstrong man, who loved Rosie so passionately. Deep down, she must still feel something for him. Ben was sure of this, but he needed more time to think it all over on his own.

When they reached the cottage, he kissed her tenderly goodbye. They had become so very close. Oh what bliss, they would meet again tomorrow.

* * * * * *

It was fortuitous that Rosie was given a few days leave before her transfer came through, so she and Ben had planned days out together. The fine weather still held, but there was a chill in the air and the leaves were starting to fall.

She took him to all her favourite places, many of which she had painted, and he observed the country through her eyes and instantly fell in love with it. The rugged Welsh landscape and quaint villages, nestling in the lush green valleys, strongly appealed to him. He liked the contrast of the houses, built with the local stone and slate and the pink and white thatched cottages, all so immaculately maintained.

They visited Anglesey one day, crossing Telford's famous suspension bridge, which linked the island to the mainland and which afforded them a magnificent view of the Menai Straits. He enjoyed hearing the Welsh speaking in their native tongue and was fascinated by this centre of Celtic culture and religion.

On another occasion they drove to the old slate mines at the head of the Vale of Ffestiniog. Rosie, as always, took a pencil and drawing pad with her and made emphatic black and white sketches of the quarries in heavy pencil – their stark bleakness dramatically relieved by the splendour of a back-cloth of woods and sparkling lakes. It was a country of contrasts. Rugged in the extreme, yet softened by the verdant, undulating fields and woodland glades – a haven for wildlife. Ben felt at home here, which pleased Rosie, as this countryside meant so much to her.

The evenings were drawing in now and they liked this quiet time of the day best, with their chairs drawn up close to a blazing log fire and Biscuit asleep at their feet. They were in perfect harmony and Ben felt for Rosie a single-hearted devotion and tenderness – a complete negation of self. He understood what her life had been reduced to, but knew that she was trying bravely to pull herself out of it. His only mission was to help her and shield her from further pain.

They had many common interests and enjoyed a lively exchange of ideas on a variety of subjects, but art and music were always at the forefront of their discussions. They often talked of their past lives but they never discussed the future – it was carefully avoided by them both. One could only live for the present.

Ben often spoke of his great friend, Mike Lovell, who was a pilot in the same squadron. "He's a wild Irishman, Rosie, and knows no fear. We're as close as brothers and I have unbounded admiration for him. I hope you'll meet him one day."

"So do I," Rosie said rather wistfully.

"Mike is king of the 'Tail-end-Charlies', whose duty it is to defend the squadron when the enemy attacks from astern. He once saved my life by intercepting and shooting down a Messerschmitt which tried to 'jump' me by diving out of the sun with all guns blazing." He grinned boyishly. "We had a whale of a party that night at the local – celebrating my survival! Thank God I was off duty the next day; flying with a hangover is pure purgatory. Mike and I tossed for it and the poor devil lost. It's rather like Russian roulette."

"My goodness, I think you pilots are quite terrific," Rosie said proudly. She thought these young men were remarkable – each day they came face to face with death. She was deeply moved by their resilience, and their devil-may-care attitude, and their comradeship was tremendous.

Sometimes they spoke of Peter – Ben tried to soften Rosie's feelings towards him, but she would not budge – her mind was closed. She had suffered too much at his hands. Ben did his best to influence her by appealing to her soft heart – describing the dreadful fatigue experienced by naval officers. "You know, Rosie, the Senior Service has the worst job of the lot. There is never any let up and through continuous lack of sleep they often behave irrationally." She listened carefully. "That's no excuse for what he has done," she answered stubbornly. Ben still hadn't got through to her.

He tried again, talking of fate. "You say you believe in fate and our lives are preordained, so even Ricky's death must be part of the plan. If you accept this, you can not fairly lay all the blame at Peter's door and, after all, his motives were good; he was only trying his best to gather his little family together again. Surely he has suffered enough, for he's lost everything and has only his guilt-ridden conscience to live with. Unless you can forgive him, you will never enjoy true peace of mind."

Finally she answered him. "Ben, you are a good man and have influenced me for the better. I no longer feel corroded by bitterness towards Peter, but he is dead as far as I am concerned. Ben, can you understand any man being so insanely jealous of his own son – and such a darling child?" She choked and couldn't carry on.

He paused for a moment before replying and his voice was tense. "It's hard to answer you, Rosie. You had Ricky too soon. You were young and immature and should have waited. For a man of Peter's temperament it was essential for him to have you entirely to himself for a time. After the honeymoon and the excitement of the early months, his attitude would have matured and the mutual longing for a child would have been a very natural evolution. He would have become a very different Peter, regarding this as the exciting consummation of your love."

There was silence between them for several minutes; she sensed tacit criticism of herself, which hurt, but she could not deny the logic of his argument.

"Oh, Ben, you didn't know arrogant Peter – that is why reason falls down, but let's not talk about him any more."

"Very well, Rosie," he replied and they sat silently by the fire, lost in their own thoughts. He longed to blot out from her life the cruel happenings which had crucified her.

Presently Rosie got up and walked over to the piano – music always soothed her. She sat down and played a little Chopin. He closed his eyes and let the music flow over him.

"You play beautifully, Rosie; all your feelings are reflected in your music – I can sense that. A means of self expression like this is a wonderful gift."

Smiling, she turned her head towards him: "Music is a great solace to me," she answered, and he saw that all her tenseness had gone. She looked relaxed and happy.

At that moment there was a gentle knock on the door and Rosie got up to answer it. Bron was standing on the step holding a basket containing a dozen lovely brown eggs. She glanced through the open door and was surprised to see an R.A.F. officer sitting by the fire.

"I'm sorry to disturb you, Mam, but I've been to Ty Croes farm today and David Pritchard asked me to bring you these new-laid eggs."

"Thank you very much, Bron, they look delicious; I love them brown and speckly – they will be nice for supper tonight."

Bron stood hesitantly on the step, not knowing quite how to take her leave, and looked rather awkward.

"I won't ask you in now, Bron, as I have a visitor, Squadron Leader Scott, who rescued me on the airfield the other day, when it was attacked. He has kindly brought back my gold locket which must have fallen off in all the confusion."

"Is that the one with Ricky bach's photo in it?" she asked anxiously, then blushed to the roots of her hair, realising that she might have said the wrong thing mentioning dear Ricky.

Rosie smiled back reassuringly. "Yes, that's the one, Bron."

"I'm so glad you've got it back, indeed I am," she said, obviously relieved. "As you have company, I'll be off now, so goodnight, Mam."

"Goodnight, dear Bron, and bless you."

She closed the front door behind her and walked into the living room, casually glancing at Ben; she was just about to speak to him but stopped in her tracks – the effect of the soft evening sun highlighting his face was most dramatic, emphasising its strong, clean lines. His penetrating grey eyes were accentuated by his Air Force blue uniform and his wings seemed to be strangely shimmering. This unusual play of light was an artist's dream and she longed to record it.

"Don't move an inch, Ben," she cried impulsively. "Not even a hair's breadth. You're a marvellous study in the sunshine and I must paint you."

He laughed merrily. "All right, Rosie, I won't even blink an eyelid."

She felt a great surge of excitement, as she rushed out to collect her easel and painting equipment. She quickly returned and was soon roughing in the outline on the canvas. She became completely absorbed in her work, anxious to apply the colour as fast as possible, before losing the light.

Her face was a study of concentration, yet the picture came so easily. Providence seemed to guide her hand to make unerring strokes with the brush. She had never before painted with such inspired alacrity.

When the light faded, there was still much to be done, but her vision was there. Not merely were his good looks faithfully portrayed, but the real essence of the man was captured and recorded. She loved the picture, it was quite beyond her expectations.

"Come and have a look, Ben, but remember it's not nearly finished yet."

He came and stood behind her, with his hand on her shoulder. The strength of the painting staggered him, for she had caught the drama of the moment. His expression was resolute, the face of a brave young man, yet the light playing on his wings gave the picture an ethereal quality. This was pure genius.

"It's incredibly good, Rosie, though too flattering. You know you could be a superb war artist. Why don't you send this picture up to the Academy as a study of an unknown fighter pilot?"

"I'll never do that, Ben," she replied sadly. "I couldn't part with it. After you've left, it will be a great source of comfort to me. It is the living image of you and through it I shall always feel that you are close to me."

He drew her gently toward him, laying his hands on her shoulders and looking deeply into her eyes.

"Rosie darling, please remember that wherever I am, whether it is in this world or the next" and he said this lightly — "I shall always be near you, be assured of this."

Her heart beat wildly as she fought back the tears.

Seeing her distress, he quickly changed the subject.

"I saw, amongst all your clutter in the cupboard a nice piece of light mahogany. Would you like me to make a frame out of it for your picture, then we could have a hanging ceremony before my departure?"

"That's a marvellous idea, Ben, I'd love that." She was obviously delighted and managed a little smile. "I have already chosen a place for it — in that niche on its own, away from all the others. That's the perfect position, as I shall be able to see you clearly from my chair."

"All right, darling — well now that's settled, I'll get cracking on the frame. It shouldn't take me too long to complete."

He departed early that evening as he was visiting the local airfield, hoping for news of his squadron. He knew they must have taken quite a battering in his absence and he was worried about his pal, Mike.

Left on her own, Rosie was still in an inspired mood — almost light-headed and longing to continue with her painting. It was hard to leave her easel, but the portrait could not be finished that night. She needed at least one more sitting.

She pondered over Ben's suggestion of her becoming a war artist. This was not practical, as she was committed to ambulance driving, but she could still find time for some painting — if only she could succeed in conveying on canvas her abject loathing of war — the hideous obscenity of it all. Could this in some small way be a deterrent for future generations? This would give her a mission in life — a purpose; then perhaps Ricky would not have died in vain — but what was the next step?

The horrific scene of Ricky's death, always with her, came to mind with vivid clarity — this was it — her first protest, but could she bear to reveal it? Had she sufficient courage? Slowly she placed a fresh canvas on the easel and almost unconsciously started outlining the ill-fated 'Oswell Terrace'. She was soon quite oblivious of her surroundings — she was back in Rochester again on that tragic morning, reliving the scenes of death and destruction, like flashbacks on a screen. She could even smell the dust and dirt rising from the rubble and feel the pain in her agonised fingers.

She was now painting at lightning speed like one possessed – on and on without respite, recording on canvas her tormented memory. As the grey dawn broke, she slumped back exhausted. The picture was finished. She had put her heart and soul into it. Beads of perspiration stood out on her forehead and her haunted eyes were enormous, as she looked down at her finished work.

The force of the picture shook her – dragged from the depths of her innermost tortured mind. Here was her unmistakable message for the world to see – the title must be right. She paused, deep in thought, then slowly wrote down the words 'The holocaust of war – here lies my innocent son.'

She left the room almost in a trance, utterly drained. She had given her all, yet she felt a great relief, the cancer had been exorcised. She was herself again.

* * * * *

Ben had only two more days left of his precious leave. He was feeling restored, but he dreaded parting from Rosie. His conscience smote him. Being off ops for even a short time seemed wrong with the Battle of Britain still raging and losses so tremendously high. During his absence several of his fellow officers had been killed in combat, but in a pilot's life there was no room for emotion – sorrow caught up later but, thank God, Mike had been spared so far.

Ben hated war and killing, but he loved his country and was determined to do his duty to the utmost. Personal glory meant little to him; he felt his medals undeserved. Many braver men than he had fought and died without recognition.

That afternoon, as the fine spell of weather continued, Rosie and Ben decided to make the most of the sunshine. They climbed the hill behind the cottage and happily surveyed the peaceful scene spread out before them. The very prospect of invasion, with Germans defiling this green and pleasant land, was utterly repugnant. The threat seemed inconceivable on such a beautiful day.

They found an inviting place to sit beneath a great oak with its massive trunk and its branches, twisted and gnarled, spreading over them like a giant umbrella. This stalwart old tree had endured for centuries and there was a certain comfort and feeling of stability in that thought at such a time of insecurity.

Rosie was soon busily sketching a distant view of the patchwork fields, separated by sturdy dry stone walls and dotted with grazing sheep, contentedly cropping the grass. Her style was changing, her delicate water colour era was over. She had matured and her drawings were strong and vigorous. A new realism had imposed itself and her mountains appeared hard and craggy in the distance.

Ben watched her as she worked – he could see she was healing. She had been a different person since she had painted the 'Holocaust'. It had released her pent-up tension. He had been shaken by the impact of the picture and the message which it conveyed. He felt it could be an important work, reflecting so vividly the horror of indiscriminate bombing.

A breeze arose, rustling the few fallen leaves around them, a reminder of autumn. It was starting to get chilly, so he decided to interrupt her.

"Let's go home now, Rosie darling, and have some tea; it's getting cold."

"I won't be a minute, Ben," she answered, as she applied the finishing touches. It was always difficult to break her away; once she became absorbed she was oblivious to everything, but she loved having his reassuring presence beside her.

"Be a good girl now, Rosie, and pack up your things," he said affectionately, kissing her cheek. "I'm dying for a cup of tea." She laid down her sketching pad.

"All right, darling, sorry to keep you waiting. I'm ready now."

Hurriedly she threw all her bits and pieces into an old knapsack and they were soon on their way, scrambling down the hill through the fields to the lane below.

They walked briskly back to the cottage, arm in arm, relaxed and in complete harmony – they were as one. He broke their easy silence.

"How about hanging my portrait tonight, Rosie – I've finished the frame and I think you will be pleased with it."

Her face lit up in anticipation and her eyes sparkled.

"Goodie, goodie, that will be most exciting, Ben."

"Let's crack the bottle of bubbly, that I got from the mess," he said with enthusiasm. "This is just the right occassion for it."

"Oh, that's a marvellous idea, Ben – we can throw our bonnets over the windmill tonight and have a real celebration."

They chatted excitedly at the prospect and were soon home, pushing open the cottage door. Ben as usual went straight over and put a match to the fire – he loved its comfort and cheer. It blazed up instantly, for the bed of ashes was always warm.

Rosie made a pot of tea and they sat close together on the couch. What bliss, he thought, to spend the rest of his life here with her – but this was not to be.

"Tomorrow is your last day, Ben," she said sighing deeply. "Is there anywhere special you would like to go?"

"No thank you, darling, I'd rather stay around here, if that's all right with you. I want to mend the back door and take out those rotting timbers, otherwise you will have trouble with the weather blowing in this winter."

She shuddered slightly – the idea of cold, dark winter nights was daunting. She hoped she would be posted soon; with Ben gone it would be unbearable alone.

"Why don't you go up and get changed, Rosie, while I prepare for the unveiling ceremony?"

"All right," she replied with forced gaiety. "I'll only be a moment. By the way are the ladies wearing long dresses tonight?"

He chuckled: "Of course not, my sweet, sea-boots and bathing drawers are the rig of the day!" At this they both roared with laughter but, as she ran upstairs to her room, she decided to make herself look as glamorous as possible for this special occasion, yet her heart ached as it would soon be over.

Left alone, Ben slipped the picture into the frame. He was delighted with it. The wood had polished to a satin finish and set off the portrait to perfection. He proceeded to hang it on the wall in the place that Rosie had chosen. He stood back to admire his handiwork and was well content.

He hurried into the kitchen and brought out a tray with the precious bottle of champagne and two glasses, placing them on a table by the couch. He then tiptoed to the airing cupboard and took out a white sheet, which he draped over the picture. He stoked up the fire and got the logs blazing away – now everything was ready.

He stood at the bottom of the stairs and called: "Hurry up, Mrs. Dunbar, they're all here and the ceremony is about to commence – but we need our celebrity."

"I'm on my way, master of ceremonies," she shouted back and there was an excited lilt in her voice. As she appeared, she looked radiant in a simple ivory

170

white dress, which emphasised her lovely figure.

"You look absolutely gorgeous, Rosie darling," he said ardently, showering her with kisses.

She gazed into his eyes and, taking his face in her hands, gave him a very special kiss. They clung together for a moment, before he uncorked the champagne with a delicious pop and proceeded to fill their glasses.

He then stepped back alongside the shrouded picture and with glass in hand he solemnly declared: "I hearby unveil a remarkable portrait by a very brilliant artist" – then, with a flourish, he swept aside the sheet, revealing the 'masterpiece'. "It is my privilege to propose a toast to the artist – my sweet Rosie Dunbar." There was a catch in his voice.

They touched glasses and sipped the champagne.

"Thank you, Ben darling," she said warmly. "Now I would like to respond by drinking a toast to my Prince Charming. The wonderful man, who inspired this picture – whom I shall love until the day I die. God bless and keep us both."

He put his arm around her and held her very close and together, cheek to cheek, they drained their glasses.

The spell of this magical moment was rudely shattered by the dreaded sound of enemy aircraft overhead, the heavy drone of their engines announcing their return as night began to fall. Rosie's heart seemed to miss a beat.

"Oh dear, listen Ben, they're here again and it sounds as though there is a great number of them. I hope to goodness they're not on their way to Liverpool."

She rushed to close the windows and pull the black-out curtains. The nights were drawing in, though it was not yet dark. He jumped up and opened the cottage door, standing on the path listening intently; he recognised the sound of German bombers – the low-pitched throb, as successive waves of Dorniers flew above. Rosie joined him, linking her arm in his, listening fearfully to the steady drone. She drew him back into the cottage and quickly closed the door, careful not to show a chink of light.

"Do you think they're on their way to bomb Liverpool again tonight, Ben?"

"I rather fear so; they generally concentrate on one city for several nights. As Liverpool is Britain's major Atlantic port and an essential link with North America, it is bound to receive special attention from the Luftwaffe."

Rosie shivered. "I wish I was with the family; it's awful for elderly people having to put up with these ghastly air raids. Thank goodness they at least have a good inside shelter."

"Try not to worry, darling – though I know that is easier said than done," he said with understanding. She realised he must be thinking of his own poor parents.

"Let's get supper ready now, Rosie, for I mustn't be too late getting back to my B and B place. I fear I disturbed them last night but, oh dear, how I hate to leave you – it gets harder each time."

Tears filled Rosie's eyes. "Oh Ben," she burst out. "I can't bear it, please don't go. We have so little time left now and I want to be with you for every minute of it."

He had waited and hoped for this, but the suggestion had to come from her.

"Rosie, do you realise what you are asking me?"

"Of course I do, darling. You know how much I love you and I need you terribly. Please don't leave me alone tonight, Ben."

Suddenly with a great rush of love and longing she was in his arms. She felt it was like returning home after a long journey of uncertainty. She smiled up at him, that enchanting, most radiant smile and there was so much trust and undisguised love there.

He carried her up the stairs to her room and gently laid her on the bed. She trembled as he sank down beside her – her whole being weak and surrendering.

"Oh Ben darling, I'm so happy," she said, her voice full of emotion.

He gazed at her adoringly. It seemed as if this bond was meant to be. In no time they were in each other's arms, her soft skin intimately close to his.

"Rosie, Rosie, my sweetheart, you are the love of my life – my first, last and only love," and as they embraced more intimately, they were carried away on a mounting wave of pure ecstasy. They came together with infinite tenderness and simultaneously they reached the heights in a blinding flash of exquisite pleasure that left them both gasping for breath.

They lay quietly, still lovingly entwined. She felt she could not bear this night to end. She hid her face against his shoulder and he felt her warm tears on his chest. He did not speak but rocked her back and forth like a baby, humming a little tune he remembered from his childhood days.

Presently she looked up at him, her face smiling and relaxed.

"I shall never forget this heavenly night, Ben darling. I have been divinely happy. It has been perfection."

"Bless you, my Rosie," he replied. "It was pure heaven for me too. You're the most wonderful girl in the whole wide world and I shall love you until the day I die."

They cuddled up together and fell asleep in each others arms. Blessed oblivion spared them the agonising thought of their inevitable parting.

Departure Platform 1942

Make me laugh to the end;
Keep a smile on my face,
As I gaze at my hero in his R.A.F. blue.
His wings seem to dazzle,
With my tears left unshed,
For soon he'll be airborne
And soon he'll be dead.

All his comrades have bought it
But still we must laugh,
For their joys and their sorrows
Are now of the past.
Oh please make his train
Be late in to-day;
So there's still time to laugh
And pretend to be gay.

B.B.

15

THE FOLLOWING day Rosie could not get a reply when she telephoned home – the line seemed dead, so she and Ben decided to meet the early morning train from Liverpool. They hurried down to the station and, as the train came chugging in, ran to the engine-driver's cab and asked him what had happened the previous night. He told them that there had been a severe raid on the centre of the city, causing great damage and that most telephone lines were down.

Rosie was very worried indeed and, as they made their way back to the cottage, she feared the worst had happened, but tried hard not to show her great anxiety. Ben held her hand tightly and could feel it trembling. He knew exactly what hell she was going through but, as they reached the gate, they heard the telephone ringing. She flew up the path and got there just in time. It was her mother with reassuring news.

"We're all right, Rosie, there's nothing to worry about. Our telephone lines are down, so I'm phoning from the post office but, apart from that, all is well."

"Thank God you are both safe, Mum, but whatever will you do if the raids continue?"

"I think we'll stay here, Rosie, your father will never leave his business."

"Well you know, Mum, there's plenty of room for you at the cottage as I am expecting to be posted at any moment. You would have the place to yourselves – do think it over."

"Thank you, dear, it is nice to feel that we can, if we need to. I must ring off now, but don't worry about us. Remember the Venables will always let you know if there is anything wrong. Take care of yourself, Rosie, and tell us as soon as your posting comes through. Goodbye, dear."

"Goodbye, Mum, and take care."

Rosie put down the phone slowly, reluctant to break the tenuous contact between them. There was a worried, haunted look on her face as she turned to Ben. Their eyes met and he reached out, touching her cheek with his finger tips; he smiled lovingly at her.

"There's nothing you can do for them, darling. They'll be all right in that reinforced shelter of theirs, so don't worry. Let's get breakfast ready; a cup of coffee will do us a power of good!"

The kitchen was not spacious, but uncluttered and very clean. Everything was always in its place. They worked silently together that morning, both lost in their thoughts. Rosie felt a quiet dread, secretly wondering if any of her loved ones would survive this terrible war. She knew she should not dwell on such morbid thoughts, otherwise how could she keep going? She must not spoil the remainder of Ben's leave and a warm excitement flooded over her, as she thought of the bliss they had shared the night before. Her spirits rose and, to his surprise, she laughed almost gaily.

"As soon as we've had 'brek', let's go and collect your gear from your B. and B. place and I'll call in at the Red Cross office in the village to see if anything has come through for me. I'm praying it's London and then we won't be so far apart and we will be able to see one another occasionally."

Ben smiled encouragingly, but he knew that there was little hope of this. On his return he would be on almost constant alert.

"Remember, Rosie, when we get back, I'm going to repair your door. You will thank me when that Welsh horizontal rain starts driving through the crevices!"

"You are a dear to think of these things for my comfort when you have so much to face yourself."

Her voice was low and she looked away to hide the tears in her eyes. She was determined that this must be a happy day — their last together for some time, but her heart missed a beat as she intuitively knew, perhaps for ever.

Swallows were collecting and swooping down over the trees, preparing for their long flight south. There is nothing as free as a bird, Rosie thought and she longed to escape from the bombs and the torture of worrying about loved ones.

They drove into the centre of the village together, then parted company and went their separate ways. Although they had not disguised their friendship, they had not flaunted it and hoped that there was no gossip. Bronwen, they knew, was loyal and would put a stop to any unkind words from the villagers. Rosie went straight to the little tin hut, at the back of the local store, which was also the Red Cross office.

Plump, bossy little Mrs. Thomas was sitting by the telephone and, as she saw Rosie, she jumped up with excitement.

"You've come in at the right moment, Rosie. I've just received an S.O.S. from headquarters, Liverpool: you are to report there tomorrow afternoon. They need a driver badly as the raids have been terrible recently."

Mrs. Thomas was so puffed up with self-importance that she always got on Rosie's nerves. Her heart sank at the thought of the distance which would separate her from Ben, but she managed to conceal her feelings.

"Thank you, Mrs. Thomas. I'll close up the cottage tomorrow and take the afternoon train."

Mrs. Thomas purred. She loved to give orders and considered herself now the pivot of all war endeavour in the village. However, as she looked at Rosie's young face, she felt pity for this girl; after losing her child in an air raid and now she was going into the thick of it all over again. Mrs. Thomas knew that she, herself, would hate such a posting in such circumstances.

"Good luck, Rosie, and take care." There was warmth and sincerity in her voice.

"Goodbye, Mrs. Thomas. I'll get there as quickly as I can."

Rosie did some shopping in the village, then called in at Bronwen's cottage to tell her of the latest developments. Poor Bron lived there all alone since her old Gran had died. Rosie hoped and prayed that she would marry; it seemed such a lonely existence. Bron looked alarmed when Rosie announced that she was being sent to Liverpool.

"Oh, Mam, I hope you'll be all right — surely to goodness you've suffered enough without this and I'm going to miss you." She made no secret of her love and admiration for Rosie.

"Don't worry, Bron. I'll be all right and it will be a relief to me as I shall be able to keep an eye on my parents."

"Always thinking of others, that's you, Mam. Well, you know I'll do my best down here. I'll take good care of Biscuit. I'll go into the cottage every day and keep it ship-shape and well aired, so it's always ready for you. Of course, I'll see that Ricky bach's grave is kept tidy."

Rosie leant forward and kissed her.

"Goodbye, dear loyal Bron. I would be lost without you."

Then, trying to conceal her emotion, she hurried down the path without a backward glance. She arrived home a few minutes before Ben. She was determined to make their last day a happy one. Each second counted and must be enjoyed to the full. I wonder how many seconds we have left, she thought. Idly she tried to work it out and, when Ben came back, she greeted him with a broad grin, announcing that they had 79,200 seconds left and must make the best of every one. He held her close, grateful for her cheerfulness and brave spirit.

"Let's do that, Rosie darling, we'll make every single one count – but how about your posting?"

She paused for a moment, then looked up at him sadly.

"Oh, Ben – it's Liverpool – but perhaps it's all for the best. I know you'll be on the go every minute when you get back, and having to worry about seeing me too might not be such a good idea."

He felt a stabbing disappointment, yet relief. The other arrangement, he knew, would never work out, and now she would be close to her parents. He was glad she had accepted it philosophically.

"Well, darling, we have no choice in the matter, so now let's start enjoying our seconds," he said laughingly. "I thought we might go to the local tonight for a pint and have dinner out for a change."

"That's marvellous, Ben, because I have to leave tomorrow afternoon and have quite a lot of packing up to do. I thought I'd get on with it while you are repairing the door."

"That's a good idea," he said, as he carefully put the gear that he had collected from his B. and B. place in an orderly pile by the front door. It didn't strike Rosie at the time as being unusual, she did not see the deliberate intention behind it.

The day was as happy as they could make it. They both kept up a cheerful front, but their heartaches were hard to bear. As she got herself ready for going out and walked down the cottage stairs, he was waiting for her. She hesitated as she reached the bottom step, then she rushed towards him – but there was no laughter now, only tears. They clung together and it was almost a relief to drop the facade for a moment. Then she drew away from him, wiped her eyes and bravely carried on with the charade.

The pub was full of locals, with a sprinkling of service men and women. There was much talk of the bombing of Liverpool and particularly the devastation of the dock area. The radio blared out Vera Lynn's most popular songs – the pathos of 'We'll meet again' was too much for Rosie, so they hastened out into the darkness to the little hotel close by for dinner. Neither of them was hungry and they hurried through the meal, longing to be on their own again. Abruptly, Ben stood up.

"Let's go home to bed, Rosie, I want to hold you in my arms for all the remaining seconds we have left." He gave a little smile, an attempt at humour which at that moment she couldn't even hope to match.

They held hands tightly and, as they walked home, they again heard the now-familiar sound of enemy aircraft overhead. This time they did not even comment on it.

Come what may, Rosie knew that this night would live with her for ever. They clung tightly together with the unspoken but obvious realisation that it might be their last. They talked intimately until after midnight, then they came together gently and fondly for the last time – finally Rosie snuggled close to him – exhausted by tears and emotion and was instantly asleep.

He cradled her in his arms and lay without moving, savouring the sweetness of their love-making, and deliberately cherishing every second of their closeness until he saw the dawn creeping in and heard the first chirrup of an awakening bird. Then, with the greatest care, he moved away soundlessly and, barefooted, crept down stairs.

All his plans had been made. He was quickly dressed, his clothes having been hidden in the cupboard below. After swilling his face in the sink, he returned to the sitting room and stood quietly looking at all the now familiar things. His feet felt leaden, he could hardly bear to tear himself away, but with a supreme effort he tiptoed to the door and, picking up his gear, went out quickly into the cold, raw dawn.

Remembering the creaking gate, he opened it carefully. Then, with one last look back at the beloved cottage, he was running noiselessly down the road towards the station.

* * * * *

Half awake and half asleep, Rosie reached out for Ben and then sat up with a start, realising he was not there. She called him anxiously until, in the dawn light, she suddenly saw an envelope on the pillow where he had lain. She instantly knew what this meant. She switched on the bedside lamp and, with thudding heart, tore it open and read

> *My dearest, darling little Rosie,*
>
> *I know you will understand my leaving without a final goodbye, I feel it is the kindest way for both of us. We have never needed words between us, for we are as close as twin souls. The love we have shared has been quite sublime. If our whole life were stretching ahead of us now, it would be sheer enchantment but, believe me darling, I have experienced utter bliss with you in the short time we have spent together. It has been sheer perfection.*
>
> *You are strong, Rosie. Be happy, for you have so much to give to others, who need your encouragement. Remember I shall always be close to you and whatever happens there is no need for sadness.*
>
> *You have all my love.*
>
> *Your Ben.*

She was as white as a sheet. Devastated, she fell back on her pillow, racked with heart-rending sobs. She knew this was the end – the seconds had run out. She would never see Ben again.

* * * * *

The Battle of Britain was now a battle of survival, a furious struggle in the face of tremendous odds. The first thin line of defence was in the air and already stretched to the utmost. Barges were massed along the French and Belgian coasts in readiness for the German invasion of Britain, Hitler's Operation Sea Lion. This could not be launched without control of the air – thus the destiny of the country depended upon an incredibly small number of brave young pilots in Spitfires and Hurricanes, fighting with grim determination to overcome the superior strength of the Luftwaffe. This was indeed their finest hour.

When Ben returned to the squadron, he was instantly aware of the heightened tension that had developed during his absence. He was greeted enthusiastically by his fellow pilots, who were sitting around on tenterhooks, waiting for their next call to scramble. He was immensely popular in the squadron, admired particularly for his steadfast courage – he had guts. There was a classic example of this when alone, he had attacked out of the sun twenty five Messerschmitt 109s and had shot down two before diving into protective cloud-cover then safely returning to base. For this exploit he had been awarded the Distinguished Flying Cross.

Seasoned pilots were at a premium now and the replacements, coming into the squadron, were young men with the minimum number of flying hours and without combat experience.

He looked anxiously around for Mike and saw him sitting alone, slumped in a corner – still alive, thank God! His fur-lined flying jacket was open, his tense face staring at the ground, lost in thought. As he saw Ben approaching, he brightened up and jumped to his feet, patting his chum warmly on the shoulder.

"Hello, old chap, did you have a nice leave? It's marvellous to have you back."

"Yes, I had a wonderful time," Ben replied, "but it's bloody good to see you again. Now tell me the score, what's been happening in my absence?"

Mike quickly brought Ben up to date with the news of the squadron – it wasn't good: several of their friends had bought it and he noticed that Mike's face was grey and drawn, his eyes bloodshot with fatigue. He was jumpy and obviously stretched to the limit.

"The heat's really on, Ben – I've just about had it. We seem to be scrambling the whole time now. Thank God you're back. The new replacements, poor sods, are terribly inexperienced – I feel like an old hen with chicks up there but, Ben, I really believe we're winning. We've knocked up some big scores lately and I don't believe the Hun will be able to keep up the pace much longer."

"Thank heavens for that," Ben replied fervently. "If we can just hold on, then that bastard Hitler will never dare to invade. To be overrun by bloody Nazis would be the dreaded end."

They were silent for a moment until Ben could contain himself no longer. He was bursting to reveal his good news.

"Mike, I've something stupendous to tell you – believe it or not, I've fallen in love with the sweetest and most beautiful girl in the world – her name is Rosie Dunbar."

Mike looked astonished, then an enormous smile spread across his face.

"Congratulations Benjamin, you old fox, but why have I never heard of Rosie Dunbar before?"

"Well, to tell you the truth, dear boy, I met her for the first time during my leave and, to use an old fashioned expression, it was simply love at first sight,"

"My goodness, old Ben, she must be quite a doll to have done this to you of all people, but jolly good luck to you both. This definitely calls for a celebration. How about meeting me at the Spotted Horse this evening for a pint, then you can tell me all about her."

"That's a splendid idea," Ben replied enthusiastically. "I'm going to need your luck, chum, tomorrow. I'm back on ops and that's what I want to talk to you about." He cleared his throat and hesitated for a moment. "Will you promise to do something for me, Mike?"

"Of course, anything."

"You are my best friend and, if my number should ever be up, will you please send on this letter and my medals to Rosie?" He produced an envelope from his pocket. "I'll leave it in my locker. I'd be most grateful if you wrote her a short note telling her the score, as gently as possible as she's had a tough time in one way and another."

"Of course, old chap," Mike said gruffly. "But don't worry. Somehow or other we'll manage to survive this bloody war together."

They grinned at each other with understanding until suddenly, interrupted by the insistent call to scramble, Mike jumped to his feet like lightning and, shouting over his shoulder: "See you chum", was gone. It was only a matter of seconds before all the others had departed, running like bats out of hell to their aircraft, always at the ready for take-off.

Ben watched the familiar yet ever-exciting spectacle of the Spits speeding down the runway and becoming airborne and, as they gained height, opening out into their battle formation. He hated to miss the party but it would be his turn tomorrow – yet he felt different now. The thought of permanent separation from Rosie was unbearable.

He remained standing there, staring at the empty runways, deep in thought. How would she manage without him? A picture flashed through his mind of a snapshot he had seen of Peter and Rosie together; Peter's arm was around her shoulder as he looked down at her with obvious adoration. Ben's whole being told him that Peter loved her and he felt certain that he was now a changed man and would make her a good husband. Perhaps this was the answer. Her happiness was the only thing that mattered, but oh how terrible if he were never to hold her in his arms again – to miss all her sweetness – it was unthinkable. He turned slowly and left the deserted building. He must write to her at once, for who knows what might happen tomorrow?

*　*　*　*　*

Since leaving the cottage for Liverpool Rosie's life had changed completely. The brief interlude of delirious joy, that she had experienced with Ben, seemed like an exquisite dream, shattered now by the grim realities of war. Yet she was so utterly close to him. He was warmly cocooned around her heart and she felt that this would always be so, whatever fate held in store for them.

She had received one letter from him so far, expressing his undying love and longing for her. She sensed that since being back on ops, his life like hers was a blur of danger, daring and death and she knew she must accept the uncertainty of their future.

She had been thrown in at the deep end the moment she arrived in Liverpool. She was assigned an ambulance and a young V.A.D. trained assistant, called Maisie, and right from the start they worked well together. Rosie liked her on sight. She was an attractive brunette with dishevelled curly hair, a high colour and twinkling brown eyes. She was strong and sturdy and would tackle anything. She came from a large working class family and was always full of jolly quips and fun. Nothing seemed to get her down. They made a splendid team.

They were on duty 24 hours a day, sleeping on bunks during quiet periods, but instantly springing into action the moment the alert sounded; they would don their tin hats and carry their gas masks, ready to proceed to wherever the bombs had rained down their deadly terror and destruction. It was a great help that Rosie knew the area so well, particularly around the docks where her father's factory was situated. Rosie was an indefatigable worker – driving, digging out, and administering first aid. Her compassion was unlimited and she was a great source of comfort and reassurance to the poor souls, whom she tended.

Once she helped to dig out a little girl of Ricky's age but by the time they reached her it was too late. Her poor little face was covered with blood and grime and her staring eyes were frozen in a mask of shock. With overwhelming compassion, Rosie had turned to the mother, and held her tightly in her arms – anything to dispel the look of horror on her stricken face.

After this incident she worked even harder, never sparing herself and ever digging, digging. Her courage was remarkable – when others sought shelter, she kept doggedly on and on. Maisie was always generous in her praise of Rosie.

Whenever she was able, Rosie went home to see her parents. The neighbourhood had taken a battering but their house was still intact. One afternoon, having a few hours off duty, she went over to see them. They were both in the garden searching among the bushes for their beloved Siamese cat, Samson, who had taken Chi Chi's place, after the little dog had died. Samson had disppeared the night before, making a bolt through the front door, as soon as the blitz started, evidently preferring the cover of the trees to the underground shelter. After much calling, to their utter relief, Samson seemed to appear from nowhere, looking delighted to see them and purring away with pleasure. Her mother swept him up into her arms, holding him close and Rosie noticed that her eyes were full of tears, showing the evident strain under which she was living.

"Why don't you come down to the cottage with me this weekend?" Rosie asked. "I've been told I must take some time off and I hate the thought of going alone. It would do you both good to have a couple of peaceful nights away from the blitz."

Her father hesitated – he was worried about leaving his factory and felt guilty of the privilege of escape. All his workmen lived nearby in the thick of the bombing and had to take it. He admired their hardy northern tradition of endurance. However, seeing his wife's drawn face and noticing how thin and fragile Rosie looked, he decided that to get away from Liverpool would do them good; they both badly needed a break.

"All right, Rosie, we'll go. I've got enough petrol coupons to take us there and back and the change will be most welcome."

Rosie's face lit up with relief as she turned to her mother. "There's no need to worry about Samson, Mum, we can take him with us. I know he hates car rides but he'll be all right in his basket."

"How do you think he will get on with Biscuit?"

"Oh Biscuit is such a darling – a super cat and I'm sure they'll become good friends."

Her mother smiled but looked sceptical – cats were so unpredictable.

"It will be lovely being in the quiet of the country," she said, "though I must admit I feel a bit guilty escaping when our faithful workers are right in the thick of it."

* * * * *

They started early the following morning, arriving at the cottage by mid-day. The weather was kind again. The sun was shining and there was hardly any wind but there was a nip in the air and the little garden was no longer gay. A sadness had descended upon it as the early frost had caught and withered some of the blooms.

Bron had everything ready for them. A lovely fire was burning in the hearth and a plate of delicious sandwiches and coffee had been prepared for their lunch. To Rosie it was coming home.

As she relaxed in her chair by the fire, she raised her eyes at long last to look at her portrait of Ben. She had dreaded doing so, fearing the pain would be too hard to bear but to her surprise she felt only comfort, as though he were there with her. The illusion of his presence was so strong that there seemed to be a direct communication between them. She no longer felt alone.

She dropped her eyes hastily, hoping that her mother had not seen her expression but it had not passed unnoticed. There was an uncomfortable silence between them, then her mother spoke.

"I see, Rosie, you have painted a new portrait. Who is the young man? It is a brilliant study, so lifelike that he almost seems one of us."

Rosie hesitated before replying. "I'm glad you think that, mother. He is a very dear friend of mine. He is a pilot, flying Spits and is on ops at the moment. It is a good likeness and I think the best portrait I have ever done."

There was a short silence then her mother, who had obviously been thinking things over, said: "Tell me, Rosie, do you ever hear from Peter?"

"No, mother, I don't but I believe that he is in command of an M.T.B., operating across the Channel."

"I see," she murmured.

Rosie felt uneasy but she carried on. "I want you to know that I feel differently about Peter now. I was partly to blame for our break-up. It wasn't all his fault."

Her mother looked across at her searchingly. "I'm glad you've told me this, Rosie. Does this mean that he is forgiven?"

"Yes, Mum, it does but our relationship is spoilt and we shall never come together again. You were right when you said I was too immature to marry."

Rosie got up from her seat and went into the kitchen to make more coffee. She obviously did not wish to prolong the conversation and her mother had far too much sense to pursue the subject.

During the afternoon they walked along to see Ricky's grave. The day was foggy and bleak, with a low sun just showing through the haze. The trees had turned to their autumnal shades.

The grave was immaculate. Only a few stray leaves blew hither and thither, their rustling the only sound in the ever-silent churchyard. The new white marble cross brought back to Rosie the child's sweetness and goodness. Perhaps now she could remember him with less anguish.

She held her mother's arm on the way home. Rosie felt protective towards her, for she seemed to have aged considerably. The loss of her grandson had been a mortal blow.

"You know, Mum, even though Ricky's life was short, it was nearly perfect. We all loved him and he was such a happy little fellow. Peter was good to him too when we were in Chatham," she conceded.

Her mother nodded in agreement "We must try not to grieve for him – he was adored by all of us," but inwardly she was quite inconsolable.

They quickened their pace and were glad to get back to the cottage to a warm fire and a steaming hot cup of tea. Mr. Greenwood was busy sorting through a briefcase full of papers he had brought with him. The last shipment of sugar, which he had expected from Trinidad, had never reached its destination. The ship carrying it had been sunk by a U-boat while crossing in convoy; his stocks were getting low. Running a business in wartime was a constant worry and anxiety. He resented being too old to be in the services. He gave a sigh – it would be so nice to be young again.

He blamed the government for their lack of preparation and especially "that fool Neville Chamberlain" lulling everyone into a sense of false security – with his slogan "Peace in our time", yet still not rearming the country adequately. Well we are suffering for it now, he thought, and if it were not for men like this nice looking chap, who Rosie had painted we would be finished. He wondered idly if there was anything between them, but he didn't say a word.

They decided to have an early night and enjoy the luxury of undisturbed sleep but no sooner were they comfortably settled in their beds than they heard the ominous throb of aircraft overhead. They feared the target would be Liverpool, but tried to dismiss it from their minds and get the rest which they so badly needed.

Rosie curled up in bed like a child, holding a pillow close to her as she so often did since being alone. That night she experienced the most vivid and terrifying dream of her life. She saw Ben in the cockpit of his blazing aircraft, fighting to get clear of his harness, with flames leaping towards him. Every time he attempted to wrench himself free, he became more entangled and the flames leapt closer and closer, until they finally engulfed him. She distinctly heard him calling "Rosie, Rosie". She woke up with a tremendous start, bathed in perspiration and sobbing uncontrollably – she felt that this was the end.

*   *   *   *   *

The family met at breakfast the next morning. Rosie's face was ashen. They switched on the wireless and heard that on the previous night there had been the largest of all Merseyside raids so far – at least three hundred bombers had taken part in it.

They all agreed that they must return home at once and, after a hurried breakfast, they packed up the car and were on their way. Rosie tried hard not to think of Ben, determined to convince herself that it had only been a nightmare. She sensed that there was trouble ahead in Liverpool and she must be mentally prepared for the worst. Her father drove fast and almost in silence. They were all engrossed in their own private thoughts and dreads.

As they approached the Mersey Tunnel, they were stopped by the police. A young officer motioned them to draw in to the side of the road.

"I'm sorry, sir, but you can't use the tunnel. No-one is allowed through today.

I'm afraid Liverpool is a disaster area – you must turn back."

"But officer," Mr. Greenwood protested, "we live there and I own a factory in the city, so it is imperative that we get to it."

"Let me see your driving licence and identity card, please sir."

After a cursory glance at these he was satisfied and beckoned them on. They all gave a sigh of relief as they drove through the tunnel entrance.

"Thank goodness he allowed us to go but I'm afraid, my dears, we must be prepared for shocks." Mr. Greenwood put his hand on his wife's knee and she turned to him with a reassuring smile. He knew he could depend on her whatever the circumstances.

It was eerie going through the tunnel which was almost devoid of traffic. When they emerged at the other end they saw numerous buildings in ruins. Fires still burned fiercely and many streets were cordoned off, with unexploded bombs and surface débris to be cleared. Their usual route was impassable, so they had to make several diversions. They tried going down a narrow side street that seemed relatively clear of obstruction but, just as they passed a burning building, a great wooden beam fell from the roof with a resounding crash and sparks flying. It narrowly missed the car and Rosie, sitting in the back seat, ducked her head as it seemed inevitable they would be hit.

Eventually, after taking many circuitous routes, they managed to get on to the main Scotland Road again, crawling along it, trying to avoid the débris. Whole terraces of slum property had been demolished and many houses stood windowless and blackened by smoke. The poor always get the worst of it, Rosie thought, and her heart bled for some of the pitiful sights before them.

Homeless families, with prams full of bedding and hastily-packed holdalls, were walking away from the blazing city, searching for somewhere to sleep, under the hedgerows or, with luck, in a barn.

There was one little group she found unbearably pathetic. A young woman, aged beyond her years through poverty and deprivation, was wheeling along a laden pram with three diminutive children beside her, clinging to her skirt and being coaxed to walk – an underfed mongrel was tethered to the pram handle by a piece of string. The poor animal was trying not to get in the way. There was abject despair written all over this young mother's face. Rosie knew she would never forget her expression – it was locked in her memory. This was another subject for her pictorial protest against the horrors of war.

As they neared the factory the tension in the car mounted and, approaching along the wide straight road, they soon became aware that something was badly amiss. They saw at once that the handsome entrance gates and pillars had been razed to the ground and, as they drew closer, they saw with horror that the factory had been completely demolished, with only enormous piles of bricks and rubble remaining. Nothing was recognisable – just a large area of devastation.

There was complete silence in the car as it drew to a standstill. The enormity of the shock had left them all speechless. It was hard to believe their eyes. Then slowly, with obvious effort, Mr. Greenwood pushed open the car door and stepped out on to the pavement. He looked bewildered, staring blankly around at what remained of his life's work – his livelihood.

Sitting on a pile of rubble, waiting for his boss to arrive, was his foreman, Bill, who had been his very first employee. He had been taken on as a lad at sixteen and through the years had been loyal and hard-working. As soon as he saw Mr. Greenwood he stood up, his old cloth cap askew and tears running down his face. He picked his way through the rubble and solemnly shook Mr. Greenwood by the hand.

"I've been waiting for you, sir, since early morning. We heard the explosion in the middle of the night and I said to the wife: 'I'm going to see if things are all right at the factory as soon as it's light' . . . " – his voice tailed off, too upset to continue, then with an effort he managed to regain his composure. "It was a direct hit from a landmine that did it, sir. Mr. Riley, the landlord of the pub on the corner, saw it all happen. He said that there was a blinding flash and then a deafening explosion."

"Has there been any loss of life, Bill? Mr. Greenwood asked anxiously.

"No, sir, old Thomas, the night watchman, sheltered under that new vacuum pan and it held. He's in the hospital now, stone deaf. The blast broke the old feller's ear drums but they say he's comfortable enough."

"Thank God for that," Mr. Greenwood said vehemently. "Tell him I will be along to see him later, if you can get the message through to him."

By this time Rosie and her mother were out of the car and looking around, horrified by the disaster. Mrs. Greenwood knew so well what a mortal blow this was for her husband. He had started this business as a young man and had put his heart and soul into it. He had worked all the hours God sends, saving each year to buy better and better plant and equipment. He had been immensely proud of his achievement, having ended up with a thriving enterprise. She took his arm, trying her best to comfort him, but she felt at a loss for words.

"I am dreadfully sorry, dear – it's a terrible blow for you but let's be thankful that nobody was killed. We must count our blessings. This is only bricks and mortar it can be built up again."

He deeply appreciated her brave words. She was always a tower of strength to him. With an anxious face he turned to Bill again: "How are you off for money, Bill?"

"I'm afraid I'm skint as usual, sir."

Mr. Greenwood took out his wallet – his hands were shaking.

"Well, don't you worry, Bill, here are your next week's wages and I'll see you're all right."

A look of relief spread over Bill's face. He lived a hand-to-mouth existence, having the weakness of being a heavy drinker. Over the years Mr. Greenwood had always helped him out, if there had been a crisis.

"Thank you very much, sir. It's very kind of you and I must say you have taken a load off my mind. My missus was terrified and didn't know where we'd get out next meal."

"Tell her from me not to worry. Now, Bill, will you gather together the workers tomorrow morning at about nine o'clock. I see part of the office building is still standing so we can meet there."

"Very good, sir, I'll try to get a message round to everyone this afternoon. I think I'd better be on my way now in case those buggers come back again."

He was obviously glad that there was something he could do to help and was relieved since seeing the boss. The missus would be glad of the lolly. "Goodbye all," he said touching his cap as he unsteadily mounted a dilapidated bicycle and went wobbling on his way. They all managed to summon up a smile.

Mr. Greenwood put a protective arm around his wife and looked anxiously across at Rosie. How lucky he was to have them both; so long as they were all right nothing else really mattered.

"I think we'd better get going, my dears, before dusk. It's no good hanging about here for there may be other shocks waiting for us at home."

They drove along slowly, picking their way through the devastation, out of the city and into the suburbs. They were shocked to see that several houses in the park had been hit but, from a distance, theirs appeared to be intact and they all felt thankful; but as they proceeded up the drive to the front door they saw with sinking hearts that all the windows had been blown in. There was shattered glass everywhere and the curtains had been cut to ribbons. They walked from room to room and this usually immaculate house was full of dust, dirt and broken glass – it was heartbreaking.

Rosie tried her best to comfort them. "You know it could be a lot worse; it's only the windows that have gone. I'll be here all day tomorrow and we can make arrangements to have them boarded up. It won't take long to get all the mess cleared away and the house put in order again."

Her mother nodded in agreement. "we can do it together, dear," she said stoically, but she was badly shaken; this was her domain and the destruction of it shocked her.

They all gave a start of apprehension as they heard the eerie wail of the air raid sirens sounding off again. It seemed almost too much to bear. Rosie felt terribly sorry for her parents. To her they now appeared old and needed protection.

"You both go down to the shelter and take Samson with you and I'll be there in a minute with a cup of tea."

For once they acquiesced without an argument. "Thank you, Rosie," her father said. "A cup of tea will do us good."

Her father took her mother's arm and down they went – almost into the bowels of the earth, she thought. She hurried to put on the kettle but, before it was ready, the ack-ack guns had opened up, shaking the very foundations of the house and their blinding flashes illuminated the rooms. She heard the sound of engines and a thunder-clap of bombs in the distance. This was the last straw; a feeling of hopelessness overcame her – would they ever survive this terrible war?

No Resting Place

No grave, no earth or stone to rest my weary head.
No place to go for solace, close to you.
To share with you the self-same earth,
Enfolding all in love,
To weep my bitter tears.

B.B.

16

AFTER THE two successive nightly raids on Liverpool, Rosie returned to work immediately. The bombing had been severe and there was heavy loss of life. She and Maisie were sent to various first aid posts to remove the dead to mortuaries. It was a grim and terrible task. There appeared to be no proper plan or organisation but somehow they seemed to muddle through by sheer initiative and guts. She couldn't have a better assistant than Maisie, this sturdy warm-hearted Liverpudlian was an absolute brick.

Rosie felt deeply about the apparent casual approach to the dead, who were hastily disposed of without ceremony. This was perhaps understandable, for the first priority was to restore order out of chaos and protect the living. Rosie instinctively treated with respect these poor, mangled and distorted remains, hunting for sheets or covering of any kind and saying a silent prayer over each victim.

Often the physical effort of carrying the stretchers was too much for the girls and they had to take snatches of rest, laying down the stretchers and leaning against any nearby wall to regain their breath. Life assumed a complete unreality at this time and, although Rosie wondered what was happening at home, she ceased to worry about it. Her parents' problems seemed diminutive compared with the death and destruction which faced her each day in the city area.

Thankfully the raids suddenly ceased, which helped considerably with the clearing-up process. The city was coming to life again and the general routine approaching normal. Pubs were doing good business at nights – theatres and cinemas enjoyed full houses. Dance halls were particularly well filled with service personnel living it up on the principle that 'Who knows what tomorrow may bring?' The general feeling of insecurity prompted a devil-may-care attitude and one of making the most of being alive.

Morale generally was amazingly good and Rosie was often astonished by the resilience and bravery of the ordinary man in the street. Lack of sleep seemed to be the most undermining factor. Many could not get any real rest in their primitive outdoor shelters so went back to their beds, taking a chance, but invariably they would be driven out again to the shelters by the deafening ack-ack gun fire and alarming fall of bombs.

* * * * *

Rosie lay on her bunk trying to rest for a couple of hours and gather together her strength. She and Maisie were being sent to a nearby hospital to help out with the changing of dressings and the treatment of minor injuries.

Since the bombing had ceased, they were temporarily given other duties. Rosie was becoming conscious of strain and the only way she survived was through sheer doggedness and a feeling of overwhelming sympathy for the injured. She tried to sleep but the memories of the day were just too vivid. As she lay there she heard footsteps and the curtain was drawn back a fraction by Maisie.

"Are you awake, Rosie? This letter has just come for you."

Rosie sat up and, leaning on her elbow, took it eagerly from her.

"Oh, thank you, Maisie, I'm so relieved," she said grasping the envelope but her voice tailed off as she saw the writing – it was in a strange hand. Maisie had gone. The small cubicle seemed to turn over and over, revolving crazily with dazzling lights. Then, as Rosie gripped the side of her bunk, it settled down again to normality. She knew this was it – what she had anticipated and dreaded ever since her terrifying nightmare.

Carefully she opened the heavy official envelope with the R.A.F. crest in the corner. Out tumbled two envelopes – one marked 'medals' and the other bearing only her name 'Rosie'. There was an accompanying sheet of writing paper and, as she unfolded it and started reading, her heart pounded so madly that it was hard to breathe. The letter was from Mike, saying how distressed he was to have to break the news of Ben's death. He had been shot down by anti-aircraft guns at Calais after heroically pressing home attacks on the harbour installations. Tragically he had been hit by flak as he was peeling off for home. His gallantry was an inspiration to the squadron.

Mike ended his letter –

I feel awful for you, Rosie, for I know how much you loved each other. I am absolutely shattered myself but I feel proud to have had such a friend. Ben asked me to send on to you the enclosed letter, together with his medals, if the worst should ever happen to him. This I do with the deepest regret. God bless you, Rosie, and never hesitate to write, if you need my help.
       Mike.

She let the letter drop and gripped tightly the 'Rosie' envelope. She held it close to her – the last communication she would ever have from Ben. Then gently she opened it and read with difficulty through her tears, cherishing every word.

My dearest Darling,
 I have a premonition that I will not survive my next few missions and I am leaving this letter with Mike to be posted if I do not return.
 Rosie, I want you to know that you have given me the greatest happiness a man could possibly have. The closeness of our relationship has been perfection. My only concern is that you can find contentment yourself again. The little money I have is yours and I am hoping that this will enable you to build the studio of your dreams and stay on in your beloved cottage after the war. You have such very great artistic talent, my darling.
 Don't grieve for me. I am one of the fortunate ones, for together we reached the heights. Darling Rosie, I adore you.
      Eternally your very own
       Ben

She turned over and faced the wall. She had a strong desire to give way to a paroxysm of grief. She had the need to cry, as she had done as a child, just cry and cry, but she knew she must not give way to this weakness now. There was work to be done.

She lay for a few minutes longer then, dragging herself up with difficulty, she dressed. She picked up her tin hat and gas mask and walked through to Maisie, looking as white as a sheet. She seemed to have aged years in a matter of minutes.

One glance was enough for Maisie.

"Was it bad news, luv? You look all in."

Rosie just nodded in reply.

"Poor dear, you've suffered more than most in this war. Sit down now, the kettle's boiling and I'll make us a quick cuppa."

"Thank you, Maisie," she said in a strangled voice.

As she drank the hot strong brew, she was grateful to Maisie – no questions were asked but Rosie was conscious of her warm sympathy. There was too much tragedy around and the least said the better for all concerned. The rest of the day was a blur for Rosie. She threw herself into her work, mechanically doing what she had to, but her limbs were as heavy as lead, almost as heavy as her heart.

* * * * *

During the next few weeks Rosie applied herself to her duties, working fanatically, treating the injured and comforting the bereaved, not allowing herself a moment to think. She went to bed at night completely exhausted, blessedly unconscious almost the moment her head touched the pillow.

The raids had tailed off somewhat and people were optimistically hoping that there would not be any more attacks on Liverpool. Rosie tried to see her parents as often as possible. Making her way home in the black-out was a misery, but she developed cat's eyes and instinctively found her way about in the inky blackness. Her father always insisted on driving her back, using his precious petrol. They would creep along through the unlit city, with only tiny pin points of light showing; she knew it was a great strain on him.

Her parents' morale was splendid, in spite of the body blows they had suffered. Already her father had arranged for another company to take over the refining of sugar for him, so that his contracts would be honoured. Negotiations were going on for the re-building of the factory. He would get government support, as sugar was such an important commodity, hoarded for jam making as shortages caused many to give it up in tea. She admired his will to start again at his age, with such odds stacked against him. He was made of stern stuff and she herself must show the same fortitude and determination.

Several more weeks passed, still without any significant bombing then, just before Christmas, there were two terrifying nights, with hundreds of enemy aircraft involved. This pre-Christmas blitz was taken remarkably well with typical northern stoicism. The two girls made a splendid team and again they pitched in unsparingly without regard for self, but Rosie was exhausted and Maisie knew that her friend had come to the end of her tether. Ever since Ben's death her strength seemed to be ebbing away. The injuries to children were the hardest for Rosie to bear – she was always reminded of Ricky. Since the previous lull in the bombing, parents had unwisely brought back their children from the safety of the country.

On the second night, during the height of the blitz, the girls were sent to a mean little street just off the dock road. The ambulance ploughed through every hazard to reach a group of slum dwellings which had been hit by a stick of incendiary bombs. In spite of heroic attempts by fire watchers to put out the flames, the houses were soon a blazing inferno. The street was in a turmoil, with whirling clouds of acrid smoke and choking brick dust. Rosie spotted a ragged little urchin with wild frightened eyes and soot-blackened face. He was screaming for his mother and running around in frantic circles; his arms and legs were covered in red weals and blisters. She swept him up in her arms and carried him to the ambulance – he was no older than Ricky. She started preliminary first aid, but he was frightened and distraught and difficult to treat. All he wanted was *my mum*. His thin little chest was heaving with convulsive sobs but Rosie managed to bandage him up and at least soothe the pain.

She felt an overwhelming pity for this little scrap of humanity and an unreasoning rage against his mother. A blousy-looking woman suddenly appeared through a vast pall of smoke from around the back of the ambulance, swearing like a bargee, but when she saw her child a look of relief swept over her face and she gave a toothless grin.

"Where the 'ell 'ave you bin, Ernie. I've been looking all over the shop for yer and any'ow what's all the racket about? Stop yer bleedin' row."

He clambered out of the ambulance and ran into her arms and all his crying ceased. He was used to harsh words – they meant nothing – he was secure again, but it was all too much for Rosie.

"You stupid woman," she shouted. "This child is badly burnt, you should be ashamed of yourself. He ought to be evacuated to the country."

She could have hit this apparently tough, uncaring woman, who turned on her with indignation.

"It's all right for yer to talk, Miss. We've only just brought 'im 'ome for Christmas – 'e was evacuated but 'e wouldn't eat and got ill – so what the 'ell could we do? We only done our best."

Rosie leant against the ambulance and said more gently, "I'm sorry, I hate to see children suffer."

This incident upset her; she knew she needed a rest. She was becoming unreasonable, making hasty judgements, without knowing the circumstances. Suddenly she longed with all her heart and soul for the peace and quiet of the cottage. To be able to shut herself away from all this and paint and paint the vivid pictures which filled her mind.

* * * * *

Christmas was over, thank goodness. In spite of shortages, everyone had made the best they could of it. Food rations were slightly increased which helped to boost morale. Normally rations were small, with only a tiny meat allowance, very little sugar and fats; eggs had virtually disappeared from the shops, but the thing that hit hardest was the tea ration. For a cup of tea was the cure for all ills and would calm the frightened or soothe the bereaved.

Rosie went home and helped to cook the Christmas dinner. It was an agonising time for the family; the three of them tried their best to put up a brave front, but however hard Rosie tried, Ricky's little face was always before her eyes. He would have been three years old now. The loss of her darling Ben was eating into her; she still could not quite believe she would never be in his arms again.

For the first time she wondered where Peter was and if he were safe; latterly she had felt concerned for him and his happiness. Her own tragic misfortunes had matured her – she was more tolerant and understanding now – she had grown up.

She asked her mother if she had any news of Peter, but she had not. Her mother confessed that she had also been thinking about him, for to her he was still part of the family. She had read in the local newspaper that Parkie had been killed in action, fighting with the 8th Army in North Africa; this grieved her deeply but she dare not mention it to Rosie at such a time.

* * * * *

Old Dr. McDonald, the Greenwood's family doctor, who was long past retirement age, had started working again. He had known Rosie all her life, indeed he had brought her into the world.

He was in the Red Cross office the day after Christmas when she arrived. He looked up as she walked in and was taken aback by her appearance and especially her frailty. She had lost so much weight and her eyes, ringed with shadows, appeared abnormally large in her drawn face.

"Hello, Rosie my dear, how are you?"

She smiled back but all her old gaiety was missing.

"It's wonderful to see you again, Dr. Mac. How are you?"

It was obvious to him that she was over-wrought.

"I have a message for you, Rosie, from an old friend of yours – a delightful fellow, a Mr. Timms."

She looked up eagerly. "Wherever did you meet him? He's such a dear."

"Well I've just been down to Chatham and he came into casualty, suffering from burns."

"Oh, no!" The words slipped out agonisingly.

"Nothing to worry about, Rosie, they were only first degree surface burns. He's a fire watcher and incendiaries hit the factory where he was. A blazing bit of timber fell on him but he's a tough little fellow and was quite unperturbed. He sent you his love and spoke of you so warmly – you have a great admirer there."

She struggled to keep back the tears but hadn't the strength to pull herself together and put up her usual facade. Without warning she burst into tears. Dr. Mac got up from his desk and patted her shoulder. His voice was gentle.

"Rosie, you look tired out. You have been overdoing it and everyone has their limit, you know. Come to the surgery this afternoon and I'll thoroughly check you over. Will three o'clock be all right?"

She was too upset to answer, but nodded in agreement and, wiping her eyes, fled from the office. Why had she made such a fool of herself?

When she returned that afternoon, she passed in the street an ex-serviceman from the First World War. He was playing a mouth organ. One arm was missing below the elbow and his empty sleeve was secured by a safety pin. A row of medals adorned his shabby old suit and on the pavement beside him was his cap, in which were scattered a few pennies. His face was blue with cold as he bravely played 'The White Cliffs of Dover'. A lump came to her throat as she threw down a shilling and hurried on.

She remembered Ben telling her of the delight he felt on returning from a mission when he saw the dear old white cliffs of Dover gleaming in the distance – he was coming home. Dear God, he would never experience that again – buried in the deep, still trapped in the cockpit of his aircraft. She shuddered as she thought of him there. She must not torture herself like this. It did no good, but seeing this shadow of a man from the First World War filled her with despair – they were at it all over again.

She arrived breathless at the surgery, but right on time. Dr. Mac was waiting. He looked searchingly at her and noticed how her uniform hung loosely on her now-slender frame. He knew most of what she had been through. Mr. Timms had told him the story of her ordeal in Chatham and the Red Cross had filled in the rest. She was at the end of her tether, both mentally and physically.

"Good afternoon Rosie, my dear" he said with a cheery smile, trying to put her at ease.

"Hello Doc.," she replied. "It's very good of you to see me. I feel an awful fraud taking up your time when you're so terribly busy."

"Nonsense, my dear, I always have time for you. Now will you go into the first cubicle and take off your dress and put on the gown provided, then lie down."

She nodded: "I'll only be a minute."

When he entered the cubicle, he studied her drawn face on the pillow and her haunted eyes gave him a painful twinge. This was a feeling that, as a doctor, he had learned to suppress long ago and was surprised that he was still so vulnerable.

He checked her thoroughly and her heart confirmed his original suspicions.

"You can sit up now, Rosie, while I talk to you."

She leant on her elbow and looked into his kindly face, so familiar and reassuring. She felt a slight lessening of her burden, as though he had shouldered part of it.

"Now, my dear, you have been overdoing it and the strain has been just too much for you. You are suffering from a 'tired heart' and you must have a long rest."

She started to protest but he would have none of it.

"You must accept what I am telling you, Rosie; I have looked after you all your life and I feel I can talk to you frankly like a Dutch Uncle. If you don't do what I say, you will have a complete breakdown. You must give up ambulance driving at once; you have done more than your fair share. You need a complete rest for at least six months."

Her voice was husky as she replied: "If this is an order, Dr. Mac, I have no choice but to obey." She said this with obvious reluctance and yet she felt a sense of relief too. A vision of her cottage swam before her eyes. She would soon be able to return to it, away from the turmoil.

She turned to him with a wan smile: "Thank you, Dr. Mac, I'll do as you say."

He held her arm affectionately. "Go straight home, Rosie. I'll explain everything to them here. They are all going to miss you and particularly Maisie."

Tears filled Rosie's eyes again and she spoke huskily. "I shall miss her too – dear warm-hearted Maisie. I wish I could say goodbye to her but she won't be here until this evening. Will you please give her a message for me, Dr. Mac?"

"Of course, my dear, I shall be working late tonight."

She seemed to be searching for the right words. "Please give her my love and tell her I will write to her as soon as I'm settled in the cottage." Then, after a pause, she said wistfully: "Dr. Mac, please say: 'Thank you' for me   she'll understand, we've been through so much together. She's a wonderful girl."

Rosie walked leisurely up from the little station. At least nothing had changed here. The peace of the country lane was like balm to her soul. She gazed with pleasure at all the familiar sights and her heart lifted as she saw in the distance the windows of 'Apple Trees' gleaming in the wintry sunshine and a wisp of smoke rising from the chimney. She knew that Bron was there waiting to welcome her so she would not have to face that first moment alone.

She pushed open the cottage door and stood on the threshold, quietly gazing around. This was her refuge. There were hurried steps from the kitchen and Bron appeared with a beaming smile.

"Hello, Mam, I'm so glad you're back home again – it's been lonely without you – Biscuit has missed you too."

There was comfort in these kindly words and Rosie smiled back appreciatively.

"It's lovely to be here, Bron," but she was exhausted and light-headed after the journey and her smile faded as she flopped down into the nearest chair. Bron's happy expression quickly turned to one of consternation.

"My goodness, Mam, how thin you've gone – you look worn out" and her face showed her evident concern.

"Oh, I'm all right, Bron. I just need a rest. I have in fact been sent on sick leave, but how kind of you to be concerned about me." The ready tears sprang to her eyes again.

"You settle down by the fire, Mam, and I'll make some tea. I've got some special news for you but it will keep until you're rested."

Rosie closed her eyes for a moment, contemplating what the news could be. Bronwen somehow looked different – more self-confident and prettier. Her hair was set in a becoming style and surely she was using lipstick! Her overall was gay with flowers and Rosie guessed what she was going to be told. It was only a moment before Bron was back with a tray, laid for two, and a home-made chocolate cake – a favourite of Rosie's.

"You shouldn't waste your precious rations on me, Bron – but the cake looks absolutely delicious."

They always had their first cup of tea together; it was something they both enjoyed.

Bronwen poured out the tea and cut the cake, handing a piece to Rosie, then helped herself and sat in an upright chair beside the table.

"Now, Bron, please tell me your news. I'm anxious to hear it."

"Well, Mam," she said shyly, "I'm courting and we're going to be married in the summer."

"How splendid, Bron, but who is the lucky man?"

"Do you remember John Pugh, son of Richard Pugh, who owns Trecastell Farm?"

"Yes, Bron, of course I do. He's a very nice young man and so handsome. Congratulations, you really have done well and it's certainly no more than you deserve."

Bronwen blushed to the roots of her hair with embarrassment and excitement. "Could I bring him along to see you, Mam?" she asked, her eyes sparkling. "He's heard so much about you and the cottage and everything." She tailed off rather awkwardly.

"Of course, Bron, come whenever you like. I'm most anxious to meet your young man. I want to tell him how lucky he is getting you for a wife; but, Bron, I hope this doesn't mean you won't be able to go on working here?" For a moment Rosie's eyes clouded with a shadow of apprehension.

"Oh no, Mam, I'll never leave you." Love and loyalty shone out of her honest brown eyes. "John's Da has given us the little white cottage at Penrhyn cross roads, so of course I'll let 'Ty glyn' go. I'm not sorry, for I've been lonely there without Gran. John will be working for his Da, so thank goodness he won't be called up as they need farm workers badly – it's a reserved occupation."

A quick smile came to Rosie's lips.

"Dear Bron, I'm so happy for you. It's the best news I've had for a long time. You will make your John a wonderful little wife."

Her eyes were heavy and beginning to close. The warm fire had relaxed her and she could hardly keep awake.

"You have a nap now, Mam, you look all in. I'll wash up and unpack your bag. I've left some cold ham and salad in the larder for your supper."

"Thank you, Bron. It's lovely to be home again, but whatever would I do without you?"

Rosie was asleep almost before the words were out.

When she awoke, dusk was falling and it was chilly. She stoked up the fire. So far she had not dared to look at Ben's portrait. She had deliberately averted her eyes but now that she was alone the moment had come.

She got up slowly and walked across the room, standing beside him. Her heart twisted painfully as she gazed yearningly at the picture. She had accustomed herself to accepting that he was lost to her forever and it came as a shock to see his dear familiar face again. The portrait was inspired – reflecting to the full his integrity and goodness – an inner peace seemed to radiate from it, an acceptance of his destiny. She remained beside him for a while. She knew that his presence would always surround her.

* * * * *

Rosie had not realised how close to breaking point she had been. The next few weeks were almost like a time of hibernation. She sat by the fire all day long, dozing and reading her art books and contemplating the pictures she would paint when her strength returned. Her intense fatigue made her think of Peter's many ordeals and now she fully understood what he had gone through. She should have been more tolerant.

Bronwen came in each day and cooked her nourishing meals. In the country it was easier to get a few extra rations and Bronwen was determined to build up Rosie's strength again. She was beginning to feel better already and for the first time wandered into her tiny studio. She saw the picture of the 'Holocaust', all crated up by Ben, ready for dispatch to the Academy. She had filled in the forms for submission earlier and it was now time to get the picture transported to London.

Idly she thumbed through some previous sketches and then carried her charcoal pencils and drawing block back to the fire. Supporting it on her knee, she started making rough sketches of war scenes recorded in her memory. She would get out her oils tomorrow and start painting.

Ironically that night, after weeks of inactivity, the Germans launched another all-out attack on Liverpool. She heard the bombers pass again and buried her face in the pillow and prayed that her parents would be safe. Ben seemed closer than ever that night and, when she finally fell off to sleep, she dreamed that she was warm and secure in his arms.

* * * * *

The following morning she woke up with a start. It was hardly light and the telephone was ringing insistently. She jumped out of bed and, barefooted, ran downstairs to answer it, noticing the time on the way. It was just seven o'clock. She picked up the receiver breathlessly, terrified at what she might hear.

"Is that Mrs. Dunbar? It's the station master here, Mam. The early morning train from Liverpool has just gone through and there was a message on it from your mother and father. The telephone lines are down, but they say they are safe and well and you are not to worry – they'll contact you as soon as possible."

"Oh, thank you, Mr. Williams, you don't know what a relief it is to know they're safe."

"Indeed, I can imagine, Mrs. Dunbar. The engine driver said it was the worst raid so far. The centre of the town's had a real pasting and there's general dissatisfaction with the authorities now. They say the shelters are no real protection – just flimsy things and very damp at that. It's a real disgrace. You begin to wonder what will be the end of it all."

Rosie could hear his morale was low, and tried to cheer him up.

"I know how you feel, Mr. Williams, but I expect we'll muddle along somehow or other. It's heart-breaking knowing what they have to put up with in the cities."

"My goodness, that's true Mrs. Dunbar. Well, now I must go home for breakfast."

"Goodbye, Mr. Williams, and thank you again so very, very much. I would never have got through the the day without that message."

She replaced the receiver and sat pensively by the telephone. She looked a forlorn little figure now in her nightie with bare feet. The gay voluptuous Rosie seemed to have disappeared entirely. She was deep in thought, wondering how Maisie and her team had survived during this fresh attack. She felt guilty that she was no longer a part of it, yet she knew inevitably that she would only have been a liability. Even this latest scare had knocked her sideways. Her hands were trembling as she sat there. She looked up at Ben's picture with loving eyes.

"Thank you, my darling, for comforting me last night," she said. The light seemed to change his expression to one of great tenderness, and she felt that he was watching over her.

That day she could not settle down to anything. She sat by the fire, gazing into it – all thought of painting had now gone. Finally she forced herself out of her lassitude and wrote to Maisie, inviting her to come to stay for a quiet weekend and a well deserved rest.

Bron came in twice that day, sensing Rosie's nervous strain. She returned in the evening with a home-made apple pie as an excuse for a second visit, and as they were talking the phone rang. Rosie's steps seemed unsure as she ran to answer it and Bronwen hurriedly drew up a chair and eased her into it. As she picked up the receiver, she heard her mother's voice at the other end, sounding tense but, as usual, strong.

"Hello, Rosie, how are you?"

"I'm fine, but are you both all right?"

"Yes, thank you, Rosie, but last night was a real terror. I'm phoning from the Venables, as we've been forced to evacuate the house. A barrage balloon was brought down by gunfire and has landed on our roof. Its steel cables are lying around like giant spaghetti all over the drive and are dragging off tiles. Unless they can disentangle it quickly, they fear it will pull down the chimney stack."

"Oh, Mum, I'm so sorry, but I'm thankful you're both safe."

Her voice sounded faint and her mother noticed it.

"Don't worry, Rosie, we're in good heart. The Heavy Rescue Squad is at the house now and, if they can dislodge the monster, we will return home tonight."

"Do keep in touch if you can, Mum."

"Of course I will. Your father sends his love and tells you not to worry. I mustn't delay now, this line may be needed. Goodbye and take care, darling."

Rosie put down the telephone with a feeling of intense relief and, turning to Bronwen, told her what had happened. Bron's eyes were wide with amazement.

"I always thought those balloons were on ropes, Mam."

Rosie smiled. "Oh no, Bron, the cables are made of steel and are enormously thick. If an aircraft were to fly into one, it would cut off a wing like a hot knife through butter."

"I never really understood before what good they were," Bron replied.

Since the phone call the tension was lifted and Rosie was almost buoyant with relief.

"Do make a cup of tea, Bron, and bring one in for yourself. I want to hear all about your wedding plans."

A smile broke over Bron's face – she was delighted. It's amazing, Rosie thought, how the small personal things still matter, even though this grim life and death struggle was taking place.

* * * * *

The endurance of the people in Liverpool was near breaking point and the feeling was that officialdom was guilty of bungling. Nobody realised the extent of the difficulties confronting local government. They were improvising and groping their way about in the dark, because of the absence of adequate preparations before the war. Now it was a question of muddling through.

Maisie accepted Rosie's invitation to the cottage and a few weeks later came to stay. Her well-being and survival were important to Rosie for they had been through so much together and she wanted her to have a brief respite from the blitz. She thought this Liverpudlian was the salt of the earth.

Maisie loved being with Rosie again and was entranced by the cottage. The environment was so totally different from anything she had ever experienced before, but secretly she preferred the livelier, vibrant atmosphere of home and the bustle of city life with neighbours always dropping in.

She could take only two days away from her post, and the girls sat up late into the night, drinking numerous cups of tea while Maisie gave Rosie a graphic account of the successive nights of terror in Liverpool.

She told heart-warming stories of fortitude and courage during this fresh onslaught. The heroism of many trapped under the débris was remarkable.

When they were freed, dazed and almost blinded and with throat and lungs clogged with dust, they generally ignored their own plight and showed concern for their families and neighbours.

"My goodness," Rosie said, "it all restores one's faith in human nature."

"Yes," Maisie replied, "it has in mine. As long as I live I shall never forget one old woman. She was over 80 and, after being pulled out of the wreck of her home, she flatly refused to go to the ambulance – 'struth she was a tough old bird! She just wiped the muck from her eyes then, bawling at the rescue squad, showed them where to dig for her daughter and grandchildren. She had her buttons sewn on all right! She knew just where they'd be. Croaking like a jackdaw she kept yelling: "They're under there, they're under there, for gawd's sake get a move on!" She was damned right; Rosie, we all pitched in, and in no time we heard voices from below – it was a ruddy miracle. The old woman got on her knees then started clawing away like a mad thing. You should have seen the look on her face. She was going to save her young and damn all else."

"God bless her," interjected Rosie, "what a wonderful spirit! Did she get them?"

"Cor blimey, yes, we found them in a hole under the stairs – the daughter and her two kids – all as bright as ninepence. The kids seemed to think it was a perishing joke – one was still clutching his teddy. They were pleased to see their tough old Gran, who although flakers was still game. The family gave her a hand up and linking arms they all stumbled down the road together, ploughing through the ruins to the mobile canteen for a cup of tea." Maisie's eyes were moist as she recalled this incident.

"You're doing a wonderful job, Maisie, I wish I could be with you," Rosie said wistfully.

"You'll be back, Rosie, when you're better. Take it easy and keep your pecker up!"

There were many other heart-rending stories but Maisie kept these to herself, telling Rosie only the positive and courageous acts of the people. She said she was proud to be an Englishwoman but, if those bloody Germans ever made it across the Channel she would give them what for!

Rosie hated to see Maisie go. This marvellous girl oiled the wheels of life with her ready humour. She was a real person.

*　*　*　*　*

Thankfully the bombing of Merseyside had ceased but now the full force of the Luftwaffe was directed against London with renewed ferocity. The capital was taking a terrific battering and one unforgettable night, 500 German bombers made a momentous assault on the city and docks, dropping 10,000 incendiary bombs and starting another 'Fire of London'. There was a strong westerly wind blowing which whipped up the flames and the fire spread rapidly. It was soon a blazing inferno. Water mains were shattered and brigades, left with only a trickle from their hoses, had finally to resort to drawing water from fire floats on the Thames.

The conflagration raged for seven hours and the firemen, with black and scorched faces, worked heroically through this terrible night. When dawn broke, the devastation and chaos stretched as far as the eye could see, like the incredible fantasies of a horrifying nightmare. Yet the mighty dome of St. Paul's — this symbol of faith — was miraculously still standing, towering majestically above the ruins. Surely this was an act of God!

17

ROSIE WANDERED out into the orchard, feasting her eyes on the smokey blue hills in the distance. Spring was here again and the apple trees were dotted with pink blossom. Her heart lifted with hope of better things to come – a new season, a fresh beginning, she thought. She felt stronger and knew that she was healing.

The warmth of the sun on her face was a delight after the cold winter months and the chirruping of the birds in the trees was the only sound on this lovely morning. She was moved by the quiet serenity of the countryside. Life was still sweet, with so much beauty to enjoy. Today she would try to get down to serious painting again. She was excited by the prospect.

When Bronwen arrived, she was surprised to find that Rosie was not curled up as usual in her chair by the fire, but instead was in her studio, sitting before an easel, busily sketching. She was wearing a gaily coloured smock and was deeply absorbed in her work.

This in fact was the turning point. The frail, apathetic Rosie had gone. She was vital again and, although she tired easily, her enthusiasm for work had returned. Painting now became the predominant interest in her life and she shrank from the thought of any emotional involvement. In future her dedication would be to her art – this, so essentially impersonal, could only bring her serenity in contrast with the traumas of the past.

During the weeks that followed she completed her series of war pictures. She had put her heart and soul into them. Her tragic experiences had matured her and added a new dimension to her painting.

One evening, after Bronwen had left and she was quite alone, she brought her collection of war studies through from the studio, arranging them around the room. She studied each one separately and then assessed them as a whole. She was a harsh critic of her own work, but the paintings exceeded her wildest hopes and expectations. They stood out with a stark realism. Their reflection of the evils of war was undeniable.

There was no flag-waving or glory here, yet each picture held a spiritual quality which lifted it supremely from the macabre. In the midst of terror and destruction the human elements of love and self sacrifice shone through.

She was well content, having achieved her objective. Her mission was completed.

She carried them back to the studio, meticulously storing each one away. She must exhibit them but first would wait to see how the 'Holocaust' was received by the Academy. She hoped desperately for its acceptance, yet disliked the prospect of the publicity revealing her personal tragedy.

It was dusk and she loved to sit by the fire in the twilight with Biscuit asleep at her feet, quietly planning her next picture. She watched the changes of light as the soft darkness fell, obscuring the panorama outside and enclosing her within the confines of the cottage.

Now that her project was complete, she felt relieved that she had recorded, for all to see, the horrors of war in terms of human suffering. She was free to return now to her tranquil pastoral scenes.

She glanced up at Ben's portrait. He seemed to be smiling. Was it a trick of the light?

"Thank you for everything, dear Ben," she whispered. "Now the pictures are finished, I feel myself again – it is a miracle and I have only you to thank for this."

A curiously warm feeling of contentment came over her.

*   *   *   *   *

She had resumed driving her mobile canteen but only part time until her health was fully restored. She grew stronger each day and was becoming more extroverted, being once again the smiling, vivacious Rosie.

She knew that the servicemen, dispersed on outlying sites, were often homesick and looked forward to her visits. This gave her a sense of purpose. She was very popular and was frequently asked for dates, but she always refused, not wishing to make her life more complicated; yet an inner loneliness gnawed at her unmercifully. Would she ever quell this terrible feeling of isolation – of having no one of her very own, who cared about her?

Recently there had been rumours that all was not well between Germany and Russia despite their non-aggression pact. It was hard to believe that Hitler would make the fatal blunder of waging war on two fronts; yet a German invasion could not be ruled out, as already there was a great concentration of armoured might established on the Russian border. During the month of June heavy German troop movements took place, all directed toward the east.

There was a great sense of relief in the country when the prime minister, in a voice charged with emotion, announced to the nation that Hitler had indeed invaded Russia. Mr. Churchill, in one of his most stirring war-time speeches, firmly pledged British support to the Russian people in their struggle against the Nazis. He reaffirmed his determination to destroy Adolf Hitler and every vestige of his evil regime. "We shall fight him by land, we shall fight him by sea, we shall fight him in the air, until with God's help, we have rid the earth of his shadow and liberated its people from his yoke." From the inspiration of this great orator, the British people again drew strength and there was a new spirit of optimism abroad, for now the German concentration would be eastward. It seemed likely that the Fürher had made his first big error of judgement – this could be the beginning of the end.

*   *   *   *   *

One day early in summer, feeling a bit frivolous, Rosie decided to go on a shopping spree to the nearby town of Bangor. She had saved up enough petrol coupons for this jaunt and had accumulated a number of clothing coupons to augment her sadly depleted wardrobe.

Her first call was at a little dress shop which specialised in Welsh tweeds and hand knitted woollens. She spent a rewarding hour there, choosing carefully, and finally used up all her precious coupons on a hand-woven dress and coat in soft blue. It suited her perfectly and when she left the shop she felt pleased with her purchases.

The town was full of servicemen and, as she walked along the winding main street, she was aware of admiring glances; in spite of all the tragic happenings in her life, she was still a beautiful girl.

She glanced casually in the shop windows as she passed by, observing their austere wartime displays. The clothes were mostly what was officially called

'Utility', bearing a special symbol. The accent was on durability and good value as distinct from style.

Her next call was to be on an art shop at the far end of the town – an old-established business which in the past had bought some of her water colours. She loved to browse around it and was eagerly looking forward to a chat with the owner. He was knowledgeable and had good artistic appreciation.

She was surprised to see that the shop had a smart new exterior. The old familiar sign above the door had been removed and in its place was a stylishly lettered board, white on grey, with the name changed to 'Contemporary Artists Ltd. Paul Anthony Crispin'.

There was only one picture displayed in the window and Rosie was quite taken aback when she saw it was one of her own – a large water-colour of the Menai Straits which she had painted shortly before the war.

Coming upon it so unexpectedly she was able to study the picture objectively. She liked the way she had applied the wash, particularly on the gleaming stretch of water. Highlights were cleverly shown by leaving the white cartridge uncovered. She felt gratified that this example of her earlier work was so good. There was a small red sign beside it – 'not for sale'. This told her that the picture was valued by the owner.

She pushed open the door and was impressed by the new décor. Instead of the old brown paint, the walls were now covered in grey hessian, a perfect background for pictures. This was relieved by vivid white paintwork and on the floor was a charcoal grey carpet – practical and smart. There were not many pictures on display but every one was of a high standard and they had obviously been carefully chosen.

As she was looking around, fascinated by the changes, a pleasant young woman appeared from the back of the shop.

"Good afternoon, madam, can I help you, or would you prefer to wander around on your own?"

Rosie smiled hesitantly: "Well actually I was hoping to see Mr. Parry Jones but I notice the shop has changed hands."

"Yes, I'm afraid so," she replied. "We have recently bought the business from him. He has gone to live in Chester with his unmarried sister. I think he was finding it all too much for him at his age."

"Oh I see," Rosie murmured. "I'm sorry he's left the district. He was a nice old man and in the past he sold a number of my pictures. In fact you have one of mine in the window at the moment – a study of the Menai Straits."

The new owner looked pleasantly surprised. "Then you must be Rosie Dunbar. I'm delighted to meet you. I am Tessa Crispin."

"How do you do," Rosie replied with a friendly smile. She liked on sight this smart young woman, so beautifully sun-tanned. Somehow she looked out of place in Bangor. Rosie imagined her in a Bond Street setting. She little realised that she herself was being carefully scrutinised too.

"My husband, Paul, and I adore your picture," she said with enthusiasm. "Parry was most reluctant to part with it but we put up a very strong argument against his taking it with him." She laughed. "In fact it was almost written into the contract!"

"Oh I'm most flattered," Rosie exclaimed and her eyes sparkled. She was genuinely pleased that they should want her picture so badly.

"Parry told us such a lot about you. He was a great admirer of yours and thought very highly of your work."

"How kind of him," Rosie said. "He was a terrific source of encouragement to me in my early days and you can imagine how exciting it was when he started to sell my pictures."

"Indeed I can. Are you still painting or have you given it up for the duration?"

Rosie paused. "I have just finished a series of wartime studies in oils – a sort of 'Guernica' theme, but I intend to start on water colours again very shortly. Until recently I was driving an ambulance in Liverpool, but the Red Cross have put me out to grass for a rest period, so I now have time on my hands for painting, though I do drive a mobile canteen twice a week."

"That's good," Mrs. Crispin replied. "I only wish that I could do more for the war effort. In fact I feel quite guilty about it. The trouble is that I'm rather tied as my husband is not at all fit. After a tough time at sea, being blown up twice by mines, he was invalided out of the Navy, so we decided to buy this small business and try to make a go of it."

"I think you have an excellent chance of succeeding here," Rosie said encouragingly. "You have already transformed the place."

"I'm so glad you like it but things are not easy. So many good artists have been called up and, as we are both perfectionists, it is hard to get the standard of work we want. This is a busy little town normally and with the additional service personnel stationed around here, we get plenty of would-be buyers so, providing we get the pictures to sell, we should be all right. My husband is very knowledgeable on art and is as keen as mustard. He was studying at the Slade when war broke out."

"That's marvellous," said Rosie. "I'd love to have gone there myself."

Mrs. Crispin continued: "Unfortunately he is out today on a painting expedition and will be terribly disappointed when he knows he has missed you."

Rosie smiled warmly. "I'm sorry too, but lucky man to be painting, that's what I would like to be doing."

Mrs. Crispin looked enquiringly across at her, then asked with some hesitation: "I am wondering if by any chance you have any pictures you would like us to sell for you?"

Rosie thought for a moment before answering. "I have a few tucked away that you might be interested in but not many, I'm afraid. However once I get going again, it will be a different matter. Would you like to come over and see what I have?"

"Yes, very much," she replied.

"Well, what about next Sunday afternoon for tea? I live in a cottage just outside Penrhyn."

"We would love that. Paul will be thrilled when he hears he is going to meet the artist who painted his favourite picture." She was obviously delighted at the suggestion.

Rosie smiled: "Well, come as soon as you can after lunch so as to give us plenty of time for discussion and for inspecting my work. Here is my card with the address. I am sure you won't have any difficulty finding the cottage."

"Will your husband be at home on Sunday, Mrs. Dunbar?"

Rosie frowned: "No, I'm afraid not, he's in the Navy too and in command of an M.T.B."

"Paul will be interested in that – does he get much leave?"

Rosie hesitated, always reluctant to discuss Peter. Mrs. Crispin noticed her slight change of colour and wished she hadn't enquired. "Actually I don't see him at all now. We have separated," she said quietly.

Mrs. Crispin felt embarrassed and tried to put things right.

"I'm so sorry to have asked – unfortunately in wartime, with such pressures on personal relationships, these things do happen."

Rosie nodded. Speaking of Peter gave her an uneasy feeling and she was glad when the door bell clanged and a woman walked into the shop.

"I won't delay you any longer now, Mrs. Crispin, but I shall look forward to seeing you both on Sunday," – and with a friendly wave she was gone.

She felt delighted with this new contact. It could be a good outlet for her pictures and she thought Mrs. Crispin was singularly charming.

*   *   *   *   *

The following day there was a real Welsh downpour and the mists hung low over the mountains, covering the peaks in thick heavy cloud. Just the sort of day to stay cosily indoors by the fire and do some sketching. This was an opportunity to finish off some drawings of local scenes to show to the Crispins on Sunday.

She heard a plop on the mat and knew it was the post arriving. She hurried to the door and opened it and was just in time to see Huw Thomas disappearing down the path.

"Huw!" she called. "It's such an awful day: would you like to come in for a cup of coffee?"

"Indeed yes, that's very kind of you, Mrs Dunbar," and with a shy smile he returned, making very sure that his feet were dry, wiping them over and over again on the mat and leaving his dripping mackintosh in the porch.

He picked up the letters and placed them on the table. He was a good, conscientious young man and Rosie was fond of him.

"Go and sit by the fire, Huw. I'll be only a moment with the coffee."

When she returned he was sitting stiffly in an upright chair.

"Ta, Mrs Dunbar," he said, as she handed him the cup.

"Now tell me, Huw, how is your young lady and when do you expect to be married?"

"She is very well, Mrs Dunbar," but a worried frown crossed his usually placid face. "I may be called up and, if so, her Mam and Dad won't let us marry. They say it isn't fair to her," and he blushed. "The trouble is if babas come along, who's to provide for them? We're both upset, my goodness we are."

"I'm sorry to hear this, Huw, but perhaps it's best not to rush into anything at the present time. Mary is a lovely girl and so pretty."

He smiled delightedly. "Thank you, Mrs Dunbar, I'll tell her what you have said. It will mean a lot to her."

He pushed the letters hesitantly across the table towards her. She turned them over quickly and saw that there was one from the Royal Academy; it was the letter she had been hoping for. Her face flushed with excitement and she could not wait to read it.

"Excuse me, Huw, while I open this one; it's rather important." She prised open the flap with care. Her heart was beating faster as she read the hoped-for words. It was a formal card notifying her that her picture had been accepted and would be hung in the Summer Exhibition.

She could not contain her excitement.

"Huw," she cried joyfully, "this is from the Royal Academy in London and they're going to exhibit one of my pictures."

"Oh Mrs Dunbar," he said, his face wreathed in smiles. "I am that pleased," and he felt almost personally responsible for this good news which he had brought along. "I'm sure you'll be famous one day, indeed I am. Bronwen always says you will."

Rosie chuckled. "Thank you, Huw, for those kind words – I hope you're right," and her eyes sparkled with unaccustomed joy.

He carefully put down his cup and saucer and stood up awkwardly. He was anxious to spread the news on his round; the villagers were all interested in the successful young artist living in their midst.

"Now I must be off, Mrs Dunbar, as I have a letter to deliver to the Pritchards of Maesteg and that's a tidy step from here, halfway up the mountain side. Thank you again for the coffee and indeed I'm very pleased about your picture."

She accompanied him to the door and waved a cheery goodbye as he hurried down the path, disappearing into the mist.

She closed the door quickly, as the rain was driving in; she returned to her chair by the fire and sat quietly day-dreaming for a moment. She was thrilled by her achievement. This was confirmation of her innermost feeling that her work had now reached a high standard of competence.

She looked up at Ben's portrait.

"Oh darling," she said quietly. "If only you were here to share my success. Without your faith and encouragement this would never have happened." A curiously warm feeling of comfort came over her.

She glanced through her other letters and one postmarked Swindon caught her eye. She knew this was from Ben's solicitor and friend, Gordon Nash, as he had written to her earlier, notifying her of Ben's legacy. She tore open the letter and was pleased to read that he was visiting a friend in the area the following week and could he call to see her?

She would reply by return and invite him to come to lunch. She looked forward to his visit, yet with a certain trepidation. She wondered how he would regard her, but she yearned to be able to talk to him about Ben.

She had often considered contacting Mike, but something told her that by now he had probably 'bought it'. If this were the case, she would rather not know.

The next day was fine and clear so, armed with easel and paints and a sandwich lunch, she set off for her favourite spot by the oak tree. Since the rain of yesterday and the bright sunshine today, the colours of the trees and grass were a vivid green and the sky a brilliant blue with dramatically dark shadows on the mountains. She settled down under the tree and started work. Everything looked crystal clear, almost brittle. She wondered if she could reflect this in her painting.

She found it strange working in water colours again and she loved the effect of the honest simplicity of this medium. After adding the last stroke, she put her brushes away and looked down critically at her picture – it was delightful. There was a magical quality about the painting which had come straight from the heart.

She slowly packed up her easel and paints, feeling reluctant to leave this special place where she had experienced such happiness with Ben.

* * * * *

When Sunday arrived, the day of the Crispins' visit, she filled the cottage with flowers from the garden and as usual had a log fire crackling in the grate. The cottage looked cosy and most welcoming and when the door bell rang she hurried to answer it. She was really looking forward to their coming.

Mrs. Crispin was as attractive as ever. Her gleaming chestnut hair, simply done in a page-boy style, pleasantly contrasted with her green tweed suit. Her husband stood beside her – he was a slim, gaunt young man; his face was deeply lined and he had an anxious look in his eyes.

"Hello, Mrs. Dunbar, how nice to see you again. May I introduce you to my husband, Paul? He is dying to meet the artist who painted his favourite picture," she said with a friendly smile.

"It is very nice to meet you," Rosie said warmly, recognising at once his sensitivity. "I'm flattered that you like my picture and it's nice to know that it has a good home! Please do come in and sit down."

She was anxious to make Paul feel at ease and he reacted favourably to her kindly approach.

"What a lovely cottage this is," he remarked. "Tessa and I have been looking for something like this for ages, but this calibre of cottage rarely comes on the market."

"I know, but I was fortunate enough to have this left to me by my Great Aunt Louise. It's almost like a fairy story. She was a recluse and I had met her only once; in fact I spent just one afternoon with her, but we got on well together. We had the same interests in common – painting – so I suppose that's what did it!"

"How marvellous for you," Tessa exclaimed, "but I think Great Aunt Louise had good judgement!"

"Hear, hear, I agree with that whole-heartedly," Paul responded warmly.

"Changing the subject rather," Rosie said, "I had exciting news yesterday. I heard from the Royal Academy that they have accepted one of my oils for the Summer Exhibition."

"Congratulations, that is wonderful," Paul said jumping up and shaking her by the hand – "you've really arrived now!" Rosie was touched by his enthusiastic response, and it was nice having someone with whom to share the good news.

"What was the subject of your picture?" Tessa asked with interest.

Rosie looked serious and was slow to reply. "It is a controversial study, entitled 'The Holocaust', depicting the evils of war. I never thought it would get past the selection committee. To me it is a very personal picture and in a way I am reluctant to have it exhibited." It was very obvious to them that she did not want to discuss it any further.

After they had finished tea and everything was cleared away, they got down to business. They were on first name terms now, chatting away like old friends. Paul during the afternoon had been quietly studying the pictures on the walls and was most impressed.

"I think your latest water-colour, Rosie, is pure genius. However did you manage to achieve such dramatic sharpness in a water-colour? The technique is quite superb and one I have never met before."

"I'm trying something out and I am delighted that you think it has come off – everything was going for me. That day the light was perfection and it was sheer joy working in water-colours again."

He looked keenly across at her and spoke without preamble, "Rosie, I love your picture, it is magnificent. I wonder if you would consider hanging it in our gallery? We would be honoured, if you would do so."

"Of course, Paul, I would be delighted but, what do you think about it, Tessa?"

"I think your work is superb, Rosie, but I'm not the picture expert. Paul is the one. I concentrate on the business side, but you know I would be thrilled if we could collaborate in this way."

"Rosie, I believe you have just finished a series of war studies. I would love to see them," he said.

She did not want to refuse him, for she liked him immensely, but the pictures were still so personal and revealing that she could not bring herself to show them to anyone yet.

"I'm sorry, Paul, but they are all packed away. Perhaps later on I can let you see them."

He looked at her long and hard and she knew he understood. She had not hurt his feelings.

Neither of them mentioned Ben's portrait until they were leaving. Then Tessa casually asked "Is there any chance of our displaying this marvellous portrait in our window, Rosie? It would really bring the customers flocking in," but one look at Rosie's face provided the answer.

She looked strained as she replied, "Sorry, but I could not bear it to leave the cottage, and I never want it exhibited." They both sensed tragedy here and quickly passed on to another subject.

They were all good friends by the time the Crispins departed. A happy relationship had developed between them and they had established a satisfactory business arrangement for the sale of Rosie's pictures. She felt she really had something to work for – her career was being established.

From now on her thoughts were almost exclusively centred on her painting. She felt a sense of loyalty to the Crispins and wished for their sakes, as well as her own, to see their gallery enhanced by many more pictures. She and Tessa kept in touch on the phone and Paul came over to see her whenever she had a picture completed for framing. This he did himself. His choice of frames was in the best possible taste and Rosie felt she could safely leave this side to him.

They had already sold the last landscape which she had painted while sitting beneath her favourite old oak tree. A wing commander had fallen for it. He had bought it partly as an investment. He said he backed this young artist and was sure the picture would be very valuable one day.

The gallery flourished and naturally the Crispins were anxious for her to complete pictures as fast as she could, but she was determined not to lower her standards and turn out pot-boilers. So far her mood had been entirely creative and she just wanted to paint and paint but this would not necessarily last. There were occasions when she loved to spend time gardening and always the cottage was a joy to her and working in it was part of her artistic expression.

She was anxious to have everything in order when Gordon Nash arrived, and the two previous days were spent in preparation. She wished to look her best for his visit, otherwise she would be letting Ben down. She washed her hair the night before and sat for a moment in front of her dressing table, reflectively studying her face. She was still beautiful but there was a subtle change. She looked older and sadder. Her child-like quality had disappeared.

She sighed as she turned away, shivering a little in the cold night air as she quickly jumped into bed and pulled up the clothes. Before dropping off to sleep she thought of Ben: his presence was always with her – they were two halves of the same person. Now that her agonising grief had spent itself, she was ever comforted by his closeness and had become reconciled to his death. Their brief idyllic relationship now seemed like a perfect dream.

*　*　*　*　*

Rosie was out in the garden when Gordon Nash drew up outside the cottage. She went down the path to meet him. He was of medium height, slim with a thatch of pure white hair.

"Hello," she said shyly, "you must be Mr. Nash – Ben's great friend?"

"Yes," he answered, "and you his lovely Rosie – he always spoke of you as that." His blue eyes held a smiling quizzical expression and she knew at once that she liked him.

He in turn thought there was something very special about her and now he understood why Ben had insisted unequivocally on making her his sole beneficiary. At the time he had thought this unwise, but now it was clear to him.

"What an enchanting old world garden," he said as they walked up the path together, "and your cottage is delightful." When they stepped inside, he was charmed by what he saw. This attractive young woman was obviously a home-maker.

Rosie felt a trifle ill at ease but did not show this even by a flicker of an eyelid; she appeared quite composed.

"Would you like a drink before lunch?" she asked.

"Yes please, that would be nice – a dry sherry, if I may."

She poured out two glasses from the corner cabinet and joined him by the fire. She noticed that he was looking with interest at her pictures.

"I believe you are an artist – are these all your work?"

"Yes," Rosie replied. "They are Welsh scenes which I did some time ago. I suppose Ben told you that I paint?"

"Yes, that is so, he considered you had immense talent. He talked so much about you and now that we have met I can understand his feelings."

A great sense of relief surged through her for now she knew that he approved and she raised her eyes appealingly to his.

"Please tell me all you know about him." She hesitated: "You see there is no-one else I can ask and I knew him for such a short time, yet we became so very close. I want to know what he was like as a little boy and how he became the very splendid person he was."

She paused and looked away and he saw that her eyes were full of tears.

"I loved him so completely and admired him more than any man alive."

He was obviously affected by what she said and answered her with gentle understanding.

"I too shared your admiration; from a child he was unusually nice, a very sensitive boy but full of courage. You have reflected brilliantly his qualities in your portrait. It shook me when I first came into the room. It is his very image and exactly as I remember him on his last visit. I think he knew then that his number was up."

"I believe so too," she said sadly. "He never expressed any hope for the future."

They were quiet for a moment then Rosie suggested that they should start lunch. The meal was beautifully served on an old oak table with a cheerful centre piece of carnations. In spite of wartime restrictions, the food was delicious.

"I believe your parents live in Liverpool. How have they fared during the air raids?" he asked.

"Not too well, I'm afraid. My father is a sugar refiner and at the height of the blitz his factory was razed to the ground which was a terrible blow; their house was damaged too on the same night."

"I am very sorry to hear this. It must have been heartbreaking. Liverpool has taken a terrible battering. Let's hope that they leave it alone now."

"It has certainly had its fair share," Rosie replied, "I was driving an ambulance through the worst of the blitz and I thought the Liverpudlians were splendid – it makes one feel proud to be British."

He listened intently to what she had to say. He felt he understood her better now. She was obviously a warm, sincere girl.

After lunch, when they were settled in front of the fire, drinking coffee, he opened his brief case and spread out a number of papers on the table before him.

"Would you like to get down to business now?" he asked. "I hope you won't mind if I call you Rosie, but that was how Ben always referred to you."

"Of course not, I would like you to."

"Now, Rosie, as you know Ben bequeathed you a legacy and I have come to tell you about it."

"Yes, he did say that he was leaving me a little money which would enable me to stay on here and do my painting. Of course I have means of my own and there was no need for this."

"Well actually, Rosie, you have inherited quite a sum of money – now that his parents' estate has been settled and as he was the sole beneficiary, it will all come to you. The figure is just over £55,000."

Rosie drew back, looking thoroughly shocked.

"This can't be so, it is far too much. His parents never knew me and I don't feel it is right and proper for me to inherit their money."

"Well, my dear, I discussed this threadbare with Ben and he was adamant about it. There are no close relations to whom either he or his parents would wish the money to go. He said that, if they had known you, they would have loved you as he did. I think this could be so, Rosie, for they were good people and I feel that in the circumstances you should respect his deeply-felt wishes."

Rosie said nothing for a while. She pensively gazed into the fire, deep in thought. He did not want to disturb her, so he sat back waiting patiently. Presently she looked up appealingly and spoke in a quiet voice.

"Mr. Nash, if you are absolutely satisfied that I am entitled to this generous legacy, then please go ahead with any arrangements which have to be made."

He gave a sigh of relief and smiled as he said in an assured voice: "I have no doubt that Ben was absolutely right in what he did. You are a lovely girl."

Tears sprang to her eyes again. "I deeply appreciate your kind words, Mr.

Nash. They mean a lot to me."

She knew she had made a friend and that Ben would have been pleased.

*   *   *   *   *

During the next few weeks Rosie was completely absorbed in her work and, as the opening date of the Academy's Summer Exhibition drew near, she wondered whether or not to go.

She felt that seeing this tragic picture, exposed to the public view, would upset her but finally decided she must go. She would spend only one night in London, not contacting any of her friends. It was a very personal occasion which she was not in the mood to share with anyone else.

She caught an early train and went straight to a small hotel, which she knew, close to Harrods. She felt strange here on her own and her thoughts kept returning to the days before the war, when she had lived in London with Peter. How proud she had been to have him as her husband and how very exciting everything had seemed. They had been so passionately in love, but now this memory held an unreal, dream-like quality.

She dined quietly in the hotel, then went upstairs early to her room with an exciting novel which had just been published. This was sheer heaven for Rosie. She felt frivolous and in another world as she read with amusement of the fun and foibles of a beautiful young woman, Claudia, who lived flamboyantly in the lap of luxury on the Côte d'Azur. Did scatty people like this really exist, she wondered? She thought about her legacy and it dawned on her for the first time that she was comparatively rich herself. After the war she could afford to travel and even live as Claudia did – this absurd character in her book. She gave a little laugh at these strange thoughts for this was not what she wanted. The cottage was her world and being close to Ricky a necessity to her.

She would of course build on the studio as Ben wished. It was an exciting prospect and before falling off to sleep she planned it all out in her mind's eye. It would be a long, low structure built of stone with a northerly exposure and with plenty of cupboards. What bliss to have adequate room for working and ample wall space for displaying her finished pictures. This would be a dream come true.

The next day, as she was reading the "Daily Telegraph" over breakfast, she was surprised to find that the 'Holocaust' had attracted favourable comment in the review of the Summer Exhibition. It was described as one of the most powerful and exciting pictures on show and by a comparatively unknown arist.

She hurriedly packed her overnight case and paid her bill. She decided she had time to walk through the park which was always a joy to her, but wartime London was bleak and forbidding with gaping holes and crumbling ruins and evidence of destruction on all sides. The bombing still continued spasmodically and indeed it had become a part of the daily life of Londoners.

As she walked up the steps of Burlington House, instinct seemed to guide her to the right room and there was her picture straight ahead. The impact of it was like a body blow – it was torture to look at her little darling's face exhibited for all to see. She sank down on a well-worn leather couch and closed her eyes until her heart regained a steady beat. Then she opened them narrowly and gazed at the picture, reliving the whole dreadful episode.

She sat there inert for many minutes; then she got to her feet and with aching heart, looking neither left nor right, she stumbled out of the building into Piccadilly and was quickly swallowed up in the crowd.

* * * * *

A close friendship had developed between Rosie and the Crispins and this made all the difference to her life. She admired Tessa's practicality and organising ability, and she appreciated Paul's brilliance and valued him as an art critic. She often asked his advice and their discussions were of tremendous help to her. He recognised her great talent and believed that she would become one of the outstanding artists of the day.

He was a remote man and Rosie often wondered how the warm Tessa reached him. His war experiences had left their mark, both physically and mentally, and he had never properly recovered from a nervous breakdown. On his bad days it was impossible to draw him out of the deep depression which stifled his enjoyment of life. His revived interest in art had saved his sanity and Tessa was a tower of strength.

Paul valued his friendship with Rosie; their mutual interests and her sympathetic understanding would often pull him up from the depths.

Since her success at the Academy, her name was beginning to be recognised and her pictures sold so readily that it was hard to keep up with the demand. Paul had increased the prices but this was not a deterrent.

There had been a sequel to the first article in the "Telegraph" which prompted a London gallery to approach her with a view to including the 'Holocaust' in their forthcoming exhibition on the theme, Great Britain at War.

She now felt emotionally ready to release her other war studies; so one morning, having made this decision, she telephoned Paul asking him if he would come over and assess the merit of the collection. He sensed her urgency and was himself most excited at the prospect of seeing the series for the first time. He said he would come at once.

She lined the pictures up against the walls. She was almost afraid of his reaction for they meant so much to her.

She was waiting at the open front door when he arrived and warmly put her arm through his and drew him into the cottage. "Thank you for coming over so promptly, Paul." He saw at once how tense she was and knew these pictures had a special significance for her. He must step warily.

"I have been looking forward to this moment very much, Rosie, and as you know I will tell you quite honestly what I think."

"That is the only way," she said, but she could hardly bear to look at his impassive face as he carefully examined them; so, to relieve her tension, she gazed out of the window at the gentle pastoral scene beyond. Autumn was here again and the falling leaves were blowing hither and thither. It was time to pick the apples and store them away for the winter. These mundane thoughts helped to calm her nerves as she waited anxiously for Paul's pronouncement.

His face was inscrutable as he studied each one from all angles. When he finally turned towards her she saw a new Paul. He had come to life, as though the blanket of his reserve had been lifted, leaving the man himself exposed – an emotional revelation that had its roots in his wartime experiences. Tears filled his haunted eyes, which he unashamedly brushed away.

212

Presently he spoke in a low hoarse voice.

"They are brilliant, Rosie – I am overwhelmed. They must be shown in London and I will make all arangements to have them despatched to the gallery which wrote to you. I believe that these pictures, together with the 'Holocaust', will have an immense impact on the art world."

"Oh, Paul," she whispered, "I so hoped you'd say that."

It transpired that his prediction was proved correct and almost overnight she was hailed as a new and outstanding contemporary war artist – which was what Ben had foreseen.

18

BRON'S WEDDING had come and gone and the honeymoon was over. It had been a joyous occasion. John's parents had insisted on holding the reception, as Bronwen was all alone in the world. They had no daughters of their own and they already loved their daughter-in-law to be – their affectionate young Bron.

Rosie was the guest of honour and it had been a lovely day with pure blue skies and sunshine. Bron's little face, peeping out of a froth of white tulle, had looked divinely happy, almost bursting with pride as she held her John's arm.

Rosie had given them a handsome cheque as a wedding present and in addition had painted them a picture of their new home as a surprise. She had done this with loving care, for nothing was too good for Bron. It looked a charming cottage – pure white with a thatched roof and a blue front door, complete with Biscuit sitting in the window. Bron was overboard with excitement when Rosie gave it to her and said she would be the envy of the village, owning a painting by such a famous artist.

Rosie was driving her canteen every morning again and painting in the afternoons. Bronwen was deliriously happy in her marriage and still came in for a few hours each day.

Rosie had asked Bronwen to call her 'Rosie' instead of 'Mam', but Bron had compromised – from now on she was to be 'Miss Rosie'.

Very soon she delightedly told Rosie there was a baby on the way.

Rosie was thrilled: "Oh, Bron dear, this is wonderful news. I am so pleased but you mustn't work as hard in future and there must be no more scrubbing. I'll do all that and you can just dust and keep me company."

They both laughed but Bron said stoutly: "I'm a strong country girl, Miss Rosie, and will go on working till my time comes. You're not to spoil your lovely hands with rough work. Remember you're famous now."

"Oh Bron, not quite. I doubt if many people have heard of me."

"You're famous here all right, Miss Rosie," replied Bronwen, her face alight. "I'm telling you I'm the envy of the village working for you."

Rosie laughed again and gave her a hug. "Bron, I'm so looking forward to your baby. I shall feel very close, just as you were to Ricky." Her voice was sad. "But that all seems long ago and so much has happened since."

Bron nodded and her heart ached. She only hoped that her baby would make up a little for Rosie's tragic loss.

*　　*　　*　　*　　*

On 7th December 1941, the Japanese launched a treacherous surprise attack on the American Naval Base at Pearl Harbor in the Hawaiian Islands. Their planes, operating from an aircraft carrier force and supported by submarines, wrought havoc and destruction on the pride of the American navy, leaving behind a shattered fleet, hidden in a pall of fire and smoke.

On this day of infamy over 2,000 Americans lost their lives and, at a stroke, control of the Pacific passed to the Japanese. This dastardly act brought America into the war – Britain no longer stood alone, and the whole country rejoiced: the tide was turning.

May was a lovely month this year and the cottage garden was again a mass of spring flowers.

Bron had just produced a bouncing nine pound baby girl in the local cottage hospital. Rosie had been the first to visit her outside of the family and was delighted when Bron, with shining eyes, announced that the baby was to be christened Catherine Rose – already 'Cassie' for short.

"John and I wondered if you'd be her godmother, Miss Rosie?"

"Of course, Bron, I would be absolutely delighted – it's such an honour," Rosie replied with pleasure. "She is a lovely little girl but what a wonderful mop of dark hair and lovely blue, dreamy eyes she has. I expect they'll turn brown like her mother's. May I hold her, Bron?"

"Of course, Miss Rosie, any time you want."

When Rosie looked down at Cassie's dark little head and her pink crumpled hands with nails like tiny shells, she knew that she already loved Bron's baby.

As the months went by Rosie became more and more attached to Cassie. Her painting and the baby filled her life and helped to combat her loneliness.

Each morning now Bron arrived with her daughter at nine o'clock and, before setting out for her driving job, Rosie had an hour to spend with the child, which for her was sheer joy.

Rosie had left the cottage early to put the finishing touches to a study she had started of sheep grazing on the banks of the mist-shrouded river. The painting had a wraith-like quality and she was pleased with the unusual effect she had achieved. When she had finished it she hurried back to the cottage. She found Bron busy as usual with her duster.

"Good morning, Bron," she called out gaily. "How is Catherine Rose today?" This was always her first concern.

Bron smiled broadly. "She's very well indeed – she's sitting up in her pram on the back porch as good as gold and chewing a rusk."

"Oh, I must go and see her – may I lift her out, Bron?"

"Of course, Miss Rosie," she said delightedly.

A minute later Rosie returned carrying the chubby little girl. Then sinking into her favourite chair, she rocked her gently back and forth and sang her some nursery rhymes. Cassie was a quiet, responsive child and was always content to be with Rosie. She seemed almost like a second mother.

They spent a happy hour together by the fire, with Biscuit curled up beside them. Rosie held the baby's plump little hand and marvelled at the perfection of her clear creamy skin, enhanced by pink cheeks and enormous eyes – now golden brown and as soft as velvet.

When it was time for Rosie's departure, Bron came in and picked up the sleepy child.

"I will take her so that you can get ready."

"She's a beautiful baby, Bron, and when the winter comes and I'm less busy, I'd like to paint her portrait for you and John."

Bron's eyes lit up with pleasure. "That would be grand, Miss Rosie – to have a picture of Catherine Rose painted by you would be nicer than anything, even a thousand pounds," she added impishly. "Indeed it would!"

Rosie smiled but there was a hint of sadness in her voice as she replied: "You're so kind the way you share her with me, Bron." She broke off. "Having a baby to cuddle makes up a bit for losing Ricky – but on no account must you let me spoil her."

"Our Cassie will never be spoilt by loving," Bron stoutly replied. "I don't believe in these new-fangled ways of bringing up children, leaving them to cry their eyes out. Poor little babas not able to tell us what's the matter."

She paused a moment. "You know, Miss Rosie, I'll never forget little Ricky, my 'carriad bach'. I loved him as though he was my own baby, my goodness I did."

"Yes, Bron, I know and I'll always be grateful to you." There was silence between them for a moment, then Bron quietly changed the subject.

"I think she's nodding off now, Miss Rosie, so if you give her to me, I'll put her back in the pram." She lifted the baby gently from Rosie's lap and, humming softly, carried her off for her morning nap.

*　*　*　*　*

Rosie spent a few days with her parents at Christmas time. The bombing had ceased and it was lovely being at home again with a caring family. She knew now that she could never be happy living alone but, although she had many opportunities for romantic involvements, she steered clear of them.

There had been one exception to this, however. She had been invited out to dinner by an older man – a Wing Commander Jeffery Harris, whom she had met socially and, feeling low and depressed that day, had accepted his invitation and bitterly regretted it afterwards.

They had previously discussed art. He was an extremely cultured man and owned an exclusive picture gallery in the West End of London, so they had much in common.

He was attractive, stocky in build with hair greying at the temples and penetrating dark eyes. She enjoyed his company – he was a sophisticate and when he invited her for the second time, she accepted. He drove her to Portmerion for dinner and she realised how much she had missed male companionship. She was completely taken aback when he quite openly suggested that they should become lovers. He told her that he was married with children and stressed that nothing must upset the tenor of his family life.

She was conscious of her rising colour and let a certain contempt show in her face as she replied: "Jeffery, you amaze me – a cold blooded affair without love would never appeal to me."

"But Rosie, my dear," he protested, "I do love you; your beauty thrills me and I admire your intellect immensely. We could have a most civilised and rewarding relationship."

"I'm sorry, Jeffery, but your idea of love is very different from mine and I don't indulge in inconsequential affairs," she said witheringly.

He looked at her intently, as though regarding every detail of her face, then with a self-satisfied smile and shrug of his shoulders said: "I'm disappointed, Rosie, but if that is how you feel the subject is now closed. Let's have one for the road and then I'll drive you home."

"I'd rather not, thank you, let's go right away." The whole episode was sickening to her.

216

It was a thoroughly nasty day. The mists hung low over the hills and the Snowdon range was invisible behind a blanket of cloud. The rain poured down unceasingly, overflowing the gutters in a steady stream. Rosie guessed they were blocked with leaves. Without a man about the house, outside work in the winter was neglected. She was always so absorbed in her painting that she hated to spend time on these mundane jobs.

Bron had come in as usual, taking her short cut over the fields, paddling unconcernedly through the mud in her wellington boots. Rosie thought she looked delightful, wearing her shiny black oilskins and a sou'wester hat, her face glowing with health and happiness.

There was no doubt Bron adored her John. It was a real love match. She had left Cassie at home today with her Nan. It was a standing arrangement between them that, if the weather was bad, Nan would look after the baby while Bron was working. Needless to say Nan always jumped at the opportunity – she loved her grandchild and would sit for hours cuddling her and singing old Welsh lullabies. She hoped to foster in the child an appreciation of her Welsh musical heritage. Her grand-dad sang solo in the Eisteddfod each year and the family were justly proud of his powerful tenor voice.

Bron was delighted she had given them a grandchild. The baby was such a source of joy to them all and the comfort she had brought Rosie too gave Bron a warm feeling.

The death of Ricky still haunted Bron – sometimes she had a nightmare about him. She had experienced it many times. It was always of vivid intensity —

There was deep snow on the ground and the wind was strong and bitingly cold. She struggled to keep her footing and reach the churchyard, but the wind kept pushing her back. Finally she succeeded and, as she approached the little cross, it shone fiercely bright in the moonlight. She tried with all her strength to move the stone until suddenly it fell away revealing the open grave, and to her horror she saw the baby clad only in a white cotton shroud. She wrapped his shivering little body in a blanket, hugging him close, and the dear little face of her 'cariad bach' smiled happily up at her, grateful for the comfort and warmth which she provided.

She would wake up sobbing at these times and would cuddle up to John and his arms would wrap around her and hold her close. Her heart ached as she knew how Rosie as a mother must feel.

Today, as she swept and cleaned, her mind seemed far away. Carefully she dusted the frame of Ben's portrait and looked searchingly into his face. She had no doubt that he was a good man and stubbornly refused to believe any gossip about him and Rosie.

She knew that all was not well between Rosie and Commander Dunbar and she felt strongly that he had been at fault. She had often seen his uncompromising attitude toward little Ricky, which was difficult to forgive, but her kind heart went out to him; she knew what he was going through at sea and she prayed every night for a reconciliation between them. Her dear Miss Rosie must not go on living alone; they both needed each other.

* * * * *

The birds' chorus woke Rosie early each morning; today instead of drowsing off again, as she usually did, she decided to get up. She ran downstairs in her nightie to put on the kettle, so that it would be boiling by the time she was dressed. She stopped for a moment by Ben's portrait and looked at him tenderly. She experienced an unfamiliar pang.

"Dearest," she whispered, "I do love you – we shall always be close," but for some strange reason which she could not understand she felt he was remote from her today. His familiar image seemed to be receding into the past. She shivered slightly and ran upstairs, glad to put on some warm clothes.

She had a leisurely breakfast with several cups of coffee then, feeling better, she wandered into the garden. How lovely being able to enjoy this morning freshness. The sun was out and the beds now a blaze of colour. She gathered a bunch of mixed flowers, holding their colourful heads close.

She heard the early morning train in the distance, chugging along and the hissing of steam, as it drew into the station. Then shortly afterwards there was a sound of the guard's shrill whistle, indicating its depature. It was almost always punctual and never more than a few minutes late. This was a great source of pride to the engine driver and many of the country folk set their clocks by the train's arrival.

She decided to wash up the breakfast dishes to save Bron, then thought she would tidy the hearth and light the fire, partly for Biscuit's sake, but she too loved the company of crackling logs and there was still a chill in the air.

When all was accomplished she ran up the stairs to her bedroom and put a comb through her hair. Then she slipped into her comfortable old coat and, gathering up the flowers, set off briskly down the lane to the church.

There was not a soul about at this time of the morning. The only sounds were of the birds and her own echoing footsteps. She quietly pushed open the churchyard gate and made her way towards the little cross. To her amazement standing beside it was a tall, thin bent figure – a stranger in this usually deserted sanctuary. His back was turned to her and he could not hear her quiet approach across the grass. She hesitated, then remained motionless, as she saw his hand reach forward to touch the stone, as though trying to establish a contact with it.

Her heart started to beat erratically, pounding in her ears. It must be Peter but he looked so different. His naval uniform hung from his shoulders as if supported by a skeleton frame.

She tried to prepare herself for this first meeting but there was not time. He had sensed her presence and swiftly turned almost guiltily towards her.

The shock was infinite. She thought she was going to faint as she looked at his poor disfigured face which stared at her through seemingly lidless eyes. His mottled skin was scarred in pink and white patches.

"Oh, God," she prayed, "help me."

Since a child she had felt fear and revulsion of any physical disfigurement and this was worse than any nightmare she had ever experienced. She knew she must not show her feelings but such a sickness overcame her that all she could do was to whisper his name: "Peter, it's you." She was appalled by this shadow of a man, who stood before her.

He moved closer to her and she saw that his eyes were haunted by the fear of her rejection, but words still would not come.

"Rosie, I'm sorry if I've frightened you with my hellish face – I never expected to meet you at this hour of the morning. I came in on the milk train and intended catching the next one back – don't look at me if it makes you sick," and he turned his face away to spare her.

Still unable to speak and playing for time, she knelt down on the grass and laid the flowers on the grave, methodically taking out the dead ones and replacing them with new. She felt less sick now, her head had stopped swimming and she was better able to cope.

With a supreme effort she got to her feet and forced out the words. "Come back to the cottage for breakfast, Peter, you look all in."

He hesitated for a moment, then nodded in assent; again he touched the little cross with loving hands as if to say goodbye. The tears ran unashamedly down his face, out of those poor disfigured eyes. Hoarsely he just said; "You know I loved him, Rosie, just as deeply as you did, though in a father's way."

"I know, Pete, I understand now," she replied in a choked voice. Compassionately she took his arm and led him slowly out of the churchyard, horrified by his frailty.

Pity overwhelmed her and she raged against the terrible fate of this handsome man, who was so horribly disfigured. Her strong maternal instinct was aroused by his vulnerability and she wished above all to comfort and protect him from further misery.

They walked slowly home and when they pushed open the front door he looked around in wonderment. So often, when tormented by pain and despair, he had imagined being back home, living with his beloved Rosie.

Everything was as he had pictured it, except that Rosie looked different. When he had last seen her she still looked a child in a way, yet here she was now, so changed. She had skipped girlhood but she was still beautiful.

Rosie was the first to break the silence. "Pete, do go and sit by the fire while I get breakfast ready. Fortunately I was able to get some fresh farm eggs yesterday and an American airman supplied me with some real coffee from the P.X. – not that ersatz stuff."

"That's wonderful," he replied as wearily he sank into a chair, closing his eyes for a moment. The lids, like shutters, were mercifully constructed by the surgeon to protect his uncovered eyes; without them life would be unbearable.

Presently Rosie brought in his breakfast; she was thankful he had chosen the chair with his back to the light, softening the impact of his poor face, though already she was more used to it. She put the tray on a table beside him and helped herself to coffee. It was hard to talk to him except in platitudes, but she sipped her coffee and told him briefly of her daily life in the cottage. There was so much to be said or left unsaid.   After he had finished she took the tray and carried it to the kitchen, washing up slowly. She needed time to think. Of course she must help him. After all she was still his wife but she was shattered by his awful disfigurement. Quietly she walked back into the room so as not to disturb him. His eyes were closed again.

She studied his scarred face and thin emaciated body – tears filled her eyes. Oh God, how he must have suffered. She thought of the old good-looking, debonair Peter, now a mere shadow of a man.

He must have dozed off for a minute then he woke up with a sudden start, looking anxiously at his watch.

"I must be off now, Rosie, if I'm going to be in time to catch that train. I am living at home at present but it isn't working out."

He struggled to his feet, holding on to the back of the chair, obviously feeling weak and swaying slightly.

Rosie walked over towards him.

"You're not fit enough, Pete, for another journey today. Stay here for a time until you regain your strength. The spare bed is aired and all your gear is still in there. Anyway," she added kindly, "I'll be glad of your company."

A look of relief came over his face, yet a curious embarrassment and hesitancy as he asked: "Do you really mean it, Rosie? Are you sure I won't be a nuisance to you?"

"Of course you won't and there are lots of things you can help me with – anyway it will be nice having a man about the house again."

She smiled and felt more relaxed with him.

"What are you future plans?"

"Well, I have been discharged from hospital and they say I have to wait a whole year before they can tackle any more plastic surgery. I'm afraid it's a slow job. They think it's possible to make me look all right again. They are going to do complete skin grafts on my face, taking it from various other parts of the body and there's a lot of work to be done on my eyes. They can even give me new eyebrows and eyelashes again."

"That's wonderful, Pete. I must confess you shocked me when I first saw you, but now I can see that with a bit of patching up here and there and you'll be as good as new again."

They both smiled and much of the tension had fallen away. They were quiet for a few moments as they sat on either side of the fire, gazing into its warm depths. Peter broke the silence. He bowed his head, searching for the right words. He spoke almost pleadingly.

"Rosie, do you think you could possibly forgive me for all that has happened? I've been an arrogant, selfish ass. I have had so much time to think during my long spell in hospital. I know that my behaviour was unpardonable – I shall always live with this heavy burden of guilt on my shoulders." His voice broke. "Ricky's death was caused all through my selfishness."

She tried to break in but he wouldn't let her.

"No, Rosie, there is no excuse for it, only explanations, but I loved you so very much and just hadn't learnt to share you with anyone else – it was as simple as that. Oh, I know I have lost your love but, if only you could bring yourself to forgive me, it would relieve me of an almost intolerable burden."

This appeal was too much for Rosie. She slid from her chair on to the hearth rug close to him and took his thin emaciated hand in hers.

"I forgave you long ago, Peter. I have also had time to think and I cannot let you take all the blame. I was a very foolish young girl, completely immature, with romanticised ideas of life. I didn't give you a chance. When Ricky was born I became all mother overnight and you didn't get the consideration you deserved." Her voice started to shake. "I'm horrified when I think of the strain you were undergoing at that time, yet I had no patience with you when you came home on leave."

He demurred and tried to stop her but she continued.

"I know now what it is like to be short of sleep and utterly exhausted. You see,

I had a taste of your medicine myself, when I was ambulance driving in Liverpool throughout the worst of the blitz, and I almost ended up with a nervous breakdown. I was sent back here on sick leave and I gradually healed with Bron's help, together with the peace and quiet.

He broke in: "Poor little Rosie. You've had a ghastly time. It's no wonder you look so frail. If I had known what you were going through, I'd have been demented."

He gave a deep sigh. "It's wonderful to be forgiven, Rosie, I can almost be happy again, the relief is so great. Thank you a million times for your generosity."

She did not like him being humble like this. She felt his pride must be restored.

"We must forgive each other," she said, "otherwise neither of us will have any peace of mind. Stay here, Pete, until you are strong again. I must warn you though that I have a busy life – in fact I must rush off now as it's my driving morning. On my way I'll tell Bron that you are home and I shall be back at lunchtime."

"Don't worry about me, Rosie, just being here is happiness enough."

She felt touched by his words.

"Pete, you look all in. Why don't you go to bed for a few hours. I'll tell Bron not to come in today so you won't be disturbed. She has a baby now, Catherine Rose, a few months old."

He hated his weakness but after the journey and emotional strain he felt completely debilitated and knew he must give in.

"It's a good idea, Rosie – I'm a bit shaky. I'll go up after you've left – but it's heavenly sitting by the fire, looking at all the old familiar things and absorbing the utter peace of the place. I'd like to stay here quietly for a little longer, if it's all right with you and then I'll go to bed."

"Of course, Pete, you do what you feel like – just make yourself at home."

It was strange to have him back as a guest in the house but this was the way it must be.

After she had left the cottage, he raised himself up wearily from his chair, really too exhausted even to cross the room, but with a great effort he went over to look more closely at Ben's portrait. He had seen it the instant he stepped into the cottage. Instinctively he had looked away, sensing there was a threat here and he was not able yet to cope with it.

He drew up a chair and proceed to scrutinise the portrait. He liked the face of this young man, with his determined chin, yet with the eyes of an idealist. He recognised at once the integrity that shone through so clearly in this inspired portrait – inspired by what – admiration or love? Instantly he knew it was love. This was the reason for the changed Rosie – her new maturity.

Oddly he felt no resentment towards this unknown pilot; he sensed that Rosie had been influenced for the better by him. He had no doubt that this was the man who had changed her. She was a more understanding woman now and Peter was grateful for this.

His emotions, dulled by his physical condition, were still sharp enough; his old bogey jealousy could well return and take over again but Rosie must never know – this hateful trait, as far as she was concerned, must be buried for ever.

He must contrive discreetly to find out about this young pilot and the part he had played in her life and, most important of all, whether he was still alive.

19

The refuge of the cottage and Rosie's care gradually restored him, but she knew he would never be the old ebullient Peter again. His youthful spirit and confidence had been lost – he was now a shell of a man. Yet she respected his quiet determination – he got on with life, never complaining or burdening her. Having literally been through the fires, he was a better man for it. His pathetic eagerness to help tore at her heart-strings; his courage in adversity and his uncomplaining acceptance of his disfigurement filled her with admiration.

Now that he was once more close to Rosie, Peter felt at peace and an enormous relief that harmony had been restored between them. His love for her had never faltered and he knew that to separate again would destroy him completely. She was his prop, without her he was floundering. He dare not think ahead, but she must never feel she was stuck with him. He knew he must not disrupt her life again and indeed now her interests and happiness came first with him.

The horrific impact of his burned face gradually receded, and progressively she grew accustomed to it. Reality returned only when a third party saw him for the first time; few could conceal their intial shock. Poor Bron, when she first set eyes on him, had fled from the room without a word, quite unable to cope with the situation.

Rosie had quietly followed her to the kitchen and found her standing over the sink sobbing and shaking. She touched her on the shoulder.

"Don't upset yourself, Bron, I understand how you feel. I was the same at first, but it's terribly important that we hide our shock and treat him as if nothing had happened."

Bron, struggling with her emotions, nodded dumbly and straightened herself up.

"I'm sorry, Miss Rosie, I couldn't help myself."

"There is no need to apologise, Bron, but just remember he's the same person inside."

"Oh, I know that," she cried, "I'd do anything for him – the poor commander. My goodness I would."

Rosie knew that stalwart Bron would cope in future, although in fact she always had to steel herself to look at him – she never could completely adjust.

Peter had become accustomed to this sort of reaction and never flinched. He behaved with quiet dignity, which Rosie admired, but she herself could not accept it. She raged inwardly at the utter futility of war and its terrible personal consequences.

Peter fought hard against the physical inertia, which so easily overtook him. He must not be a drag on the wheel and he did all he could to help Rosie. They became great friends; never was there a word of acrimony between them. Circumstances had matured and changed them both, but their new relationship was a happy one.

Rosie no longer felt the awful pangs of loneliness which used to assail her; with the passage of time, her work and her dedication to Peter's recovery had tended to lessen the intensity of her heartbreak for Ben. She would never forget what he had meant to her, but their joyous interlude was of the past; she knew he would wish it that way.

No longer did Ben's picture seem vitally alive in the room. Now she saw it as a canvas on which she had reproduced his image; somehow he had drawn away from her.

She knew that Peter must be told about him, but she would await the right opportunity. The picture had become an embarrassment, as neither of them ever referred to it and each knew that the subject was being deliberately avoided – until one evening after supper Peter casually mentioned that he liked the portrait she had done of the airman.

"Is he a friend of yours, Rosie?" he asked and, in spite of his effort to sound normal, his voice trembled.

Rosie replied without hesitation: "Yes, Pete, he was a very good friend of mine, but he is dead now. He was a fighter pilot and was shot down over Calais several months ago."

"I'm sorry," he said quietly.

There was a pause, as she started clearing away the supper dishes, while she was considering whether to tell Peter now of their relationship. Yes, she thought, this is the right moment.

As she carried the tray out to the kitchen, she called back over her shoulder: "I'll just bring in the coffee and then I'll tell you about Ben."

Peter knelt down and put another log on the fire. He felt weak about the knees. He desperately wanted to hear what she had to say, yet dreaded this moment of truth. He braced himself for he was afraid of his own reactions. He knew that if he was not careful he could break for ever their still-tenuous relationship. It was so important to him and, whatever she disclosed, he must not over-react to it.

When she returned with the coffee, he was sitting reading the newspaper, seemingly relaxed and unconcerned, but she knew this was a cover up. There was an uneasy feeling inside her – she would be glad to get everything out into the open. Subterfuge was not in her nature.

She sat down opposite him and handed him his coffee; a faint blush came into her cheeks. He stirred uneasily in his chair, gazing intently into the fire as she started telling him her story. She left nothing unsaid – it was like a knife turning in the wound and yet he felt it was fitting justice.

He was slow in his response but when his considered words were formed they were sincere; it was how he truly felt. He could speak with honesty.

"Bless you, Rosie, for your frankness, but that is you. The happiness which you found with Ben was no more than you deserved, after what you went through with me. It's awful the way that war claims the best."

She admired him for his brave words. She knew what it cost him to say them. The icicles round her heart seemed to be melting and a genuine affection and warmth broke through. Impulsively she jumped to her feet and lightly kissed him on the cheek. He held her hand for a moment and said with a sigh; "You know, Rosie, I still adore you. That will never change."

* * * * *

Paul still visited the cottage each week, giving Rosie constructive advice and appreciation of her pictures. Happily a close friendship developed between the two young men. Paul had not shown any visible reaction when he first saw Peter's mutilated face. He recognised that they were both casualties of war in different ways and must be accepted as such.

They enjoyed long discussions on art and architecture and both had great respect for the other's opinions. Curiously enough they rarely discussed the war, which had so nearly destroyed them both.

Peter was anxious to increase his knowledge of painting. He listened avidly to the exchanges between Rosie and Paul and quickly developed a keen critical appreciation. These visits were a great help to both of them, each with his individual problem of rehabilitation.

Rosie had made it clear from the start that her painting came first and that she had no intention of changing her life style; over this she need not have worried for Peter was tremendously proud of her work and greatly impressed by her growing reputation in the art world. He no longer felt any resentment when she was just too busy to be with him. He accepted the fact that her work was important and indeed, as time went she valued his opinions and listened carefully to his comments on her painting. His shrewd appreciation was helpful to her.

One afternoon Paul arrived unexpectedly at the cottage. He was obviously in a jubilant mood when Peter answered the door.

"Hello, Pete," he said excitedly. "I have some interesting news for you."

"Good, do come in and have a cup of tea with us."

Peter was always pleased to see Paul and so was Rosie.

"What's this I hear about good news?" Rosie asked, emerging from her studio.

"Well I think you will be delighted," he said. "I have just heard from the London Gallery about your 'Guernica' studies, Rosie. They are most enthusiastic about them and would like to exhibit the series in the autumn. They intend to collect the 'Holocaust' from the Academy, when the Summer Exhibition is over, and arrange the series around it."

"That is good news, Paul," she said with a smile, "though I must admit that in a way I rather dread it, for those pictures are so very personal, yet they were done for a specific purpose. I wanted so badly to bring home the evils and utter futility of war by putting over my message forcibly, yet in an uncomplicated way which all could understand." She spoke almost apologetically.

"You have done just that, Rosie. I am sure the pictures will make a terrific impact and certainly 'The Holocaust' is the most moving picture I have ever seen."

After Paul had left, Peter took the initiative.

"Rosie, there's something I want to talk to you about, so let's have a drink for a change. I know I really shouldn't with all the pills I've been taking, but it won't matter for once."

"That would be nice, Peter. I'd like a gimlet, how about you?"

"I don't think I'll risk gin, probably whisky would be safer for me."

He prepared the drinks and they sat together in companionable silence, gazing into the fire. Peter looked up and smiled at her.

"Rosie, there is no need to worry about my seeing your war series. I expect it's the 'Holocaust' that is bothering you — well actually I have already seen it."

She looked astonished.

"However did you know about the picture?" she asked.

"It was mentioned in a review of the Summer Exhibition, so I went up to London the very next day. It was a terrible experience, Rosie. You had caught completely the atmosphere of that dreadful scene and Ricky's face – it took me right back in time; it was the nightmare of Chatham all over again."

Rosie put her head in her hands.

"I'm truly sorry you saw it, Pete, that was just too cruel. Painting the 'Holocaust' seemed to help me. It was really part of my crusade against war – a picture to shock and to release the pent-up grief inside me, but I never thought you would be exposed to it in such a shocking way."

Her face was wet with tears as she turned aside. This time she was suffering for him too.

* * * * * *

Rosie had written her mother a long letter about Peter, telling her of his exhausted state and facial disfigurement. She explained that he would be staying on at the cottage until he was well enough to undergo the next stage of plastic surgery. It would be a protracted and painful process.

It was a difficult letter to reply to and her mother wrote back briefly, expressing her sympathy for Peter. The news of his injuries had affected her deeply, for she was fond of him and horrified by this grim turn of events.

She knew how much Peter must have suffered during the period of his estrangement from Rosie and now, poor man, he badly needed the comfort and affection of a good wife.

The thought of Rosie's living alone also haunted her and she prayed for a complete reconciliation between them. She felt that his dreadful experiences must have mellowed and changed him – they needed each other and in spite of his faults she knew that Peter loved Rosie.

Peter grew visibly stronger each day. He was gaining weight and his lassitude was slowly leaving him; even his face had improved. The livid scars were toning down and now it was possible to look at him and visualise the old Peter, his previously-handsome face being fleetingly revealed. His mouth mercifully was unchanged.

Occasionally though, when Rosie came upon him unexpectedly, the shock was still great and it was hard to conceal her natural reaction. He was in fact quite aware of how she felt and it hurt him deeply.

* * * * * *

Catherine Rose was struggling to walk now. She was a dear child, with her mother's loving temperament. Bron still brought her to the cottage each day and to Cassie it was as familiar as her own home. She was quite blind to Peter's facial injuries and obviously adored him. She would look up with a shy smile when he came into the room, her eyes alight with pleasure.

One day she struggled from Rosie's lap and ran towards him and, as Ricky had done, clung to his trouser legs. For the first time he picked her up and swung her gently in the air. Her trusting little face studied him seriously for a moment, then she smiled and gave him a kiss, her soft cheek pressed against his, quite oblivious of the roughness of his deeply-scarred skin.

"Love you, love you, Unc' Pete," she crowed softly with the delighted cry of an infant.

He was touched and obviously overcome by her unreserved acceptance of him.

"I love you too, Catherine Rose," he said seriously, yet straight from the heart, and from that moment on there was a close bond between them.

Peter decided he would make a little chair for her. He had a flair for woodwork and for the first time he felt he wanted to be up and doing. Rosie was delighted when she found him busy at the lathe in the tool shed. He was working with enthusiasm and she instantly recognised a new extroverted Peter, completely wrapped up in his labour of love.

When finished it was a delightful little chair in cherry wood and of a most unusual design. Her name, Catherine Rose, was carved on the back in simple lettering, above which was a small nosegay of Christmas roses.

He carefully placed the little chair by the fireside and when Rosie first saw it a lump came to her throat. It was obvious that a lot of love and devotion had gone into its making.

They both eagerly awaited Cassie's reaction and when she came toddling into the room that morning, holding Bron's hand, she saw the chair at once. She drew in her breath with excitement. "Baba's chair," she said with a little squeal of delight. She left her mother's side and ran unsteadily over to it and sat down with a bump, her eyes alight with joy – she knew it was for her.

Peter's face was a picture. Her obvious pleasure had amply rewarded him for his pains. He strode over and picked her up, chair and all, and held her above his head with outstretched arms. She loved this and chuckled merrily. From now on, it was always called 'Baba's Chair'.

Bron turned away, her eyes moist when she saw his devotion to her child. It pleased her, but if only he had been like this with his own son, she thought.

* * * * *

Rosie had encouraged Peter to visit the Crispins in Bangor, for she felt it was good for him to venture out more, but so far he had not felt like going on his own. She was also anxious for him to see their set up, so when Tessa invited them over for tea, she dropped everything and took the afternoon off.

It was a bright, clear winter's day and they enjoyed the drive. The Crispins gave them a wonderfully warm welcome and Paul was delighted to show his new friend what they had so far achieved.

They were considering building on a small extension to the workshop and were eager to consult Peter, as an architect, on the best way to go about it. He was most helpful and full of good ideas. He agreed to come over again the following week with rough plans and talk to the builder.

He was very interested in the gallery and seeing Rosie's pictures so beautifully displayed there gave him great satisfaction. It was early closing day and Tessa had really pushed the boat out, using up their rations and raiding their store cupboard to provide a delicious tea. She had made a traditional Welsh barabrith – a rich fruit loaf, full of currants and raisins, which she had thinly sliced and buttered. Tea was served in the Welsh tradition on the dining room table on a white linen cloth.

It was a cosy room at the back of the house and, in spite of fuel shortages, a coal fire burned brightly. Rosie's Menai Straits study was now hanging over the fireplace. It was the only picture in the room, which gave it a special aura.

Inevitably the main topic of conversation was art and the great success of the gallery. Paul generously gave Rosie the credit for this.

"Are you both going to London for the opening of the Great Britain at War Exhibition next week?" Tessa asked.

Rosie hesitated and her colour changed a little.

"No, I don't think so, Tessa – the pictures are rather harrowing and I believe it is best for all our sakes not to dwell on them."

There was a strained silence in the room for a moment, but Peter took it in his stride.

"Rosie is trying to protect my feelings over this and obviously doesn't want me to see them, which is fair enough."

Rosie looked up and smiled at him. She realised she was being foolish for, after all, he had already seen the 'Holocaust', though she hoped he would never have to again.

"Well, it's up to you, Peter. If you really want to, we can go." But there was no enthusiasm in her voice. She hated to hurt him.

Paul deftly changed the subject and soon they were talking lightheartedly as before.

It had been a lovely afternoon, but it was time to go home. Reluctantly they said their goodbyes and left the warm fireside and the company of their good friends, stepping out into the cold winter's night. There was a full moon and the sky was dotted with stars. They were in high spirits as they drove home, discussing the plan for the extension of the Crispin's gallery.

Rosie was pleased with this new interest for Peter. She knew it was what he needed to bring back his old self-confidence. He had so much to offer and must be made aware of this.

*   *   *   *   *

Their relationship took on a new closer dimension, yet physically they were poles apart. Peter lived in constant fear of her rejection but he longed for them to be together as one, for her body to assuage his hunger and loneliness.

Rosie no longer found him the strong vital man whom she had so passionately desired. His interest in her painting, however, was a great source of joy to them both and they had long and stimulating discussions on various techniques. His own enthusiasm for design was reviving and he was thoroughly enjoying the small project in hand of the Crispin extension.

He went over every week to inspect the progress. Mr. Lewis, the builder, was an earnest little man, conscientious and a reliable craftsman. He was making a good job of it, but Peter watched him with an eagle eye; he ensured that the fabric was up to standard and that the interior, with its additional shelves and cupboards, was functional and would provide Paul with exactly what he needed.

One afternoon, arriving unexpectedly, he found Paul crouched over the fire, looking thoroughly miserable. He had caught a severe cold and knew that the only thing to do was to coddle himself, but enforced inactivity did not suit his temperament. During his time in the navy he had been on Russian convoys for months – the extreme arctic conditions and lack of sleep had so undermined his health that he had developed pleurisy. Now he caught colds easily and unless he was careful complications set in.

"How nice to see you, Peter, I was feeling rather low," Paul said, cheering up visibly.

"As a matter of fact, I wasn't feeling so hot either – but I'm all the better for seeing you, Paul. I started to worry about our lives when the war is over."

"I am thankful to be established in this business," Paul replied, "and it is particularly reassuring to be doing so well with the local residents. No doubt, when peace comes and the holidaymakers return, it should be even better. But how about you, what are your plans?"

Peter hesitated before answering.

"Well, I shall definitely go back to architecture. My old firm in London has promised to keep my job open for me." He paused again, wondering how much to say. "Rosie will never leave the cottage; she says she will always stay close to Ricky and, so long as I still fit into the picture, it will mean working around here."

Paul looked at him sympathetically; he knew what their situation was. Rosie had told Tessa just the bare bones of the story.

"There is a small firm of architects here in Bangor. David Owen is the boss and he turns out exceptionally good work. He is a traditionalist and uses mainly local stone and slate, but his designs are excellent. My great ambition is to have a 'David Owen' house one day. I met him last week when he came into the gallery – incidentally he bought one of Rosie's pictures, 'The Bluebell Wood'.

"His only son, Wilf, worked as his right-hand man, but he's a gunner in the R.A. now, fighting in the North African Campaign. He is sorely missed in the business, particularly as they are inundated with official contracts. Why don't you go along and see the old man?"

Peter felt this was an excellent suggestion.

"What a good idea! I think I am fit enough now to do a part-time job and perhaps after the war he might keep me on."

He was quiet for a moment, deep in thought.

"Tell me frankly, Paul, do you think my face will go against me? It's pretty bloody at the moment, isn't it?"

"No, I certainly don't think so, rather the reverse. Mr. Owen is a good chap. He has an excellent reputation around here for being a straight-shooter. Anyway you look much improved and, after more plastic surgery, you'll be a regular lady-killer again!"

Peter smiled wryly. "I'm afraid I'll never be that, but thank God Rosie's getting more accustomed to me. She used to try so hard not to flinch every time she saw my face but I think she's learned to live with it now. If the plastic surgery isn't a success, I sometimes wonder if I'll just disappear from the scene. It doesn't seem fair to her, being tied to a Frankenstein's monster."

"Now take it easy, Pete, you're exaggerating. I never notice anything is wrong and Tessa said the other day that your attractive personality more than counteracts your scars. In any case Rosie is obviously genuinely fond of you and by nature a very loyal person, so I wouldn't worry on that score."

Peter looked him squarely in the eyes.

"Thank you, Paul, you're a good friend. I'll certainly take up your suggestion and call in to see Mr. Owen on my way home."

He looked at his watch. "It's after four o'clock already, so I'd better be pushing off. Goodbye, old fellow, and take care of yourself. I'll call in tomorrow and tell you the score".

He found his way easily to Mr. Owen's office. It was tucked away at the back of the town, overlooking the Straits. He was received kindly by the elderly receptionist and, after stating his business, was quickly ushered into Mr. Owen's private domain. He was a man of medium height with grey hair and a high broad forehead. His eyes were commanding yet his expression kindly.

It was obvious from the start that Peter's disfigurement touched him. He thought of his own son and wondered how he was faring – but for the grace of God the same thing could happen to him.

"Have you been invalided out of the Navy?" he asked.

"No, sir," Peter replied, "I am at present on sick leave. My MTB was blown up and caught fire. In a few months' time I have to return to hospital for more skin grafts so, if I worked for you, it could only be on a temporary basis."

"We are extremely busy here at the moment and any help at all would be most welcome. Tell me about your background."

"Well, I graduated from the Liverpool School of Architecture with a First Class Honours degree and then worked for a short time in London for Jonas Carr, until I was called up with the Naval Reserve. I now live just outside Penrhyn. My wife is an artist and I believe you bought a picture of hers from Paul Crispin last week."

Mr. Owen smiled broadly.

"My goodness, yes – we are great admirers of her work and my wife is delighted with our latest acquisition. Actually we have been wondering if we could commission her to do a view from our living-room window across the Menai Straits?"

"I know she'd be delighted to do it, sir, but I'm afraid she's very busy at the moment. She drives a mobile canteen each morning, and for the rest of the time has her work cut out to supply Paul with sufficient pictures for his gallery. You see they are selling like hot cakes, particularly to American servicemen but, providing you're not in too much of a hurry, I know she would be pleased to do it for you."

"No, of course not, we can wait, but the Spring or Summer would be the best time."

"Well, I will speak to her about it tonight, sir, and will let you know in the morning."

"Splendid, well now back to our business – how many hours a week do you think you can put in? As far as I am concerned the more the better."

Peter looked thoughtful. He didn't want to undo all the good the rest had done for him but on the other hand he was itching to get back to work.

"Would it be all right if I started doing just mornings and, if I can manage more later, I will?"

"That would be ideal," Mr. Owen said with enthusiasm. "But how about money? We haven't discussed that yet."

Peter smiled. "I will leave that entirely to you, sir, when you've had time to assess the quality of my work."

"That's fair enough, young man, I feel sure we won't fall out over this. We shall expect you next Monday at nine a.m."

They both stood up and shook hands warmly – they were sure the arrangement would work.

Rosie was astounded when she heard the news; it was so completely unexpected. She was pleased, but worried in case Peter's health would not stand up to the strain.

* * * * *

The next few months flew by. Peter enjoyed his new job immensely and had great respect for Mr. Owen; it was manifestly obvious that his boss was well satisfied with him. They got on extremely well together and Peter was treated more like a son than an employee. Mr. Owen felt the utmost sympathy for this young man, so hideously scarred. He was obviously most anxious about his own son and frequently made reference to the war and particularly the front on which Wilfred was fighting.

One day, when Peter was talking to him in his office, a yellow telegram was delivered and hurriedly brought in to Mr. Owen. He knew the implication and instantly his face was drained of colour – he first stood frozen with apprehension, then he opened the envelope with fumbling fingers and read the dreaded message. As the telegram fell from his hand, fluttering to the ground, he turned blindly to Peter, tightly grasping his arm as if for support.

"Peter," he said hoarsely, "my Wilf has been killed in action." He looked on the point of collapse as he choked back the tears.

"Oh God, how can I ever tell Mary?" he asked as this fresh horror dawned. "This will break her – Wilf was her life."

Peter felt shattered – it was almost as if a jinx were following him around. He knew what it meant to lose a son and it seemed too cruel that this kindly man had been dealt such a blow.

"This is terrible news, Mr. Owen, I cannot tell you how deeply sorry I am," he said as he led him to a chair and eased him into it.

"Sit down quietly, sir, and I will go and get you a cup of tea."

The poor man slumped down and buried his head in his hands; his shoulders shook and tears trickled between his fingers.

When Peter returned with the tray, Mr. Owen had pulled himself together somewhat. Peter wished with all his heart that there was something he could do to ease the poor man's distress.

He handed him a cup of tea. "Drink this, sir, it will help you," but Mr. Owen seemed to drink with difficulty; his hand was shaking so badly that the cup clattered in the saucer.

"If you feel up to it, let me drive you home now," Peter said with infinite kindness. "Mrs. Thomas can close up the office tonight."

Mr. Owen nodded as he wearily got to his feet. Peter helped him into his overcoat – he seemed absolutely stunned. Wilf, his only son, had been the apple of his eye.

He clutched at Peter's arm again as he got into the car.

"How can I best break the awful news to Mary? Whatever can I say?"

Peter replied gently: "I am afraid there is no easy way, sir. You can only tell her the truth and do your best to comfort her. I know what you are up against. We lost our son a few months ago in an air raid."

Mr. Owen looked up – he was shocked but his resolve strengthened.

"You have suffered terribly in this war, Peter. I mustn't burden you. We must bear up as best we can."

He was silent as they drove along. When they reached the house and Peter helped him out of the car, Mr. Owen thanked him in a muffled voice then squared his shoulders and walked unsteadily up the path.

There was a certain determination in his stride, however, and Peter knew he would be a tower of strength to his poor wife. He was a splendid man.

20

SOUTHERN ENGLAND was now a vast military camp, bulging with trained men, weapons and equipment. The Allies were massed in great strength and it was obvious that the invasion of France was imminent. The question was when and where? The country waited with bated breath for the crucial hour. Secrecy was essential and every loyal citizen guarded his tongue. "Careless talk costs lives." These posters were prominently displayed as a positive reminder to the public of their responsibility at all times.

June 6th 1944 started off as a wet and blustery day with driving rain pattering against the windows. Peter had arrived home for lunch, dripping wet, to the welcome refuge of the cottage.

As they sat down to their meal, Rosie had switched on the wireless to listen to a piano recital from the National Gallery; it was one of their lunch-hour concerts. Dame Myra Hess was playing, as she so often did, Bach's 'Jesu, joy of man's desiring', and before the last soothing notes had faded away, there was a dramatic interruption by the B.B.C., announcing that the Allied Forces had landed in France – D-Day had arrived at last. The whole country held its breath.

The news was brief, but encouraging. The invasion had started well. Security had been effective and the enemy, convinced that an attack would not be made in such unfavourable weather conditions, had been caught completely off guard. The whole operation had miraculously taken place in secret.

Peter's initial reaction was one of excitement and optimism.

"Thank God, it's started at last," he exclaimed triumphantly. "Now we are fighting back and will soon have them on the run."

"This is marvellous news," Rosie replied joyfully. "It was a miracle that we caught them unawares; now we will be able to get cracking and finish off this damn war quickly."

"It really seems as though we've fooled them. Apparently they were expecting us to land elsewhere; so far luck seems to be with us, but we mustn't be too optimistic yet," Peter said cautiously.

Rosie carried out the dishes and left Peter glued to the wireless set, but when she came back she found him looking pale and distressed.

His mood had changed.

"Is there anything wrong?" she asked anxiously, fearing the Allies had suffered a reversal.

"Only with me," Peter replied disgruntledly. "I'm just a useless bastard on the scrap heap. I should be taking part in this operation."

"You've done your bit and more," Rosie replied stoutly, "and I for one am thankful you are not in it."

There was no way she could reason with him and, when he started pacing the floor like a caged tiger, she left him and went to her studio. She felt he was better alone.

Later in the afternoon Paul arrived, his strained face tense with excitement. He was obviously anxious to discuss the invasion with another man. Like Peter, he was crushed that he had been destined to miss the show – the supreme climax of the war. They sat huddled together over the wireless, listening avidly to all the commentaries on the progress of the assault. The mind boggled at the complexities of such an operation and marvelled at the planning and organisation of the venture.

After their talk they were more reconciled to their personal situation, though it was hard to accept that they had played their part and were now just onlookers.

* * * * *

The Normandy landings were going well and it soon became apparent that the Allied Forces had indeed achieved a great tactical surprise. Their superiority in the air was immense; the coastal defence guns and shore batteries were quickly silenced by the heavy bombers of the R.A.F. and a naval bombardment from the sea, thus preparing the way for the infantry to get ashore.

The American forces at Omaha Beach were the only exception. Here the enemy had been very much on the alert. The Americans ran into severe resistance and tragically lost several thousand men before the defences were finally penetrated.

Once the Allies had consolidated their positions on the beaches, they expanded and established new fronts further inland. After the initial hold-up, the American thrust westward went according to plan and within a few weeks they occupied the whole of the Cherbourg Peninsula. The general feeling was of tremendous relief that the end of the war was within reach. This was the last great stride that would lead to victory.

The highly disciplined German forces, however, were still resisting strongly – their war machine must not be under-estimated.

Peter listened religiously to all the B.B.C. broadcasts and kept a map at hand, tracing the rapid advancement of the Allies. Inevitably talk was focused almost exclusively on the war and the successful strategy employed against the enemy, who was finally in full retreat. Brittany and Normandy were now released from the German yoke. On 26th August General de Gaulle made his triumphant entry into Paris. This liberation was heralded with great joy and thanksgiving – it was a milestone on the road to victory.

* * * * *

Peter had just heard from the plastic surgery unit at Stoke Mandeville that he was to report back there on 1st September. He dreaded leaving Rosie, yet it had to come – this was the parting of the ways. Would she want him home again after it was all over or was it just her kind heart that had allowed him to stay there up to now?

The thought of being separated from Catherine Rose disturbed him. Would she forget him in his absence? She was a most affectionate child and all his pent-up love was centred on her. She always searched him out – her Unc' Pete. They would often walk hand in hand together in the garden. He would draw her attention to the wildlife, teaching her the names of the flowers and the birds they saw. This quiet, tall, ugly man and this serious tot with the thoughtful brown eyes – they were happy together.

He dreaded breaking the news to Mr. Owen that he would be leaving shortly.

Since Wilf's death, they had grown close and Peter knew he would be sadly missed. A week before his departure, however, he had to tell him.

"I've just heard from Stoke Mandeville, sir, and they want to start work on me again next week."

Mr. Owen was obviously upset.

"I hate the thought of your leaving, my boy. We shall all miss you and I only hope that you will return after your spell in hospital. I know these are uncertain times and you probably can't commit yourself."

"Thank you very much, Mr. Owen. I am delighted that you want me back but at the moment I'm afraid I am not able to give you an answer."

Mr. Owen got up and put his arm round Peter's shoulders.

"I shall pray to God that everything turns out well for you, Peter and, if you should decide to rejoin the firm, I would like you to take Wilf's place as a junior partner."

Peter had not expected this and for a moment hardly knew how to express his appreciation.

"Thank you enormously, sir," he said in a voice charged with emotion. "I can't tell you how grateful I am for all your kindness and now this generous offer."

He felt quite overcome. It was a terrific boost to his morale.

* * * * * *

Rosie was uncertain of her reaction to Peter's departure but she knew that, in spite of her great preoccupation with painting, she would sorely miss him and be lonely again.

Bron seemed particularly upset over his forthcoming operation and went out of her way to do all she could for him.

On the morning of his departure, little Cassie came running to him and wound her arms tightly around his neck.

"Don't go, Unc' Pete," she cried and her eyes were swimming with tears. He tried to comfort her.

"I'll soon be back again, little one. They're going to give me a nice new face," he said jokingly.

"Don't get a new one, Unc' Pete, I like your face," the child said solemnly, looking at him with loving eyes.

"All right little one, I'll tell them you like it as it is and not to alter it too much," he said seriously. He was obviously upset at the parting for this child's love and acceptance meant so much to him.

He had woken up that morning with a feeling of dread and insecurity. He had been sheltered and accepted here. Now he would have to face the outside world again without his Rosie's soothing presence.

After lunch, she drove him to the station. They were subdued and obviously sad at being parted. They arrived early for the train, so they sat in the car talking.

"Do you think you will be back for Christmas, Pete?"

"I rather doubt it," he replied. "I know the surgeon will be working on me for months and, anyway, I'd rather not see anyone until I'm fixed up."

He was determined not to commit himself, or her, for that matter; they both must have time apart to be able to think clearly. She must not be trapped by her kindly nature.

As they heard the train approaching, Peter leaned forward and kissed her lightly on the forehead.

"Goodbye, Rosie dear, take good care of yourself. Thank you for everything and God bless."

He jumped out of the car and slammed the door, hurriedly disappearing through the station entrance just as the train pulled into the platform. He didn't trust himself to look back. He must not weaken, but life without Rosie was impossible.

She drove slowly back to the cottage. Autumn was approaching and the country had a sad, untidy neglected look and already there was a nip in the air. She pushed open the front door and saw that the fire had burned down to ashes in the grate – there was not even a comforting glow. She looked at Peter's empty chair and it brought a lump to her throat – poor darling, he still had so much to go through.

She was alone again and the silence and isolation which surrounded her seemed to cut her off from the outside world. For a moment she felt panicky and her heart ached indescribably. She wandered round the room, idly shaking up the cushions and returning books to their respective shelves.

She had intended finishing a painting that afternoon of an old cobbler's cottage, hidden away in the trees, which she and Peter had discovered on their way to Portmadoc the previous week. It made a charming picture, but she had wanted Peter's advice before completing it. She knew her painting had improved with his guidance, though his opinions had to be considered with caution, as she had to guard against the atmosphere and cold precision of an architect's drawing.

He, himself, always warned her of this, for he recognised the life which radiated from her work and was always so generous and honest in his opinions.

After a rather half-hearted attempt to finish the picture, she wandered back into the living room. For the first time in many weeks she studied Ben's portrait and tried to analyse her feelings for him now. He would always be close to her heart – but it all seemed so long ago. She turned away and gazed through the window. The moon was veiled behind the clouds, only tipping the ghostly peak of Snowdon. She shuddered then drew the curtains.

*　　*　　*　　*　　*

Hitler had indeed made a disastrous decision when attacking Russia. Fighting on two fronts was leading to his inevitable downfall. He continued to make his vitriolic speeches against the enemy and still forecast ultimate victory for the Fatherland. His rantings and ravings became less and less credible and rumours were rife that he was no longer sane.

His latest threat of a secret weapon, "which would utterly demoralise the British people", had caused a certain apprehension, though many dismissed it as an idle boast – but when the first V-1 pilotless aircraft was launched and hit the south east, it came as an unpleasant shock. It carried a high explosive warhead and was nicknamed "the doodle bug" or "buzz bomb". It could be heard approaching from a distance until suddenly the engine would cut out – the silence was ominous, for the missile would then plummet earthwards, striking the ground with a deafening explosion. The blast damage was particularly vicious. They were launched day and night, so there was not any let up. This latest weapon was exceedingly frightening and disconcerting even to the most stout-hearted citizen.

Gradually the fighters of the R.A.F., with the help of radar, were able to intercept many doodle bugs over southern England. These fighters together with anti-aircraft gunfire, finally mastered the flying bomb.

Hitler's next secret weapon, the V-2 rocket, was infinitely more lethal, as it was pure rocket. It approached in silence without warning, and it caused a state of uncertainty and mental tension even greater then the V-1. The attacks continued for seven months until in due course the Allies over-ran the launching sites and the relief was overwhelming at home.

It was hard to believe that the Londoners' ordeal was finally over. They had bravely endured and survived the unleashed fury of the enemy and now their well-deserved victory was in sight.

* * * * *

Rosie tried hard to settle down on her own again but she was afflicted by her old bogey – loneliness. She had far more time to spend on her painting now that Peter had departed, but she missed him painfully. Without the stimulation of his sharp brain and their shared experiences there was a void in her life.

She had derived a sense of achievement from nursing a broken man back to health. Now her sense of purpose had gone but at least she had done her duty as a wife – what of the future?

She felt restless as she sat at the window looking out disconsolately at the peaceful scene. The weather was uncertain and today Snowdon looked black and menacing; yet in the sunshine it was so green, then changing magically to a deep purple at sunset. She would wait until later then venture out hopefully with her paints.

She picked up Biscuit and returned to her chair by the fire. She must soon make a decision about Peter. She knew how badly he wanted a reconciliation but respected him for not exploiting his misfortune as a lever to achieve his aim. She surely would have given way, if he had pleaded with her. Soft-hearted Rosie would not have denied him, but as it was he had manfully left her to make the choice, probably the most difficult of her life.

She knew that self-sacrifice alone was no good – there must be love too, otherwise the sacrifice would turn to bitterness and disillusion for them both. She was still young and full-blooded; she longed for a physical relationship such as she had enjoyed with Ben and Peter in the early days, but this feeling for him had completely gone.

She analysed herself and was troubled by her own character weakness. As a child facial abnormality in others frightened her. Once she had seen her mother's face badly swollen and bruised after a car accident. She had run away screaming from the room. Masked faces too had always terrified her and at fancy dress parties and carnivals she could not cope with them at all – even today she had to take a grip on herself, if she saw anybody wearing a mask.

With Peter this horror had passed. Her overwhelming pity for him had dispelled it, but what was she left? She needed soft lights, sweet music and glamour to switch her on, not scarred faces. She shivered as she contemplated running her fingers over his pitted, uneven skin and looking into his disfigured eyes. She thought of beauty and the beast and despised herself for it. Would her desire for him ever come back and, if it did not, could she live without the return of his erstwhile charisma.

She went upstairs to her bedroom and dug out some old photographs of him. She marvelled at his tall, handsome positive image. Something stirred within her. She adored his vigorous masculinity – would this ever return? Suddenly she knew the problem was not 'skin deep', but the power of the man himself which was missing – this important ingredient that she needed in her love-making. She could not settle for less. She turned away from these thoughts with a feeling of selfish guilt.

*   *   *   *   *

It was a clear, crisp autumn morning with sharply etched white clouds in the sky. Rosie had decided to paint a picture of the cottage to send to Peter as a Christmas present. Today the conditions were ideal, so she packed up her old satchel and easel then, putting on a warm coat and heavy walking shoes, she set off early.

It was chilly and she realised this would be one of the last painting expeditions of the year. She had already made an exploratory search before choosing her point of vantage and had settled on a site high up on the hillside.

She walked briskly along the lane, passing the little church, then round the next bend to a five-barred gate. This opened on to a narrow path which weaved its way through steeply sloping fields dotted with sheep. Some glanced up from their grass cropping as she passed them by, then dropped their heads and munched on contentedly.

The fields rose sharply until finally she reached an outcrop of rock at the summit which was her objective.

She was breathless after her climb and was glad to sit down and admire the view. It was magnificent, stretching away as far as the eye could see – neat, vivid green fields, enclosed by grey stone walls. The leaves were already turning a russet brown and there in the centre of it all – her little jewel – 'Apple Trees' nestled in the fold of the hills, looking as always a welcoming retreat. She hoped she could capture this image for Peter – she knew it would please him.

She unpacked her satchel and set up her easel and started to paint. Her brush strokes were purposeful and decisive. She was never happier than in these creative moments, when she had a clear vision of her objective. Then her brush seemed to guide her, taking its own course without effort.

When the painting was finished, she examined it with half closed eyes. She was satisfied; she had caught the atmosphere which they both treasured.

She packed up her gear and light-heartedly ran most of the way down-hill to the lane. She felt delighted that her picture had gone so well, but was anxious to be home in time to play with Catherine Rose.

She pushed open the cottage door and shouted gaily: "Where is my Catherine Rosie?" knowing the little girl would be waiting for her.

There were tiny pattering footsteps and in a moment the plump little girl was in her arms, hugging her tightly. "Wosie home – Wosie home," she cried joyfully. She loved "Wosie", but still missed her Unc' Pete. She had been tearful for several days after his departure. They had a special relationship and nobody could quite replace him.

"Bron dear," Rosie called, "I'm home. May we have our refreshments please?"

Bron's smiling face appeared in the kitchen doorway. "It's all ready, Miss Rosie," she said, carrying in the tray. She knew the routine. Baba's chair was drawn up close to Rosie's and Biscuit, as usual, was dozing in front of the fire. They always had their 'elevenses' together, if Rosie were home – it was one of the high spots of the day, especially for Bron. She put a saucer of milk down on the floor for Biscuit, who was too sleepy to respond but Catherine Rose was all agog to make him drink it.

"Silly Puss, d'ink Puss, d'ink," she said, pushing his face into the saucer of milk and wetting his whiskers which, like all self-respecting cats, he hated; but after much spluttering and a few sneezes Biscuit proceeded to do her bidding and lap it up. She gave a little squeal of delight: "Good Puss d'ink," she said stroking him gently.

"How is the commander getting on, Miss Rosie?" Bron asked anxiously.

Rosie felt a little uneasy as she had heard from him only once recently and Bron must be aware of this.

"They are operating on his eyes at the moment, Bron, so it is difficult for him to write. He says how much he misses Catherine Rose."

"Poor, dear man," she exclaimed. "Please tell him how much she misses him too and that every night she says in her prayers – God bless Unc' Pete."

"That will mean a lot to him," Rosie replied sincerely.

Bron smiled, her deep brown eyes thoughtful, reflecting her serenity and steadfastness of character. She adored this child of hers in a completely selfless way. She felt the child's destiny was strangely linked with that of Rosie, and John felt the same way. He was proud that his little daughter was so well thought of by this famous artist.

It had become apparent that Cassie was musical. She would climb on to Rosie's lap and cuddle up to her then, with little pushes and shoves, she would indicate that she wished to be rocked.

"Ting Wosie, ting," she would say, quietly yet insistently.

Rosie was excited by the little girl's interest and was most anxious that it should be fostered.

Cassie drank up her milk quickly that morning then ran over to the piano and gently struck the keys. She did this thoughtfully as though testing out the sound of each note, then she hastened back to Rosie and started tugging at her arm.

"Wosie, play lullby," she wheedled, trying her best to hum the tune.

Rosie smiled; "All right, Catherine Rose, I've time for just one tune," and as Bron carried the tray through to the kitchen Rosie sat down at the piano stool and, with Cassie on her knee, played the little girl's favourite German lullaby *Guten Abend, gut' Nacht.* It was exciting to watch the reaction of this tiny child, humming and nodding her head to the gentle rhythm. There was no doubt that like her Welsh ancestors she had music in her soul.

After she had finished playing, Rosie sprang to her feet as it was getting late.

"I must be going now, my little sweet," she said reluctantly as she kissed the crown of Cassie's shiny dark head; then with a hurried farewell to Bron she was quickly on her way to her driving job.

It was the last Christmas at war and Rosie as usual went to spend it with her parents.

The tide of victory was flowing strongly now, but the killing still went on – what a terrible price to pay in human life and suffering.

Her mother probed her with questions about Peter's health and her own future, which was unlike Mrs. Greenwood, but she hated the thought of Rosie being all on her own. Rosie, however, refused to commit herself.

"How is Peter's plastic surgery getting on?" her mother asked concernedly. "Your father and I are most anxious about him. Poor boy, he's had such a ghastly time."

"I haven't heard from him recently," Rosie replied, "but the last report was good. He is evidently progressing well."

"Wouldn't it give him a boost, if you were to go and visit him, Rosie?"

"I don't really think he wants me to," she said, unwilling to be drawn.

"Your father and I are both very proud of our brave son-in-law and the gallant part he played in the war," her mother said, obviously angling for information, but Rosie only nodded. She wouldn't budge an inch. Her future must be decided without outside influence and anyway she was doubtful now how Peter felt about her.

She had in fact written to Peter several times and had received only brief notes in reply. He said his skin grafts were going well, but he looked rather like a patchwork quilt. She sensed he was depressed, so to cheer him up she wrote asking him to design a new studio for her, the present one now being far too small.

It was a warm letter full of encouragement but he was a long time replying and, when his letter arrived, it was almost indecipherable. He said they were still working on his eyes and he was a 'pretty sight'. The studio project had given him something to think about and he welcomed the challenge. He would send her a rough plan when he was able.

She heard nothing for many weeks, until a letter arrived from Stoke Mandeville in a strange hand. It was written by a Sister Howard, dictated by Peter, telling Rosie that his eyes were bandaged, so he could not write himself. This was to let her know that the final operation had been completed and it seemed to be a success. He ended up by saying how well he had been cared for by everyone at the hopital.

Sister Howard enclosed a covering note expressing her admiration of his courage and endurance. She was obviously a fan of his and Rosie sensed that perhaps she felt something deeper than admiration.

A few weeks later Peter wrote himself. It was a brief reply to her last letter, saying that he was being sent to a convalescent home in the country. He did not give an address which surprised her and made her feel more remote from him than ever. Perhaps he had met someone else. Could it be Sister Howard? When she thought of this a stab of apprehension ran through her. It made her realise that, in an odd sort of way, she had always depended upon his love. Even during their estrangement it had been there, secure in the background.

She had found some old snapshots of herself and Peter in their early happy days together. She had them framed and displayed them on the mantlepiece. His previous good looks saddened her, but what he had lost in appearance he had undoubtedly gained in other ways. He was now a mature and kindly man, dependable and easy to live with. She knew now that she wanted him back, yet feared she might have lost him.

****

It was hard to believe that five long years of war had passed, though the widespread havoc and destruction, wrought on all sides, was beyond comprehension. It made Rosie shudder to think of it.

She was proud to be British when she recalled the terrible scenes during the air raids and the remarkable bravery and fortitude shown by the people – bloody, but unbowed by the German blitzkrieg.

Russia,in her heroic fight to defend her motherland,had suffered most of all – millions lay dead, ravaged by a ruthless enemy who gave no quarter.

The savage, searing episode of the siege of Stalingrad would be recorded in the annals of history as an example of remarkable courage and dogged endurance; every house had been fought for in this beleaguered city and the devastation and obliteration spread out endlessly as far as the eye could see.

Germany had received her just deserts. Retribution had come at last. Her key cities were being virtually wiped out by relentless air attacks from British and American bombers – the death toll was enormous. Finally the destruction of Dresden, the fairy-like city, which Rosie had visited and loved as a child, was in ruins. It all seemed so senseless.

When peace came, would there be anyone sagacious enough to unscramble this chaos and make the right decisions for a fair and honourable peace or would there be the same bitterness and injustice, felt by the enemy after the First World War?

A wave of depression swept over Rosie – what was life all about? As ever, when unhappy or disturbed, she turned to her painting for relief.

She had been commissioned to paint an oil of the South Stack lighthouse. It was situated on the western coast of Anglesey and, viewed from the towering cliffs above, it was a dramatic sight. The vivid white structure was built on a rocky promontory, reaching out into the Irish Sea. In stormy weather it was viciously lashed by the thundering waves, sweeping up the spray to a great height.

She had made rough sketches on the spot and hoped to be able to finish the painting at home. She was a keen nature lover and was entranced by the colourful profusion of wild flowers on the cliff top. She was particularly fascinated by the colony of puffins, the clowns of the bird world, who frequented this area, their nests precariously balanced on tiny shelves in the rock face.

She did not seem to be in the right mood – she could not capture the atmosphere of the scene to her satisfaction, so she decided she must finish the picture *in situ*. She put away her brushes and wandered through to the other room, disconsolate that she had made so little progress.

She heard the front gate opening with its tell-tale creak and footsteps approaching up the path; then the door bell rang. She jumped up, straightening her skirt, and after a peremptory look in the mirror and a few pats to her hair, she hurried to open the door.

Standing on the threshold in the pouring rain was a middle-aged man with the rain dripping off his slightly battered trilby. He quickly removed this with a flourish.

"Mrs. Dunbar?" he asked hesitantly.

She nodded and smiled.

"I am David Owen and, as you will know, your husband worked for me for several months last summer. I wonder if I could possibly speak to you for a few moments?"

"Of course, Mr. Owen, do come in. I am delighted to meet you," she said with a genuine welcome.

He carefully removed his soaking raincoat and shook it vigorously outside, before hanging it up in her hall.

"Do come and sit by the fire and dry out," she said as she threw on another log.

"I have been meaning to come and see you about the picture of the Menai Straits, which you wish me to paint, but Peter told me to forget about it for the time being," she paused. "I was terribly distressed to hear about your sad loss and Peter was very upset too, as I am sure you know."

He replied quietly: "It has been a body blow for us, Mrs. Dunbar, but we must try to carry on; we're not the only ones to suffer in this terrible war."

"Please do sit down," she said kindly. "I won't be a moment. I'll just pop on the kettle for some tea."

"That will be most welcome; it always seems to hit the spot – my poor dear wife, Mary, almost lives on it these days."

Rosie murmured sympathetically as she left the room.

When she returned with the tray, he was looking around with interest.

"I love your cottage, Mrs. Dunbar; it's just the sort of place I would like myself. Our house has a beautiful view over the Menai Straits, but it lacks the homely comfort you have here."

"Thank you, Mr. Owen, I'm glad you like it. I think the large open fireplace makes a world of difference. We have plenty of our own wood, so I seem to have a fire winter and summer. When Peter is home he does the chopping and before he left he filled the tool shed with logs for me, bless him!"

Rosie poured out the tea and handed him a piece of Bron's home-made cake.

"I'm so glad to meet you at last, Mr. Owen. I very much appreciated your kindness to Peter. You gave him back his self-confidence, which he needed so badly at that time."

"How is he now, Mrs. Dunbar? We think of him often."

Rosie frowned. "I think he is getting on well, but it's a depressing business – very painful and infinite patience must be shown on all sides and of course one must not expect too much."

"I am a tremendous admirer of your husband. His acceptance of his disfigurement without bitterness shows great strength of character. Then, apart from that, he has a brilliant brain. He did a mammoth job for my little firm and, inspired by his original ideas, I have been flooded with enquiries for rebuilding after the war."

"I'm delighted to hear this," she said and her face lit up with pleasure.

Mr. Owen thought he had never seen a prettier woman, except for his Mary, of course.

"Now, Mrs. Dunbar, I must tell you the reason why I am here. I hope I can be perfectly frank with you?"

"Please do," she replied.

"Well, Wilf's death has knocked us completely sideways and I feel I can no longer carry the burden of the firm on my own. Yet I know that to sell up this old-established practice would be like breaking faith with the past."

Rosie nodded understandingly. She knew exactly how he must be feeling.

"I am sure that Peter will have told you that I have asked him to join me as a junior partner as soon as he is well again."

"Yes indeed," she replied. "He was deeply appreciative."

"Well, the purpose of my visit today is to find out if he has made up his mind yet. I have talked it over with my wife and she is delighted at the prospect. She saw Peter only once – you see I was afraid she would be upset by his appearance," he said almost apologetically, "but I underestimated her. She was deeply impressed by him and the splendid way he faced up to it all. She prays for him every night."

Tears came to Rosie's eyes; she refilled his cup, playing for time. She was in a dilemma, not knowing how to answer him. Finally she looked up and spoke with sincerity.

"Peter is a fine man and I think he will come back to you, but of course I cannot speak for him. I know he will be in touch with you just as soon as he has made up his mind."

"Thank you, my dear, but please don't feel that I am pressurising you. I can certainly wait until the war is over and of course expect to do so. It shouldn't be too long now, thank God," he said with feeling.

Rosie sighed: "War has become such an accustomed way of life for us all; it is hard to remember what things were like before it started." Her face looked sad, for she knew she would never be the same person again. Her youth seemed to have slipped away.

"I don't want to add to your burdens, my dear, but I wonder if you could come over and see us one day. I would like you to meet my wife and talk to her about the picture. It would give her a new interest. She is very lonely now and I feel a young and vital person like yourself could help her."

"Of course, I would be delighted to do so," she said warmly. "I am having lunch with the Crispins next Thursday, as I have a picture to deliver to them; could I call some time during the afternoon to see you?"

"That would be splendid," he replied. "Come and have tea with us – say about three-thirty."

His expression changed and, for a fleeting moment, he looked almost boyish, she thought, then his face settled down into its accustomed lines of sadness.

He stood up to go. He was reluctant to leave but he must get back to his wife; it was a compulsion to share that silent grief-stricken house – he could not bear to leave her alone for long.

Rosie wished she could console him – she knew what he was going through and she struggled for the right words.

"This dreadful time will pass for you both, believe me, for I have been through it – gradually your grief will lessen and you will feel life is worthwhile again. You have each other which is a great blessing." She looked with kindness into his eyes. "Spring is just around the corner and peace for our country not far away."

"Thank you, my dear, for your encouragement; I know you have lost a son too

242

and you give me fresh hope."

"Please call me Rosie," she said. "I feel I know you well, for Peter talked about you so much and I particularly want to thank you again for helping him in his hour of need. I shall always be grateful to you for that."

He shook her hand warmly as he departed, hurrying now to be home before dark – Mary hated to be alone at night. He felt comforted and reassured by Rosie and, if Peter should return, then it would all seem worthwhile – some reason to keep the business going for he almost regarded Peter as a son.

Strangely enough Rosie felt comforted too; the day seemed less bleak, as though a link had been forged between her and Peter again.

* * * * * *

Victory was now in sight, so it become imperative that the Big Three – Churchill, Roosevelt and Stalin – should meet again to discuss on the complex arrangements to be made once the enemy surrendered.

Yalta, on the Black Sea, was chosen as the venue. Churchill had developed a close understanding with Roosevelt and there was a special relationship between the two great nations. Unhappily, however, Britain's bargaining power was weak, as the country had been completely drained, whereas America and Russia were both strong in resources.

Roosevelt was now an ailing man and this did not help the situation as he tended to appease Stalin. Churchill left the conference with decided reservations and anxieties about the future of Europe, for the Russian approach was uncompromising – the future was now in the lap of the gods.

21

SPRING WAS here again – the dark winter nights were over and nobody doubted that the black-out curtains would soon be taken down for good. Only those who had lived through these dreadful years of adversity could understand the emotional relief that their long ordeal, and that of their loved ones, was finally coming to an end – it was almost unbelievable.

The last few months had passed swiftly for Rosie. Her reputation as an artist had grown and she became more deeply involved than ever in her painting. In the art world her War Series was considered of exceptional merit.

In spite of her achievements, she was not happy; she missed someone to share with her the joy of success – on her own it all seemed rather hollow.

She was in low spirits as she had not heard from Peter, but she tried to be as cheerful as possible for the sake of those around her. Catherine Rose was a joy and Rosie loved her as much as she would a child of her own. She was now teaching her to play the piano and already the little girl could memorise a simple tune. There was no doubt she was talented and Rosie was determined that everything possible must be done to encourage and further this gift. Rosie felt that Cassie might even become a child prodigy.

One evening, after an arduous day's work in her studio, Rosie came through to listen to the six o'clock news. Alvar Liddell was reading it. In his calm, clear voice he made the dramatic announcement telling of the suicides of Adolf Hitler and his mistress, Eva Braun. Rosie felt an enormous sense of relief. The world was a cleaner place now – rid of this monster, who had sent millions of innocent people to the concentration camps and had been responsible for the most dastardly acts of inhumanity – his evil deeds spreading like a cancer through the German nation. His infamous regime was now mercifully in its death throes.

*   *   *   *   *

Church bells were ringing joyfully all over the country, for it was VE Day and the war in Europe was over. The people of England celebrated their well-deserved victory with a great outburst of triumphant jubilation. There was singing and dancing in the streets and the pubs were full to overflowing. There were thanksgiving services in the churches and bonfires on the hills and beaches.

The British reserve was swept aside in an unrestrained outpouring of delight and relief. This great nation, drawn close together through adversity, rejoiced in full voice. The war had been won!

Rosie felt that a great burden had been lifted from her shoulders, but in no way could she share in the jubilation for she had lost so much. She went to a thanksgiving service at the little church, then stood for a moment at Ricky's grave – it was hard for her to rejoice.

May was beautiful that year and her garden was in all its glory, but today it did not bring her any happiness – there were only heartaches.

Tessa and Mrs. Owen had both telephoned, inviting her over for lunch, but she had declined as she wanted to be alone at this time, quietly remembering her loved ones, and she must not blight this day for others.

She would stay at home and just be thankful that these terrible pages of history had been turned and one could now look to the future. At least her parents had been spared.

The telephone was ringing when she arrived back from the church, and she rushed to answer it. She was pleased to hear her mother's excited voice.

"Hello, Rosie dear, isn't it wonderful that it is all over at last?"

Rosie admired her spirit and tried to reply in the same cheerful way.

"Yes, Mum, it's absolutely marvellous – now you can have those old boards taken down and the windows reglazed. I know how much you have hated them!"

"Yes dear, that's our next job. I've already pulled down the black-out curtains and life should soon be back to normal again."

"But what are you doing today, Rosie?" She could not hide the anxiety in her voice.

"I'm going to spend it in the garden. It's beautiful here, so I'm staying put. I've had invitations out for lunch, but I have declined them. It's always such a treat for me to be out in the sunshine and anyway I would prefer to be on my own today."

Her mother understood how she was feeling, so didn't pursue the subject but her heart ached for this only daughter of hers.

"Come home soon, dear, and we can have a quiet celebration together."

As Rosie replaced the receiver, she saw Bron's cheerful face peering round the back door. It was a national holiday, so she was not expecting her in today but this was so typical of Bron.

"I just popped in to see if you are all right, Miss Rosie. I've put a cooked chicken and a home-made cake on the kitchen table for you – so you shouldn't be short."

"How sweet of you, Bron. I do appreciate it but don't worry about me – it's a day for celebration not work."

"Should I come in later and tidy around for you, Miss Rosie? We're not going out until this evening."

"Oh no, Bron, there's no need for that. You mustn't work today."

"John bach, says there are going to be bonfires on the beaches. They're already setting up the trestles for refreshments and of course there'll be a sing-song – trust the Welsh!"

Bron's eyes were alight with excitement; but as she spoke of the beaches Rosie's mind quickly switched back to her solitary walks along the shore at night not many months ago, when she heard the fearful drone of enemy aircraft overhead making for Liverpool.

Memories were short, thank God, and people were tough and resilient. She pulled herself together and forced a smile.

"It's nice and warm today and the garden looks so lovely that I think I'll go outside and potter about. I don't think I've ever seen it so full of flowers – it's a real joy."

Bron's face cleared with relief.

"Well, if you're sure you're all right and there's nothing more I can do, I'll be off. Goodbye and I'll see you in the morning."

"Goodbye, dear Bron, enjoy yourselves. Please give Catherine Rose a big hug for me."

She turned quickly away so that Bron would not see her expression. They must part on a happy note, otherwise it might worry this dear girl and spoil everything.

Memories – her mind seemed full of them today. She walked over to Ben's portrait and touched his cheek lightly with her fingers.

"It's all over now, Ben dear," she whispered. "We've won – you did not die in vain."

For a fleeting moment she sensed the old communication between them which had been missing for so long – then she turned away sadly and wandered out into the garden.

Presently she sat down on the front door step, basking in the sunshine. She closed her eyes, trying to imagine what her future would be. She dreaded the thought of the long years stretching ahead and being completely alone.

She knew that she must reshape her own life as so many others would have to do. She thought of the men in the forces returning home, gathering up the old threads, trying to fit into civilian life again. Experiences and time change people dramatically and she knew there would be many disappointing homecomings, as well as joyful family reunions and for some no homecomings at all.

Her deep musing was unexpectedly disturbed by the familiar creak of the gate. Idly she wondered who could be calling today?

She opened her eyes lazily and looked up, dazzled by the brilliant sunshine. Her heart missed a beat – she must be dreaming. There was Peter, standing as though spellbound, gazing at the cottage which he loved so much, drinking in the peace of this familiar scene.

To her he looked like the handsome, debonair hero of her youth – his distinguished figure in naval uniform, upstanding and well-built. His face was lightly tanned from his open air life. He was wearing dark glasses but as he approached he deliberately removed them, so that nothing was concealed from her.

She drew in her breath sharply and she jumped to her feet. Looking at him almost shyly, she experienced the same heady excitement of their first meeting in the classroom almost a decade ago. It was like putting the clock back.

The scars on his face, now barely perceptible, seemed to add rather than to detract from him. 'Honourable battle scars', she thought. Her feelings were clearly reflected in her eyes and, as he looked at her searchingly, a tremendous relief surged through him, for here again was his loving, almost child-like Rosie of the past.

He stepped forward confidently – this was the strong, vital Peter as she had first known him. Her prayers had been answered and without hesitating she rushed into his outstretched arms.

Epilogue

THE DAY was ending and the twilight gently falling on the patchwork quilt of hills and dales. Inside the cottage the fire had burnt low, leaving only a few glowing embers in the hearth; but the pervasive and pleasant smell of burning wood filled the room.

Rosie stirred slowly and opened her eyes. It had been so long since she had thought as deeply of her dear ones, their weaknesses and strengths; but how painfully she still missed Peter for they had become blissfully close during the remaining years of his life. He had paid dearly for the misdemeanours of his youth, but his retribution had wiped the slate clean and he had finally brought her contentment and peace of mind.

Ricky was tucked snugly beneath her heart, a solace now – no longer a sorrow. Ben was eternally engraved upon her mind – as an idyllic interlude of pure perfection.

Catherine Rose, as precious to her as a daughter and now a brilliant concert pianist, filled her thoughts. She had brought Rosie and Unc' Pete so much love and happiness – and ever Bron, dear Bron.

Now her reverie of those bitter-sweet memories, so full of joy and pain, had ended. She did not hesitate over her decision. She would not write her autobiography – it was a private matter, the mosaic of her life. She did not wish to expose her loved ones, her friends and many who had passed her way, to the public gaze – this would be a betrayal of trust. Any pain in her life was buried deep now – so be it!

She turned to her easel, always close at hand, and looked at her latest portrait. Her thoughts, so vivid and alive, were still lingering in the past but, when she examined the picture more closely, her interest quickened and her heart lifted with pleasurable anticipation as she picked up her brush and palette – then gently she wiped away her tears.